Where We Keep Our Indians

The Cherokee Vanishment

Historical Novel
By: Barney Beard
1st Edition

I0665328

If history were taught in the form of stories,
it would never be forgotten.

Rudyard Kipling

Where We Keep Our Indians

The Cherokee Vanishment

Historical Novel
By: Barney Beard
1st Edition

Edited by: Connie Schultz and Gaila Perran - Reader: Beth Kalamanka

ISBN: 978-0-9964328-4-9

Dedicated to my constant parents

Alyce Helene
and
Samuel Emerson Beard

who provided a loving home every day of my life
and taught me to read at an early age.
If I had one wish, it would be they could read this book.

Other Books by Barney Beard

Chapter Books

The Bow Window

The Amazing Adventure of Carter and the Pie Rats
New England Book Festival-Award Winner

The Book Visitors

The Incredible Adventure of the Eight Cousins
FAPA Silver Medal Winner

The Horrible Word Hole

The Great Alphabet Adventure

Summer of '19

Their New, Big, Old House

Shut Up and Dance

The Ordinary Man and the Book Dragon

Luke and Carter: Their Summer Adventure

Melody and Connor: Christmas with Grammy

Melody and Connor: Their Visit with Grammy

Oliver and Quinn Travel in Space

Luke and Carter's Winter Adventure

Books for Early Reading

Five Little Monkeys

Conner Can Read

Our Favorite Nursery Rhymes

Luke's Great Adventure Begins

Carter Finds His Imagination

Quinn's Great Adventure

Oliver Learns to Read

More Books by Barney

The Old Man and the Book

Where We keep our Indians
Historical Novel

The Ordinary Man: A Poem
New England Book Festival Winner-First Place

Golf for Beginners
Double Award Winner-FAPA Silver & eLit Bronze

Letters to My Grandchildren

My Collected Poems

The Adventures of Bouncy

Letters to My Grandchildren: Volume II

The Official Rules of Canasta

Golf for Beginners: Left Hand Version

How to Write: A Primer
New England Book Festival Winner-First Place

Writer's Journal
Award Winner-eLit Bronze

A White Killing Frost
New England Book Festival Honorable Mention
Historical novel woven around the Cherokee Nation's
deportation from northwest Georgia. 1820-1838. 744 pages.

Foreword

This is the abridged version of my historical novel, *A White Killing Frost.*
If you have read the unabridged version of Moby Dick, Les Misérables, or
Don Quixote you'll know what I mean by the usefulness of an abridged
version of a long novel by a wordy author. Samuel Clemens himself told me
I would have a much better book if I would cross out the parts people skip.

Here is the book with all the parts removed that readers skipped. Some may
say I didn't leave out enough, but perhaps one day I'll come out with an
abridged version of the abridged version. Until then, enjoy.

The many newspaper articles in this book are real. Not one is fiction. The
newspaper quotes are exact reprints from extant American newspaper
archives with references in each case. I did not delete any of them in this
abridged version. They were invaluable source documents which helped me
understand what happened in northwest Georgia in 1838.

This novel is classified as historical fiction. The framework for this novel is
not a creation. It really happened. I wish that were not the case.

Barney Beard

Table of Contents

Prologue

I mentioned one evening to a dinner guest I was writing a historical novel about the Cherokee Trail of Tears. My guest was interested. He immediately shared a story from his military experience in Oklahoma as a young serviceman in the United States Army.

He re-counted how in 1970 when stationed at Fort Sill he and a fellow soldier were driving through the rural Oklahoma countryside when the landscape suddenly changed.

My friend asked his army buddy about the curious change.
        'Why does the landscape look so different here?'

His friend replied,
        "That's where we keep our Indians."

Barney Beard

Copied from the Georgia Journal Newspaper
9 March 1829 – page 2

"The benevolent and enlightened policy which the Government has invariably pursued towards its Indian neighbors ought to quiet the fears of the Cherokees on the subject of their territorial rights…."

Where We Keep Our Indians

Our Indians

The Cherokee Vanishment

Chapter I
Where We Keep Our Indians
Chapter 1

"Greg, you're from Oklahoma. Why does this landscape look different?"

"Because that's where we keep our Indians," Greg said.

"What do you mean? Who keeps Indians? Are you making fun of me?"

"No, I'm not making fun of you, Katie. That's the Cherokee Indian reservation we're passing."

I could hear Greg laughing under his breath.

"Greg, what an ugly thing to say," I shot back.

"If I said 'that's where we keep our Mexicans' or 'that's where we keep our Japanese people', like we did in WWII, what would you think? How can you joke about something like that?"

"I was trying to be funny," Greg said.

"I don't think you're funny."

"You're taking me wrong," Greg said, defending himself. "We like Indians out here. We don't have anything against Indians."

"It didn't sound that way," I answered.

"Out of context the remark could sound bad, I guess, but that's what people say out here, Katie. We're not racist or bigots. We're good folks."

"We've got all kinds of Indians out here, Katie—Cherokee, Choctaw, Chickasaw, Pawnee, Cheyenne, Apache and more tribes I can't pronounce. The east end of Oklahoma is full of Indians. We're good people out here, Katie, patriotic as you can get, the salt of the earth. Everyone out here likes Indians, always have. Indians are different, but we like them."

The more he explained the more bigoted he sounded.

Greg is a good man. I knew he was telling me how people thought but I was unprepared for his remark and less prepared for his defense. I was angry at myself for being surprised and snapping at my boyfriend. Up to this point, Greg and I had been having a great time on our trip west.

As we drove along Greg's phrase kept ringing in my mind. I was determined to understand his remark. I needed to think. It was going to be all picture and no sound. I stared out the car window. I knew nothing about Oklahoma, Indians, their reservations, culture or history, not a blessed thing.

I've lived in Walker County, Georgia all my life, in the northwest corner of the state. I went to primary school in Rock Spring and high school in

1

Lafayette. I studied history, but at the moment I couldn't recall a thing about Indians in Georgia. Everything I know about Indians I learned from Hollywood. There had been Indian occupation before Georgia was colonized, but I don't know where they came from or why they disappeared. No Indians lived in our community. Growing up I never heard anyone talk about Indians, much less a place to keep them. I realized when Greg said, 'it's where we keep our Indians', he had implied, 'it's where we Americans keep our Indians'. I guess that's what disturbed me.

Why was I surprised by the humorous terminology Americans used for Indian reservations in Oklahoma? Why should I care? I'm a journalist, educated and well read. I didn't like being unable to connect the dots.

Maybe I was pouting because my business major boyfriend knew more about United States history than I did.

I finally spoke in a sharp, staccato voice, "Can we visit the reservation?"

"Of course, Katie. It's American soil. We can go anywhere we want to."

"I want to see the place where you keep your Indians," I said sarcastically.

"Tahlequah is just north of here. That would be a good place to visit if you want to see a reservation."

"Let's go. Can we go now, today, right now?"

"This whole trip west is your project, Katie. I'm just your limo driver."

"I want to go now," I said petulantly. "I want to go to Tahlequah, I want to see what's there."

"No problem. We can be in Tahlequah for lunch."

Greg squinted at the big road sign ahead.

"It's Highway 82 to Park Hill and then it's just a few miles north to Tahlequah, if I remember right. You want to stay the night, Katie?"

"Sure, let's stay the night. I've never been on an Indian reservation. We don't have Indians in Georgia. I wonder why that is?"

"Well, we got plenty of them out here," Greg answered.

It was interesting how he kept referring to Indians as 'them'.

"Why don't you get us a reservation at a nice motel."

He suddenly laughed louder than before, a big belly laugh.

"Get a reservation on the reservation. How appropriate, don't you think."

Greg kept laughing. I was liking him less and less.

Despite myself, I giggled at his reservation joke. It was clever.

Greg made a right turn onto Highway 82 and headed my Camry north into the heart of the Cherokee reservation. What kind of adventure lay ahead?

I made reservations near downtown in a nice bed and breakfast that advertised itself within easy walking distance of the historical section.

I sat with my back to Greg. My entire knowledge of Indians was limited to Hollywood movies like *The Searchers* and *Last of the Mohicans*. There are dozens of Indian place names in my part of Georgia but no Indians, none that I knew about. Why? Did they simply vanish one day?

I knew vaguely the entire South had a history of Indian occupation but I had no facts to call on from my school days.

As Greg drove towards Tahlequah, the place names from back home began swirling through my mind.

I currently live in Chattanooga not far from Chickamauga Dam which is on the Tennessee River. I had driven by the Ocoee and Tellico Rivers and the gorgeous Nantahala River over in North Carolina. I had a little job in Catoosa County, Georgia. Farther south I had some relatives in Chattooga County and east of that was Cherokee County, but none of these places had Indians.

Georgia had rivers like the Altamaha, Chattahoochee, Oconee, Ocmulgee and the beautiful Hiwassee. Georgia had Indian names everywhere but no Indians. In Walker and the surrounding counties white folks owned all the farmland. All the farmers I knew were white with European ancestry. When did my part of the world turn from red to white, from Indian to American?

I told myself I was wasting time being overly concerned about irrelevant history, but the other side of my mind was curious. I wanted answers but I didn't know the questions. Why did I know so little about our past? I continued thinking as I watched the Oklahoma landscape pass by. Why did my knowledge of history have a void between the Revolutionary War and the Civil War? I tried to think of just one important event in American history between 1800 and 1860. The only mental peg that came to mind was, *'In 1814 we took a little trip, along with Colonel Jackson down the mighty Mississip'*.

Did nothing happen in America between 1800 and the beginning of the Civil War? I've gathered wonderful stories for my writing project, stories portraying a marvelous kaleidoscope of diverse Americana. Each vignette fit comfortably with what I know about our country and the modern American education I'm receiving at the University of Tennessee at Chattanooga.

I felt a growing disquiet in the shadows of my mind that didn't fit my comfortable view of America. My emotional unease was because of Greg's offhand remark. Why was that?

There was more to this, I was certain. My journalism training was kicking in. I could smell a story in Greg's flippant, chauvinistic comment. I felt a determination growing inside of me to understand, to know more about this whole thing with the Indians, American history and the curious place names I was so familiar with in my part of the world.

What was drawing me to Tahlequah? Have I allowed Greg's narrow-minded remark to redirect my summer project? How could I grow up in northwest Georgia and know almost nothing of its history? Maybe I'll get some answers in Tahlequah.

Chapter II
The Old Woman
Chapter 2

We drove straight to the bed and breakfast in downtown Tahlequah. Our room was clean and smelled nice. We were hungry. We decided to sample the authentic Cherokee fare advertised at a local mom and pop restaurant. Their specialties were fried chicken, real mashed potatoes, turnip greens, green beans cooked with fatback, foods I learned to love at my grandma's house.

After we ordered I noticed one older waitress, I guessed she was Cherokee. There was a kindness about her I liked. I got her attention. She came to our table with a smile. I asked if she was Cherokee. She was. I asked if I could ask a few questions. Maybe she could tell me a few stories about the reservation and life in Tahlequah. She shook her head no.

"I'm not a story teller but my grandma will talk about anything. I'm getting off for lunch in a bit. If you follow me home my grandma would be tickled to talk to you. She don't have many visitors."

We finished our lunch and followed the waitress' car into the driveway of a small, sturdy, two-bedroom wood frame house badly in need of a coat of paint. We followed the waitress inside. The living area was tidy, furnished with an old, three-piece stuffed suite covered with clean, white bed sheets.

"Elisi, I met this lady who writes people's stories. I told her you like stories," the waitress said in a louder than normal voice.

The old woman stood with a pleasant smile and extended her hand.

"It's a pleasure to meet you two. I'm Maude Bliss Allen. You've met my granddaughter, Kari. She's really Karen, but she's been Kari since she was a baby. Sit you two down. You're welcome here.

"Forgive my old house," the old woman continued. "Kari wants us to sell and move into an apartment out from town but I like living in my old home place where my Elisi was born.

I knew I was in the right place. The old woman's eyes were dark like her granddaughter's. Her coarse white hair, tinged with yellow, was pulled back in a severe bun. Her back was bent because of a hump that made me think she had some kind of spinal arthritis.

4

"I hear you're quite a storyteller, Mrs. Allen. I'm a journalism major and I love to record stories. Today is my first visit to an Indian reservation. We don't have Indians or reservations in Georgia."

I couldn't help but notice the old woman's eyes, alert and penetrating.

"Nope, no Indians in Georgia," the old woman said, "but there's over three hundred thousand registered Cherokee now. Quite a bunch, ain't it?"

"Yes, ma'am. It is."

"Lots of folks left the reservation but my people stayed. We was always homebodies, I guess, but I got relatives all over. I got a nephew who's an architect in Chicago, another who's a mathematics professor at Vanderbilt and a niece who works for the government in DC. We're all storytellers. My momma told stories. Elisi told stories. Elisi told me stories her momma told her. I mostly tell other people's stories, I guess."

I was taking notes as fast as I could write.

"We Cherokee are mostly in Oklahoma now," the old woman continued, "but I got cousins in North Carolina. Ain't seen 'em in years. We got stories how the government took our land and then took more land. I hate the damned government. The Federal Government owns sixty-three percent of land west of the Mississippi and takin' more. You didn't know that did you?"

"No, ma'am. I didn't know that."

"Forgive me, dear. I got carried away, didn't I?"

"That's alright, Mrs. Allen. We enjoy listening."

"Thank you, dear. Well, if you want to hear a story, did you know the famous Mr. Ed is buried right here in Tahlequah. I can close my eyes and hear him say, '*Hello, I'm Mr. Ed'*."

She laughed until tears ran down her cheeks.

"It don't take people long to forget. When I was young, ever'body knew Mr. Ed. He's a thing of the past, an old relic like me. Mr. Ed was a Hollywood star. He was a talkin' horse, dear, a beautiful palomino 'bout sixteen hands, the star of his own TV show in the sixties called *Mr. Ed*. He's buried right here in Tahlequah. I don't figure you're interested in a story about a dead talkin' horse, dear. I been expectin' you all morning."

"You were expecting us?" I asked. Before I could ask how that was possible Kari returned with a loaded tea tray.

The teapot, cups, saucers, sugar bowl and milk pitcher were elegant, obviously antique. The workmanship was exquisite, classic. Kari carefully set the tray between us. The tea service looked out of place on the green plastic serving tray next to the old couch covered in bed sheets. I wanted to ask her why she was expecting us, but she began talking. I didn't want to interrupt.

"I got more stories. How about the story of this tea set?" the old woman said as she began pouring our tea. "Would you like to hear that story, dear?"

"I love that kind of story," I answered.

5

"This tea service came here to Oklahoma with my family on the Trail of Tears in 1838. Have you heard of the Trail of Tears, my dear?"

I had heard of the Trail of Tears but knew little about it.

"This tea service came with my great-great grandmother. It was a gift from a friend during that journey. That's all I know. Not much of a story, is it? I don't know where it was made or where it came from. I don't really know who the friend was. I've always wondered how they managed to carry this tea set eight-hundred miles without breakin' it into pieces. Do you like it?"

"I think it's beautiful."

I examined the delicate cup and saucer in my hand with new interest. Where did this tea service come from? Where was it manufactured? Who owned it? How did it arrive in Tahlequah? I wanted to know.

"Would you like to know where and when this tea set was made?"

"Oh my, yes, I would like that," the old woman answered quickly.

"If you will allow me to take photos of the bottom of the pieces, I can do an Internet search and tell you the date and place of manufacture. Have you ever watched *Antiques Roadshow*?"

"No, ma'am. Never watched that show."

I took photos from different angles and close-ups of the markings.

"I'll find out what I can and send you the information. It won't take more than a few days after I get back," I told her.

"I would like to hear more stories about the Cherokee and their history. I don't know much about the Trail of Tears."

The old woman chuckled to herself and patted my knee again.

"No offense, but you folks who moved into our country have forgotten all about us. Out-of-sight, out-of-mind, you might say. Things change, don't they? In the '60s everyone knew who Mr. Ed was. Nobody knows him now. We used to be the Principle People. I ain't surprised you don't know about us. You asked me why there ain't no Indians in Georgia, Katie. I didn't avoid your question. I was waitin' for the right time to answer."

"First, my people have always lived in what you call America. You're American, we're Cherokee. My people was here when yours got off the boat. I don't think my people ever thought of themselves as Native American, indigenous, First Nations or aborigines. Americans are always trying to put a handle on anybody different. We called ourselves the Principle People, 'Aniyunwiya', but you can't say that word, can you?"

"No, ma'am," I said.

I knew I was in the right place for a story.

"Before your people came we spoke Cherokee. Today we're talkin' in a language you Americans brought from England."

She leaned over and patted me affectionately on the knee once again.

"Forgive me, dear. I don't want to make you mad. There ain't no Cherokee in Georgia and I know why. You're sweet for listenin' to an old woman babble. Some white folks would get mad at what I'm sayin'. Thank you for being polite. Do you still want me to tell you about Georgia and why there ain't no Cherokee there, Katie?"

"Oh yes, please," I answered quickly.

"The reason there ain't no Cherokee in Georgia is you Americans forced us to leave. It was our country, Katie, and your people took it from us. You deported us here in '38, lock, stock and barrel. One day in May, American soldiers rounded us up and brought us out here."

The old woman had just begun and already I had goosebumps.

"Their motives weren't complicated," the old woman continued. "Americans wanted land. They took it. They marched us out here. Oklahoma was the end of the earth in those days. It didn't even have a name."

She paused again and patted my knee.

"I don't mean to offend you, but if you don't know anything about how you Americans got your land you need to read some history, don't you?"

"Yes, ma'am. I'll do that as soon as I get back to Chattanooga."

The old woman continued, "Nobody likes that old stuff, do they? Readin' history is like lickin' old carpet. Borin' ain't it?"

Suddenly she sat taller.

"But, my dear, a well-told tale is another matter, isn't it? That's the way to learn history, ain't it? There's always time for gossip. You're in the story business. You know what I mean, don't you?"

"Yes ma'am. I know exactly what you mean. Everyone loves stories. Humans have an insatiable desire for story. That keeps the media in business."

"You're right, dear. Everbody loves a good story."

The old woman was a lot smarter than she let on. I suspected her country girl vernacular and intentional misuse of verb tenses was assumed, a device used as a cover-up for an intelligent, penetrating mind. She was sharp.

"Katie, I'm eighty-eight years old. I was born right here in the back room of this old house in '27. My mother was born in that same room in '92. My Elisi was born after the Civil War in Park Hill. When she married, her brothers built this house for her. Nice house, ain't it?"

"Yes, ma'am. It is," I answered.

"I've heard lots of stories right here in this room and out on the porch in them old rockers. I've heard stories how my great-grandma, Elisi's mother, walked the Trail of Tears when she was a little girl. That's a story you won't hear folks tell where you're from. All I know is Elisi's mother was born somewhere in Cherokee Country in what you folks call Georgia, couldn't be far from where you grew up. Soldiers brought her and her momma here in '38. Now, how would that be for a story?"

"Oh yes, please," I begged. "And you say your family is from Georgia?"

"You call it Georgia now," the old woman said, "but that's not what we called it. My people came from Cherokee Country. We had our own nation with borders. We had our own language and newspaper. You didn't know that, did you?"

"No, ma'am. I didn't know that," I answered.

"We had our own constitution. We was civilized, like you Americans."

She pronounced the word civilized with extra stress and laughed out loud.

"Folks on the whiteside called their country Georgia. The Americans took it from us piece by piece. They said their king had given them our country."

I could tell this woman was saying what every Cherokee knew.

"After they took our country they called it Georgia," she continued. "That's all I know, dear. Don't know where my great-grandma was born. I guess this story is short, like the story about the tea set. I've often thought about our country where you live now. I never met my great-grandmother. She died before I was born, but Elisi, my grandmother, told me stories she heard from her Elisi. I know those stories, stories about the Trail of Tears."

The old woman stared out the window. She was remembering things she had heard in this very room.

"My Elisi's grandmother was five when she left Ross's Landing. I think Ross's Landing is near Chattanooga, isn't it, dear?"

"Yes ma'am. It's on the Tennessee River."

"Elisi told me the stories her Elisi told her about the Trail of Tears. She remembers it being hot summertime, dry and dusty. She remembered walkin' barefoot for weeks and weeks. Ever'body slept on the ground."

As the old woman talked, her visual focus drifted beyond the horizon as she stared through the walls of her old house, reliving each sentence of her grandmother's narrative. She was communicating the sights, sounds and emotions of the Trail of Tears with such an accuracy I imagined her great-grandmother sitting before me rehearsing from actual memory.

"Wagons carried the old and the sick. Soldiers didn't leave anyone behind, they took everyone. Even though she was only five, she walked barefoot ever' step of eight hundred miles. Imagine that, Katie."

The old woman continued with something I could not imagine.

"Sometimes I dream about walkin' barefoot all that way. Can you imagine soldiers makin' kids walk eight hundred miles barefoot?"

"No ma'am. I couldn't imagine that."

"Nobody told you that story in your Georgia schools, did they, Katie?"

"No ma'am. This is new to me."

"Americans don't tell their grandkids they're livin' on farms they stole from us and they don't talk about what they did to the folks they stole from."

I couldn't imagine our own American Army forcing children and their grandparents to walk eight hundred miles barefoot just to take their land. What she described would be prosecuted as war crimes today.

"The soldiers kept us away from towns and farms. I guess the government didn't want the white folks to see what they was doin'. One of their friends died in childbirth. Those were hard times, Katie, the hardest of times.

She patted me on the knee again.

"If we couldn't walk the soldiers piled us into wagons and kept goin'. Many a Cherokee took their last breath in an army wagon and then was buried in the clothes they was wearin'. That's all I remember, Katie. Not much, is it?"

"No ma'am," I said. It was an emotional story.

The old woman stood.

"I'll be right back and tell you why I was expectin' you."

She walked slowly towards her bedroom. In a few minutes the old woman shuffled back carrying a large tattered book under her arm.

She rested a moment.

"I dreamed last night, Katie. I dreamed about this book in my lap. This old book has been in our family since '38. My family has two things from the old days. We have this tea service and this book. They both came on the trail."

She patted me on the knee and continued without waiting for a response.

"Last night I dreamed about this very book and today you show up asking about stories, stories from these old pages. Strange, isn't it?"

"Yes, ma'am. It is strange," I agreed, wondering what she would say next.

"I guess you want to hear my dream?"

"Yes, ma'am," was all I was able to say.

"I dreamed I was a girl walkin' barefoot on a dusty road with my great-grandmother and other Cherokee folk. There was a blue sky, so blue it would hurt your eyes. The sun was shinin' on the green grass beside the road. There was a red bird under a tree, bright as a fire engine, his mask black as night. A tall woman with a newborn on her back was walkin' with us. She handed me this book, this very book I'm holdin' now. She was pretty. Her hair glistened like a coal pile after a rain. She told me I was to give this book to the woman who tells stories. She gave me this book and the dream was over."

Mrs. Allen tilted her head forward, looking over the tops of her glasses.

"You, Katie, are the woman who tells stories I dreamed about."

The old woman laughed and broke the tension and pushed the book into my lap under my unresisting hands.

"This book is for you, Katie. I don't have the story you came lookin' for. I never did. You didn't come to Tahlequah to hear about a talkin' horse or an antique tea service. The story you came lookin' for is in this book."

The old woman put both her hands on top of mine and looked into my eyes as I held the old book in my lap.

"You were called, Katie. I'm supposed to give this book to you. When you tell the story, don't sugar coat nothin'."

"Yes ma'am. I promise."

9

"Keep the book. Tell its story. This book has been waitin' for somebody who grew up in Cherokee Country. This book wants to go back home."

The old woman's serious mood suddenly changed to one much lighter as she slowly lifted the stained cotton tea cozy and poured us another cup of tea. I felt the weight of the book on my legs. She finally broke the silence.

"It's an ugly book, ain't it? It's been waitin' on you."

As we got up to leave the old woman spoke.

"There's one last thing, Katie. When you're writin' I want you to answer me this, 'When does the thief legally own that which he stole?'

Chapter III
Return to Chattanooga
Chapter 3

When we got back to the room I decided to walk around and decompress before I began to peruse my new treasure. I noticed unusual street names: Choctaw St., Chickasaw St., Keetoowah St., Shawnee St. and Cherokee Avenue. I walked past the Cherokee Nation Courthouse on S. Muskogee Avenue. Across from the courthouse was the Cherokee Supreme Court Museum and the Cherokee Arts Center. After two hours walking around town I was ready to relax and study the journal.

When I got back Greg ordered our favorite pizza, got himself comfortable on the king-size bed to watch a movie and let me do my thing. Greg is a TV person. He never reads. How anyone can get through college without reading I'll never know. My parents taught me to use my imagination. They told me watching television is like having someone do your imagining for you. I like to write, be creative and use my own mind.

I turned on the bedside lamp and picked up the old book that a white person hadn't seen in over a hundred and fifty years? I felt my pulse quicken.

I began flipping through the pages reading an odd passage here and there. The thick book was full of old-fashioned, handwritten text with only a few blank pages remaining at the end.

The journal was a re-purposed business ledger printed on foolscap. The ledger's opening date was January 1818. It recorded pricing, sales and receipts from a shipping business in Savannah. I could see an overworked clerk hunched over his desk in a straight-back wooden chair beside an oversized sash window in a dockside Savannah warehouse. The man was recording bills of lading, shipping manifests, receipts and expenditures in a masculine hand so neat it looked as if it had been printed mechanically.

My imagination swirled with antebellum images of the unknown clerk dipping his pen into his black inkwell. Outside his window tall ships would have been moored stem to stern as far as you could see with scurrying stevedores handling freight from around the world.

The unnamed clerk wrote in perfect columns within printed guidelines. After the book was repurposed, the subsequent journal writer began writing on the first available blank space on the inside front cover and wrote over, under, between and beside everything recorded by the clerk. The journal

11

writer wrote in English, using small characters with almost no space between lines until no blank space whatsoever remained. When the journal writer filled all the pages used by the clerk, the writer began filling the unused blank pages towards the end of the ledger, edge to edge, top to bottom, front and back.

Following the sequence of the journal writer's winding entries was a trick. I laughed out loud when I saw the crowded text. Greg had to know what was funny. I told him the journal writer reminded me of my grandmother's letters. My grandmother wrote as if she was using the last piece of paper she would ever be allowed. Her writing was small with sentences jammed together. When my grandmother ran out of room on the front she would continue on the back. When she ran out of room on the back, she turned the paper sideways and wrote in the margins until the paper was filled, edge to edge, top to bottom, on both sides in an impossible to follow sequence. I miss her terribly.

In like manner, the pages of the journal were crammed full of text, top to bottom, edge to edge, front and back. Whoever wrote this journal didn't waste paper, not one square inch.

The journal entries, unlike the business entries, were in a feminine hand. The penmanship was more ornate than anything one sees today. It looked like professional calligraphy, like artwork.

The business ledger began in 1818. The first entry in the feminine hand was dated 1820, written in English by a Cherokee girl named Cassie. I suspected the writer was classically educated and appeared to have a stronger vocabulary than mine and possessed a keen interest in her political milieu.

The writer had been involved in the Cherokee removal. Sadly, the journal entries ended abruptly in July, 1838. Why?

I had a desire to learn everything about this young woman, every detail of her life. I felt a pang of disappointment to think the end of her story would remain a mystery. How poignant to think someone would faithfully keep a journal for almost two decades and leave it incomplete. What happened? I felt an overpowering desire for a happy ending.

There was a huge amount of material in this journal, much more than I first thought. I read odd passages until long after midnight. Greg had fallen sound asleep halfway through his movie. My mind was tired. My emotions had been drained. I leaned back on the soft pillows without turning off the lamp, laid the open journal face down on my stomach and fell into a deep sleep. I dreamt about that mysterious place where people keep their Indians.

That night in my dreams in Tahlequah, Oklahoma, I first heard the voice.

My dream was vivid. I was looking through an immense picture window at a bright landscape. The sky was blue with scattered black clouds. I saw myself walking alone down an unpaved country road. I stopped at a tree and listened to bluebirds singing. The colors were intense.

I don't remember seeing a person, but I did hear a voice. I would remember the woman's voice forty years from now, a kind, musical, friendly voice. I knew instantly the person behind the voice needed my help.

As I walked the voice said three times, 'Tell my story.'

I sat bolt upright grasping the open journal. It was as if the voice came from someone in the room. The light was still on. I jumped up to check the room. The door was double locked, the window was permanently closed with screws, no one was in the bathroom, shower, closet or under the bed. We were alone. Greg was snoring. The voice must have come to me in my dream. There was no other explanation. How could that be?

I remembered the old woman saying the story was pursuing me. I shivered from a sudden childish fear of the dark. This thing with the journal, the old woman's dream and now a voice invading my own colorful, Disney-like dream was making me believe I was in some kind of sci-fi story.

I recall little about our visit with Greg's parents in western Oklahoma or the return to Chattanooga. I gathered material on the return journey for my university project, but I can't bring to mind the gist of one story without referring to notes. Since my visit with the old woman I have been obsessed with one thing. Since I returned I've been spending time in the Chattanooga library's third floor trying to understand the journal and its historical milieu.

If I wanted to understand this woman's life and her journal, I would need a crash course in Cherokee history. The journal was written between 1820 and 1838. I couldn't tell you one thing that happened during those eighteen years, nothing, nil, zero, zilch, nada.

To satisfy my own curiosity I asked friends, classmates and casual acquaintances if they knew one event in American history between 1820 and 1838. No one knew anything. Everyone was as ignorant as I was. I have a lot to learn about this blank space in Georgia, Tennessee, and American history.

I quickly came to realize nothing much remains of hundreds of years of Cherokee culture that had existed around Chattanooga and north Georgia. It's as if Cherokee history had been removed along with the people.

Ross's Landing is slightly upriver from Riverbend. There's nothing at the site to indicate the precise location of the old Cherokee trading post and village. John and Lewis Ross's trading post was of wooden construction and long gone. Common photography wasn't in general use until after 1839, so there is no photographic record of the Cherokee and their removal.

I found no extant drawings of Ross's Landing and pitifully few eyewitness accounts of Cherokee occupation or their removal. About all I could find were terse military reports, ration books and emigration rolls. I did read the Reverend Daniel Butrick's journal and found it somewhat useful. He lived and worked at the Brainerd Mission seven miles east of Ross's Landing on the other side of Missionary Ridge, where Brainerd Village is today.

13

Just up river from the Riverbend venue is the Market Street Bridge, erected in 1930. The bridge has been graciously re-named the John Ross Bridge. The text of the brass plaques placed at the ends of the bridge reflect the mindset of the citizens of Chattanooga when the bridge was constructed.

The 1930 plaque reads:

"This Tablet marks the site of Ross's Landing--Here a Cherokee trading station was maintained by John and Lewis Ross during the early part of the 19th century. From this point, in 1813, General John Cocke led the East Tennessee troops through the Cherokee Nation to join General Andrew Jackson in the Creek war. Ross's Landing was designated as one of the three places of rendezvous for the removal of the Cherokee in February 1838. A ferry was operated at this place and around it grew up a flourishing village called Ross's Landing. On 14 November 1839 the name was changed to Chattanooga."

The military action of the American Army against Creek Indians was given center stage in this brief memorial. My curiosity was growing about our sanitized view of American history, especially as it pertained to the Cherokee. The United States government referred to the Cherokee removal as emigration, the Cherokee problem or the Cherokee disturbance. Our government's use of language reminds me how we euphemistically refer to the killing of civilians in wartime as 'collateral damage'.

I visited the Cherokee memorial near the old Blythe Ferry. The seven raised stones record 2,537 households from the 1835 Cherokee census. My grandfather crossed the river many times near here on the old Birchwood Ferry with his grandparents, the same crossing as the 1838 Blythe Ferry.

The Passage memorial is on the hill just above where Ross's Landing may have had their docking facilities for the big steamboats. The Passage is a permanent outdoor exhibit showing the seven Cherokee clans, a weeping wall, seven six-foot high disks recording the Cherokee story and a fourteen-foot-high stainless-steel sculpture of Cherokee stickball players.

In 1835, Ross's Landing, on the Cherokee northern boundary, was a small Cherokee owned trading post and ferry with maybe two hundred full time residents, maybe not that many. The Tennessee River was the northern and western boundary between the Cherokee Nation and the states of Tennessee, Alabama and Georgia. Before 1838, travelers from Nashville to Milledgeville or Savannah were required to pass through Cherokee Country and pay a toll to the Cherokee ferry owner. These tolls created a small Cherokee upper class and resentment by American business travelers.

By the spring of 1838, with the influx of the U.S. Army, government officials, Tennessee and Georgia militias, multitudes of contractors, hordes of squatters, scavengers and the incarceration of thousands of Cherokee in prison camps, the population around Ross's Landing would have swelled to as many as twenty thousand, probably more. Add horses, mules, donkeys, cows, oxen, dogs, chickens and hogs and it would have been a disorganized maze of camps, hastily constructed wooden structures, houses, barracks, forts, inns, stables, barns and corrals impossible for us to imagine in our modern world of automobiles and electricity.

Before 1838, there were few permanent structures on the Cherokee side of the Tennessee River. In 1837 and 1838, temporary camps were erected as far as one could see in every direction preparing for the government ordered removal. Just forty miles up the road in Charleston, present day Cleveland, there was another large military operation rounding up and imprisoning the Tennessee and North Carolina Cherokee, another ten thousand souls.

In 1838, Ross's Landing would have been a madhouse, generating a cacophony of sounds and odors. Morning and evening smoke from cooking fires would have filled the sky, an unforgettable sight. No one would see anything like it again until November of 1863 when the American army returned and violently removed another group of uncivil folk.

Seven miles east of Ross's Landing was a long-established Christian mission to the Cherokee, opened in 1817, visited by President James Madison. It housed fewer than a hundred Cherokee residents and staff. It was located where Brainerd Village and Eastgate are today. It was overseen by the *American Board of Commissioners for Foreign Missions*. Resident youth were taught the English language and American customs. Young Cherokee men were taught trades and farming. The girls were taught to be keepers of the home, to spin, cook and sew. The 'general government', the term used to describe what we today call the federal government, used Christian missionary societies as a tool to accelerate the absorption of Indian cultures into American society and thus expedite their disappearance.

Nothing remains of the Brainerd mission except their graveyard. It's still there. The graveyard is one of the few places in Chattanooga where the final resting place of any Cherokee who died during the removal are honored. It's located directly between the old Eastgate Mall and Brainerd Village. Look for the out-of-place square of mature trees in the midst of concrete and asphalt.

The hundreds of native Americans who died in detention around Ross's Landing and Cleveland remain in unmarked graves under buildings, sports facilities, roads and farmland. In 1913, the new Hales Bar dam flooded more native American gravesites. In 1915, progressive government bulldozers unceremoniously pushed all remaining Native American burial sites into the Tennessee River to make way for Chattanooga's Riverside Drive.

In 1830, the American Congress, led by president Andrew Jackson, passed the Indian Removal Act authorizing the 'extinguishment' of all Indian land rights. U.S. Army General Winfield Scott accomplished that mandated removal in the first weeks of June of 1838. In October of 1838, the Christian mission at Brainerd closed. The remaining Cherokee were deported in the autumn of that year. By 1839, the Cherokee were gone, 'extinguished', the word federal and state governments used.

In 1838, the deportation was enthusiastically welcomed by the surrounding American populace. Georgia, Tennessee, Alabama and North Carolina opened up Cherokee Country to legal American settlement.

On 14 November 1839, Chattanooga was incorporated. The 'Scenic City' was built on what was the year previous sovereign Cherokee soil.

I tried to visualize the location of the ferry and the steamboat docks and the center of Ross's Landing. I found the task impossible. I tried to imagine the 1838 scene among the modern buildings and streets and the tidy lawns of the peaceful park on Riverside Drive beside the river.

Why don't we have more detailed accounts of the removal? Non-military records are scarce to non-existent. No one, military or civilian, cared to chronicle the deportation of the entire Cherokee Nation.

Two large Cherokee prison camps were located near Ross's Landing. Their exact locations are lost. From the top of the hill I looked down and tried to imagine those two camps, crowded with Cherokee families held under twenty-four-hour guard. They were packed together in open areas with little shelter, no sanitary facilities or provisions for cooking. They were supplied with a few tents. They slept on the ground. Where did Cherokee mothers cradle their babies while they waited deportation?

Where were the docks where hundreds were herded into noisy steam vessels? As I stood on the hill overlooking the river I imagined a young Cherokee mother separated from her husband, struggling with terrified children as impatient American soldiers ordered her and her little ones down the hill into the noisy, smoking contraption floating at the water's edge, intending to transport her and her babies to a far-away land she knew nothing of. The American soldiers threatened the young mother with violence if she disobeyed, in a language she would not understand, all for one reason, to possess her land.

Where were the United States Army barracks located? Where were the Tennessee and Georgia Militia camped? Where were the several hundred Creeks imprisoned who were rounded up with the Cherokee? Where did the civilian contractors and wagon drivers eat and sleep and keep their thousands of draft animals? Who was housing, feeding and shoeing the thousands of horses and mules? Who supplied the immense amounts of grain and fodder necessary? Who hauled the water? Who carried off the mountains of manure? For those who were there, the sights, sounds and smells of the Cherokee removal would be indelible.

I tried to envision the 1838 scene. My imagination failed me.

Chapter IV
The Second Journal
Chapter 4

I sent the old woman the information I discovered about her tea service. I enjoyed the research. I was surprised to learn her tea set was manufactured about 1790 in the Meissen factory in Germany, the oldest porcelain factory in Europe and still in business.

A few days later I got a phone call. I had a premonition it was the old woman. I was right.

"I received your letter this morning. Thank you so much for the information on the tea service," she said. "I appreciate you taking the time to do that research for me."

"You're welcome, Mrs. Allen."

"I would never guess after all these years you could find that information," she said. "Thank you, Katie. Your visit has renewed my interest in family history. I've been searching every nook and cranny in this old house. I've discovered things I haven't seen in sixty years. Just yesterday I found a small box I never remember seeing. In that old box I found a sheaf of yellowed papers. I suspect they may be another journal. They're written in a cursive hand like the one I gave you. Do you want these papers, Katie?"

"Yes, please," I answered quickly. "I'll send fifty dollars today, and you can overnight them to me and keep the difference."

Two days later I received the FedEx envelope. The handwriting of this second journal was in a cursive hand much like the first journal, though not quite as neat and apparently with no pages missing. What a find.

It was a personal journal similar to the first one and probably from the same time period. Was it possible this document was related to the first journal? If the two were connected, it could provide clues to the missing conclusion of Cassie's journal. Since the two documents were found in the same house, they must be associated in some way. They had to be. This was my lucky day. I should go buy a lottery ticket.

The facts are coming together. Cassie's journal began in 1820 in a Cherokee community near New Echota, near Calhoun, Georgia not far south of where I was reared. Her journal ended abruptly on an obscure country road in Tennessee north west of Ross's Landing in early July 1838. A Cherokee woman named Cassie wrote the first journal. I don't know the author of the second, but I'm sure I'll eventually find out. I'm amazed at the historical details I can uncover so many years after the fact.

The author of the second journal was deported in the same detachment with Cassie and was about Cassie's age. The author of this second journal completed the eight-hundred-mile journey. It appears this second journal writer had been associated with the Brainerd Mission in some kind of teaching capacity. My guess is the author of the second journal would be the correct age to be the great-great-grandmother of the old woman I visited in Tahlequah.

Cassie's journal ended in early July, shortly after her detachment left Ross's Landing. The second journal, thankfully, chronicled the entire eight-hundred-mile trip. It recorded detailed information about the writer's children and a small group of expecting women, recording sickness, deaths and births and the like. But why did Cassie's journal end so early in the journey? Why did she stop writing? Perhaps I would never know.

Now that I have the second journal, I want to know what happened. I want to know why. I want to know every detail. I want to know Cassie's story. Will I ever learn the truth or will this brave young woman's life lie hidden forever beneath an impenetrable historical shroud?

I don't suppose there's anything I can do to right an old wrong, but the big question for me is why I didn't know about this? I grew up in the middle of what used to be Cherokee Country and until recently I didn't know a thing about Cherokee history. The events of Cassie's journal are new to me.

I didn't know that at the end of May, 1838, the entire Cherokee Nation was imprisoned, supplied with little in the way of shelters, latrines, utensils, clean water or fuel for cooking. Cherokee families slept on the ground and were supplied by the army with meager rations. It wasn't unknown for Cherokee families to eat uncooked or partially cooked food while in detention. The few doctors supplied by the government spoke a foreign language, American English. That sounds strange, doesn't it?

The Cherokee prison camps echo those I've read about in WWII. They weren't in Poland or Germany or some impossible-to-find Pacific island. The Cherokee were arrested by our own American army and confined in the middle of our beautiful country. Hundreds of Cherokee prisoners were held within a stone's throw of my university in Chattanooga. How could that have happened?

Everyone knows something of the Battle of Chickamauga, the Confederate siege of Chattanooga and the Union charge up Missionary Ridge. Every child in school knows about Robert E. Lee and Ulysses S. Grant. It seems no one, including myself, knows anything about Andrew Jackson, the 1830 Indian Removal Act and the Cherokee deportations of 1838. Why?

I grew up in the middle of what had been sovereign Cherokee Country. When my grandfather was a child he lived in Rossville, Georgia, named after the Cherokee chief, John Ross. My great-great-grandmother was born in 1892 in Lyrely, Georgia, Gordon County. She grew up almost within walking distance of New Echota, the old Cherokee capital. I'm guessing, according to my recent research, her grandparents came into what had been Cherokee Country very near the time of the removal. According to my grandfather, his mother and her family never talked about the removal. Did they know? Had the memory of what happened in 1838 disappeared by the late 1800s? Did her folks choose not to talk about how they acquired their farms?

I remember feeding ducks in the pond near the old John Ross house in Rossville. The two-story log structure is tucked just behind the old Rossville Post Office near the intersection of McFarland Avenue and Chickamauga Avenue. I learned the John Ross house was moved down the hill from its original location beside the main road to its present out of the way location. For a second time John Ross's house was in the way of progress.

I don't remember being told why John Ross and his wife left their home or where they went. I don't think my parents or grandparents knew, to be honest. I suppose they thought John Ross and the rest of the Cherokee unexplainably disappeared one day. John Ross and his wife, Quatie, had six children. John Ross and his wife were not wanted inside the borders of the United States of America. She died 1 February 1839, during her deportation. She was buried in the old city cemetery in Little Rock, Arkansas.

I am determined to learn more. The second journal is a factual treasure trove detailing the daily life of the Cherokee during their eight-hundred-mile deportation. I was especially moved when I read of a pregnant woman dying in childbirth during the removal. The second journal gives the exact location where the poor woman died, directly opposite twin peaks of the ridgeline resembling the breasts of a woman, the right peak slightly taller than the left.

Could I find those twin peaks? They weren't far from Chattanooga. If I found them, would I find an old grave close beside the road? There's a good chance I have enough detail from the journals to identify their route, and I have the second journal's daily reckoning. I might get lucky.

A civil engineer, my history professor and I studied topographical maps to determine the exact route of Cassie's detachment. They highlighted several locations that seemed to match the topography described in the journal where they thought the pregnant woman may have died. They told me not to be surprised if I found nothing, but it was obvious the journal writer had noted prominent landmarks so they could return, perhaps to erect a memorial.

The second journal recorded the pregnant woman's death near a certain place. I thought it logical she would be buried there, but I had no way of knowing. Even if my search was fruitless, I would have a nice outing in our beautiful Tennessee countryside.

The endless hills and valleys of Tennessee are confusing, even to professionals. On the other hand, the topography of Tennessee hasn't changed since 1838. If I were to accidentally find the two hills, they would appear exactly as described.

The following day was the Fourth of July. I want to transcribe Cassie's journal. I must be focused. I have no time to waste. The two hills and the grave were out there somewhere, a short drive from Chattanooga. Perhaps I would use my Fourth of July outing to celebrate my personal independence as well as our country's independence. Perhaps I should talk to Greg and tell him I want to re-evaluate our relationship. Re-evaluate didn't sound nearly so bald as breaking-up, like using the word emigration instead of deportation or today's distasteful modern pejorative, ethnic cleansing.

With luck, I might actually find the two hills and the burial site, though that wasn't likely. Historians estimate between four and five thousand Cherokee died while under arrest. If I add to this number the many thousands of Choctaw, Chickasaw, Seminole and Creek deaths, each with their own Trail of Tears originating in the American south east, I learn we Americans are directly responsible for many thousands of Indian deaths, all because we wanted what they had—land.

On the Cherokee Trail of Tears there were upwards of twenty different groups deported on various routes, some routes are traceable, some not. The records of the deportations are scanty at best, sometimes nonexistent, and the written accounts we do have often contain inconsistencies. There is no accurate record of the hundreds and hundreds of Cherokee burial sites along the various routes. Most of the unfortunates were hastily buried in shallow, unmarked graves. After their arrival out west, even more Cherokee died. I feel overwhelmed when I think of the hundreds of unmarked roadside graves, and I'm looking for one, a needle in a haystack. I decided to go alone on my Fourth of July quest, but then, after thinking about what the old woman in Tahlequah had said, perhaps I wasn't alone after all.

Chapter V

Reunion

Chapter 5

I left the morning of the Fourth with the journal riding in the passenger seat beside me. I stopped at scenic locations along the way trying to visualize the deportation. I wanted to imagine what happened. It was educated guesswork figuring how far Cassie's detachment traveled each day, although the second journal gave clues to the exact route.

I kept my eye out for the distinctive ridgeline as I neared the area I had marked on my map as the most likely spot of the woman's death but, to be honest, I had prepared myself for disappointment.

Suddenly, there were the two hills on my left exactly as described in the journal. Could these be the ones? They were where they should be according to the journals. I stared at the ridgeline recalling the description of this very valley. I transported myself to that day in July years ago. In my imagination I watched a pregnant woman struggle past my car with the help of friends. Not far from where I sat, she went into labor and died. My vision wasn't a make-believe Hollywood script.

I studied the two peaks. The hills were steep and wooded top to bottom with no structures or clearings. They were much too steep for agriculture. Without a doubt they looked precisely as they did when the Cherokee walked past them in 1838. I marveled that so little had changed.

Up the road to my right was a three-story red brick house on top of a small hill. A long black asphalt drive bordered with ornamental cherry trees wound its way to a house that looked as if it belonged on the cover of *Southern Living* magazine. The driveway was packed with cars and pickup trucks.

I decided to enquire at the house. I probably wouldn't learn anything but it felt like the right thing to do. I was pretty sure the road I was on must be close, very close, to the 1838 road. The spot where the woman died must be near. It had to be.

I rang the doorbell. An elderly man opened the door, introducing himself as Mr. Johnson, the owner.

"What can I do for you, young lady?" he asked politely. "You're the only person today who has rung our doorbell. You must be a stranger?"

"I would like to ask a couple of questions about the history of this area if you have the time," I asked.

"No problem. My daughter and granddaughter are here. They know all about the history of this place. Would you like to speak to them?"

"Sure, if you don't mind."

"Follow me. I'll introduce you. They're our family historians. Lately, my granddaughter has been interested in the history of this place before the war."

"Before World War II?" I asked.

He laughed out loud.

"No, ma'am. THE War. The Civil War. The War of Northern Aggression we call it around here."

He led me down the back stairs into the huge celebrating crowd and introduced me to his daughter, Ann. I loved the holiday atmosphere.

"I'm proud of Ann," Mr. Johnson said. "She made straight A's and graduated with honors from UT. Her daughter is eight and the smartest kid in Tennessee, even smarter than her mother. Let me introduce you to Cassie," Mr. Johnson said proudly.

"That's odd," I said.

The words slipped out. I had not intended to speak.

"What's odd about my daughter's name?" her mother said.

"Please forgive me," I answered. "Of course Cassie isn't a strange name. It's a coincidence your daughter is named Cassie, that's all. May I tell you the story that will explain?"

"Sure," Cassie and her mother answered in unison.

"I was in Oklahoma collecting everyday stories about American life to finish my journalism degree at UTC. I talked to an old woman on the Indian reservation in Tahlequah, the Cherokee capital. She said her great-great-grandmother was on the Trail of Tears and may have passed right in front of this house, if I read the documents correctly."

"What documents?"

"The old woman gave me a journal," I answered. "Entries began in 1820 and ended in July, 1838. The old woman gave me a second diary that chronicled the entire trip of that detachment from Ross's Landing until their arrival in Park Hill. According to the text of the second journal, a woman died in childbirth very close to this house. I stopped here today because I recognized the physical location described in the journal where the mother and baby died. They died beside the road across from a southern ridgeline with two peaks resembling a woman's breasts, the right slightly taller than the left, precisely like the ridgeline across the road."

Ann and her daughter immediately turned to look.

"Here's the coincidence I was talking about."

I couldn't help pausing for a bit of added drama before I continued.

"The journal was written by a Cherokee woman named Cassie."

"That is a coincidence, isn't it?" Ann said. "It's also a coincidence that we have an old grave down by the road but it's a pioneer woman and her baby, not Cherokee. My family has been here since 1809. We would know. The historical society investigated the grave. Their results were conclusive, the grave wasn't Indian. We've been told there may be a few unmarked Indian graves in this valley, but no Indians were buried here."

"I'm happy to share anything I have learned with you," I volunteered. "I've enjoyed the journal and learning Cherokee history. I grew up in northwest Georgia, but I never knew anything about the Cherokee deportation. Cherokee history is new to me."

"We appreciate you coming by, Katie," Ann said. "If you're not in a hurry, you can hang out with us for a little while and we'll talk?"

"I would like that," I answered.

"You picked a good day for collecting stories," Ann said lightly. "The only problem is not many of the stories are going to be true. There'll be more tall tales told today than you can shake a stick at. You'll get all the stories you want. Give us a few minutes to help Mother and then we'll talk."

I was beginning to relax. Ann left me by the pool and promised to return as soon as she was finished with her chores. I wonder what twist of fate persuaded me to turn into this particular driveway. I thought about Cassie's journal lying on the passenger seat of my car. Why am I here on this day?

There must have been more than a hundred people at the reunion, judging by the cars. Folks were everywhere. I loved everything about this place. It wouldn't be long before the picnic's main meal would be served. Who wouldn't love to be a part of this extended family? As I looked around I realized every person here, including me, was of European ancestry, English probably. I wouldn't have noticed such a thing normally, but I was planning to write a story about dispossessed Indians, dispossessed by white folks, Americans. This farm was in the area of that seizure.

There were no Africans, Asians, Mexicans or Native Americans at the reunion. Everyone was of Western European ancestry and spoke American English. I realized my quest to understand the journal would also be a quest to understand my heritage, a heritage that was inextricably joined to this story. I wanted to understand my family and my family's history. Where did we come from? How did we arrive in north Georgia? What part did we play in the local history of this area?

Three hundred years ago the property where I was standing belonged to a prosperous non-European, non-American culture. The Cherokee Nation was happily raising their children in this valley, growing corn and vegetables surrounded by forests filled with game. If I could be transported back in history to a Cherokee holiday gathering, I would have witnessed a similar scene as I was witnessing today. There would have been no asphalt driveway or swimming pool, but the joyous gathering of extended families with noisy children running everywhere would have been the same.

I felt a tinge of sadness. Three hundred years ago the Cherokee were unaware of the impending disaster. The Johnson family was a part of a European ethnic migration which violently supplanted the inhabitants they encountered. Today the Cherokee are gone and this entire area belongs to immigrants, immigrants who call themselves Americans, who love their families and this day are enjoying the Cherokee homeland immensely.

I sniffed the delicious aromas that filled the air and realized I was hungry. I saw all my favorite foods: homemade slaw, country style potato salad, trays of southern fried chicken, green beans and real mashed potatoes with plenty of homemade gravy, huge bowls of butter beans, fried okra and stacks of corn on the cob dripping with butter.

Mr. Johnson asked if he could get me anything.

"No sir," I said, "but I would love to hear your stories. Since you're the host, I would love to hang around and listen, perhaps ask a question or two."

"My dear, stay all day, you'll get all the stories you want."

One of the boys shouted, "Hey Grandpa, you want a lemonade?"

"No, Dustin. I'm watchin' everyone havin' fun," Mr. Johnson answered.

"Ok, Grandpa," his grandson replied. "If you need something, let me know. Grandpa, are we going huntin' again this fall? Are you going to take us to your special valley? I love that place where I killed my first deer."

"Sure, Dustin," his grandfather said. "I've already set aside that week. I can't wait. I got pictures of all of you boys with your first deer. It won't be long before I'll be puttin' a great-grandson's picture on my wall."

"Don't worry, Grandpa, I'll teach my kids to hunt. I love to be with you in the woods and hear the crunch of leaves under our boots."

I was taking notes. My mind was going from the reunion to the journal and back again.

"Come with me, Dustin. I got somethin' to show you. I was goin' to wait, but come with me now. Get your cousins and follow me up the hill."

"You want to come with us, young lady?" Mr. Johnson asked me. "You might find this interestin', maybe write about it."

"I would love to," I answered quickly.

I tagged along while Dustin's grandfather led us up the hill behind the old log cabin and showed us his new archery target cleverly tucked into the edge of the underbrush. From fifty yards the target looked exactly like a proud buck in profile with his head turned looking straight at me. It looked alive.

"I'll bring you boys up for some bow practice later," Dustin's grandfather said. "I bought a compound bow this summer and I want to try out an antique Indian bow I got from a dealer down in Gadsden. He said it was over a hundred and fifty years old but would string and shoot like new. He said it's the best handmade bow he's ever seen. Want to try it?"

"May I have a look at that old bow before I leave, Mr. Johnson?" I asked.

"Of course you can, Katie. It's in a display case over the mantel."

On the way down the hill I passed several college-age men tossing a football. One was wearing a Florida State football jersey with the profile of their Seminole warrior mascot with his two stripes of maroon war paint. In my recent research I had learned Thomas Jesup, an American army general, had been unable to capture the elusive Osceola. Under pressure from Washington, Jesup ordered his subordinates to deceive the Seminole Chief by luring him to a white flag meeting, promising him safe return. Shortly after his arrest under an American white flag, Osceola died in a South Carolina prison. I can't imagine a Florida university choosing Chief Osceola as a mascot to bring good luck during American sporting events.

From my research I've learned most folks know nothing about our history before the Civil War. My schoolgirl impression of American history was that Columbus discovered an unoccupied continent. The fact that we celebrate Columbus Day as a national holiday tells me how Americans think when it comes to Indians and their history.

I was surprised to learn I didn't know the answer to the simple question, 'Which is the oldest city in America?'

The answer in Jeopardy form: 'What is St. Augustine?'

I've been taught since primary school St. Augustine is the oldest city in North America, founded in 1565 by the Spanish.

Nope. Now I know I was wrong, badly wrong. It's not the oldest city on the north American continent by a long shot.

When the Spanish founded St. Augustine, there were hundreds of densely populated cities all over the North American continent from Canada to South America. There were long-established towns in North America from sea to shining sea, but since the inhabitants of those cities didn't maintain a standing army, didn't speak a European language and had no knowledge of gunpowder, they were easily swept aside and ignored in our history books. I was reminded of a sentence in the Little House on the Prairie books. Laura Ingles Wilder wrote about their trek west. She wrote exactly as she had been taught by adults, "There were no people, only Indians."

I recalled an old Johnny Cash song about the Seneca my father listened to. We wanted the Seneca's land. We didn't want the Seneca. They were forced by New York into a tiny reservation in the Allegheny mountains and guaranteed a permanent home by our federal government, by George Washington himself.

In 1965 the United States decided we needed even more Seneca land. We Americans confiscated the Seneca's last ten thousand acres of arable land by right of eminent domain and built the Kinzua dam. The Seneca's objections to the American seizure fell on deaf ears. Per usual, a treaty with the Indians was ignored. The Seneca were dispossessed once again. The unwanted dam and the ignored treaty got the attention of both Johnny Cash and Bob Dylan, but neither are generals or have a seat in the American Congress.

I headed on down towards the pool. I noticed little Cassie was still sitting and reading where I had left her under her big orange umbrella. As I watched, a young woman sat down beside her. I was curious and joined them. Cassie introduced me to her cousin, Ashley.

"Nice to meet you, Katie," Ashley said.

"Cassie, it's nice to see you again," Ashley said to her little cousin.

"I'm happy to see you, Ashley," Cassie said. "Isn't this reunion wonderful? I love celebrations and holidays and I'm glad you're here. I'm glad everyone is here. I love it when our family gets together."

"Yes, it is a wonderful day," Ashley answered. "There's not a cloud in the sky. We got a nice little breeze blowin' down the valley and this is a perfect day. We're lucky to have grown up in Tennessee. This is the greatest country on earth and we live in the best part of it, don't we Cassie?"

"What ya' reading, Cassie? What's so important you don't want to talk to your relatives?"

"Oh, this is a library book I brought home for the summer," Cassie said, holding the book up for us to see. "It tells about the people who lived here before the settlers came. There are things about Tennessee history I didn't know. Do you know much about Tennessee history, Ashley?"

"I know nothin' about history, Cassie," Ashley answered. "When I was in high school I was havin' too much fun teasin' boys. The only reason I went to college was to get my M.R.S. degree."

"What's an M.R.S. degree?" Cassie asked.

Ashley and I laughed out loud.

"My M.R.S. degree is my Mrs. William Benson degree, silly," Ashley said, still laughing. "It means I went to college to find a husband and not for an education. I wanted to find an ambitious man who would provide."

Ashley continued laughing, "I didn't want to marry some backwoods, television-watchin' redneck. I didn't want to live in a trailer and work night shift. I married Bill. He's finishin' his law degree. He's goin' to be a real estate attorney. We're buyin' a place close by. It's much nicer here than Nashville. Rural Tennessee is a lovely place to raise children. I wouldn't want to live anywhere else in the world. Nothin' could make us leave."

Cassie's mother, coming up from behind, affectionately embraced both her daughter and Ashley.

"Isn't my little girl lovely? And she's smart, too," Ann said.

"Yes, ma'am. Cassie's as cute as a button," Ashley replied.

Ann sat at our table beside her daughter.

"My Cassie does love to read. When I kiss her goodnight, I have to turn the light out or she'll read till dawn."

"Katie, I have an interesting story for you," Ann said. "I didn't tell you earlier, but there's a reason I named my daughter Cassie. After listening to you tell us about the old woman in Oklahoma, you got me thinking."

"I would love to hear about that," I responded.

"I got pregnant for the first time right here on this farm," Ann said and paused for a moment staring south over the trees with an expressionless face. "My fiancé came to spend Thanksgiving with me and my family. Momma always fixes a big Thanksgiving dinner. It's quite a tradition. I'm the youngest of four. My siblings left that Thursday evening after the football games. My honey and I had the rest of the weekend to ourselves. He brings flowers and leaves sticky notes around the house. Sometimes I'll find a note in a pocket or a sock or he'll put one in a book I'm reading. I found one yesterday in the freezer on the chocolate peanut butter ice cream."

I was envious. Ann continued her story.

"The weather was warm that weekend. Friday afternoon my honey and I wandered up to the old cabin while my parents were resting. Our youthful hormones got the best of us. John and I were planning to wait till after the wedding, but we decided we couldn't delay. We made love right there on the dusty floor of that old log cabin. I wish we had waited, like you did, Ashley, but we didn't."

In unison we looked up the hill at the old Johnson log cabin, long empty.

"That was a special day and the result of that special day was a special child," Ann said, as she kissed her daughter on the forehead.

"In case you're wondering, Katie, Cassie knows the story of her conception. That moment was special. When I tell you the rest of the story, you'll understand why I told Cassie. I don't know how I knew the exact moment I conceived, but that very night I had a dream I remember as if yesterday."

I was the one staring now.

"My dream had colors," Ann said in a low voice. "I don't usually dream in color. I think I dream in black and white and I never remember dreams. This dream was dazzling, like the colors in *Wizard of Oz*. I can close my eyes and see the colors now. I could sketch every scene. The sun was bright orange, the cabin a rich chocolate brown like a Hershey bar, the leaves and grass brilliant shades of springtime greens and the butterflies were like neon signs at night. In my dream I walked up the path toward the cabin and felt a warmth. That's when I heard the voice."

"What happened next?" I whispered.

"The voice said, 'Your baby will be Cassandra'. And then the voice repeated that same exact sentence twice more, and that was all. In my dream I was walking up the hill, but the voice was coming from behind me, from the direction of the old headstone down by the road."

"That sounds spooky, doesn't it?" was all I could manage to say.

"No, the voice wasn't spooky. It didn't frighten me. I know it sounds eerie now, but the voice brought comfort, still does. I'm telling the truth."

"You heard voices?" I was barely able to get the words out.

"I didn't hear voices, plural," Ann said. "I heard just that one friendly voice, Katie. The voice was as real as if the person was in the room with me."

"I know exactly what you mean," I said to Ann.

Ann continued, "I haven't had a dream like that since. I don't remember dreaming in color again either. I thought my dream was connected to the cabin and the grave, but I have no idea how, and that is a guess. It was as if some benevolent spirit wanted to bless my unborn child and the benediction began with this dream. As you can see, I obeyed and named my child Cassandra."

"Ann, may I ask you a few questions? Are you busy right now?"

"No, I'm not busy. What do you want to know?"

"I would prefer our conversation be just you and me. Would that be ok?"

"That would be fine," Ann answered.

"Would you two be offended if I took Ann away from you for a few minutes?" I asked Ashley and Cassie. They didn't mind.

Cassie took her book and wandered towards the kitchen. Ashley went to sit with her husband. Ann and I walked onto the lawn.

"Ann, I want to tell you something that happened in Oklahoma."

"Tell me. I'm all ears," Ann said as we walked along.

I told Ann about my interview with the old woman, how she heard a voice telling her to give me the journal. The old woman said the story was chasing me and not me chasing the story. I told her about the voice I heard that very night in my dream. I told Ann everything.

"This whole story, from the time I went to Oklahoma until I arrived here today, is so Twilight Zone. That's three of us connected by dreams and voices. Wouldn't it be bizarre if it were the same voice, if all this were linked?"

Ann and I went back to the pool deck and sat in the shade.

"You're right, Katie. It's creepy. I have no idea what's going on here with our dreams, the voices, the old woman's journal and the story you're writing, but I have a suspicion all this is connected and the old woman is correct. This story is chasing you. How else could you have ended up here on the only day you could have possibly met me and my daughter?"

"All this does make me wonder," I said.

"Katie," Ann said, "I think you should continue your quest. That's my advice. The old woman is right. The story needs to be told. I think you're the teller. You've been chosen. I also think you may have some answers I've been lookin' for myself. We shall see."

Chapter VI
Cassie's Paw-Paw
Chapter 6

Cassie walked up the hill to the old log cabin to get away from the noisy celebration. She wanted to read. The cabin, on the National List of Historic Places, had been acquired in a land grant in the early 1800s. Cassie often tried to imagine what life was like on this farm back then. The book she had brought from school had piqued Cassie's interest in her family's history and the visit today by the journalist had increased her curiosity. She was also curious about the history of all of Tennessee before her ancestors moved here. Who had lived in Tennessee before her family had been given the land grant?

Cassie's grandfather followed her up the hill, moving as fast as his old hips would allow. He found Cassie sitting in the doorway reading.

"Honey, some of our relatives have driven a long way and would love to visit with you. Can't the book wait, sweetheart?"

"Paw-paw," Cassie asked, ignoring her grandfather's question, "did you read about the history of Tennessee? I've read some interesting things in this book, things I didn't know."

"No, sweetheart. I don't know much about history," her grandfather answered. "I never was one for readin'. I leave that to your maw-maw."

Cassie's grandfather paused for a moment as he admired his farm.

"Yep, I done pretty well. I never did learn to read good, Cassie. Your grandmother, now she can read. She's educated. She taught fifth grade. Anyone who can teach a room full of fifth grade boys is a saint. I don't do much readin', Cassie. If I want to know somethin', I ask her. If there's somethin' in the paper I want to know about, I ask her to read it."

"Paw-Paw, do you know anything about the grave down by the road? Why is there no name or date on the headstone?"

Her grandfather sat beside Cassie in the doorway to the old cabin and put his arm around his granddaughter.

"I was the one that found the grave, Cassie. We had a terrible wet spring. It rained and rained. Water gushed down the hills where we had never seen water run before. Our whole bottom was a lake where the cornfield is. We replanted twice that year. When the rains were over that spring, I found the skeleton in the wash right behind that big white oak beside the road."

"That's scary, Paw-paw," Cassie said, leaning against her grandfather.

"If I close my eyes, I can still see that skeleton plain as day. Daddy called the sheriff. The sheriff called Nashville. The forensic folk from UT came down. They told us they believed the bones to be those of a twenty-five or thirty-year-old female. They also discovered the skeleton of a newborn. The woman and baby had been buried together, wrapped in a quilt. They also found two gold rings."

Cassie remained quiet and listened to her grandfather.

"They told us the quilt and the rings were probably German. They concluded this was an unfortunate immigrant woman who died in childbirth."

"That's so sad, Paw-paw."

"Yes, it was," her grandfather agreed.

Cassie snuggled against her grandfather.

"Daddy re-covered the bones and put some stones on top to keep it from washin' again. He made it look like a proper grave like Momma wanted."

Her grandfather's voice took a brighter tone.

"The pioneers, like the woman and her baby, they made America great."

"This is interesting, Paw-paw. Thank you for telling me," Cassie said.

Cassie's grandfather, sensing the discussion had taken a depressing turn, changed the subject. He impulsively took a twenty-dollar bill from his wallet and held it up in front of Cassie. Cassie thought her grandfather sometimes behaved like an impulsive little boy. She loved him dearly.

"See this man," her grandfather's calloused finger pointed at the portrait on the twenty-dollar bill. "This is Andrew Jackson, seventh president of these United States. He's from Tennessee. How's that for knowin' history?"

Cassie knew about Andrew Jackson, but she didn't interrupt her grandfather's speech. Her grandfather held the twenty-dollar bill up close to his face and inspected the image of Jackson carefully.

"There he is, right here on our twenty-dollar bill," he said, holding the bill at arm's length and punching the portrait with his gnarled old finger as if he were playfully punching the real Andrew Jackson on the chest.

"Your great-great-great-grandfather once fed and watered Andrew Jackson and his Volunteers right here, right here on this very spot where we're sittin' now. Ain't that somethin'? Mr. Jackson sat right here where we're sittin', Cassie, in this same doorway on this same piece of old wood we're sittin' on. Mr. Jackson looked out over this same valley we're lookin' at."

Although his granddaughter had heard the story of Jackson's visit before, she wanted to encourage her grandfather. His marvelous rehearsal of family history was as welcome as if she was hearing it for the first time.

"Mr. Jackson said, 'Abner, you got a beautiful place here. You're a true American. This is what me and my boys are fighten' for. We whipped the British and we gave the Indians what for. Mr. Johnson, but you can call on the volunteers anytime. We'll be back in two shakes if you need us. Me and my boys won't let anyone stand in our way, or your way, of building America and bringin' peace an' prosperity to our families. We discovered this country. America is rightfully ours. We'll defend it.'

"Owning land is important, Cassie. Daddy told us boys ownin' land is the most important thing in this world. He said 'they ain't makin' no more land, ain't never goin' to make more land, so the value of land will always go up'. Daddy was right. Ever' time I saved a little, I bought land."

He smiled again as he looked with pride across the farm.

"Paw-paw, you know a lot about history," Cassie said.

Her grandfather stretched his legs and sat back down beside her without a word. He put his arm around his granddaughter's shoulders again.

"We're proud of Jackson, Cassie. Every American owes a debt to Mr. Jackson. He brought unity to this country. He made America great."

"Paw-paw, I love to hear you talk about those things."

He gave his granddaughter another squeeze.

"Our family came here in 1809, Cassie. Bet you didn't know this farm used to be North Carolina land, did you? North Carolina was given this land but they gave it back to the government. You didn't know that, did you?"

"Didn't Indians live here?" his granddaughter asked.

"Oh, I guess so," her grandfather said. "Nobody ever' talks about them."

Her grandfather wanted to talk about Andrew Jackson.

"Jackson was a great Indian fighter, an American hero. The pioneers loved him. Jackson even went down to Florida and fought Indians down there when Florida belonged to Spain. You didn't know that either, did you?"

"No, I didn't know that, Paw-paw. Tell me more."

Cassie wanted to keep her grandfather talking.

"Jackson is the one who got rid of the Creeks but he wasn't finished. He went down and whipped those trouble-makin' Seminoles a second time, yes-sir-ree-bob. Jackson and his Volunteers flew right into the thick of things. That's why we elected him twice. He wasn't scared of nothin'. Men like him made America great. He's the reason we have this farm."

"Why did the Indians leave? Where did they go, Paw-paw?"

"I don't know. They're gone. I guess they disappeared."

She was asking more questions than he had answers.

"To tell the truth, sweetheart, nobody cares," her grandfather answered. "Indians weren't smart and they were lazy. Indians didn't like to work. They didn't know how to build things so they left. History about Indians ain't important. All you need to know is when the first Americans came here, they found a land with no people—only Indians."

"Paw-paw, why would Indians leave a beautiful place like this? That doesn't make sense to me. Where could they go that would be better than here? How were they inferior to Americans?"

Her grandfather didn't have answers to her questions. He didn't want to discuss a difficult subject on a happy day like his family reunion. He gave up.

"We're havin' a picnic, Cassie. This is an American holiday. You don't need to be thinkin' about dumb history. Those old books don't mean nothin' now. That book you're readin' don't have nothin' to do with us."

Cassie wasn't ready to end the conversation.

"I've been reading, Paw-paw. They say the Indians didn't want to leave."

"Cassie, when you're older stories like this won't be important. What we did was right for back then. What Jackson and his Volunteers did wasn't wrong. There wasn't much government out here then, Cassie. People took care of themselves. Folks needed land and they took it. Americans had to work hard. There was no electricity, running water, telephones or cars. Can you imagine that? It was a hard life. Tennessee was the frontier back then."

There was a hint of annoyance in his voice.

"Sweetheart," he continued with his patronizing tone, "we're good people. We've always been good. The Indians left. No one made them leave."

"This book says Andrew Jackson killed Indians," said Cassie quietly.

The old farmer took his granddaughter's hand.

"Jackson didn't fight good Indians, sweetheart. He only killed bad Indians, Indians who couldn't learn. Indians ain't important—never was."

He paused to catch his breath.

"It's not like they was white folks, Cassie. They weren't American. It ain't the same thing at all. Come on, dear. Let's get back to the party?"

He took one last proud look at the portrait of Jackson, folded the bill in half and put it back into his wallet.

When they got back everything was ready to ring the old bell up at the cabin to call the family together. Mr. Johnson, a Southern Baptist Deacon, led the traditional prayer.

"Thank you, Lord, for this beautiful day and this beautiful country you've given us. Thank you for our families and our children gathered here once again this year. We're grateful for your bountiful gifts. Make us mindful of the needs of others. We ask you to bless America as we gather together to celebrate our freedom. Watch over our soldiers defending American liberty in far-away places. Bless our missionaries. Bless our children and our children's children. May they have a happy home, free from oppression in the greatest country in the world. Bless this good food and the hands that prepared it for the nourishment of our bodies. In Jesus' name, Amen.

After we had eaten, I thanked Mr. Johnson for a lovely afternoon.

"Before you go, Katie, I'll show you that old bow. Follow me."

I followed Mr. Johnson up the stairs to the living room. He took the bow from its display case over the mantelpiece. As I held it, I was impressed by the delicate carvings on the handle. There were five feathers carved in a curious running design and a buck's head in relief. Both carvings were exquisite with perfect perspective.

"Do you know the significance of these carvings, Mr. Johnson? Do you know who made them, where and when?"

"No, ma'am. The dealer said this was an authentic Indian bow maybe a hundred and fifty years old, but that's all he knew."

I wondered what piece of history I was holding in my hands? I had the disappointing feeling I would never know the answer.

Chapter VII
New Echota
Chapter 7

I made an appointment with my journalism professor. I needed advice. I showed him my notes, the two journals and recounted my story from the beginning, including Greg's offhand remark, my visit with the old woman, the coincidence of Cassie's name and the series of dreams. When I finished my disjointed recital, my professor smiled.

"Young lady, you have the gift, don't you? In all my years I haven't had many students like you. You're a born storyteller. You have a passion that can't be taught or acquired. It's in your blood. I'm privileged to have you as a student, Katie."

"Thank you, sir."

"As far as I'm concerned your mind is lucid and chomping at the bit to express itself. Writing is what you do, Katie, what you were born to do. If you want my opinion, you should embrace this project. I think your systematic mind is telling you to pursue this undertaking to its logical conclusion. My advice is to go somewhere and write, write, write. Allow your enthusiasm full rein. Let your passion infuse your work in a non-distracting atmosphere and you'll produce something we'll all be proud of."

I took his advice to the letter. I told Greg I would be working alone for a while. I found a little bed and breakfast on an out-of-the-way working farm about twenty-five miles south of Chattanooga near Rock Spring, in Walker County, Georgia. There would be no traffic noise. I could write undisturbed day and night. Appropriately, I would be working smack in the middle of the last piece of land the State of Georgia took from the Cherokee.

I planned to spend at least the next four weeks in journalistic hibernation, buried in Cherokee research. I intended to spend every waking hour reading and transcribing Cassie's journal. When I needed rest, I would do some casual exploration of what used to be the Cherokee homeland.

As a starting point I decided to drive down to New Echota and look around the old Cherokee capital. I don't remember ever being there. I didn't expect to find much, but maybe something there would give me a connection to Cassie and her journal, her culture and her people. A little poking around where the journal was actually written would be an auspicious beginning. I wanted to look at the same landscape, the same hills, the same mountains, the same rivers. I wanted to see and hear the same birds. I wanted to see the clouds and feel the air. I wanted a taste of the same weather. According to MapQuest, the old Cherokee capital was just south of Dalton, near Calhoun and only thirty-five miles south of my bed and breakfast.

I remember the old woman's personification of the journal, so I placed it on the passenger seat beside me. It would be an appropriate symbol to take the journal back where it came from as if it were my companion in research, as if Cassie were actually sitting beside me.

As I drove south from Rock Spring, I glanced occasionally at the book beside me. Then I imagined a young woman my age in the passenger seat. As my imaginary passenger watched the passing countryside, I felt her rising emotion as we approached New Echota and the home she hadn't seen since that day in May long years ago. As I visualized, my eyes filled with tears. This was going to be an interesting trip.

For the next couple of hours I drove slowly getting a feel for the Cherokee homeland around New Echota. I headed down the Chatsworth highway and crossed the Oostanaula River towards the east. I turned around and went back and turned right on Craigtown Road and then left on Gee Road. I was going in a big circle around New Eschota. I turned left onto Industrial Boulevard, then left on the Old Dalton Road, left again onto the Chatsworth Road and then under I-75. I had completed the circle.

I stopped at several convenience stores and asked about the Cherokee but no one knew anything. I thought it interesting no one could tell me a thing about the Cherokee right in the heart of the old Cherokee Nation. They were as ignorant as I was. How could that be? Evidently, the only remaining human memory of the Cherokee in this part of the world was the state park at New Echota. It seems when the Cherokee were removed everything that marked centuries of their national existence was erased as the old woman in Oklahoma had said. The Cherokee had been deleted, vanished.

Around Chattanooga there are thousands upon thousands of signs, memorials, inscriptions, markers, plaques, statues, monuments, museums and tributes to the Civil War, but nothing to speak of regarding the Cherokee who lived there for hundreds of years. I remember driving along the top of Missionary Ridge on Crest Drive and enjoying that breathtaking view of Chattanooga and the river below. Every other house had two plaques and a cannon in the front yard. Americans have a macabre pride concerning our cherished Civil War, a war between Americans we remember and re-enact. The war against the Cherokee has been forgotten. No one re-enacts the Cherokee removal.

Before 1838, our United States government recognized where I had been driving all afternoon to be sovereign Cherokee Country and not governed by Georgia or United States law. It was entirely Cherokee by longstanding treaty.

As I circled I saw picturesque agricultural farmland dotted with homes, barns, outbuildings, fences, fields and livestock, with the noisy I-75 running north and south through the middle. There was nothing in the countryside to indicate Indians had ever lived here. According to my research, the Georgia Militia, the Georgia Guard, fortunate drawers and squatters who came into Cherokee Country in the spring of 1838 seized all Cherokee homes, property, assets, livestock and even ransacked Cherokee graves looking for valuables. A few days after the deportation nothing remained of the Cherokee Nation, not even their graves.

I decided to end my quest by having a brief look around the state park at New Echota. When I arrived at the gate I was disappointed. It was after five. I was too late to get in. Mine was the only car in front of the locked gate. I got out and leaned lazily over the hood resting my chin in my hands and watching the setting sun. I tried to imagine what this area looked like in 1838.

This part of Georgia marks the end of the Piedmont and the beginning of the mountainous region. I especially love the stretch of road past Sonoraville, Fairmont, Talking Rock and up through the narrow mountain roads to Ellijay. I remember my Sunday outings with my grandfather long ago.

As I was leaning over the hood of my car watching the setting sun, I thought how the State of Georgia proudly proclaims ownership of New Echota and operates it as a tourist attraction. I have to pay the State of Georgia seven dollars to visit the old Cherokee capitol. What a paradoxical turn of history.

In 1838 the State of Georgia took possession of New Echota. Near where I was standing several hundred Cherokee families were held prisoner for days and then marched north on foot by the Georgia Militia to be held briefly at Ross's Landing on the Tennessee River before being deported.

I don't understand. Why hasn't New Echota been given back to the Cherokee? It was theirs, wasn't it? It wouldn't be the last time the actions of the American government would puzzle me. I wondered where the removal fort had been built. What did it look like? Where was the open ground where the Cherokee families were imprisoned, guarded night and day as if they were dangerous criminals. I closed my eyes. In the peaceful evening stillness I imagined I could hear children crying in their mother's arms.

I heard, "When does the thief legally own that which he stole?"

As I mused about things long ago, a small yellow butterfly landed on the sleeve of my white blouse. I didn't move. It sat on my arm for quite a while gently moving its bright yellow wings. I imagined I was being welcomed to New Echota by a benevolent spirit. The spirit was blessing my quest. After my welcome, the butterfly flew into the Georgia dusk and disappeared.

In silence I watched the last crimson rays of the Georgia sun disappear behind the mountains. As the light began to fade, the twilight shadows crept from their hiding places, embracing all of New Echota. The long-abandoned

Cherokee capital, with no living residents other than myself, lay still and silent before me, no lights, no sounds, no people.

In the gathering gloom New Echota seemed to quicken. I imagined shadowy silhouettes rising from the soil, Cherokee sentinels, wispy, majestic, giants of honor standing their sacred guard over their old capital, safeguarding hallowed ground in their nightly vigil, preserving the dignity of their dispossessed nation.

In the gathering darkness I suddenly heard what sounded like distant voices, soft choral harmonies that swelled into a gentle crescendo, pouring over me and New Echota. They sang, "Tell our story."

I heard the voices sing, one moment in sweet consonance, the next in an unpleasant dissidence. What was I hearing? The voices grew louder, surrounding me with their song. For a second time I heard the sweetness followed by a strange discord.

I looked around but saw nothing.

Then I heard the chorus singing a third time, or did I? Did I really hear voices? More likely it was my out-of-control imagination manipulating the sounds of whining eighteen-wheelers on nearby I-75.

I am weary of voices and dreams. I am becoming emotionally involved in a historical drama whose last act had begun right here under my feet in the spring of 1838. I was tired. I wanted the familiar security of my car, to lock the doors, drive to the safety of my room and pull the covers over my head.

I need to come to terms with the truth that it is impossible for a single person to right old wrongs a hundred and fifty years after the fact. No one will ever be allowed to re-write the wretched end of the Cherokee, especially me. What was done was done. The milk has been spilt. The genie cannot be put back into the bottle. Pandora's box can never be shut. I need to write the story I was given and get on with the next project in my life, case closed.

Perhaps I should gather happy stories about people who are alive, helping nice people become nicer. Perhaps I should let sleeping dogs lie. I don't believe I should forget the story but I'm worried. I remember the old woman staring at me and saying the story was pursuing me. I know the journal contains a great story, but I am feeling like a dog on a leash, tugged this way and that by an invisible master.

I need to quit thinking so much. I drove straight back to my room without stopping. As I got out of my car the oversized full moon was rising over the nearby Peavine Ridge. It lit up the landscape like daytime. It was huge, yellow and beautiful as only a summertime moon can be when it first appears. It was a welcome omen and an auspicious ending to my long day. The rising moon made me feel better. I went inside and decided I didn't need to unwind. I locked the door and went right to work transcribing the journal.

Chapter VIII
Katie Sets the Stage
Chapter 8

Since Greg's 'that's where we keep our Indians' remark and the meeting with the old woman, I've thought of nothing but preparing Cassie's journal for publication. The following will be the foreword.

The Cherokee once occupied most of the vast area we call Georgia, Tennessee, Alabama, North Carolina, South Carolina, Kentucky and some Virginia. By 1820, the Cherokee had been squeezed into the mountainous land where Georgia, Alabama, Tennessee and North Carolina intersect.

Cassie, a young Cherokee woman, details her life from her girlhood in 1820 until the deportation of the entire Cherokee nation in 1838. She tells of joys, heartaches and loss. She talks of family, her nation and the complicated politics of those last turbulent years. She tells about her love for her handsome fiancé. She describes in detail how her land was seized and her people deported en masse west of the Mississippi River, outside the borders of the United States to the end of the earth.

Who were the foreign invaders who seized the Cherokee Nation's land and deported her people at gunpoint? They were Americans, mostly English immigrants with a small number of Scots, Welsh, Irish, French, Dutch and Germans. All were white Europeans. They were Americans just like me. In fact, they were my relatives.

It was Cassie's lifelong wish that her story be told, her journal published. It seemed best to my editors to let Cassie speak first person. We want this courageous woman to have her say. I want you to hear her brave voice, a voice denied for a hundred and fifty years. This book is her story.

Cassie's Cherokee name was Walela. Until I accidentally wandered into the Cherokee Indian Reservation in Oklahoma, I never knew the area where I grew up in northwest Georgia was once independent, sovereign Cherokee Country, Cassie's home.

To my surprise I learned that before 1838 the entirety of Walker County where I was reared was considered outside the legal jurisdiction of both Georgia and the United States. How strange that seems to me. Walker County once belonged to Cassie's people, the Principal People.

The Cherokee have vanished from northwest Georgia. They're long gone. Their villages gone, hunting paths gone, structures, barns, fields and houses gone. Their stories, culture, language and even their graves have disappeared. Nothing remains, absolutely nothing. Even the authentic looking buildings at New Echota are modern reproductions constructed by Americans, descendants of the same people Georgia sent to burn the originals.

I remember my grandfather taking us on long circuitous Sunday drives around northwest Georgia. On Sunday afternoons my parents, grandparents and I explored every highway and byway. Sunday was family day.

One of my grandfather's favorite Sunday outings was a drive to Chickamauga. We always stopped at Crawfish Springs for a drink of cold water from the big stream that bubbled out from under that huge rock on the other side of the road from the old Gordon Lee Mansion. We would read the cast iron plaques, some grey, some blue, detailing local Civil War activity and the big battle that was fought in and around the sleepy town of Chickamauga.

We would sometimes go out Cove Road through Mountain Cove Farms, for many years a working farm that filled the perfect triangle where Lookout and Pigeon mountains join. My grandfather had worked on that farm.

Other times my grandfather would head east from Rock Spring and then south. As I write I can see the rolling hills, the dark green forests and the carpet of uninterrupted trees that climbed the mountain sides to the sky, or so it seemed to me as a little girl.

We would drive through Lafayette and east through Naomi, Villanow and then down through Sugar Valley to Resaca. The road through Sugar Valley ran south through the hills beside the pristine Chattahoochee National Forest.

Sugar Valley, what a beautiful place name. As a child I imagined small country grocery stores in Sugar Valley that sold nothing but five-pound bags of Dixie Crystal sugar. What a memory.

According to Cassie's journal, it was in this same picturesque Sugar Valley young white soldiers arrested every Cherokee family at bayonet point and herded them into prison camps at nearby Calhoun, Lafayette, New Eschota and other strategic locations. A few days later every Cherokee family was marched north to Ross's Landing on the Tennessee River.

Other times on our outings my grandfather would drive us south on Highway 27 through Trion. When we went through Summerville he turned left and then immediately back right onto 114 into Gordon County towards my great-great-grandmother's home place in Lyerly, in a beautiful valley where my great-grandfather's mother and her siblings were raised on a working farm before WWI and where my relatives still live.

If we continued south past her old homeplace, we would go down towards Cedar Bluff and Lake Weiss and end up in Gadsden and Rainbow City just across the state line in Alabama.

Every acre we drove past on our Sunday outings had been sovereign Cherokee soil under sovereign Cherokee law. I don't understand why I never knew that. Maybe I was told and I forgot. Maybe no one thought it important. Maybe there was no one who cared.

If my grandfather turned more towards the southeast on our Sunday drives, we would go towards Rome and Cedartown. We never went much past that. We had to be back by dark. Sunday was bath night.

We would sometimes come back through Calhoun, Resaca, Dalton and then maybe cut back through Ringgold and pass through Fairview by Lake Winnepesaukah, then down McFarland Avenue by the old John Ross house, through McFarland Gap and then past Happy Valley Farms. We would go around the ninety-degree Happy Valley curve, turn left onto Dry Valley Road and then back through Chickamauga, Shield's Crossroads, where my great-grandfather caught his car pool ride to Dupont for thirty years, and then back down 27 to Rock Spring. I love every inch of that country. I can call up this entire area in my mind at will, pretty much every turn in every road.

Even after reading Cassie's journal, I can't visualize what happened in the peaceful county of my youth. Hard as I try, I can't picture my blood relatives removing terrified children, parents and grandparents at gunpoint in order to occupy their land. I can't imagine my kinfolk seizing the Cherokee's every possession and herding them into prison camps and soon afterward deporting them eight hundred miles west, all sanctioned by our American Congress. The Cherokee deportation was, and still is, quite legal according to American law.

My memories of Walker County are all happy memories of enchanted high school days, afternoon band practice, Friday night football games, cruising John's Drive-in, family outings and riding our horses through the endless maze of bridal paths in the enormous Chickamauga Battlefield, the largest military park in the United States.

Is the graphic account of the Cherokee being imprisoned at Fort Cumming, located not far from the old Lafayette High School on north Cherokee Street, a made-up story? Is the arrest of every Cherokee and subsequent seizure of all Cherokee assets, every house, barn, smokehouse, pot, pan, hoe, plow, horse, mule and cow, historical fiction?

On the morning of the twenty-fifth of May, 1838, young American soldiers began arresting every Cherokee family. Three weeks later Georgia newspapers boasted the Cherokee had been extinguished as a nation, vanished. The entire state had been ethnically cleansed.

Soon after the removal American families occupied every acre of Cherokee land. They registered their new deeds at the new courthouses in Lafayette, Ringgold, and Dalton and the other new county seats.

When I began my research I was puzzled why I knew nothing of the history of the removal. Now I understand.

Can you imagine a jovial American grandfather with his white hair and bright smile taking his wide-eyed grandchildren on his knee saying, "We Americans are proud of our country. Let me tell you young'uns about the day we rounded up the Cherokee with our pretty bayonets glistening in the morning sun. What a glorious sight. You should've been there. Yep, we took everything they had. We sure did. We took their homes, cows and hogs. We took their barns and fields. We took every pot, pan and stick of furniture. We cleaned house you might say. We even dug up their dead relatives. A new broom sweeps clean. Then we made those lazy, good-for-nothin' Indians walk barefoot to the other side of the Mississippi. Yep, we shoved them outside the borders of our country. We Americans have no use for Indians. It was some sight to see. I'm proud to say this farm will be yours one day. We passed laws and got rid of ever' last one. We did everything legally. Americans are good people. We did everything by the book."

No one could tell that story, could they? The Cherokee removal was erased from the corporate consciousness of an entire nation. What America did in 1838 was swept under the rug where it lies today.

Cassie, an avid newspaper reader, included numerous quotes from Georgia newspapers. Those newspapers are extant and available online.

There are no Indian reservations or Cherokee towns in Georgia, no modern Cherokee farms with Cherokee families in Walker County or any county. After reading Cassie's journal, you'll know why.

I had a small part in telling her story. I shall be content to be her amanuensis. I commend her story to you. She is yours.

Chapter IX
1820 – Cassie's Gift
Chapter 9

18 February 1820 - Month of the Bony Moon -*ka ga li*

Today I received the best gift of my life, a journal.

I am Walela. I am eight years old. My name is hummingbird in Cherokee. My parents died soon after I was born. I live with Elisi and Edudu and my brother, Five Feathers. Elisi and Edudu are my grandmother and grandfather. We live in Cherokee Country at the southern end of the great mountains near New Echota, our Cherokee capitol, the most beautiful place on earth.

Mr. Lowry is my teacher. Today he gave me my special gift.

"Hello, Cassandra," Mr. Lowry said, still in his saddle.

"Bonjour, Monsignor," I answered.

"I'm doing well in my French studies, am I not, Mr. Lowry?"

"My dear Cassie, your French is splendid," Mr. Lowry said as he dismounted, "and your accent near perfect."

"Thank you, sir," I answered.

"I'm pleased you're in my school. I'll see you there tomorrow, will I not?"

"Yes sir, I'll be there," I answered.

Mr. Lowry dismounted and handed me a small bundle of newspapers.

"Thank you for the newspapers. I read them every day as promised."

In one smooth athletic motion, Mr. Lowry's son, Ben, jumped from his horse and landed in perfect balance beside me. Ben is my best friend. I see Ben at school and some days when we don't go to school.

"Cassie, I adore your love of learning," Mr. Lowry said. "If everyone wanted to learn like you, this world would be a better place."

"Thank you, sir," I answered again.

"If I can pull the right strings, I'll get you into a college one day."

"I would love that, Mr. Lowry. I would love to go to school."

"If you keep learning at the rate you're going, it won't be long before you're ready," Mr. Lowry said. "Learning to communicate is the most important thing for any young person, even for a woman," Mr. Lowry continued. "If a person has a small vocabulary, they will have a small mind and think lesser things. You don't want to be small-minded, do you?"

"Oh no, Mr. Lowry. Of course not. I want a big mind."

"A person with an extensive vocabulary can think big thoughts and roam the universe in their mind. One's imagination is fueled by words, each word an idea. The human mind is powerful and yours, young lady, is more powerful than most and you have a marvelous memory. Trust me, Cassie. Learn all the words you can and see if what I'm telling you isn't true."

"Give her the gift, Ben," Mr. Lowry said to his son.

"You're going to like this, Cassie," Ben said. "Father got it just for you."

Ben handed me an old bound book with tattered corners. Two thirds of the pages were blank. It was bigger than my slate.

"Thank you, thank you, thank you, Mr. Lowry," I said.

"I've known you've been wanting to write, Cassie. Now you can write all you want. When I came across this old book, I knew you would love it. You could write in that big ole' thing for years."

"This is the best gift ever in my life."

"Eleanor also sent you a gift, Cassie," Mr. Lowry said.

Mr. Lowry pulled a small package from his coat pocket. I unwrapped it immediately. Mrs. Lowry gave me a beautiful new pen to go with my journal. I will never have to use an awkward turkey feather again.

"Cassie, this is your journal and pen to keep. Some folks write daily and some now and then. Some write for pleasure and some to remember what they did. Write anything you wish as often as you wish."

"I shall write, Mr. Lowry, I promise," I said. "I shall begin tonight."

"You can record daily activities, write prose, poetry or stories. You can write about what happened or write the marvelous things you conjure in your imagination. Write whatever you please, but write, write, write."

"I'll start this very day."

"May I give you some advice about writing?"

"You can always give me advice, sir," I answered.

"First, write for pleasure. Above all enjoy writing. Write about things that give pleasure and things that make you sad. Write about things you love and things that make you angry."

"Yes, sir, I promise I shall do that," I added quickly.

"Secondly, be yourself. Don't imitate books or newspapers. Write like Cassie, not like me, or Ben or anyone else. Use words the way Cassie uses words. You can invent words as long as they come from your mind."

"I love to make up words," I answered.

"Thirdly," Mr. Lowry said, "write in English as we do in school. I wouldn't be surprised if one day your journal becomes a treasure for those who want to understand your culture. There's a dearth of literature by citizens of your nation. You're unique, young lady. I want you to write. You're intuitive. Tell your story from your Cherokee perspective. Let your heart flow down your arm and through your pen onto the paper."

"I shall do that, sir."

"Mother and Father knew you would like your gift," Ben said.

"Cassie," Mr. Lowry added, "watching you with your new journal and pen is special. I can't seem to stop from giving you advice. Forgive me."

"I love your advice, Mr. Lowry. Please continue."

"I'm almost finished, Cassie. Always remember that writing isn't like mathematics. There is no wrong answer in writing. You can't write anything incorrectly if it comes honestly from your mind."

"Yes, sir. I promise I shall write," I said.

"Eleanor and I already know what Americans think. Write about anything you want, but it would be my wish you write about your Cherokee life."

"I would like that, sir. I love to write. I often listen to Edudu and his friends when they talk on Elisi's porch. Sometimes they talk all afternoon."

19 February 1820

What a grand gift is my journal and pen. I shall be writing the rest of my life. What a lovely thought. What shall I write this evening? I can write about the moon hanging above the mountain, how it throws soft light over my legs like a blanket. I can write about Elisi's fire keeping us warm. Who will read these words? I feel a joy, as if my body were packed full of jumbled words begging to be allowed out to play.

20 February 1820

I am by the fire again. It is cozy inside our house. Whoever you are that may read this, I promise to think about you as I write. I share my fire, my words and my mind. Who might you be? Are you my child or grandchild? Are you an old friend or relative? Why do you read? How did you find my journal? I promise, dear reader, to write from my heart, to tell you the truth.

21 February 1820

I pledge to write as if you were here and we were having a marvelous conversation. One day I shall sleep with my ancestors. When you read, I shall wake and we shall walk together. We will sit on Elisi's porch listening to Insect, Frog and Owl. We'll listen for Whippoorwill's call. I wish you well. I imagine us walking arm in arm under the pines with the moonlight dancing like scattered silver on the pine straw as we whisper our deepest secrets.

Who knows what is on the other side? Perhaps in another time and place we shall laugh and share. I would like that. I look forward to your visit. I shall wait for you, you who will waken me to things yet unknown. When that first star appears in the twilight, remember it was upon that star I have pledged to write just for you.

Chapter X
1820 –Newspapers - Rabbit & Terrapin
Chapter 10

19 March 1820 - Month of the Windy Moon -a nu yi

Agin'agi'li, a Cherokee leader, visited Edudu today. Agin'agi'li means Rising Fawn in English. His name calls up the most charming image. Cherokee names are from the world around us, like Red Bird, Dragging Canoe, Five Feathers, Calm Eagle, Corn Tassel and White Path. I am Hummingbird. Our names are musical when spoken in Cherokee. Agin'agi'li has an English name similar to my teacher's name.

24 March 1820

My teacher gave me the Greek name Cassandra, a Trojan princess, blessed with the gift of foreseeing the future.

I told Edudu about Mr. Lowry giving us an English name to help us to be civilized. Edudu laughed so much he got his gun from above the mantel and went hunting. I could still hear his laughter echoing as he disappeared into the woods with Spinner. I think I heard Spinner laughing, too.

4 April 1820

At the far end of our community, close to the river, is our seven-sided lodge for meetings and ceremonies. The seven sides represent our seven clans, Long Hair, Blue, Wolf, Wild Potato, Deer, Bird and Paint. My brother and I are Deer Clan, the clan of our mother. The men in Deer Clan are known to be fast runners and have great respect for animals. Our clan is recognized for delivering messages quickly.

The members of our clan are like brothers and sisters and must not marry one another. When I marry, my husband must be from a different clan or a different country. We welcome people of all nations.

If a Cherokee woman marries an American or African, the children are Cherokee, not half Cherokee. If a woman marries a man who has children, the children are considered of the current marriage. There are no half people or add-on children among the Cherokee. All children are fully Cherokee and fully welcomed into our families.

When a Cherokee woman marries, she owns her home and the children belong to her. If her husband is bad, she can throw her husband's things out and send him back to where he came from. The wife keeps her house, property and children. Her decision will be defended by her family.

6 April 1820

Ben and I walked to the river. I showed him my special place where I come to write. It's hidden by laurels. Ben loved it. That afternoon Mrs. Lowry gave us a cup of tea and a treat. She is a charming woman. Ben and I sat on the front porch with Mr. and Mrs. Lowry. Ben had been reading how different groups of animals, birds or insects are named.

"What do you call a group of fish, Cassie?" Ben asked.

"That's easy. They're a school," I answered quickly.

"Your turn, Cassie," Ben said.

"How about whales?" I asked. "What do you call a group of whales?"

"That's too easy," Ben said. "Whales in a group are a pod."

"May I play your game?" Mr. Lowry asked.

"Of course, Father," Ben answered. "You and Mother both may join."

"Cassie," Ben's father said. "What do you call a group of bees?"

"Everyone knows that, Mr. Lowry. Bees are in a hive."

"What do you call a grouping of cows?" I asked.

Ben laughed, "That's about the easiest of all. Cows together are a herd."

"May I have a turn?" Mrs. Lowry asked.

"Of course, Mother. We would love for you to play," Ben said.

"Very well," Ben's mother said, "what do you call a collection of geese?"

"Geese together are called a gaggle," Ben answered.

"What do you call a bunch of quail?" Mrs. Lowry asked quickly.

"Mother, everyone knows it's a covey of quail."

"My turn," I said. "What do you call a bunch of hogs?"

"A group of rooting, wild pigs that ought to be shot are called a passel."

Mr. Lowry asked the next question, "What is a group of salmon called?"

"A bunch of salmon are called a run." Ben answered.

"Very good, son," Mr. Lowry said. "I thought you would miss that one. Before I lose my turn, what do you call a group of beavers?"

"That's simple, Mr. Lowry," I answered. "Beavers are called a family."

I said, "Does anyone know what to call a group of buzzards?"

"Would that be a flight or a flock?" Ben asked.

"I know the answer, Cassie," Mr. Lowry said. "What buzzards eat makes them sinister. Buzzards together are called a wake."

"Very good, Wilbur," Mrs. Lowry answered with a grin. "What do you call a group of camels?"

"A group of camels is a caravan. That was too easy."

I asked my next question quickly, "What do you call a group of coyotes?"

No one could answer.

"Coyotes in a group are called a band," I said proudly.

Mrs. Lowry asked, "What do you call a bunch of ducks when they're swimming on a lake? Does everyone give up?"

"Ducks swimming on a lake are called a raft. I knew I would stump you with that one," Mrs. Lowry said. "I have enjoyed our animal quiz and if you will pardon me, I need to go inside now. You three please continue."

"What do you call a group of possums?" I asked.

"It's a grin of possums," Ben said.

I asked again, "What do you call a group of owls?"

Mr. Lowry clapped his hands. "It's a parliament of owls. And, of course, along those same lines, it's a congress of crows. Let's go inside and have a cup of tea."

18 April 1820

Ben rode over today and we spent the afternoon at my spot beside the river. We often talk about books we have been reading and lands far away.

29 April 1820

Mr. Lowry loaned me *The Swiss Family Robinson*, an English translation originally in German by Johann David Wyss. He also loaned me the story of *Rip Van Winkle* by Washington Irving. My favorite stories will always be fairy tales and animal stories like Edudu tells on our front porch.

28 June 1820

> Copied from the *Georgia Journal* – 20 June 1820 – page 3
> "And a hunting we will go. Thirty-three persons in N.H. determined to hunt for one week. They divided into two parties, and commenced the pursuit of game on Monday the 15th ult. continuing until Saturday evening.—The following is the number and description of animals killed: 43 Foxes, 10 Hedgehogs, 2791 Squirrels, 18 Crows, 44 Woodchucks, 148 Woodpeckers, 6 Hawks, 20 Blue Jays, 14 Blackbirds, 9 Threshers and 4 Polecats for a total of 3107 animals and birds."

I read this to Edudu.

"Walela, Americans shoot everything that moves. Killing animals is sport to them. The Americans have forgotten they are connected to the earth. We hunt to survive. When we harvest an animal we ask forgiveness, which is right. Americans in the forest behave like naughty boys."

"They are a strange bunch," I answered.

"Mark my words," Edudu continued, "one day when the Americans have taken all our land there will be no game. They are bringing a great evil upon our land. What will these men do with three thousand dead squirrels? I can't imagine someone boasting as these men have done. It was a bad day for our earth when the Americans came to our shores."

22 July 1820

Copied from the *Georgia Journal* – 18 July 1820 – page 2

"The drawing of the Land Lottery will commence on the eighteenth of August."

22 August 1820

From the *Southern Recorder* – 15 August 1820 – page 3

"The Floridas….The country is divided into East and West Florida…the present population, excluding Indians does not exceed 12,000….Pensacola is the capital of West Florida and is situated on the west side of Pensacola bay….The Indians principally reside in the neighborhood of Aplachia bay, are called Seminoles, and as their name imports, are principally runaways from the Creeks, and other nations to the north of Florida. They are a horrible band associating with runaway negros and live by plunder….In 1763 Florida was ceded to England in exchange for Havana, and while in their possession was divided into West and East Florida. During the American war in 1781 both the Floridas were captured by the Spaniards, and it has remained in quiet possession of Spain, until the late war, when Pensacola was entered by Andrew Jackson. In 1818 war broke out between the United States and the Seminole Indians; the latter being protected by the Spaniards, Gen. Jackson pursued them to the Spanish ports, St. Marks, Pensacola, &c, which he captured, and transported the Spanish governor to Havana….Since that period the United States have acquired the Floridas by treaty, but which has not yet been ratified by the Spanish government.

(New York Daily Advertiser)"

13 October 1820

Edudu seems to tell his stories just for me. I love to watch his eyes and listen. His stories come alive. People love Edudu's stories. One day we were having a ballplay. People came and asked Edudu to tell the story about rabbit.

Edudu began, "Rabbit is a fast but boastful fellow. Rabbit is proud of his feet. When Rabbit runs in a straight line, he cannot be beaten. Rabbit can outrun everyone. He can even outrace Deer for short distances."

Edudu paused and put his hands on his hips. He leaned his face far forward, almost to the edge of the porch, looking around at everyone.

"But Rabbit is not always wise. Rabbit can be annoying when he boasts again and again about his speed. Terrapin, on the other hand, is slow and dependable. Terrapin is the kind that will finish every project. Terrapin never boasts. If Terrapin says he will do something, you can count it done."

"This day, because Terrapin was weary of listening to Rabbit's boasts, he devised a plan. He challenged Rabbit to a special race that would teach Rabbit a lesson to end his annoying boasts and make Rabbit a better person. Rabbit accepted Terrapin's challenge to race."

"Terrapin asked his friends to help. They would teach Rabbit a lesson he would never forget."

"The day came for the competition. Terrapin and Rabbit agreed to race across four ridges. The first one to cross the finish line on the crest of the fourth ridge would be the victor. Rabbit was arrogant, sure of himself. Because Terrapin was slow, Rabbit allowed Terrapin to get to the top of the first ridge as a head start. Rabbit, irritating everyone as usual, said he would rest on the grass and wouldn't begin to race until Terrapin crossed the top of the first hill. 'It's only fair I give the slowest animal in the forest a head start. Until I see Terrapin at the top of the first ridge, I'll take my rest', Rabbit said."

"So," Edudu continued, "the animals gathered to watch. The race began just that way. The confident Rabbit, lying on his soft patch of grass beside the start line, watched Terrapin, with his stubby legs and heavy body, struggle through the grass and weeds. Rabbit rested and watched Terrapin until he finally reached the top of the first ridge."

"Rabbit knew he could easily catch Terrapin and win the race. This race would be easy. Rabbit watched Terrapin labor on and disappear beyond the crest of the first hill. Rabbit walked casually to the top of the first ridge. He was surprised to see Terrapin already beginning to disappear down the far side of the second ridge. How did Terrapin get to the second ridge so fast?"

"What was happening? How could Terrapin be so much faster than Rabbit? Rabbit couldn't understand how Terrapin could have passed the second ridge. Rabbit must hurry. Still confident he would win, Rabbit began jumping faster. When boastful Rabbit got to the top of the second ridge, he saw Terrapin crossing the top of the third ridge. This was a fast Terrapin."

"Rabbit began to panic. 'I'm behind. I must run faster, as fast as I can.' So that's what Rabbit did. Rabbit began running, jumping and hopping as fast as he possibly could through the grass until he was exhausted. When he got to the top of the third ridge Rabbit saw Terrapin climbing up the fourth hill and approaching the finish line. Rabbit tried to run even faster but, despite his best effort, he wasn't in time to win. Terrapin crossed the finish line first."

Edudu laughed and Spinner voiced his approval with a long howl.

"Just a few moments after Terrapin crossed the finish line, Rabbit fell to the ground in exhaustion and cried mi, mi, mi, mi, mi as rabbits do to this day when they're too tired to run any longer," Edudu said.

"How did Terrapin win the race, Edudu?" I asked, as if I had never heard the story.

"Walela, everyone knows how dependable Terrapin is. Terrapin finishes any task he begins. Terrapin had many friends and family who wanted to help with his plan. Terrapin posted his look-alike friends at the tops of the hills in the tall grass waiting for the signal to join the race. When Rabbit came across the hilltop it appeared as if Terrapin was about to cross the next ridge when it was really his friend who had been hiding in the tall grass and waiting. Terrapin's look-alike friends were deceiving Rabbit. The real Terrapin was concealed near the finish line so when he won the race and the animals asked questions, they wouldn't be suspicious."

"And that's not all of the story," Edudu added with another laugh. "Even today, when young men go to a ballplay, someone will boil a soup of rabbit hamstrings. They pour it across the path the opposing ballplayers must travel to arrive at the competition. When the players cross the line of hamstring soup they become tired like Rabbit and unable to run fast. I must confess on many occasions in my youth I poured hamstring soup across the path of my competitors."

21 October 1820

Last night Bear Paws caused a disturbance. He was drunk. He came to our house after drinking whiskey. The last time Bear Paws came he was so drunk he soiled himself. No one can stop the Americans from selling whiskey in our country. Bear Paws and his friends cause trouble every time they drink the white man's whiskey. Americans give our men whiskey in order to steal their money and destroy our communities. They have an evil purpose. Mr. Lowry says many Americans have also been ruined by whiskey.

They consider themselves superior, yet they sell whiskey and destroy our families.

16 October 1820

From the *Georgia Journal* – 10 October 1820 – Page 3

"The military road is completed from this place (Florence, Alabama) to New Orleans...it has been opened under the immediate direction of General Jackson...Houses of entertainment have been erected at short stages to render every comfort to the traveler. This road runs through a delightful and romantic country and eventually must become the great thoroughfare of the southern states...the day is not far distant when a line of stages will be established from Nashville to New Orleans which must necessarily render the military road the most important of any on the continent."

Edudu has been to the great river often. The road the Americans have completed runs through the beautiful lands of the Creek, Choctaw and Chickasaw nations. Americans build wide roads for heavy wagons and for their army. They love to fight. One day, Edudu says, our nation will disappear down one of those long roads.

Chapter XI

1820 – Deerslayer
Chapter 11

12 November 1820 - Month of the Trading Moon -nu da de qua
This is the story of my brother's new bow.

"How do you like your bow, Five Feathers?" Edudu asked.

"I love my new bow, Edudu," my brother answered.

"It is a good bow," Edudu said.

Edudu let his fingers glide gently down the bow's length, feeling the flowing texture of the perfectly polished hickory.

"Your bow was living when a tree and it continues to live. When you are old, this wood will remember. It will be as alive then as today. With this bow you shall harvest your first deer in the same valley where my father killed his first deer and I killed mine," Edudu said. "It is the same valley where your mother's brothers and your father brought down their first deer."

"I look forward to that day, Edudu," my brother answered.

"You will see the same looks of approval when you return with your deer," Edudu said. "I remember the boys' envy."

Five Feathers and Edudu prepared for the hunt in Cherokee fashion, observing every ritual and fast. Just before they went to bed that last evening, Edudu handed Five Feathers the bow they had made together.

"Look at your bow, Five Feathers. What do you see?"

Carved into the hickory were five eagle feathers in a clever design. Below the handle was a carving of a bust of a big male deer and his proud antlers.

"Edudu, the feathers are my name. The deer is my clan. Thank you."

"You and your sister are Deer Clan, Ani'-Kawi', Deer People," Edudu said. "This carving is for you to carry with you the rest of your life."

"I love being with you in the forest, Edudu. Truly the land doesn't belong to us. We belong to the land. I wouldn't want to live anywhere but here in Cherokee Country and be with you," my brother answered.

When the rosy fingers of dawn crept over the eastern mountains, the two hunters had already traveled far. Curious squirrels, interrupted in their morning's play, peeked from behind tree trunks at the single-minded hunters. The two rarely spoke. The silence was as comforting to them as lively conversation to some, their camaraderie as rich as the land they traversed.

There are misty days in winter when it would be difficult to see our barn down the hill, but this autumn day had dawned so clear and brilliant it would hurt your eyes to look at the cloudless sky.

There would be no hunting until they reached their chosen valley. Five Feathers would harvest his first deer where Edudu, his mother's brothers and his father harvested their first deer. After a long trek they arrived.

Edudu felt excitement as the familiar valley opened before him. The enchanted scene was precisely as remembered. He recognized trees, paths, boulders and streams as his mind flooded with memories of past hunts with men he would never forget.

The two hunters surveyed the valley. They were carefully searching for the deer runs to identify the perfect spot to position themselves for the hunt the following morning. They must not leave their smell anywhere near the paths. Deer see extremely well and have excellent hearing, but their nose is superior to any animal, detecting humans at great distances.

They saw fresh signs of deer on a well-worn path leading to the boulder-strewn stream. They made certain the healthy odor of decaying vegetation would be the only scent detectable to a cautious deer. At first light a thirsty deer would be drawn irresistibly to the cool water of the gently flowing stream. All the hunters had to do was make certain they were carefully concealed downwind and wait quietly for an hour or two. Waiting silently was not always an easy task for an active hunter, but it must be done. Patience, of all the virtues, is perhaps our greatest asset.

A large tree close beside the run was chosen by Five Feathers. All was prepared. The two had been fasting as required, obeying our customs for harvesting the forest's bounty. They lay side by side in dreamless sleep.

Long before they could tell a black thread from white, the hunters rose and arranged themselves beside the trail, carefully obscured from the sharp eyes and ears of the vigilant deer and downwind of his expected path. As they waited the autumn dawn created welcoming shadows. Little by little the sun turned the invisible clouds high above into ridges of pink cotton.

They would soon learn if their preparations had been adequate. The deer would come down the path and a young Cherokee man would draw his bow in earnest, leaving his boyhood behind.

Five Feathers was in his chosen perch eight feet off the ground in the first fork of a gnarled white oak, close beside the path they believed the deer must surely use to slake his morning thirst.

The sun's first rays had reached the tree tops on the distant mountains when Five Feathers heard footfalls. With great care the young man peeked around the trunk of the tree from high above the trail. Six mincing does came down the path in search of water. It wasn't a doe Five Feathers wanted. It was never wise to kill a doe. The six does walked past Five Feathers, unaware of the sudden death lurking above. The doe doesn't possess the fear and intensity of sense of the proud buck. Five Feathers let them pass unmolested. He wanted the buck who remained obscured somewhere in the shadows on the path above. Five Feathers wanted the big deer he knew must surely follow the prancing does. The wary buck, though yet concealed somewhere in the half light of dawn, would be drawn to the water on the same path as the female deer. The big deer's thirst must be quenched. He must have water.

The graceful brown does, with their little white tails and careless manner, came down the path together, unaware of the young Cherokee man balanced above them in the fork of the old white oak tree. Then, as Five Feathers knew he must, came the noble buck. The suspicious male deer, antlers held high, walked down the trail in the smoky haze of early dawn following the six females in his care, pausing every few steps to scan the forest for danger.

Five Feathers, hardly breathing, watched the buck's timorous approach. The big deer and the young man were now engaged in a struggle as old as the earth itself. The wary deer would take a few careful steps and pause once again with his nose elevated, sniffing for the least trace of hidden menace, listening constantly for any unusual noise that would warn him of a concealed threat and mortal danger. If the young man were to make the slightest sound in the morning silence, the deer's keen ears would hear. The slightest mistake by Five Feathers and the magnificent animal coming down the path would instantly bolt out of the valley and disappear into the trackless mountain never to be seen again. My brother hardly breathed.

The deer and the Cherokee, though ancient adversaries, share a mutual reverence. Young Cherokee men have been harvesting deer for centuries. The primordial contest is one in which the opponents have reciprocal respect that commenced with time itself. Some days the crafty buck anticipates danger and escapes. Other days the buck will be carried home on the shoulder of a proud hunter. This morning Five Feathers was hoping to be the victor. He had made every preparation and taken every precaution.

Edudu, farther from the path, was also perfectly concealed and quiet. Edudu would not draw his own bow this day. On this trip only one deer would be killed. Only one man would receive the adulation of his peers.

The splendid white-tailed buck took a long time to come abreast the tree where Five Feathers was concealed. The buck, with his magnificent rack, had survived past encounters because he was never careless. Five Feathers was not the first human who had attempted to take the life of the cautious deer.

Drawn irresistibly by the clear, cold water he must have, the big deer made his way warily down the worn path towards Five Feathers. His small black hooves seemed to test the very soil for danger. My brother waited, his blood running hot, his heart pounding as the deer approached with agonizing slowness. Would he ever arrive? The wait was maddening. Surely the cautious deer would sense the danger. Could the animal not hear the furious thumping of a human heart coming from the fork of the old white oak tree just above the path? If the deer heard anything, even the smallest sound, he would turn and fly. Five Feathers must not make the slightest noise.

Now is the time, thought Five Feathers. Slowly. Carefully. Place the arrow silently. Not a sound. Draw the bow slowly, slowly, carefully, silently, carefully. Wait. Steady. Smooth. Make No Sound. Breathe. Breathe in quietly. Wait. Wait. WAIT. Exhale quietly. Make not a sound, not a whisper of a sound. Hold the arrow still, perfectly still. Hold with strength. Hold steady. Hold still. No wavering. Hold steady. Wait. Wait. Draw. Wait for the moment. Draw. Draw. Hold—Wait—Hold—WAIT—WAIT—WAIT—RELEASE."

The truest arrow in Five Feathers' quiver was on its way.

"Edudu," the boy shouted as the arrowhead buried deep in the deer's side.

The terrified deer, with burning pain in his flank, his worst fear realized, bolted up the hill through the underbrush away from the danger that had surprised him, away from the monster overhead. The graceful body of the buck soared between the tree trunks, flying like the wind over the carpet of dry brown leaves, almost faster than the eye could follow.

In his panic, the buck's small, sure hooves were hardly touching the forest floor as he fled the unseen danger that somehow escaped his detection. The frightened animal, darting this way and that to avoid trees and underbrush, strove to outrace the pain. He flew between the leafless trees, effortlessly brushing aside the limber branches. The deer's instinct was to fly, to fly fast and far without pause. In a moment the deer was out of sight.

Bow in hand, in one graceful leap, without bothering to climb, the lithe Five Feathers jumped to the path below from his hiding place, landing perfectly in balance. Edudu appeared instantly at his side. Without a word they began their pursuit. If Five Feathers' arrow didn't immediately sever an artery, the chase could take long hours. At all costs they must not lose the deer's trail. To lose the deer's trail would be to dishonor the deer himself.

Though both men had been still for well over an hour, they were breathing deeply, stretching their muscles with the welcome excitement, their keen eyes scanning the forest floor, missing no sign of the deer's path. Without a word, using all their senses, they followed the wounded deer.

The deer ran hard and fast, sailing like the wind in a mad panic to escape the unseen enemy which must surely be close behind. Flight is the deer's only defense. The majestic animal was bounding high over fallen tree trunks and boulders. In the briefest of moments he had crossed the ridgeline out of the valley, out of the sight and hearing of the hunters.

Five Feathers and Edudu pursued. They ran through the hardwood forest with the effortless pace developed through long years of practice, a pace they could maintain all day if pressed, and had done on many occasions.

My brother followed the path by observing the telltale droplets of blood, broken twigs and disturbed leaves. The deer would run as fast as he could to put as much distance as possible between pursued and pursuer. Although wounded, the buck was strong. The telltale droplets were far apart. Fear continued to propel the frightened deer.

Even a mortally wounded deer can run miles before his collapse. When exhausted, he can conceal himself in dense underbrush, hoping to escape detection and recover strength. The two hunters must be patient yet must not lose the trail or the deer will die unobserved, obscured in some hidden cluster of brambles and the hunt would end as a dreadful waste, a dishonor to both deer and hunter. They must be vigilant as they track the deer. The telltale drops of blood, still quite far apart on the leaf bed, told the hunters the deer was running as if uninjured.

As the morning sun continued its slow rise into the autumn sky, the two hunters ran on without a word, Five Feathers expertly following the nearly invisible trail on forest floor. With each succeeding footfall the hunters' skilled eyes found the precise spot to place their feet in order to avoid unseen dangers concealed under the layer of dead leaves, at the same time dodging low limbs, vines and underbrush that slashed and pulled as they flew past.

The sun rose. The misty valley filled with the first rays of sunlight. In the long shadows of morning the two Cherokee men ran on without pause. The hunters were moving fast. Edudu, following Five Feathers, was avoiding the whipping limbs and the vicious green saw briars my brother pushed to the side. The metal-like thorns of the saw briars are cruel knives that can penetrate leather and lacerate the careless. They dodged the dense underbrush, leapt over the fallen tree trunks and avoided hidden stones. They leapt concealed cavities in the forest floor, hollows full of nothing but soft leaves where the stump of an old tree had rotted away, some as deep as a man is tall, a hidden danger that could snap the leg of a careless runner. All the while their eyes were scanning the leaf bed before them to follow the telltale path of blood and disturbed leaves without which all would be in vain. The young Cherokee man was still in the lead. This was his hunt. Our Edudu followed. The morning sun, now shining brightly in their faces, gave renewed strength. They had been running without pause since daybreak, yet were not winded.

As the dry brown leaves crunched under every footfall, the drops of blood began appearing more closely together. The deer, losing strength, at last was slowing. They continued to follow carefully and quietly. The signs said the deer was not far ahead. They climbed the side of a ridge. As they topped the rise quietly they made no sound with their feet, not wanting to spook their quarry if he had paused to rest. In a laurel thicket about a bow shot away they saw the antlers of the big buck as he knelt on the ground breathing heavily. They could hear the animal as he labored with each breath. He could run no more. The big deer had collapsed, exsanguinated, hoping to avoid detection in the laurels, regain his strength and somehow escape the pain in his side and elude his relentless pursuers.

My brother knew what to do next. He removed his knife from its scabbard. Rehearsing the traditional Cherokee prayer for forgiveness for taking the life of a forest creature created by the Great Spirit, he quietly walked to the deer which was giving the entirety of its existence for the sustenance of the Principle People, thus participating in the ordained cycle of life. Today, the young Cherokee man was the victor, the magnificent deer the vanquished. The world was in balance. The deer had fulfilled his existence.

Edudu nodded approval. They must be grateful. Evil follows those who kill for pleasure.

Five Feathers cut out the hamstrings, leaving them as required on the leaves beside the deer. They would cut off the tip of the tongue and offer it in the fire later. All must be done according to tradition. The hunt was successful, a life-giving gift given by the Great Spirit. As the two hunters rested under the bright morning sun, all was in balance. This was a large animal. It would be a heavy burden, but the two would share the labor. There was no urgency. The return journey would be pleasant. They would take all the time required. This was a long-awaited day of joy.

From behind a boulder on the crest of the opposing ridgeline, two Americans came stumbling down the slope with guns at the ready. They shouted from a distance that Edudu and Five Feathers were not to move, accusing the two Cherokee men of trespassing and poaching.

"No one gave you permission to hunt our land. You're poachers, god-damned Indian poachers. We told y'all to stay away. This is private property."

The Cherokee hunters quietly stood their ground.

"You Indians keep traipsing through our land. You reckon they understand English, John?" one man said.

"They might not understand English, but they understand powder and lead. Keep your gun on 'em. You can't trust these sneaky Indians."

The two Americans, out of breath, were shaking with rage and the excitement of the moment. They were cowards, Edudu thought. These nervous men could accidentally pull their triggers at any moment. Edudu looked from man to man planning what to do. Both men were armed with smoothbore guns, deadly at short range. The two Cherokee men dare not turn and run. They were at the mercy of the two angry Americans.

"What in the hell are you damned savages doin' slipping around my farm? That's my buck you got there. You two lazy bastards stay off my property."

Edudu knew they were many miles inside the legal borders of Cherokee Country. Even the greedy government of Georgia would grudgingly admit that fact. The Cherokee had been plagued by American squatters with no respect for boundaries, a steady encroachment of men seeking free land. Edudu's only thought was survival. He must get the boy home safely.

If they were to retrace the men's steps, they would find a newly constructed cabin under a shade tree near newly cleared bottomland, a lean-to, mule, wagon, vegetable garden, smoke house, pig pen, chicken coop and milk cow. They had seen it many times. Today the American squatters were welcome to return to their new cabin unmolested. In their arrogance, they were capable of killing without compunction. He must act instantly.

The anger that flooded the young man's heart was unbearable. If my brother were to respond violently the American men would shoot them both and leave their bodies to rot. Before my brother could make his ill-fated decision to defend himself, Edudu grabbed his right wrist with all his strength, making it impossible for Five Feathers to use a weapon. Edudu whispered calming words telling my brother to look at the men's feet and slowly back out of their sight, saying nothing, not a word, no sudden movements. Edudu, with his iron grip on my brother's wrist, pushed my brother backwards and partially behind himself so Edudu's body would shield the young man from the first shot. If one of the men fired his weapon, Five Feathers might escape the second blast.

"Do as I do. Get behind me," Edudu warned. "Look at the ground in front of the men. Do not look into their face, not a glance."

He squeezed my brother's wrist even harder.

"Do not turn your back on these men. Stay behind me."

The painful pressure on my brother's wrist kept his mind fixed on Edudu's warning. Calm Eagle, Edudu's Cherokee name, knew the Americans would not likely shoot if he and Five Feathers kept their faces towards the men and backed away slowly, giving no challenge. Bold eye contact with the cowards might provoke the jumpy American men.

The shouting man shoved the muzzle of his smooth bore straight towards Edudu's chest. There was no chance of a miss if the gun discharged. The two men, now almost within an arm's length of the two Cherokee, were recovering from their run, beginning to breath normally.

"Stay the hell away like you been told. If I catch you here again, I'll shoot you on sight. I'm tired of you stealin' everything we got."

Five Feathers and Edudu slowly backed away from the men, bending in mock reverence, not looking the Americans in the face. Edudu continued to hold my brother with a rock-hard grip. They would abandon packs, provisions, and the coveted deer. The men might shoot them in the back if they turned, ran, protested or hesitated. The only course of action was to slowly shrink backwards, like dogs with their tails between their legs.

Cherokee hunters were often dispossessed. Unskilled American hunters routinely robbed Cherokee men at the end of a successful hunt.

A bad situation suddenly turned worse. Before they had taken five steps backwards, one man ran forward. He pressed his smoothbore into Edudu's chest with his right hand and with his left ripped the precious bow and quiver from Five Feathers. Nothing could be done. Five Feathers and Edudu backed slowly until they were out of sight of the two American men.

When Edudu made certain there were no sounds of their being followed he held the heartbroken Five Feathers in a firm grip and scanned his face a long time before he spoke.

"My dear Five Feathers, you are a man," Edudu said proudly. "You have been tested. You killed your first deer according to tradition. You kept faith with our ancestors. We maintained balance. You just now accomplished your greatest deed. You shall bring home something of much greater worth than a deer. You bring honor," Edudu said. "Unlike the carcass of the big deer that will be gone in a few days, the honor you have earned this day can never be taken. Your name will be known. You touched your enemy in battle and never once turned your back. Today you became both deerslayer and warrior. In battle, you faced guns with only your knife and bow and did not flee. When we return you will bring something of much greater worth than a deer. The honor you bring will last forever."

My brother vowed to me that the next time an American attempted to rob him, it would not be my brother who would be dispossessed.

Chapter XII

1821-22 - Spain Sells Florida – Two Wolves
Chapter 12

9 January 1821 - Month of the Cold Moon – Du no lv ta ni

When we awoke this morning Bear Paws was on our porch, filthy with a dreadful odor, hardly breathing. He appeared dead. We brought him to the fire. When Bear Paws awakened he said he had come to tell us he had decided to never drink whiskey again. He asked if we could help.

He told us his story.

"Yesterday I wakened under chestnut trees. I had no idea where I was. Hogs were rooting around me. When I tried to lift my head, I couldn't move. I was paralyzed. I thought I was dying and would be eaten by hogs and no one would know. All day I lay paralyzed, alone, with hogs coming and going. I was sick. Hogs are not good company. I went to sleep. When I woke the second time I felt worse. My head was hurting terribly. I could not move. As I lay under the chestnut trees I thought of my mother, my mother's brothers and friends like you who are happy and never drink whiskey. I thought about hunting, fishing and ballplays with Five Feathers. I don't want to drink whiskey. I almost died surrounded by hogs."

"Drink this," Elisi said, giving Bear Paws hickory milk. "It will help you stop shaking. Stay here today. We will care for you."

Bear Paws drank.

"The hickory milk is good. I will not stay. I came to tell you when I was under the chestnut trees I could see my life clearly. I would not want my mother to know I was eaten by pigs. I want to live. I want to live again. I have tried to stop but Americans are everywhere selling whiskey. I have tried to resist but I can't do this alone. I need help. Will you help me?"

"Come to us," Edudu said, "and we will help you resist."

Bear Paws' eyes were bruised as if he had been fighting. His arms had ugly wounds and scabs. His unwashed clothes stank of manure.

"Dear Bear Paws," Elisi said, "stay away from Americans. They sell whiskey in order to rob you. Whiskey steals the mind. They do not think it wrong to take what belongs to you. There is not one good thing to say about whiskey, Bear Paws."

"Your decision to stop drinking is small but powerful, like a single corn seed," Edudu said. "If you plant that seed and give it water, the sun will turn

60

it into a tall plant to feed your family. Your small decision will grow day by day. Whiskey leads to death. No one should consider it. It's not good for anyone. Whiskey destroys. We can't live your life, but we can help. Today is the only day that matters. We'll worry about tomorrow when the sun comes up tomorrow. When you were a child you were happy. Everyone loved you. Everyone still loves you. The American's whiskey has stolen your happiness. Whiskey cannot be trusted. Come see us again in the morning," Edudu said, "and we shall pour more water on your little seed of corn. We'll go to the river and get us a fish."

Bear Paws smiled, "I would like to go fishing with you tomorrow."

19 January 1821

I read every newspaper Mr. Lowry gives me. I sometimes read aloud in school. Mr. Lowry says the more words I understand, the bigger, deeper and wider I can think. If I know few words, I will be like a carpenter who can only build crude structures because he had few tools.

16 February 1821

Mr. Lowry gave me two books of poetry. I read both as soon as I got home. He said, because I am Cherokee, I have a colorful understanding of the world and a rich command of words. He said poetry helps capture emotion and convey a person's deepest thoughts. There are no mistakes in poetry. There is no wrong poem.

23 March 1821

From the *Georgia Journal* - 6 march 1821-page 2

"The Florida Treaty Ratified – The Senate yesterday gave its consent…to the ratification of the Treaty between the United States and Spain, concluded in the City of Washington on the 22nd day of February, 1819. It is understood that the votes against the treaty did not exceed four or five in number. The completion of this long-suspended transaction has afforded us great satisfaction. We facilitate our readers generally that Florida is now attached to the territory of the Union."

On 10 March 1821, the American president, James Monroe, appointed Andrew Jackson to be Florida's first territorial governor. In the past Seminoles, Creeks and Africans have fled to Spanish Florida to escape oppression. Andrew Jackson will hunt them. That's what Americans do.

9 June 1821

For the fourth time, Georgia gives away our land.

From the *Georgia Journal*-5 June 1821 page 2

"...And be it further enacted, that the territory acquired aforesaid (from the Creeks and Cherokee), shall be disposed of and distributed, in the following manner, to wit: After the surveying is completed and the returns made thereof, his Excellency the Governor, shall cause tickets to be made out, whereby all the numbers of lots in the different districts intended to be drawn for, shall be presented, which tickets shall be put into a wheel and constitute prizes. The following shall be the description and qualification of persons entitled to give their names for a draw or draws, under this act: Every male white person 18 years of age and upwards, being a citizen of the United States three years..."

30 December 1821

From the *Georgia Journal* - Page 2 – 25 December 1821

"Measures have been adopted to procure a further extinguishment of Indian title to lands within the limits of this state. We trust they will be attended with success."

4 February 1822 - Month of the Bony Moon – Ka ga li

My cousin and I were throwing stones at an old white cloth, pretending the cloth was a white man. Edudu was watching us. He called us to the porch to tell us a story.

"I saw you throwing stones at your white man."

"Yes, Edudu. We hate whites," I said in reply.

"All Americans are not bad, all are not good. Would you throw stones at Ben or Mr. Lowry or Ben's mother?"

"No, Edudu. We would not throw stones at them," I answered.

"There are good Cherokee men, but some might hurt you. If you two girls had a few bad blackberries in your basket, would you throw all your blackberries away?"

"No, Edudu, we would never do that."

"What is true with blackberries is true of people," Edudu said.

"Hate is an enemy more dangerous than white men."

"Would you girls keep a pet rattlesnake?"

"No, Edudu. No one would have a pet rattlesnake. That's silly."

"You wouldn't bring a rattlesnake into your home and you can't bring hate into your heart. Neither can be a pet."

"We are here because Mother Earth and Father Sky made this world, both Cherokee and white. You will become a nuisance if you hate."

"We don't want to become a nuisance, Edudu," we answered quickly.

Edudu leaned over close to us.

"Do you hate your cousin Red Bird because he was born deaf?"

"No, Edudu. We don't hate Red Bird. He is a good man," we answered.

"Just because someone is different, we don't hate them. Do you hate Africans because of their skin and curly hair?"

"We love Africans, Edudu. They are gentle. They tell stories like you do."

"Africans belong to Mother Earth and Father Sky just as we do, just as Americans belong. It is time you learned about the two wolves. There are two wolves living inside you and inside me. There are two wolves living inside of everyone, including Americans and Africans. Your two wolves will live inside of you the rest of your life. One wolf is good, the other bad. One wolf adores you. The other despises you. Both wolves want your attention. They constantly struggle with one another. One wolf is hateful, deceptive and a liar. The other wolf is good and kind."

"One wolf will grow stronger, the other weaker," Edudu said. "The bad wolf wants to bend you to become like him. He wants to deceive you and make you think he is the good wolf. Your bad wolf wants to deceive you because he hates you. Your good wolf loves you. He wishes you well. Both wolves want to be petted, even bad wolf. One will become stronger and the other weaker. The bad wolf will teach you to lie to yourself, which is the worst lie of all. It would be a terrible thing to lie to yourself, wouldn't it?"

"Yes, Edudu. We always tell the truth. It is a terrible thing to lie."

Our Edudu continued, "Your good wolf will never deceive. Your good wolf never lies to you. You must choose which wolf will grow stronger. You have the ability to make one wolf stronger and the other weaker. You have the power to protect yourself from the bad wolf. You, and only you, have that power. As you grow you will sometimes find yourself confused. You will not always know which wolf is lying and which is telling the truth. Your struggle will never end, but don't be afraid. You decide which wolf becomes strong."

"Edudu, which wolf will win? Which will grow? Which will become strong? How can we know the answer? Which wolf will grow inside of us?"

"You have asked the question I wanted you to ask. You have asked the question Mother Earth and Father Sky want you to ask. You have asked the most important question of all."

"Which wolf will grow inside of us?" We asked again.

Edudu answered.

"The wolf you feed will grow. The wolf you ignore will wane. He will become smaller until he almost disappears."

"Feed the good wolf and you shall live long and well and your path shall be full of light. Today, when you girls were throwing stones, you were feeding your bad wolf. He was teaching you to be a hater. Choose to feed your good wolf and be happy all your days. Feed your good wolf and he will become strong, you will be happy and live long and well."

26 February 1822

From the *Georgia Journal* - 19 February 1822 - Page 1

"Florida-A bill is now before congress, providing for the government of East and West Florida, under the name of the territory of Florida. The executive power to be vested in a governor...appointed by the president for three years. The legislature, to be composed of the governor and thirteen discreet and fit persons--the latter to be appointed, annually, by the President....The laws of the United States are declared to prevail in the territory from the passage of the act."

21 May 1822

From the *Georgia Journal* - 14 May 1822 – page 3

"...Mr. Gilmer submitted the following: 'for the purpose of holding treaties with the Cherokee and Creek tribes of Indians for the extinguishment of the Indian title to all the lands within the state of Georgia pursuant to the fourth section of the first article of the agreement and cession concluded between the United States and the state of Georgia on 24th April, 1802, the sum of $30,000.00'."

30 December 1822

I walked to visit Ben. When I arrived, Mr. Lowry and a friend were enjoying a conversation on an unusually warm winter's day. I heard their animated discussion on the porch long before I reached the house.

"Hello, Cassie," Mr. Lowry said. "Ben's gone hunting, but you're welcome to visit with us if you want to wait until he returns?"

"I would love to visit with you," I answered.

"Cassie, I want you to meet my dear friend, Mr. Ellemander J. Warbington, a Moravian missionary from Spring Place over on the Federal Road. I'm afraid we're discussing history. You might find our discussion rather dry. Eleanor sat with us for a short while but excused herself. Would you like to join our conversation or wait inside with Eleanor?"

"I would love to listen. I do not find history dull in the least," I answered.

"This young lady, Mr. Warbington, is perhaps the most astute student I have ever taught. She is bright, quick with logic and wit. Language is her forte. Most of the time it's not me teaching her, but she teaching me."

"Thank you for inviting me to join your discussion," I answered. "You know I like history, Mr. Lowry. Studying history is the key to understanding human motivations in any era. Governments change but people live as people have always done. Human behavior hasn't changed."

"Before you walked up, Cassie," Mr. Warbington began, "Wilbur and I were examining the flow of history leading to the current political situation in your Cherokee Country, a rapidly deteriorating situation, if you want my opinion. My heart is with your nation. The Cherokee are under increasing pressure. It may not seem like it to you, Cassie, but there are some on the whiteside who wish your nation well, a meagre few, I'm afraid. When push comes to shove, we Americans take the easy road."

Mr. Lowry interjected, "Cassie, just before you arrived, Mr. Warbington and I were talking about the formation and addition of the new frontier states. For example, before 1776, the State of Virginia included enormous tracts of land that extended across the mountains to their west, what we today call Kentucky. Virginia found those western lands too cumbersome to govern and ceded their western land to our new general government in Washington City and asked nothing in return. Shortly after Virginia ceded its western territory, Kentucky was organized and admitted to the union as the fifteenth state. That was thirty years ago. Political events have moved rapidly since."

"Pardon me, Wilbur," Mr. Warbington interjected. "Keep in mind, peace wasn't signed between the colonies and the British until 1783. That was only thirty-nine years ago. Seems longer, doesn't it? Although England granted their colonies independence, the Crown did not cede its westernmost holdings, forts and assets in the Treaty of Paris. Most folks don't know that."

"The British and the new American government granted one another perpetual navigation rights to the Mississippi River. The British wanted to maintain influence beyond the United States' western frontier and limit the influence of France, England's arch enemy who at that time owned all the land west of the Mississippi, land Napoleon acquired from Spain. Some say those British addendums to the peace of 1783 were the primary cause of the War of 1812 which, as you know, gave General Jackson occasion for his military fame and launched his political career."

Mr. Lowry interrupted, "I want to follow the previous line of discussion about the state of Virginia ceding its western lands. Georgia, imitating Virginia, ceded its vast western lands, what we call Alabama and Mississippi, to the general government in 1802 but, unlike Virginia, Georgia wanted something in return. Georgia wanted money and assistance from the Federal government to remove all Indians from its chartered boundaries. Virginia gave away their western land with no compensation. Georgia made a lucrative deal, the Compact of 1802, with devastating political repercussions for Creek and Cherokee. Out of the land ceded by Georgia in the compact of 1802, congress admitted Mississippi in 1817 and Alabama in 1819. Since then, Cassie, vast Indian nations on our North American continent have been gobbled up by this voracious political monster we call America. The Cherokee Nation has survived, but barely."

"The last few years have been a disaster," Mr. Warbington said. "Indians have lost most of their holdings east of the Mississippi and since the Louisiana Purchase, Indians west of the Mississippi are threatened."

"I am confused," I said. "I often talk to Edudu about these things. Americans say they purchased land from us when, in practice, they intimidate, threaten and bribe. Americans are like men who swindle children and then boast of their deception. We Cherokee are not a nation of lawyers, soldiers and surveyors. We do not have a powerful army. We are surrounded. When it comes to Americans it's Veni, Vidi, Vici. They came, they saw and they conquered. Victori Spolia, is it not, Mr. Warbington?"

Mr. Warbington silently nodded in agreement.

"I'm afraid you're right Cassie," Mr. Lowey said. "With the admission of Alabama and Mississippi as new frontier states, and now Florida as a territory, the Cherokee are indeed surrounded. America intends to own every acre of land between the Atlantic and the Mississippi River. They'll take it by force of arms if they have to. The Creeks are almost gone from Georgia and Alabama. The Cherokee are the only Indians left with any land to speak of. Cherokee leadership has made many agreements with the American government but I don't trust the fidelity of American politicians."

I interjected quietly, "Edudu says no one can stop the white killing frost that is coming. The *Georgia Journal* recently reported two thousand immigrants came into New York in one week alone. It seems all of Europe has heard about land for the taking in the New World. I am bewildered why so many leave their homeland? They must hate it there."

Mr. Lowry asked, "Tell us your thinking, Cassie. Els and I want to know what it is you're pondering."

"We have lived here for hundreds of years," I answered. "It is inconceivable we shall not continue. The world changes, Mr. Lowry, but we Cherokee are not changing. We are a happy people. We have everything we desire. Why would we change and become miserable? If we were unhappy like the Americans, we would leave our country and go somewhere else, but we are happy here. We have houses, barns, fields and farms. We grow our crops and raise families. We have our own country. We have strong communities. We have plenty to eat and we take care of our own."

Mr. Warbington interrupted with a sad tone, "The general government and Georgia agreed the continued seizing of Cherokee land would end with current 1822 boundaries. Chief Ross and his fellows worked long and hard for this agreement. I want this treaty to be the last, but American governments have broken every treaty in the past. The United States has demonstrated it cannot keep promises, not one. Will this be a landmark agreement or will America break its word again?" Mr. Warbington asked. "We shall see."

"The American government makes piecrust promises, my wife says."

"And what, pray tell, is a piecrust promise?" Mr. Warbington asked.

"My good wife has taken up that phrase popularized by Jonathan Swift. She says our government makes piecrust promises, a promise easily made, easily broken."

"That would be humorous, Wilbur, if it wasn't so very true," Mr. Warbington said quietly.

Mr. Lowry concluded, "And what is worse, I'm afraid, Andrew Jackson will one day have a greater say in the Cherokee future."

We sat in the darkening December afternoon. Our shared melancholy was tangible. The mid-winter sun hanging low above the distant mountains seemed to reflect our despondency. There was not a cloud to be seen in the cold December twilight as we concluded our discussion on Mr. Lowry's porch. The first twinkling stars of dusk warned of a bitter chill that would descend in the darkness as we slept, covering us with a white killing frost.

Chapter XIII
1823 – Right of Discovery
Chapter 13

26 April 1823 - Month of the Flower Moon -ka wa ni
From the *Georgia Journal* - 4 March 1823 - page 2
"Gen. Glascock, one of the Commissioners appointed on the part of our state, to treat with the Cherokee Nation...returned home on Tuesday last. We learn...an indisposition strongly prevails among the Cherokee generally to make any further cession of their lands: but this...proceeds from the influence of a few...who would monopolize themselves to the injury of the tribe, and to the exclusion of our claims--Our Commissioners flatter themselves, however, that at the convention in August they will be enabled to do away with the false impressions which have been made on the minds of our Red Brethren and thereby effect the object of their mission."

From the *Georgia Journal* - 11 March 1823 - Page 3
"The results of the late attempts to hold a Treaty with the Cherokee Indians, has been truly unfortunate. And from the disposition manifested by that nation there is but little hope that the meeting in August next will be more successful. The Commissioners...procured a large supply of provisions and had tents built. Some few did attend, but so scrupulously did they observe the orders in Council, which had been previously passed, that, although the weather was very inclement, they would not touch a ration or venture inside a tent. We could wish that civilized society should always present such examples of obedience to the laws of the land. A deputation of Commissioners waited on Hicks, the Principle Chief and remonstrated with him on the course that had been pursued by the nation. He heard them through their story very patiently and dryly asked: "Will you give us two dollars an acre for our land?" Being answered in the negative he answered, "Very well, we know it's value and can keep it--as for the claims your people

have against us, we do not regard them. We can pay them without selling our land, whenever they are properly presented."

"My dear Walela," Edudu said laughing, "Americans think themselves unfortunate when they don't own everything. I am proud our people obeyed Chief Hicks and didn't take government rations or sleep in government tents."

From the *Georgia Journal* - 18 March 1823 - page 2
>"Congress - In the Senate- Mr. Ware, of Georgia, delivered the following remarks...on the Militia claims....Considering Georgia, then, as a member of the Union she was entitled to the support...of the general government whenever her rights or sovereignty were invaded...It should...be recollected that at the period of time which gave birth to the claim under consideration the frontiers of Georgia, nearly four hundred miles in extent, were bordered by a race of people whose...predominant passion was war, and who readily embraced every opportunity to satiate a jealous and revengeful disposition with the blood of the innocent. Against those savages, who were numerous and warlike, the state, with a thin population and limited resources, had to defend herself. At a time when neither sex or infancy afforded security against unprovoked massacre and slaughter, when the most harassing hostilities were carried on against the unprotected frontier settlements of Georgia, under practices of Indian barbarity and warfare, calculated to arouse all the feelings of hatred and vengeance, and the utmost abhorrence and detestation against the authors and perpetrators of such cruelty...He informs the President...the Creeks and the Cherokee are unfriendly and hostile, that murders and other wrongs have been committed by them...that already blood had been spilt in every direction and that such was the havoc and carnage making by them, that retaliation by open war became the only resort."

"How can men print such lies?" Edudu asked. "The Georgia senator lies for money. He never mentioned the wrongs Americans committed."
"Please read more, Walela."
"Edudu, an American judge says white Europeans have the right to occupy our land because they have been given the right of discovery. Whites divided the world among themselves as directed by the Christian Pope in Rome. Right of Discovery is a law among white nations."

>"On 28 February 1823, Chief Justice John Marshall of the American Supreme Court delivered a landmark ruling that the

Right of Discovery superseded any Indian right of occupancy in all disputes concerning land ownership."

"The United States ... maintain, as all others have maintained, that discovery gave an exclusive right to extinguish the Indian title of occupancy, either by purchase or by conquest....The power now possessed by the government of the United States to grant lands, resided, while we were colonies, in the crown, or its grantees."

"Mr. Lowry gave me another quote."
"Romanus Pontifex, January 8, 1455 - ...we bestow suitable favors and special graces on those Catholic kings and princes, ... athletes and intrepid champions of the Christian faith...to invade, search out, capture, vanquish, and subdue all Saracens and pagans whatsoever, and other enemies of Christ wheresoever placed, and... to reduce their persons to perpetual slavery, and to apply and appropriate... possessions, and goods..."

"What is Right of Discovery, Walela? How can this white chief across the sea give away land not his and make slaves of people he has never seen?"

"Mr. Lowry says Christian governments claim possession of the entire world by right. They believe themselves superior." I answered.

Edudu spoke after a long silence, "Walela, the whites were lost when they came here. They thought this was India, a remarkable mistake for those who believe themselves superior."

"Europeans gave the world to themselves. The American judge affirmed that in this newspaper," I answered.

"Americans have strange ideas, Walela. They think themselves privileged. They think they know what is best for everyone. They force everyone to become white. They believe their way the only way."

"I think you're right, Edudu," I said. "According to the judge, we can only sell our land to white governments, to Americans."

"Americans are like the Blue-Jay," said Edudu. "They steal the eggs and devour the young of other birds."

Edudu and I talk. Men often come to Edudu for advice. I listen. This evening Edudu and I were silent for a long time. We listened to the quiet sounds of the forest. We watched the lengthening shadows. Edudu continued to stare as if he could see beyond our shadowy perimeter. He absently stroked Spinner's head. Our big mountain to the west disappeared in gloom.

"Darkness has come upon us, Walela. I have little hope. This is not something I say to others, but I say it to you. You know the Americans,

Walela. You are clever, wise beyond your years. You go to their school and talk to their men. You read American newspapers and books. Your mind is strong. I want you to write what I say in your book."

"Why have you no hope, Edudu?" I asked. "We have been here a thousand years. Why do you say such things? Why would we leave this beautiful land in which we live? We are strong and have many villages. We have agreements with the Americans that assure us we can keep our borders."

Edudu gently touched my face and let his fingertips slowly trace the length of my arm, then held my hands softly.

"My hair is white, Walela. My eyes are old. I cannot see the dogwoods because of the fog in my eyes that never goes away. I have been here a long time, Walela. I have learned how things are. Long ago the Americans asked us to trade. We agreed. We traded furs for axes, pots and knives. We welcomed their goods. They asked permission to build dwellings. We agreed. We traded for more furs and more guns. They built more shelters."

Edudu was silent. I felt a sadness as I sat with my Edudu. We were quiet for a while. We heard the first whippoorwill of the evening.

"More traders came. The Americans asked permission to bring women. We didn't know they came to stay forever. They multiplied. We complained they were occupying land without permission but they laughed from inside their big forts. They said our land had become their land according to their law. Too late we realized our folly. We gathered our families and moved. They followed. They took more land. We gathered our children and moved once again. Once again they took our land. Walela, Americans love taking. They love war. Americans brought war with them from across the waters. They have a passion for fighting. They made war against us again and again. They fought the Spanish and the French. Those wars weren't enough. They fought their fathers. Americans love war. More whites came from their homeland and took more land from us, from the Creeks, Seminoles, Choctaw and Chickasaw. Americans are the same wherever they go. They want everything they see. They fight to acquire the desire of their eyes."

"We moved our homes and children again and again and again and now you read to me they demand we move once more. They want us to move far away, across the great river. One day they will push the Principle People off the western edge of the earth. When we fall into nothingness they will rejoice and all will be forgotten."

I heard whippoorwill again. Hoot owl called.

"In my youth," Edudu continued, "our country was filled with children playing by the rivers, more children than could be counted. Americans have taken the river land that grows the best corn. They forced us into the mountains. It is hard to grow corn in the mountains. Americans spread a pall of death everywhere they go. Your mother and father died in this very house from disease they brought among us. Americans have taken our past, they are taking our now and you read to me they plan to steal our future. They seized everything between the sea and the mountains, but everything isn't enough. They want more, always more. They want to reach into our tomorrow and steal the light from our sky."

The last purple color retreated above our mountain silhouette until we were surrounded by darkness. I had never heard Edudu talk in such gloomy tones. I knew he was right but I hope for something better.

"I remember Overhill," Edudu continued quietly. "I remember our rivers, the Little Tennessee, Hiwassee and Tellico. Life was good. I can see our happy towns of the past, Tuskegee, Toque, Tanasi, Chota, Citico, Chilowee, Great Tellico and many others. Our children had plenty to eat when we lived beside our rivers. Then Americans came. They wanted our rivers."

"Those Cherokee towns are no more, burned. They destroyed our corn, beans and squash. They burned our homes. They killed women and children. I buried my mother and father in the Overhill. I alone survived. They chased us. We escaped across our big river to New Echota."

"After they destroyed our nation, the Americans named their home Tennessee after our people, as if it were an honor. They have no feeling for the dispossessed. They honor no one but themselves. Now Americans want the little we have left. They want everything. They would have more, always more. Americans are buzzards with glazed eyes, fussing and hopping among the bones of their rotting prey, pushing and shoving one another, gobbling the decaying flesh of their enemies until their belly is too fat to fly. They never have enough."

"When Jackson mercilessly destroyed the Creeks, I knew our days were few. We helped Jackson. We were wrong. We should have killed Jackson and died with the Red Sticks. Tecumseh was right. It would have been better to die with the Red Sticks than have my flesh removed a little at a time. Soon, when the Americans have more men and wagons, they will build roads and forts and take everything we have. One day soon an American family will live in this house and work Elisi's corn. This will be, my dear Walela. This will be."

I sat close to Edudu in the twilight, my head snuggled on his shoulder as he spoke softly. He stroked my hair.

"Before the Americans came they fought great wars," Edudu continued softly. "Americans will fight among themselves once again. It is their way. Their greedy eyes burn in the night as they consume their own. Their next war will be ugly. There are a great many more of them."

I felt a strange emotion, as if I were eavesdropping, as if I were listening to thoughts not meant for my ears.

"But Mr. and Mrs. Lowry are good. What about them, Edudu?" I asked.

"My dear Walela, I see the future. Nothing can be done now to save our nation. Americans are too powerful. You and your brother must find a way to survive. We Cherokee are givers. We share. We welcome white and African alike. Americans love only themselves. They believe they will be satisfied when they have taken everything from the sea to the Great River. One day they will cross the Great River and take everything there. It is a surety. Their appetite is never-ending. Perhaps the Great Spirit will right all wrongs. If that day comes, Walela, it shall be the Americans who will be found lacking. I am tired."

As the fire was dying, the last charred sticks fell into the bed of glowing coals sending bright, crackling sparks like busy fireflies towards the tops of the trees, tiny torches disappearing into the black canopy overhead.

Our village was at rest.

We were serenaded from all sides in a minor key.

A lonely dog barked once in the distance. Spinner raised his ears.

An owl sounded his solitary call from a nearby tree.

I heard the song of a whippoorwill ring out of the gloom by the river. Edudu's hair shined white and red in the final glow of the fire, both soon to fade. We were surrounded by blackness. Edudu rose, his form dim by the light of glimmering stars. He touched my face and turned to go inside.

We heard the last echoing call of the whippoorwill.

"Walela, we go to our beds. On that last morning we will wake and open our doors. The icy ground will crunch under our feet. In the night everything green will have died, covered by a white killing frost."

Chapter XIV
1823 - 1824 – Ben's Future
Chapter 14

1 May 1824 - The Planting Moon – A na a gv ti

From the *Georgia Journal* - 20 April 1824 - page 2

"...The Cherokee Nation have now come to a decisive and unalterable conclusion, not to cede away any more lands. The limits reserved for them by the treaty of 1819 is not more than sufficient for their comfort and convenience, taking into consideration the great body of mountains and poor lands which can never be settled. It is a gratifying truth that the Cherokee are rapidly increasing in population; therefore, it is an incumbent duty on the nation to preserve unimpaired the rights of posterity to the lands of their ancestors. We have told you of the decisive and unalterable disposition of the nation in regard to their lands. John Ross, Geo. Lowrey, Major Ridge, Elijah Hicks, A true copy--January 28, 1824."

3 May 1824

From the *Georgia Journal* April 20, 1824 - page 2

United States Department of War - 30 January 1824

"Gentlemen--The president has received your letter...he has directed me to communicate to you the following answer."

"By the compact with Georgia the U. States are bound to extinguish...the Indian title to lands within the state as soon as it can be done peaceably, and on reasonable conditions, and the Legislature and Executive of Georgia, now press for the fulfillment of that...This government is anxious to fulfill the agreement....With a view to this object...You must be sensible that it will be impossible for you to remain...in your present situation, as a distinct society, or nation within the limits of Georgia, or of any other State. Such a community is incompatible with our system, and must yield to it. This truth is too striking and obvious not to be seen by you surrounded as you are by the people of several states, you must either cease to be a distinct community, and become at no distant period, a part of the state within whose limits you are, or remove beyond the limits of any state. For the United States to fulfill the compact with Georgia, the title which you hold to lands, as a distinct community, must be extinguished, and the state, objects to the extinguishment of it, by vesting in you, or in any of you, in lieu thereof the right of individual ownership...I have the honor John C. Calhoun"

From the *Georgia Journal* – same newspaper, same page
The Cherokee response to John C. Calhoun's letter.
"Sir—We have received your letter of the 30th ult. containing the answer which the president directed you to communicate to us...in this answer we discover new propositions for the extinguishment of Cherokee title to lands, for the benefit of Georgia...the Cherokee Nation are sensible, that the United States are bound by its compact with Georgia to extinguish...the Indian title to lands within the limits claimed by the state as soon as can be done *peaceably,* and on *reasonable* conditions, and are also sensible that this compact is no more than a conditional one, and without the free and voluntary consent of the Cherokee Nation, can never be complied with on the part of the United States;..." the Cherokees have come to a *decisive* and *unalterable* conclusion *never* to *cede away* any more lands." And as the extinguishment of Cherokee title to lands, can never be obtained, on conditions, which will accord with the import of the compact between the United States and Georgia...the government should adopt some other means to satisfy Georgia...the United States have by treaties, solemnly guaranteed to secure to the Cherokee forever, their title to lands, which have been reserved by them. Therefore the state of Georgia can have no reasonable plea against the Cherokee..." JOHN ROSS, GEO. LOWREY, MAJOR RIDGE, ELIJAH HICKS

From the *Georgia Journal* – same newspaper
Governor Troup's response to the Cherokee letter.
"Sir I have received this day your letter of the 17th Inst. Be pleased to present to the President my acknowledgements for the attention he has given to the requisition of Georgia...to adopt any measure in his power, which may tend to the fulfillment of the convention with the state of Georgia, with the least possible delay...In your effort to open negotiations with the Cherokee Delegation for the extinguishment of claims, you are met by a

flat negative to two fair and liberal propositions. The 1st to purchase for valuable consideration in money. The 2nd to accommodate them with equivalent Territory…beyond the Mississippi—It has been made known to me for some time before, that a Council has been formed…to enable the Chiefs to present themselves before the President with a boldness bordering on effrontery…with an emphatic No!…not the spontaneous offspring of Indian feeling and sentiment, but a word put in his mouth, by white men, who are nourished and protected by the power of the U. States—…From the day of the signature of the articles of agreement and cession, this word ceased to be available to the Indian…On that day the fee simple passed from the rightful proprietors to Georgia, and Georgia after a lapse of twenty years…are now told in answer to their just and reasonable demand, that this compact is only conditional, depending on its fulfillment on the will and pleasure of the Indians…" G.M. Troup

22 May 1824

Ben's conversation with his parents.

"Father, I've made my decision. I want to do something noble for the Cherokee. I want to dedicate my life to the service of others."

"Good for you, son. Your mother and I will help any way we can."

Ben answered.

"Cassie and I believe an American lawyer who understands Cherokee culture would be helpful. Do you and Mother think law would be a good profession for me?"

"Son, your mother and I want you to use your God-given intellect in the way your passion leads you. We can't tell you what to do. Our passions are not your passions. What you choose doesn't matter as long as it's an honest decision. Solomon's advice remains unequivocal, 'Whatsoever thy hand findeth to do, do it with all thy might.' Whatever you choose to do, give it your best. If you choose to be a farmer, be a good one. If you want to be a lawyer, be a good lawyer."

"Yes, sir. I promise. I will do my best."

"Son, the final choice is yours. You have a kind heart and a strong sense of justice," his mother said. "I'm very proud of you at this moment."

"It makes me angry, Mother, that people want to take Cherokee land. That isn't right," Ben said.

"Son," his mother said, "anger can be a destructive evil or it can be the fuel of great achievement. Righteous indignation is divine. If you're angry at the right things at the right time in the right measure, you'll be fine."

"Your mother's right, Ben," his father said. "If your anger towards injustice leads into an honorable law career, that would be good, but you must choose. We can give advice, but we can't make your decision. We trust you to make the right decision, son. You're well educated and hardworking. You have a great start in life. You understand language, reason and logic. You have a systematic mind, plus you're highly skilled in language arts. I have no doubt you'll make a good lawyer, if that's where your heart leads you."

"I'll be a good lawyer. I know I will," Ben said proudly once again.

"I believe you, son. I admire your wish to do something noble for the Cherokee. To my knowledge, not one Cherokee man I've ever heard of has been professionally trained as a lawyer. The Cherokee leadership are wise, experienced, skillful men, but they aren't expert in American law. Except for a few men like Chief Ross and a handful of others, they know little about law, government or the legal profession. There would be plenty of honorable work for a lawyer in the Cherokee Nation, but it would not be lucrative. As a lawyer for the Cherokee, you would make enemies. The entire population of Georgia would view you as a traitor. Even though I'm a missionary, I'm often viewed by my fellow Americans as a turncoat. Without exception they believe my work to be wasted."

"I know, Father," Ben answered, "but I wouldn't be working just for the money. I want to do what's right."

Ben's father said, "I came to teach the Cherokee, but it is they who have taught me. Robert Burns was right, Ben, 'O would some power the gift give us, to see ourselves as others see us.' To see our voracious, selfish American culture as we really are would be a divine gift."

"It would be tragic for Cherokee customs to disappear," Ben's mother interrupted. "I wish you well in your decision to become a lawyer, son, and work for the Cherokee. The biggest crime of our American society in regard to the Cherokee is the demand that the Cherokee become like them. I agree with your father. He and I have loved the Cherokee and their culture since the day we arrived and, of course, your friendship with Cassie will be good for you in that regard. She's as smart as you are, if not smarter."

"I agree with your mother," Ben's father said. "The Cherokee need help. They could use the assistance of a hardworking lawyer. Georgia is expanding rapidly. Milledgeville is Georgia's fourth capital in its short history. Savannah was the first, then Augusta, Louisville and now Milledgeville. Sadly, Georgia's westward expansion has been at the expense of the Creek and Cherokee. I wish we Americans could arrange a long-term lease of Cherokee land, but we don't want that. We want ownership. This is definitely a clash of cultures. Cassie's right, I'm afraid. I see no end to Georgia's desire to occupy the entirety of the Cherokee homeland. The Cherokee need help. Therefore, the short answer to your question is, your mother and I will support you if you decide on law."

"Thank you, sir," Ben answered.

"Ben, you've been patiently listening. I've said too much, but let me conclude with this," his father said. "Things change, son. No matter how hard we strive for continuity, things change. Change can't be prevented. Your mother and I wish you to be part of a change for good. One determined person can sometimes do more than an army. Do you remember David and Goliath?"

"Yes sir, I remember."

"One young man armed with confidence can accomplish great things with Him on his side. You'll never know what a single righteous decision will accomplish unless you make the attempt. If you choose to support the Cherokee, you'll have chosen a parallel path. If David had stayed home, he would never have known what he could have accomplished. Such is life. You'll never know what could have been if you stay home and do nothing, but you can always find out what can be if you make the attempt."

"I see your point, sir."

"Good for you, son," his father said. "There's been an active debate about Georgia's Indian problem, as they call it. Georgia is full of immigrants who know nothing about the Indian culture. Are you familiar with the popular song about the Cherokee I've been hearing, Ben?"

"Yes sir," Ben answered. "It's not nice."

"The lyrics go like this," his father said:

> *All I ask in this creation,*
> *Is a pretty little wife and a big plantation,*
> *Way up yonder in the Cherokee Nation.*

"The song's popularity reflects the mind-set of Georgians. Americans believe Cherokee land is theirs for the taking."

"You've mentioned your interest in law on more than one occasion," Ben's father continued. "We've noticed your developing sense of justice. I don't think a young man as quick as you will have any problem finding a place in a good law school. You could skip law school and be apprenticed straightaway, but if you want to be at the top of your profession, law school is imperative."

"Yes, sir," Ben said. "I would prefer a law school over apprenticeship."

"Good for you, son," his father said. "In the meantime, continue to discuss current political developments. Defend your intellectual positions verbally and in writing. Use unemotional logic as you develop your arguments, but remember to debate both sides of any position you truly wish to understand. You must be able to debate both sides of an issue or you'll never fully understand the complexities of the problem."

"Think about what we have talked about. Your life's vocation must be your decision and your decision alone. Your mother and I won't make the choice for you. Whatever you choose as a career, your mother and I will support. Count on us to stand behind you."

"Yes, sir. I'll be considering my future, but I'm determined law will be my calling," Ben answered proudly.

Chapter XV
1824 - The Green Corn Festival
Chapter 15

13 June 1824 - The Green Corn Moon – De ha lu yi

Ben and I walked to my special place on the river's edge where I read, think, write and dream. I feel our hearts entwining. Ben had something important he wanted to tell me.

"Cassie, I have decided to go to law school in Connecticut, a school my father suggested. It's a great distance but Father says it's the best. I will miss you terribly. Maybe you could go, too?"

"This isn't bad news," I answered. "I think you were meant for a career in law. You'll learn and be back before you know it and we'll be together like old friends. You shouldn't delay. I shall wait for you."

"I haven't made the final decision, Cassie. You make it sound like I'm leaving tomorrow."

With Ben I feel alive, content and carefree. He is my best friend.

"We are the most fortunate of people, are we not?"

"Yes, Cassie. Everyone needs a confidant, you're mine."

"That's probably the most wonderful thing you've ever said to me."

"Cassie, I don't understand how folks can call you and your people savages. If people could live here they would see a strong community that would be the envy of any society. I love your people. I love living here."

"It's true. If Americans lived here and understood our language, the forest would come alive for them, they would understand the birds, animals and fish and how we relate in community."

"Cassie, let's forget the world's troubles. Tell me good things. Tell me about the things that you love."

"Oh, I love many things, Ben. I love family, the faces of children when they hear Edudu's stories, making pine baskets with Elisi. I love to watch the chickens scratch and peck as I toss their feed. Each morning when I gently take the warm eggs I call each hen by name and tell her thank you. I enjoy shutting them in their little house for the night when they come home to roost. We are a happy people. I wouldn't want to live anywhere else."

"Keep going, Cassie," Ben said. "I want to hear more good things."

"I love the trees when they wake from their winter's sleep and dress in their new green clothing. I love the dogwoods and redbuds in springtime."

"Keep going," Ben said.

"I love the Green Corn Festival. I love fresh corn and all the other new vegetables after a long winter. I love hot cornbread with melted butter. I love stories, traditions, dances and happy children. I love seeing friends and relatives I haven't seen since last year. I look forward to our reunion during the Green Corn Festival. It's quite a holiday. I love the melons. I love to watch my brother's ballplay. Do you want me to continue, Ben?"

"Please, please continue. I love listening to you," Ben said.

We reclined side by side as we lay looking up at the lazy clouds.

"I love persimmons when they're ripe. I love to find the talvladi vines. No one goes hungry in our country. I've spent many wonderful days with Elisi and Edudu in the forest gathering its bounty."

"Did you know," I said to Ben with a serious tone in my voice, "no fruit, nut or berry is poisonous if it tastes sweet?"

"No, I didn't know that."

"Edudu says nothing that tastes sweet can be poisonous."

"Well, I know one thing, Cassie. You could never be poisonous, you're the sweetest person I've ever met."

"What a nice thing to say."

"Keep going, Cassie. What's your favorite? What do you like the best?"

"When I was little we would find honeysuckle blooms. We would pick the bloom, bite off the end and suck the nectar. There's just the faintest hint of sweetness, but we loved it. Do you think that silly?"

"Of course not," Ben answered. "I think it precious."

"I've been reading too many newspapers," I said laughing. "The most wonderful thought of all is my future with you. Being with you is even better than living here. I want to be close to you day and night. I wish I could borrow the songs of the birds to sing my love for you. If you took me away, I would miss our country, but I love you more. I have been happy here with Edudu and Elisi. As a woman, I will only be happy with you, wherever you are."

Ben and I said nothing for a long time as we listened to the river and the wind, both wishing us well.

"One day we'll be together, Cassie," Ben said quietly. "We must be patient. It will be a while yet, but that day will come."

"I know it will," I said. "It will be just as we imagine."

We lay quietly talking about different things. We discussed the future and tried to avoid talking about the problems we have with greedy American settlers.

Finally, there in our special place, we said out loud what we had believed for a long time. We confessed our mutual love. On my big rock beside the river we became adults with our future certain. We left our childhood behind.

"Ben, I want you to know I'm yours. I'll wait for you all my life, if I must. I'm yours and only yours, now and forever. I want to belong to you."

"I know you'll wait," Ben said, holding me tight as he never had before. "I shall never worry about you. I know you're mine."

"Elisi says you are special and worth the wait. She likes you, Ben, and thinks you handsome. All the girls think you handsome."

Ben leaned back and put both of his hands behind his head and stared up at the passing clouds and grinned.

"I knew you were mine, Cassie. I've known for a while. I love you."

The moment he said he loved me, I threw my arms around him.

"Ben, I love you, too. I loved you when I first saw your smile. I feel our spirits intertwined like dozens of honeysuckle vines twisting upward on a tree trunk, the many strands so interwoven with one another they're incapable of being separated. You are my soul, Ben Lowry. I was meant to be yours from the day I was born."

I felt him breathe deeply as he held me.

"What a lovely thing to say, Cassie. I have loved you since you were a cute little girl in my father's schoolroom. You're in my thoughts every day. We'll have a good life. You'll never want for anything. I promise. I'll take care of you."

"I know that, Ben. I know you don't lie. You don't know how to lie."

My soul overflowed as we kissed. With that kiss two childhood friends left their playthings and embarked upon the road to maturity, becoming adults, lovers, partners, building a life together.

Our kiss was the seal of commitment, more enduring than any ring.

"Cassie, you make me want to tell you everything. You make me want to break open my chest and expose my deepest secrets. I want to tell you everything about myself, even things I'm ashamed of. Does that sound silly to you?"

"Of course not," I answered. "I know exactly what you mean. I feel the same. I want to take my heart out and give it to you for safe keeping."

"Cassie, I want you for my wife. I want to provide for you. I want you to be the mother of my children and I want them all to look exactly like you. I want to make you happy. That's what I want. I want to give you things. As long as this river flows and birds sing, I shall love you."

We heard leaves crunching on the path above. A young Cherokee fisherman had come to find a likely spot. The spell was broken. With sheepish, adolescent grins, we descended from our new-found romantic heights and returned to the innocence of childhood. As we walked up the hill from the river, we were oblivious of anything except one another. We were different than when we had walked down the hill. Our lives would never be the same. The inoffensive intruder had no idea what had taken place behind the laurels.

We giggled and whispered like school children. I have never felt the comfort, assurance and safety in the care of my Edudu and Elisi as I feel with

Ben. Ben will keep me safe, of that I'm sure. Elisi says the way I feel is the way it should be. There comes a time, Edudu says, when the little bird's nest becomes too small. I wish my mother and father could be here. I wish I could whisper to my parents of my love for Ben.

25 June 1824

Tomorrow begins our Green Corn Festival. Our people have been gathering for some time. There is great joy. Families are re-united, we eat, dance, tell stories, pray, we are cleansed. We play games, forgive debts, grudges, crimes and betrayal. It's a time of renewed purity, commitment and healing. We have the stomp dance, feather dance and buffalo dance. There will be ballplay. Elisi's porch is already crowded with people listening to Edudu's stories. Five Feathers asked Edudu to tell the story of the famous ballplay between the birds and the animals.

"That was some ballplay," Edudu began. "No one thought the birds could win. I talked to some old birds whose ancestors were at that ballplay. They told me the story."

"The animals were excellent at ballplay," Edudu said. "No one could remember the last time the animals had lost. The animals, weary of playing among themselves, invited the birds to a great competition. The birds reluctantly accepted. They met at the ballplay ground on the day. There were crowds of both animals and birds gathered for the ball dance and the festivities. Nothing like this had been seen in our country in many years. The birds danced in the tree tops. The animals danced on the grassy bank beside the river. It was a great day, a great day indeed."

Every eye was upon Edudu as he told the story. No one made a sound.

"Bear was captain of the animal team. On the way to the ballplay Bear would pick up heavy logs and smash them to the ground to demonstrate what he would do to any opponent who would dare to take the ball from him. Terrapin was boasting he would crush any bird who would get in his way. Terrapins in those days were much larger than terrapins today, as you know. Their shells are hard so they can resist any blow delivered by a stick, stone, beak or claw. Terrapin boasted no bird would take the ball from him. I'll crush them if they try, he said. Deer boasted he was the fastest of all the animals and no bird could catch him to take the ball. He could run under and through the forest unlike the birds who had to fly over the trees. Not even Eagle, the birds' captain, could take the ball from Deer."

"Eagle, with his powerful wings and strong talons can carry great weights over long distances. Eagles never tire. The birds also had Hawk but the birds needed a plan to have even a small chance to win. No one believed the birds could defeat the animals."

"After the ball dance the birds were in the trees preening their feathers getting ready for the ballplay. Two tiny animals slowly climbed to the treetops. They politely asked to talk to Eagle. Their request was granted."

"We want to join your team in the ballplay today, the animals said."

"Majestic Eagle looked down at the two tiny animals with admiration. Eagle was impressed with their boldness."

"You are brave but you are animals, little animals at that," Eagle said. "You should be on the animals' team. You are not birds. You don't have wings, feathers or a beak. You don't lay eggs. You could not take the ball from Rabbit, much less from Deer, Terrapin or Bear," said Eagle.

"Why do you want to be on the team with the birds?"

"We asked to play on the team with the animals but they laughed at us. They wouldn't let us join them. They said we should watch. We want to participate. Therefore, we humbly ask to compete in the ballplay with the birds."

Eagle felt a great compassion. He reasoned their tiny heart must be a great deal bigger than their little bodies. Anyone with such courage should be allowed to join the ballplay. Courage does not always come in big packages.

"If you join the ballplay you may suffer great harm, but because of your greatness of heart, I have decided to allow you on our team. However, we must equip you like a bird. We must be fair to the animals."

"Thank you, Eagle," the two little creatures said.

"You two must have wings if you compete with us birds," Eagle said.

"There was a long consultation with Hawk and the other birds. Someone remembered the drum they used earlier in the ballplay dance. They decided to take a portion of the dried skin of the drum and use pieces of cane to stretch the skin into the shape of wings. They could attach the wings to the front legs. Then the valiant little animal could fly like the birds."

"The birds went to work and that's exactly what they did. They fastened the cane and the new wings made from the dried skin of the drum to the front legs of one creature. That is how there came to be Bat, Tla'meha. They threw the ball to him. He seized the ball and dodged this way and that. He kept the ball in the air no matter what the other birds tried. Not one bird, no matter how swiftly they flew, could take the ball from Tla'meha."

Edudu leaned forward and asked, "Do you know what happened next?"

Edudu's audience was enthralled as if this were the first time they had heard of the great ballplay between the birds and the animals.

"The birds saw Bat would be one of their best players. They wanted to make more wings for the other furry animal, but they had used all the leather from the drum. What could they do? Two wise owls noticed the other little animal had plenty of loose skin around his legs. The two old birds took hold of the little animal's fur and stretched and stretched and stretched. They pulled the skin out from his front and hind legs and that was how we came to have

Flying Squirrel, Tema. The birds threw the ball to Flying Squirrel. He jumped, sailed and caught the ball. He glided across the clearing to the next tree far above the ground and kept the ball safe."

Edudu laughed, clapped his hands.

"This was going to be some ballplay. Perhaps the birds had a chance after all. The birds couldn't take the ball from Flying Squirrel and now you know how the two teams prepared for ballplay. When both teams were ready, the great ballplay began. Flying Squirrel caught the ball first and carried it high into a tree. He sailed across a clearing and gave the ball to other birds. One of the birds dropped the ball to the ground. Bear almost picked it up but Martin swooped down and threw the ball to Bat who dodged and darted this way and that."

Edudu stood, demonstrating how the ballplay progressed with wide sweeping motions of his arms. Everyone was excited.

"The animals were surprised. Bat, showing the animals his quick, skillful maneuvers, dodged this way and that way and avoided every thrust, kick and swing from the frantic animals. Bat finally threw the ball between the posts and won the game for the birds. It was the greatest ballplay victory ever for the birds. Bat won the game but Martin saved the day. As a reward for his quick thinking, Martin and his family were given gourds for a home, which they have to this day."

"And that's how the birds won the first ballplay against the animals."

Everyone voiced their approval and thanked Edudu for his story. Edudu promised they could come again later to hear more stories.

Five Feathers showed everyone his ballplay stick. Attached to the top were the wings of Bat and Tema, Flying Squirrel. With these attached to his ballplay stick, Five Feathers calls on the agility of both Bat and Flying Squirrel when he competes. Victory comes from the quickness of Bat and Tree Squirrel, Five Feathers reminded us.

30 June 1824

During the Green Corn Festival, the men in training for ballplay are forbidden to eat the flesh of rabbits. Rabbits are quick but confused when running from an enemy. When Rabbit is frightened he runs erratically or even in circles and is easily caught. Rabbit has great speed but often cannot escape his slower pursuer. Ballplayers don't want to be caught by their opponents. They don't want to run in circles so they avoid eating rabbits before a ballplay.

As the Green Corn Festival continues we give respect to our ancestors and fast. When the fast is ended we will feast with the most delicious foods of the year. We will rinse our bodies in the river and pray. We cleanse impurities and bad deeds from our life. Edudu leads this ceremony. Edudu knows how to keep the balance.

The third day Edudu will lead the most important dance. He will lead the many dancers in front of our seven-sided council house with one dancer behind the other. He will have a gourd with small stones inside to make a rhythmic sound so the dancers can stay in step. He will lead the dancers. Everyone will be in step, one behind the other, a beautiful sight.

The Green Corn Festival is the happiest of times. Our corn is beginning to ripen. There will be plenty. Life is good in Cherokee Country. I love the bread Elisi makes from the new corn during the festival. It is better than any other time of the year.

Our festival will last four or five days. Every year we have a wonderful reunion of our families. Many will come from surrounding villages and some from far away. During this festival I believe we remain the Principle People.

Chapter XVI
1824 – Presidential Election - Law School
Chapter 16

23 July 1824 - Month of the Ripe Corn Moon – Gu ye quo ni

"Father, who will be America's next president," Ben asked.

"I don't know, son," his father answered. "Four are running. I would prefer Adams over Crawford, Jackson or Clay."

"What about Andrew Jackson, Father?" Ben asked.

"General Jackson is definitely the front runner. His victory at New Orleans, success in the Indian wars, his invasion of Spanish Florida and now the recent acquisition of the Florida territory has made Mr. Jackson appear personally responsible for America's achievements."

"What about Mr. Crawford?"

"I don't think Crawford can win. He's confined to his bed with a stroke but he'll split the vote because he's from Georgia. I think it's between Adams and Jackson. Because Adams is from Massachusetts, he'll carry the northern states, but he's running against three southerners. This may be a problematic election for the electoral college."

I interrupted, "What is this electoral college, Mr. Lowry? I thought a college was like the University of Georgia?"

"That's a good question, Cassie. The Latin word collegium means partnership or association of like-minded folks, people who come together for a common purpose. Our words 'collect' and 'collection' come from the same root. The electoral college is an American political mechanism for selecting the president of the United States. The electoral college votes in the second of two elections to choose the American president."

"Could you please explain?" I asked.

"Sure, Cassie. The American president is elected by a small number of representatives of the states, not by popular vote of all the states. Here's how it works. Each state determines who they want for president in the general election. Then, about a month later, each state sends representatives to vote in a second election. The group of men who vote in that second election are called the 'electoral college'. In that second election each state has the same number of votes as they have seats in congress, both House and Senate. The results of this second election determine who will be president."

"Here's how it works. Let's use the state of Georgia for an example. First, the thousands of Georgia citizens vote in the general election to determine who the state of Georgia wants for their president. Once the state of Georgia knows who they want for president, Georgia's chosen representatives are sent to Washington City where they are allowed to vote in the second election to determine the president. Georgia has seven seats in the House of Representatives and two seats in the Senate for a total of nine seats in Congress. Therefore, Georgia is allowed nine votes for president in that second election in the electoral college. The electoral college, the group of all the electors from all the states, will meet about a month after the general election to vote for the president of all the states. You can be sure all nine of Georgia's votes will go for Crawford in the vote in the electoral college, since he's from Georgia."

"Connecticut has six seats in the house and two in the Senate. Therefore, Connecticut has eight electors and thus eight votes for president in that second election. Vermont has two Senators and five house seats for a total of seven electors. The huge state of Virginia has twenty-two house seats but, like all the states, only two Senate seats for a total of twenty-four electors and so it goes for all twenty-four states."

"I think I'm following you, Mr. Lowry. This is interesting," I said.

"In the second election in December, each elector casts one vote for president and one for vice president. The electors vote for the man who won the popular vote in their state."

"Are you following me so far, Cassie?"

"Yes, sir. This is interesting. Your explanation is clear," I answered.

"The twenty-four states have a total of 261 representatives in congress. Therefore, there will be 261 electors in the electoral college, each allowed one vote for president when they meet a month after the general election."

"I understand about the two elections and how the electors are chosen," I said. "Why not have just one election by popular vote?"

"Good question. We have two elections so the president can be chosen by the states."

"I don't understand, Mr. Lowry," I asked. "What is unfair about having one election and allowing everyone to vote? Why would one election by popular vote be unfair? A popular vote seems less complicated."

"My word, Cassie, you keep me on my toes. Let's see if I can present this logically. The United States began as a collection of thirteen diverse colonies, some large, some small, some very small. After independence each colony was self-governing. Each had their own unique charter. There was no common government. There was no common congress. After they declared independence those thirteen colonies became thirteen separate, self-governing political states. Each newly independent colony viewed itself as an independent country, an autonomous political state. The United States began as a collection of thirteen independent countries who chose to band together for the common good and yet retain individual freedoms. Some states were large, some small. Rhode Island, although exceptionally small, wanted to maintain its identity. The small 'countries' would not allow themselves to be swallowed by the bigger 'countries'. When the thirteen countries decided to band together, each of the thirteen wanted to maintain their unique identity. They didn't want to disappear into one homogenous mass, one big country."

Mr. Lowry continued, "The little states didn't want to be marginalized when they joined the union. The small states, like Rhode Island, Vermont and Connecticut wanted the same rights as the big states like New York, Pennsylvania and Virginia. That's why each state, large or small, has two Senators and why the Senate has more power than the House. The small states would not have agreed to a Federal union otherwise. Having two Senators gave the small states a larger measure of political power. As you know, the final say on all laws is voted on in the Senate.

When it came to electing the chief executive of the new federation, the small states knew a popular vote over all thirteen colonies would be unfair to them. If the presidential election were decided by a national popular vote, the densely populated states, like New York, Pennsylvania and Virginia, would forever control the executive branch. If the president were elected by popular vote, the smaller states like Rhode Island, Vermont, Delaware and Connecticut would become meaningless. States' rights were central to the Constitution in the beginning, Cassie, still are as a matter of fact. I guess you know that from reading the endless talk about nullification, but that's another story."

"Yes, sir. I'm reading about nullification. It's becoming quite an issue in the newspapers. Please continue."

"Thank you, Cassie. When it came to electing the president, tiny Rhode Island wanted the same rights as Virginia or New York. The smaller states wanted constitutional protection from voter domination by the larger states. This protection came in the form of a compromise election for president. The compromise between the big and small states was to elect their chief executive by a secondary electoral election, not by popular vote. In other words, the states elect the president, not the popular vote. That idea is key to understanding the presidential election. Simply put, the second election gives the smaller states more say in who is elected president."

"I think I have the idea," I said. "It seems quite simple."

"Well," Mr. Lowry continued, "I don't know if I would call it simple. There's one more important thing to understand. According to the Constitution, the winner in the electoral college must win with a majority, not just a plurality. Majority means at least fifty-one percent of the votes. Plurality means one more than the others. A plurality could be less than fifty-one percent. The word plurality in election nomenclature means 'more than'.

"In the electoral college the winner must have a majority, more than fifty percent, not just a plurality. The framers of the constitution wanted to make certain the president would be elected by more than fifty percent of the vote. If a candidate has thirty or forty percent or even forty-nine percent of the vote in the electoral college, he cannot be president. That might very well happen this year with four men running."

"The men who wrote the Constitution didn't want a man leading all thirteen states, doing the job of president, who didn't represent more than half the states. The president is tasked to represent all states, not some states. You can see it would be difficult for the president to govern if he didn't receive a mandate from majority of the states, therefore a majority of electoral votes is required. If the president were elected by popular vote, Pennsylvania, New York and Virginia could elect the president against the will of the other ten states because of a large population. The small states wouldn't join the union without more say in the presidential election, thus the electoral college compromise."

"Yes, sir, I understand that now and it makes sense to me," I answered.

"There are four candidates in this year's election," Mr. Lowry added. "They may split the vote and no one receive the required fifty-one percent in the electoral college.

I asked, "What happens then? What happens if no candidate receives a majority in the electoral college? Would you keep the old president or would the United States have another election?"

"Excellent question, Cassie. Here's the caveat. If no candidate receives a majority in the electoral college, there must be a third election."

"A third election?" I asked. "This is getting complicated, Mr. Lowry."

"It does get complicated," Mr. Lowry answered. "The electoral college votes one time and one time only. If a presidential candidate doesn't get a majority in the vote by the electoral college, the election then goes to the House of Representatives. If a man doesn't get the required fifty-one percent of the vote in the electoral college, then the House of Representatives will vote one time to determine who will become president. The House of Representatives will elect the president from the top three candidates in that third election. The framers of the constitution wanted to make certain their president would be elected by a majority of the states, thus the third and deciding election would go to the house where all the states are represented. Does this help at all with your confusion?"

"Yes sir, I understand the electoral college now," I said.

6 August 1824

Ben's parents have secured a place for Ben in a good law school. The term lasts fourteen moons, fourteen months. I will miss him.

We need a lawyer like Ben who will have our best interest at heart. We have no legal standing in American courts. Men from the whiteside rob our barns, smokehouses and corn cribs, sometimes in daylight. They squat on our land with impunity. We don't have anyone to stand up for us. Henry Clay famously said we are "essentially inferior and not an improvable breed" and "on our way to extinction".

"Son, your mother and I have been talking about law school. Your mother and I want to know what you want to do?

"Sir, do we have the money? Law school would be expensive. I've saved only a little. Wouldn't school be impossible?"

"Son, your mother and I have been saving in anticipation of this day. We couldn't do better than invest in you and your education. What do you think, Ben? Once you are established as a lawyer, could you repay your debt and care for us when your mother and I are too old to work?"

"Father, in that case I'll do it. I'll go. I want to go. Yes, of course I want to go if I can. I would love to go to law school. I'll be the best son and lawyer you can imagine. You can count on me, Father. You'll be proud."

"Son," Ben's mother said, "we want to help you with your education like all good parents should. We want you to be happy doing something you love. Your father and I have taught you as much as we can. We need to take advantage of this moment, don't you think?"

"Yes ma'am, I'm ready," Ben replied enthusiastically.

"Your mother and I thought you might say that, son," Ben's father said. "This special breakfast this morning was your mother's idea. I received a letter yesterday from Professor James Gould with *The Litchfield Law School*. Per my request, he's holding a place for you in his next class. What do you think? Should we confirm or wait? Professor Gould says there are other young men from Georgia accepted next term. If you choose to go you'll have good company. Do you want to stay with us another year or go to Connecticut and read law?"

"I want to go. I want to go to law school," Ben said. "I do want to go. I'll be the best lawyer in Georgia. I'll stand up for the Cherokee, Father, just like you have. I promise. I'll learn to do all the things you and I have talked about."

"Well, it's settled then. Let me share with you what I know about the Litchfield school. It's the second oldest in our nation, founded in 1774 by Tapping Reeve. You couldn't do better. I'm impressed with the achievements of their students. Litchfield is quite a distance, but it's the best. It has a strong fourteen-month vocational curriculum. Mr. Gould tells me the school has produced successful lawyers, politicians, judges and members of congress working throughout all twenty-four of these United States. You could apprentice in Milledgeville and bypass law school, but I'm told you'll begin your career with a head start if you go to Litchfield. Can you keep your nose to the grindstone and finish what you start? Fourteen months is a long time."

"I want to go, Father," Ben said proudly.

A departure date was set. Ben was going to read law in Connecticut.

8 August 1824

"Cassie, I'm not sure what I'll be able to accomplish as an American lawyer on behalf of the Cherokee, but I can do good over time if I'm patient. At least I can help my father and his fellow missionaries. I can do that. Cassie, I respect my parents and share their beliefs about the rights of the Cherokee, the Creek and others, even Africans. If Americans lived among the Cherokee, like I do," Ben said, "they wouldn't be afraid. Perhaps, with time, things will change. I hope so."

"I remember you from the first morning in your father's schoolroom," I said. "We need men like you. People like you may make all the difference. Your father said there is nothing more honorable than giving one's life to support the vulnerable. You're going to do good work. I know you are."

"I dislike injustice," Ben answered. "Especially what I've seen here. Americans put great stock in Rule of Law. With patience I could make a difference. Perhaps a lifetime of patience would be required. I won't be popular, but I don't care. Father never cared about reputation or wealth. I want to do what's right. Father didn't choose to be fashionable, neither will I. The Cherokee are at the mercy of the American legal system. American land lust must be controlled. I don't want to see you dispossessed."

14 August 1824

"Cassie, we decided my journey will be easier by coaster. I can sail from Savannah to New London rather than travel by stage."

"I've never seen the sea, Ben, but I love to read about sailors' adventures. I envy your journey. Edudu tells many stories of Cherokee who used to live close to the sea before the Americans forced us inland. You won't forget me, will you?"

"Cassie, how could I forget you? I'll write reams and reams. I'll share everything. I want you to write, too. You will write, won't you?

Chapter XVII

1824 – Bookends
Chapter 17

22 August 1824 - Month of the end of the Fruit Moon -ga lo nii

Ben will be gone for fourteen months. The birds have forgotten their songs. The moon has covered its face.

23 August 1824

Ben shared his mother's advice before his departure.

"Son, I need to talk to you. Allow me to worry a little. I know you're grown. You're no longer a child. You stand taller than your father. You're as capable as any, but I can't help wanting to give you some motherly advice. Ben, may I ask you a question?"

"Oh, Mother, you can say anything you wish."

"Ben, I've lain awake rehearsing this moment. When you return from Connecticut you won't be my little boy, not that you're little now, but you know what I mean. When you return you'll be your own man making your own decisions. Today is the last talk I'll ever have with my little boy.

Please don't be offended if I think of you today as my child. Allow me this one last indulgence. When I woke this morning I had a nostalgic parade of visions. I remember your first little red hat and how you wore it to bed. I remember the first time you helped your father bring in firewood. I can still see that little boy with blond curls and two little sticks of firewood in his arms as proud as could be for helping his father. You're tall, handsome and smart. You'll be successful at whatever you choose. May I give you one last piece of advice?"

"Of course you can, Mother," Ben answered.

"I knew this day was coming. I've dreaded it," his mother said. "In other ways I've rejoiced. Not every parent is as fortunate to have such an intelligent and obedient son as you, Ben. Let me share with you something I've learned. When older children are far from parental authority for the first time they sometimes do things they would never do at home. Like little birds flying from the nest, they test their wings, sometimes unwisely. Tomorrow you begin your adult life without your parents near. I wish I could keep you a few more years, but it's time. Beginning tomorrow you'll carry adult responsibilities and bear adult punishment. Your father and I won't be near to protect you as we have in the past. There comes a time when young birds must leave the nest. Son, do you remember our visit to the big stone mountain last year? It was spectacular. The mountain is one big round rock. Your father says it rises almost seven hundred feet and is about five miles around. We could see it long before we arrived."

"Yes, ma'am. I remember. It's the most unusual mountain I've ever seen."

"Do you remember the Indians? I think they were mostly Creek and Cherokee. It's their favorite meeting place. Anyone can find it."

Ben listened, still a little embarrassed at his mother's formality of speech.

"Ben, do you remember the view? I was astonished. I could see for miles in every direction. From the top it seemed as if God had covered the world in a carpet of trees, one of the most beautiful things I've ever seen."

Ben's mother stared into the distance remembering her trip.

"Do you remember our hike up the mountain? Right in the middle on the top is a flat spot where Indians stood on a tall pile of stones looking this way and that. They stayed up there all day. I was never sure for what purpose. We admired the view and came back down for lunch. Do you remember?"

"Of course I remember, Mother. I'll never forget that trip."

His mother looked Ben in the eye and held his gaze without blinking.

"Do you remember Cassie's grandfather's warning?"

"Yes, ma'am," Ben replied, a little nervously. "Cassie's grandfather said the mountain is dangerous because its sides are not sheer. The mountain is shaped like a round loaf of bread. The sides become imperceptibly steeper as a person walks from the middle toward the nonexistent cliffside. Cassie's grandfather insisted I must not try to look over the side of the mountain."

"That's right," his mother said. "The mountain is deceptive, dangerously so. Many have fallen to their death trying to look over the side, looking for something which didn't exist. There is no cliff to look over. They ignored advice, lost their footing and slid off the rounded mountain to their death."

"Yes, ma'am," was all Ben could answer. His throat was dry.

"You, your father and I heeded the warnings. We stood on the top, enjoyed the spectacular view and went back down by the safe path. Some things you can't afford to find out for yourself, son. Some lessons are too dangerous to learn the hard way."

His mother looked away and let her words sink deep into her son's mind.

"Son, if you had been alone on the mountain that day would you have ignored advice? Would your youthful curiosity have led you to look over the edge?"

"No, ma'am, I wouldn't have tried to look over the edge," Ben responded. "You know I would obey you and Father, even if you weren't there."

Ben felt a quiver inside. He wasn't lying, but he knew he had gone places and done things in the private thoughts of his mind against his parents' advice.

"Son, the mountain is innocuous on one hand and deadly on the other. Such is life. After today you'll be on your mountain alone without parents to protect you. Remember this. Some lessons are too dangerous to learn the hard way. Only a fool wants to experience everything for himself and ignore advice. Never be tempted to see how close you can get to the edge."

"Yes, ma'am," was all Ben could manage.

"For fourteen months you'll be in the company of unsupervised young adult men. Like a little bird, you'll want to test your wings. Turn a deaf ear to those who say, 'Let's look over the edge. Nothing bad will happen if we take a little peek. Your mother and father will never know. Let's have some fun? I won't tell your parents if you won't tell. No one will ever know."

Ben's throat was dry. He couldn't have said a word if he wanted to. His mother's speech was unlike anything he had heard in his life.

"Your friends will invite you to accompany them to the edge of your moral mountain. Be the same person then as now, Ben. Never allow peers to bully you into foolish actions because you're afraid of rejection. You'll never regret choosing the safe path to the mountaintop. Life should be enjoyed from the high ground, but there are forbidden pleasures. They're forbidden because they lead to your death. They're called pleasures because they give real pleasure. Never believe something is right because it feels good. When you're an old man you'll never regret good decisions. Good decisions will cause you to prosper. Live on the top where the best views are found. Don't let so-called friends lead you in a search for the nonexistent edge that leads to your death."

His mother looked up again at the beautiful clouds in the August sky.

"Every night I pray the Lord I might live long enough to hold my grandchildren, your children, Ben."

His mother paused again and looked her son in the eye.

"I want my grandchildren to have a good father. Experimentation with the forbidden destroys, like the use of ardent spirits. You know about that. Whiskey ruins American and Cherokee alike. I hope you never have anything to do with such. There's not one good thing to say about it. Ben, I have one last question. If you walked slowly and carefully, would it be safe to look over the edge of that big stone mountain?"

Ben swallowed again until he could speak.

"No, ma'am. No matter how slowly and carefully a person places their feet, there is no edge. Once a person slips, they're gone."

"That's correct," his mother answered. "There is no prudent way to participate in evil. Wickedness can never be taken safely in measure. If you are unwise you'll discover the danger of some temptations only when it's too late, when you've gone too close to the edge. You have the good Book. Read it. Guard your heart. If you listen to advice, your life will get better and better. You'll finish on the top of the mountain and leave marvelous legacies for my grandchildren. You'll be stalwart. You'll have good company on that mountain. Wilbur and I will be there. Your grandparents are there now."

"Ben, I have a present for you," his mother said.

His mother handed him two strings of braided homespun cord.

"Ben, these are yours. Maybe you could use them to bookmark your Bible. These were the ties on the apron I wore to prepare your breakfast this morning. I spun them myself when you were a baby. I cut them off my apron just now before I walked out here. Son, from this moment you're no longer tied to my apron strings. These are yours as a token of your adulthood. You're no longer a child. You're a grown man. Remember who you are. Remember my advice. I know I must let you go, but I wish you were a little boy again. Your father and I cannot be with you to protect you, but what we have taught you can protect you. Continue on that path. Enjoy the view from the top of the beautiful mountain. Resist the temptation to look for the edge."

Ben's departure was the saddest day. Ben brought me to their house before daylight to share their last quick breakfast before Ben and his father left in the carryall for Milledgeville.

"I promise I shall write often. I promise," Ben said.

"Your return will be the happiest day of my life," I said.

Ben and his father headed down the road on Ben's great adventure. His mother and I continued waving long after Mr. Lowry's old carryall was out of sight. Ben will be gone for over a year.

7 September 1824

Ben's first Letter - Savannah – 2 September 1824

My Dear Cassie,

The trip to Milledgeville was lovely. On the journey Father gave me his parting advice. Along with Mother's, it's like moral bookends to frame my life. On the first part of the journey Father and I talked of various things. Just before we arrived in Milledgeville, Father gave me his final word of advice. I want to share that with you.

"Your mother told me about her talk with you about the stone mountain. Do you want to hear my advice, son?"

"Yes, sir. I would very much like your advice, Father."

Father's horse pulled the little carryall at a steady pace, the big wheels slowly trundled over the uneven roadway.

"Ben, we've split a lot of firewood over the years. You remember how we split straight grain red oak with one smooth blow of an axe? I love the smell of red oak just after it's split open. Some logs are too difficult to split with just an axe. Hard to split logs require a hammer and wedge. Do you remember splitting the long chestnut logs for rails? We chose the straightest trunks with the fewest limbs and knots. We used steel wedges along with our big, wooden persimmon wedges. Remember how patiently we worked to split those rails? You can't split a long log with one mighty blow, can you? Splitting fence rails requires patience, a wedge here and a wedge there, tap-tapping here and tap-tapping there until the job is done. Splitting wood requires patience. If you hit a wedge too hard before it's in far enough, it'll jump out and hit you between the eyes. You can't get in a hurry when you're splitting wood."

"That's right, sir. I remember well," I answered.

"The thin end of the wedge has to go in slowly. We lightly tap-tap-tap the wedges into the log. After patient, soft tapping, the wedge is finally in deep enough for a stronger blow. That powerful blow drives the thick end of the wedge deep into the log and we can cut the stringers with our axe."

"That's right, sir. I enjoy splitting wood."

"When you were softly tap-tap-tapping the thin end of the wedge into the log, the wedge was hardly going into the log, right?"

"Yes, sir. I understand what you're describing perfectly, Father."

"Were we wasting time and energy when we were softly tapping the wedge with our hammer?"

"No, sir. A soft tapping of the wedge is required to get the wedge deep enough to apply the final big blow that splits the log."

"That's right, son. With enough soft tapping for long enough, anyone can split a big log. You can break down the resistance of the mightiest oak log with many small taps of the hammer and wedge. The thin end of the wedge cannot split open the log, but it opens the way for the thick end of the wedge. I can split the most difficult log if you give me a hammer, wedge and enough time."

"Yes, sir. I understand."

Father stopped the carryall in the middle of the road.

"Son, beware the thin end of the wedge of evil. Like your mother said, one day you'll be around folk of dubious character. You'll not immediately recognize these folks as dangerous. You may think of them as your friends. They'll influence you using the same method we use to split logs. They'll use friendship to slip the thin end of their immoral ways into your life. If you're unmindful you'll not notice them slowly changing your views about right and wrong. Bear Paws wasn't hooked with one drink."

"No, sir," I answered. "Bear Paws had no idea of the danger behind that first temptation."

"That's right, son," Father said. "Neither Bear Paws or anyone else would touch that nasty stuff if they knew the misery it has caused in this world. Alcohol in any form is dangerous. Someone asked Bear Paws to take his first drink. Someone will ask you to do something you disapprove of but give you a very good reason to do it. They'll coat the temptation with sugar but evil is always evil, even when well-dressed or sugar coated."

Beware the thin end of the wedge. Your friends will entice you. They'll do their best to insert the thin end of their godless reasoning into your mind in an attempt to slowly separate you from your integrity. No one splits a log with one blow. Evil cannot destroy in one blow either. Blatant evil is easy to avoid. It's the evil that disguises itself as your friend, as the thing you have always desired. Beware. After I leave you in Milledgeville, your mother and I will not be near to warn you of danger. From this day forward, you're in charge."

Father stopped the horse in the middle of the road once again, "Keep reading the good book, son. I have an additional gift for you."

While the horse was stopped Father took two short pieces of leather from his pocket.

"Son, before we left the house I cut a short piece of leather off the end of the reins of my old bridle, the bridle I've had since you were born. I tied the two together. They're yours. From this day your mother and I are observers and advisors. Our task is complete. I hand the reins to you."

12 September 1824

26 August 1824 - Milledgeville
My Dear Cassie,

I can't wait to board the coaster in the morning and begin my great adventure and get back to you. I miss you terribly. I understand now why some never leave home. I am already friends with the four boys going with me to Litchfield. We'll have a grand time. Write soon.

I can't wait to finish school and get back and go to work in Milledgeville on behalf of you and your people.

I'm missing you more than you can possibly know.
Your Ben Forever, xoxo

26 September 1824

Saturday - 9 September 1824 – Litchfield, Connecticut
My Dear Cassie,

I loved the sea journey to New London. I had one thought the entire trip, that you should have been with me.

I arrived in Litchfield this Saturday evening and was met by Mr. Gould. He showed me to my lodgings which I found spartan, but satisfactory. A country boy reared in the bucolic mountains of Cherokee Country needs little diversion beyond books and education. Mr. Gould and I will get along famously.

Our studies begin Monday morning. I'll have a dreadful time composing myself for sleep. I'm thinking of you.
Impatiently yours, Your Ben Forever xoxo

19 November 1824

Ben writes every week. How slowly will days pass before I see him again.

Chapter XVIII

1825 – Creeks Removed
Chapter 18

10 January 1825 - Month of the Cold Moon – Du no lv ta ni

My Dearest Ben,

I'm thinking about you so far away on your birthday. Do good work.

Wish you were here.

I awoke to deep snow and my first thought was of you. As far as I can see the glistening blanket is perfectly smooth, untrammeled by man or beast, not a footprint to be seen.

Wish you were here.

It is quiet, as if I alone observe the bejeweled landscape, a landscape greater than any royal court.

Wish you were here.

The fairy-tale panorama is like a grand illustration of Hans Christian Anderson. The birds and animals remain snuggled in their winter beds. All is silent.

Wish you were here.

The silvery landscape made me think some marvelous magician in one enchanted night wrapped the world in joy. Dazzling sunbeams stream through snow laden limbs flashing millions of jeweled facets in the morning sun as if the trees themselves were alight, bowing to one another, displaying their winter garments on a carpet pure and soft, with glittering slippers they dance in the shimmering light of dawn.

Wish you were here.

Although the sun has risen, it is as quiet as midnight. The only sound is the gentle crackle of the fire. There is not a cloud in the pale winter sky nor a breath of wind. Today, for this one day, the earth has paused.

Wish you were here.

Icicles hang from the eaves, fiery gems, brilliantly adorning the corners of our home, now become a mighty castle amidst a land of wholesome innocence in which all corruption has disappeared, a perfection given by heaven itself. This winter's day my thoughts are of you.

Wish you were here.

Cassie

11 January 1825

Yesterday I walked in the snow through the meadows and woods to enjoy the winter scenes. I felt like my footprints spoiled the work of a great artist. It was the most beautiful landscape I have ever seen in my life. I truly do wish you were here.

19 February 1825

From the *Georgia Journal* - 15 February 1825, page 2

"...the removal of the Indian tribes from the lands which they now occupy within the limits of the several states and territories, to the country lying westward...is of very high importance to our Union, and may be accomplished on conditions and in a manner to promote the interest and happiness of those tribes..."

"For the removal of the tribes within the limits of the state of Georgia, the motive has been peculiarly strong, arising from the compact with the state, whereby the United States are bound to extinguish the Indian title to lands within it...In fulfillment of this compact, I have thought the United States should act with generous spirit...the removal of the tribes from the territory which they now occupy...would accomplish the object for Georgia under a well digested plan for their government and civilization which should be agreeable to themselves would not only shield them from impending ruin but promote their welfare and happiness...in their present state it is impossible to incorporate them, in such masses, in any form whatever, into our system...it will be difficult, if not impossible, to control their degradation and extermination will be inevitable."

"...the removal proposed is not only practicable, but that the advantages attending to it, to the Indians, may be made so apparent to them that all the tribes, even those opposed, may be induced to accede...to...make them a civilized people, is an object of very high importance...by the establishment of such a government over these tribes, by their consent, we become, in reality, their benefactors...There will be no more war...Accepting such a government their movement will be in harmony with us and its good effect be felt throughout the whole extent of our territory, to the Pacific."

A speech delivered to congress on 27 January 1825.

From the *Georgia Journal* - 15 February 1825

"...resolved...the committee on Indian affairs be instructed to enquire into the expediency of making an appropriation for the extinguishment of the Indian title to land lying in the state of Georgia..."

"The president...has connected the performance of the obligations of the United States to Georgia, with the great plan of collecting all the Indians in our Western territory, for the purpose of civilizing them."

The Americans steal from children and boast about their theft. Governor Troup threatened the Creeks with war if they did not agree to Georgia's terms. The missionaries say both the negotiations and treaty with the Creek are a sham. Georgia wants to make their seizure of Indian land legal. Mr. Lowry says divide et impera, divide and rule.

From the *Georgia Journal* - 15 February 1825

"We invite the attention of the people of Georgia to the message of Mr. Monroe...It is based on principle which will be approved by philanthropists everywhere...Hence it is contended...that the discharge of these obligations (the compact of 1802)...should be made a separate and distinct matter, claiming the FIRST and undivided attention of the general government."

25 February 1825

I long for Ben's return. Perhaps we are wasting time negotiating. Some say we should remove peacefully while we can. Elisi and Edudu are too old to leave the only home they have ever known.

27 February 1825

Governor Troup, a supporter of Andrew Jackson, is a proponent of the removal of all Indians, not just the Creek. Older men say the worst thing we ever did was allow Americans to build roads. Allowing roads gives permission to invade, Edudu says.

Troup's cousin, William M'Intosh, a Creek chief, signed the treaty to give away all Creek land and in return received a large sum of money. The treaty said Georgia purchased Creek land. Immediately upon signing the treaty the Georgia Militia forced the remaining Creeks to remove, even the ones who didn't want to give away their house and farm and go west.

Civilization and soil belong to Americans. Divide et impera.

According to Edudu, the Creeks do not recognize William M'Intosh, the governor's cousin, as their legal representative in the new treaty. There will be trouble. Governor Troup's corruption is obvious, even to whites.

What Troup did is legal. Law is justice. Georgia has what it wants, a piece of paper with signatures which gives them the right to dispossess. William M'Intosh is rich. Troup and his political friends are happy. Creeks are homeless. If the Americans want something, they make a law to get it, exactly as the Romans did.

Horseshoe Bend severely weakened the Creek Nation. Now the Creeks are helpless. Edudu said it would be better to die honorably defending one's nation than have our flesh slowly flayed from our bones. Edudu said not one Cherokee would have participated in the Creek war if they had known all the American promises were false. Edudu said he should have fought for the Creek rather than against them.

The missionaries say the treaty of Indian Springs will be rescinded, but it is too late. Creek land has been surveyed and the lottery is in place.

Ben does not like the way Milledgeville justifies all their actions. Over a million acres of Creek land have been transferred to Georgia ownership. Edudu says one day the Americans will pass a law and come for our land.

8 May 1825

The Creek chief sold his nation for personal gain, now William M'Intosh is dead. Edudu said he would have killed him himself for signing away all their land without the tribe's permission. Our land doesn't belong to us, we belong to the land. Where will we be without our land?

From the *Southern Recorder* – 31 May 1825 - page 3

> "...The bill for disposing of the lately acquired territory (from the Creeks) by lottery, it is expected will pass the House of Representatives...in the course of the week..."

"Walela, Americans fuss with everyone. They can't see past their fence. Every Cherokee family enjoys our land as far as our eyes can see. How can people from across the ocean have a legal claim on our land? They're invaders who can't speak our language.

22 June 1825

Alabama is removing all Indians. The Creeks, Choctaw and Chickasaw will be extinguished in turn. Hurry home, Ben. Andrew Jackson and his Volunteers boast they have rid themselves of savages. Maybe it is they who are untamed. Maybe our leaders can find a solution in Washington City. Maybe Ben, with his law degree, can help.

24 June 1825

My Dear Cassie,

I miss you terribly. My main recreation is correspondence with you, reading and my sketch book. I cannot express my excitement about the school and my future. The woodsman is not wasting time when he sharpens his axe.

As Mother and Father correctly assessed, I am advantaged by my knowledge of Latin. Law uses Latin almost exclusively for technical nomenclature. Latin lives. Roman law, the mortar of their empire, has flowed across the ocean to America. Quite remarkable, don't you think?

I cannot wait to return to you. Your loving Ben, xoxo

18 June 1825

My Dear Ben,

I included a newspaper clipping. Do good work and hurry home. You are needed. I send all my love, Cassie.

From the *Southern Recorder* – 14 June 1825 - page 2

"Be it enacted by the Senate and House of Representatives of the State of Georgia…that the territory acquired of the Creek Nation of Indians…shall be divided…after surveying…the governor shall cause tickets to be made…which tickets shall be put into a wheel and constitute prizes…"

12 September 1825

My Dear Cassie,

I love the endless hours allowed for reading. I have few chores but I miss the routine of home. I miss Mother's cooking most of all. Other than that, and the fact that I can't be with you, I am perfectly happy spending long hours preparing for my career. Do not worry. As Father says, "Yesterday was the best day of his life and today is already better".

I remember your grandfather's advice about complaints and complainers. I do not complain and I avoid keeping company with anyone who does. Loving you always, Ben xoxo

11 October 1825

It would be great fun to ride on a steamboat.

From the *Southern Recorder* – 27 September 1825 - page 2

"Steamboats on the Ocmulgee and Oconee…a steamboat and four tow boats, will run constantly from Savannah to Macon and Milledgeville, stopping at the intermediate landings for the reception and delivery of Produce and Merchandize on Freight. The steamboat is now ready...starting on her first trip from Savannah on the fifteenth day of October next...they will be prepared to receive cotton...direct without the delay of landing and reloading in Darien...John T. Lamar Macon – G. B. Lamar – Savannah."

12 November 1825

From the *Georgia Journal* – 8 November 1825 – Page 2

"One thing is certain—the contract with the state of Georgia must be fulfilled. The Indians must be removed, 'peaceably if they can—forcibly if they must,"...A very high obligation is imposed upon the Federal Government to relieve the Southern States of their Indian population. In this respect the North and South are upon a very unequal footing—the Northern States...exterminated their Indians before they became partie to the Federal Constitution...Not so in the south...Georgia, Alabama, Mississippi and Louisiana are covered by an Indian population which contribute nothing to the wealth of the states, and subtract from their strength by the necessity of watching them. The Federal government alone can put these states on an equal footing with those in the North...we would beg them to refresh their memories by reading...from their own histories...'The government increased the premium for Indian scalps and captives to one hundred pounds...This encouraged John Lovewell to raise a company of volunteers to go out upon and Indian hunting'....After reading this...we would ask which is the most humane—to remove Indians from Georgia by treaty to a country west of the Mississippi...or exterminate them under a law..."

Chapter XIX

1826 – Ben Returns - The Sketch Book
Chapter 19

18 June 1826 - Month of the Green Corn Moon -de ha lu yi

Ben is home. Words cannot express my joy.

"Ben, you are more handsome than I remember."

"I don't know about that, Cassie, but I know you're lovelier than I remember, but I don't see how that's possible since you were the most beautiful woman in the world when I left."

"Tell me about law school."

"I've already told you everything in my letters but there's one thing you don't know, Cassie. Please forgive my boasting. I graduated first in my class. I wanted to tell you that in person. I had an advantage. My language skills were superior, thanks to my parents."

"You underestimate yourself, Ben."

"I give my parents credit, Cassie. They taught me to read at an early age. If not for them I would have ended up a farmer, but I did have multiple job offers. Governments over the United States were seeking graduates. North Carolina, Virginia, Maryland and South Carolina offered me a job. I turned them down. I want to work in Georgia. I want to be close to you. I couldn't bear to be away from you one more day."

"Whatever happens, we will find happiness, Ben. You're my best friend. I'll wait for you another fourteen months or fourteen years."

19 June 1826

Ben brought me a special gift.

"I can't stay long, Cassie. Mother sent me to ask if you would spend the afternoon with us? We would love to have you. Would you come?"

"Of course, I would love to," I answered.

"I knew you would," Ben replied. "I have a special gift for you. I was embarrassed to give you this in my parents' presence. I suppose I didn't want them to see it or at least see me give it to you. It's just for you. You'll understand when you see it."

Ben took a small folio from his saddlebag.

"You probably don't remember, but a few days before I left for school we were by the river in your special place. I recited a list of things I liked about you. Do you remember?"

"Of course, I remember," I answered."

"When I was lonely in Connecticut I would sketch to make me feel closer to you. The inspiration for those sketches often came from that single afternoon when we had the picnic by the river. I studied you carefully that day. As I would sketch, I would challenge my memory to call up the finest details of your body, of specific parts of your body I have committed to memory."

Ben explained as he handed me the sketch book, "I've never forgotten you or that day, Cassie. Look here. The more I thought about you, the more I wanted to sketch. It was the only way I could feel close to you. The charcoal brought you near."

I was astonished. Ben had sketched simple line drawings with uncanny precision. The first drawing was of my nose and nothing else. The second, my eyes alone, no other part of my face. The third was a profile of one of my feet and so on. There were three dozen beautiful charcoal sketches of different parts of my body in different poses. Each drawing perfectly detailed and all from that single day. I was amazed. Of all the romantic things Ben has done, this is the most special.

19 June 1826

I guess absence does make the heart grow fonder because I love Ben more than ever. When the Americans are lonely they say "I miss you". The French say, "you are missing from me".

20 June 1826

Ben and I had a long, wonderful day together.

"I must tell you, Cassie, I missed Mother's cooking every day I was away but it wasn't my mother's cooking I longed for most of all. It was you I missed more than anything when I was in Connecticut," Ben said.

"Ben, you can tell me things like that anytime," I said playfully, as he held me like an infant. "The way you express your longing is most romantic."

"I want to make you happy, Cassie. That's what I think about. After I get a job I'll save so we can set up housekeeping. We'll be together. I promise you that. I want to make you the happiest woman in the world. When I was away I can't describe the horrible feelings of loneliness I had. When I walked into town I would try to catch a glimpse of a woman who looked like you. The smallest resemblance to you would have been a vision that would have momentarily satisfied my heart. In all the time I was away I never saw such a woman."

"Ben, you are more romantic than ever. You know what I imagine?"

"Tell me, Cassie. I would love to know."

"I remember the freshness of your breath, your white teeth, your playfulness and the sunlight reflecting off your hair. I love your hands and arms. I love the soft melody of your voice, but my favorite memory of all is when I lay my head on your chest and feel your beating heart. It's then that I'm reminded that everything attractive about you comes from the inside. Ben, I have known for a long time how men and women express their love in literature. I have seen love in my community. Now I am experiencing a living romance with you. I yearn to be with my beloved. I want to know my beloved feels the same."

Later when I tried to describe my love for Ben to Elisi, her face beamed.

Elisi caressed my hair as she spoke softly of her love for Edudu.

"I cannot tell you precisely how your love will grow, Walela, but it will grow. No two trees are exactly the same. Each day with your love will be happier than the last. That I know. I am glad for you, Walela. Your Ben is a good man and will be a good husband.

22 June 1826

Another grand day with Ben.

"Ben, I brought your sketch book with me today. Turn to the last page. While you were away I read a Robert Burns poem. Please read it to me, Ben."

"Cassie, this is one of my favorites. There's something about reading poetry aloud that brings the meaning home, doesn't it?"

O my love's like a red, red rose, That's newly sprung in June.
O my love's like a melody, That's sweetly played in tune.
As fair are thou, my bonnie lass, So deep in love am I.
And I will love thee still, my dear, Till all the seas run dry.
Till all the seas run dry, my dear, and the rocks melt with the sun.
I will love thee still, my dear, while the sands of life shall run.
And fare thee well, my only love, and fare thee well a while.
And I will come again, my love, Though it were ten thousand miles.
Robert Burns

24 June 1826

I think about reading, writing and education every day. I wish my ancestors had left a written history. We have been and are now a happy people. I would love to know the details of our history, where we came from, who our leaders were and what they did but I know literacy alone will not make a people happy. The Romans were highly literate and civilized. They were not the happiest of people.

26 June 1826

I am officially Mr. Lowry's assistant and permitted to teach children and older girls. Ben and I could teach every Cherokee child to read and write if we were given the opportunity. Since our nation adopted Sequoya's syllabary last year, we have an official written language that many are learning. I'm proud. Our Cherokee dream of literacy is becoming a reality.

1 July 1826

"Cassie," Ben said, "Father and I are going to Milledgeville next week to find a placement for me in a law firm."

"This is an exciting time in your life. I'm going to miss you," I said sadly.

"Don't worry, Cassie," Ben answered. "Everything will be good for us. Milledgeville isn't far. Things will work out, you'll see. I know one thing. I'm the luckiest man in the world to have the most beautiful woman in the world care about me. I can't wait to get to work and do all the things we've talked about. I'll write and I'll be up here visiting you so often you won't even know I've been gone."

18 July 1826

Ben and his father are back from Milledgeville. They met with quite a few lawyers looking for placement. It won't be long before Ben will make a decision about his future.

25 July 1826

If Ben is to help our nation, he has no time to spare. He must find a job with a good law firm. We talked about his work as a lawyer on the whiteside.

3 August 1826

We Cherokee have begun to set up our nation with a constitution, laws and law enforcement. Next year we may ratify our own constitution. Every American newspaper says we must be removed. We are in danger of being washed away by a flood, a flood not of muddy water but of American immigrants who want to take the very last thing we possess, our land.

Chapter XX

1826 Zach

Chapter 20

6 August 1826 - End of the Fruit Moon - Ga lo nii

Ben met me in my special place.

"Cassie, it's finally happened. I'm going to be a lawyer in Milledgeville. They asked me to go to work as soon as possible and I accepted. I'm sure it's the right choice. Father agrees. Isn't that wonderful?"

"I am proud, Ben. You're going to make a great lawyer. This is the fulfillment of your dreams, of our dreams, and Milledgeville isn't far, is it?"

"No, Milledgeville isn't far. I'll visit and write so often you'll hardly know I'm gone. Father and I found a boarding house within walking distance of the firm. Would you like to ride down with us when Father takes me back? I could show you around town?"

"I would love to. What an adventure. I know a lot about Milledgeville from the newspapers but I've never seen a big town. Are you sure it's alright with your father if I come?"

"Father would love you to ride with us, Cassie. You can keep him company on the way back. You'll love Milledgeville. There are dozens of shops. I'm going to love it there. There's lots to see. You won't believe the books. I'm sure I'll spend all my extra money in the book shops. We can spend all afternoon looking at books if we want to. Do come, Cassie."

Ben was suddenly embarrassed.

"Oh, Cassie, I'm so sorry. Don't look so sad. I didn't mean it to sound like I would be happy when we're apart. I'll miss you every day I'm away. I'll be coming back regularly and I'll write often. I promise I'll write. I don't want you to think I'm happy about leaving you. I'm just happy about beginning my work, that's all."

"Ben, I'll miss you every day, but I'm proud of you. I'm glad you're going to work in a profession you love. I would never take that from you. I'm not offended you will enjoy Milledgeville. You can't stay here. I know that. I know you don't want to be a farmer. If you're going to help your father and the Cherokee, you must leave. I'll think of you every day. You have chosen the right path, Ben. I believe in you. While you were at school your mother and I talked often about you, about us. Your mother fully approves of our relationship even though I'm not white. She thinks we will have the most

110

beautiful children in the world. Your mother is special, Ben. I want to name our first little girl Eleanor."

Ben took my hands.

"Well, you and Mother feel free to talk about me behind my back, don't you? So, you and my mother think our children will be beautiful? I think my mother's right. Our children will be beautiful, but before we get married we have to make preparations, a lot of preparations. I must save to set up housekeeping, or would you rather live in poverty?"

"I know, Ben. We will have a wonderful marriage. Elisi thinks you'll be a worthy husband and good father. The only thing my family cares about is that you love me and our children. They wouldn't care if you were African, Spanish, French or English if you treat me right."

"Cassie, every night when I say my prayers, I thank God I found you. You're the best thing that has ever happened to me. I mean that. I brought you a gift. It's in my saddle bag. I was so excited I forgot it. Let's go get it. Before I give you your gift, Cassie, you'll have to guess what it is."

"It's a book," I answered quickly.

"You peeked," Ben said laughing.

"No, I didn't."

He handed me the gift wrapped in plain brown paper.

"I hope you like it, Cassie. My father would think it a frivolous waste of money, but I knew you would love it. It's popular on both sides of the Atlantic."

It was a copy of *Pride and Prejudice* by Jane Austin.

"You are the best friend ever, Ben, I love you, I love you."

"I've read about this book," I said. "I'll enjoy it."

"I knew you would," Ben said. "It's about a bookish country gentleman and his wife. Her task in life is to find prosperous husbands for her five daughters. I can't get away from young women looking for husbands, can I?"

"I haven't read it, Cassie. I thought I would wait until you're finished and then we can discuss it. I know the kind of books my father loans you. I thought you would enjoy something a little lighter. You may even write your own novel one day."

"I think I could," I answered. "Maybe I shall. A romantic historical novel about a young American man who falls in love with a beautiful Cherokee princess. They live happily ever after, have fifteen children and fifty grandchildren. That would be fun, wouldn't it?"

10 August 1826

The morning of Ben's return to Milledgeville dawned dark and dreary. Low scudding rain clouds covered the sky. It would be a warm but nasty day. The blustery wind brought intermittent showers.

Mr. Lowry planned for us to stay the night with his friends on the Hightower Road. We were leaving early to make certain we wouldn't be required to travel on the Sabbath.

I helped Mr. Lowry make final adjustments to the harness. Ben was checking to make sure our things were properly secured and covered under the oilcloth in the bed of the little carryall. Ben's mother brushed away wisps of her greying hair blown across her emotionless face by the gusting wind. As she watched her son, her hands dropped into her lap. She twisted her apron nervously. I could only imagine her feelings.

This parting was different than when Ben left for law school. This time Ben would leave never to return. He was leaving the nest, spreading his wings, beginning his adult career. I asked Five Feathers to help Mrs. Lowry with the chores.

Mr. Lowry flicked the reins. Gunsmoke started us down the hill. I felt sorry for the poor horse.

"It is going to be a long trip for Gunsmoke, Ben," I said. "Milledgeville is a long way for your poor horse to pull this heavy wagon."

"You have a tender heart, Cassie. You needn't worry. Father loves his old gelding. This little carryall is light as a feather for Gunsmoke. He's a strong horse. Father won't work him too hard. He'll let him rest every mile or two with a well-deserved rest at the top of every hill. Father has a soft heart for his animals just like you do.

"What if it rains?" I asked.

"If it rains, we'll sit close together and cover up with an oilcloth. I won't mind sittin' close to you. In fact, I've been praying for rain."

"I think I shall pray for rain, too."

"Father has two big oilskins tied tight with grommets around our things in the back. Nothing can get wet back there, no matter how hard it rains. He has two more to cover us, one for Father and one for you and me. Our feet might get a little damp, but that's all."

On that first morning we passed an orchard and picked apples off the ground for everyone, Gunsmoke included. I laughed at Mr. Lowry who would only take apples that had fallen. He said it was stealing if we took them off the tree. Ben cut the apples into small pieces. I fed Gunsmoke who would softly nibble the apple pieces off my open hand ever so carefully, tickling my palm with his whiskered lips. What fun to spend four days with Ben. I hope I will be allowed to make the journey again. I want to see every shop on every street in Milledgeville.

13 August 1826

We arrived late Saturday afternoon at the Branswell's just as we were entering the whiteside on the Hightower Road. The Branswells and their six children were expecting us. Mr. Lowry knew they would be keeping the

Sabbath. We had a wonderful visit and slept soundly in their comfortable home. I was allowed to peruse their many books, what a pleasure.

15 August 1826

We arrived in Milledgeville in the early afternoon. Everywhere I saw finely dressed people, carriages, wagons, horses and African servants. Everyone was busy.

There were tall buildings, some old, some new. Americans love to build. No wonder they think us lazy. Ben asked his father to drive by the Capitol building on Greene Street before going to his boarding house. What a magnificent building.

I realized my tiny rural nation could never resist these industrious people. I understood why they think us an obstruction. Nothing would be denied those who could build such a city in so short a time. Who could possibly stand in their way? Our once magnificent council buildings at Crawfish Springs and New Echota became crude and insignificant. We can no more stop American expansion than I could hold a runaway horse.

Mr. Lowry halted the carryall in the street in front of Ben's boarding house. The proprietor hurried out.

"I'm sorry, sir. Indians must use the back entrance with niggers. A servant can assist you but only through the back entrance. I'm sure you appreciate we do our best to keep a reputable establishment."

"Yes sir," Mr. Lowry answered politely. "We'll go around back."

Life on the whiteside became clear to me. Those I observed walking, riding and doing business around Milledgeville are the same people who write about uncivilized savages destined for extinguishment. Now I understand why Edudu and Elisi never travel to the whiteside where every sidelong glance is meant to thrust us into our place.

"I'm sorry," Mr. Lowry said quietly. "Eleanor and I have been secluded far too long. We've forgotten. I apologize."

We delivered Ben's things to his room from the back entrance. As we were mounting the carryall to leave, the proprietor once again spoke politely to Ben, not caring I would hear every word.

"Sir, we're pleased you've chosen our establishment. It's a pleasure to have our own resident attorney. You can count on us night and day to meet your every need. My door is always open to a gentleman."

The proprietor cleared his throat and continued in a more subdued tone, but I heard every word.

"Sir, we appreciate your business, but if you'll pardon me sayin', in the future it would be better if you didn't bring Indians here. We run a reputable establishment. Indians are not welcome anywhere, sir, for good reason. It wouldn't do if folk saw Indians hanging about, even in the back."

22 August 1826
Ben's first letter from Milledgeville
Huff's Boarding House - 16 August 1826
My Dear Cassie,

I am missing you terribly and can't wait to see you again. I remain embarrassed by your reception. I wish there was something I could do. Perhaps in the future things will change.

Your company made the trip down so much more enjoyable. I loved every moment with you.

I have been assigned a desk by an adequate window. The owner's son, Zach, a lawyer about my age, is in charge of my orientation. I believe Zach and I will complement one another. He needs help applying himself and I need assistance adjusting socially in this strange town. I have a lot to learn about the world.

You are indeed missing from me, as the French say.

Ben oxox

4 September 1826
Milledgeville - 27 August 1826 - Huff's Boarding House
My Dear Cassie,

This short note is to remind you how much I'm missing you. I think of you especially as I compose myself for sleep.

Zach, my new friend, doesn't like the practice of law. His main interests are clothes, food, wine, parties and the daughters of his father's clients. I am learning rapidly. I have much to share with you but I shall wait till I can talk face to face. I miss you.

I shall use my education and do my best to help Father and the Cherokee. I'm determined to work diligently on your behalf and learn as much about the legal profession as I can. I'll tell you more about Zach and the law firm on my return. You're missing from me. Can't wait to see you.

Yours always and forever, Ben xoxo

12 September 1826
Ben came home today and we talked. He talked and I listened. He was like an excited boy. He told me all about his job, his new friend and his assignments. He related some conversations with his new friend, Zach.

"Ben," Zach said, "being a lawyer is easier than working and a lot more profitable. I work just hard enough to prevent Father from putting me into some boring mercantile business or farming. Can you imagine workin' on a farm? Growing cotton and managing niggers is not for me. Our referral business is growing. I need an assistant who can help me put together legal arguments for clients. I need someone to spend time in the boring law books on my behalf. We'll make a good team, don't you think?"

As instructed by his father, Ben said he listened more than he talked.

Zach continued without pause, "My father includes me in most interviews. He says learning how to handle rich folks is my main education. I'm good at it. That's why father keeps me. The key to wealth is the ability to understand the wealthy, Ben. Money is found in the company of gentlemen and politics. Father says a successful law firm depends on who you know. We want to get to know everyone in Georgia with influence. Our business is understanding money, power, prestige and, of course, electing our friends to office. There is nothing so lucrative, my father says, as having your friend in the legislature. That's the quickest way to wealth. If someone we don't know gets elected, it's my job to make them our friend as fast as possible."

Zach continued as if giving a lecture.

"Ben, maneuvering legislators and judges is the key. If your judge owes you a favor, it doesn't matter how well your opponent argues. You see my point. It's the way the world works. We need smart lawyers. That's why we hired you. We want to be a step ahead. If you want to make money, the judges need to be in your pocket, that's what father says. I do a lot of social work, you might say, with judges and their families. I listen and I provide, if you know what I mean. I'm always willing to go out of my way for a judge or member of the legislature. Quid pro quo, Ben, quid pro quo, that's our motto. That's the most important thing I've learned, quid pro quo."

26 September 1826

Ben is home.

"Cassie," Ben said, "Zach's father has done well practicing law, but he has also been successful in land speculation and the slave trade. Zach says his father knows how to be in the right place at the right time. Because of his legal practice his father can purchase slaves at bargain prices. When a man dies or goes bankrupt, they sell his slaves along with the estate. Zach's father often gets first choice."

"Are you going to be involved with the slave trade, Ben?"

"No, of course not. I'll never own a slave. Zach's father does all that on the side. That's not part of the law firm. I'll have nothing to do with anything like that. The firm's big interest is land. Zach's father was on the good side of the Yazoo land fraud, and because they were seen to be honest, they have acquired a sterling reputation. Zach's father has a front row seat for land speculation in Georgia and beyond. People are looking for land and driving prices up, and sadly, they want Indian land."

Ben continued, "Now that I'm in the firm, Zach plans to use my legal knowledge to help them make more money. It's strange being around someone with so much ambition for money and little else. I'll work as hard as anyone, maybe harder, but I don't want to work simply to acquire riches. I want my motto to be an honest day's work for an honest day's pay."

"You're right about money, Ben," I said. "One of the reasons your father has been welcomed is he's not here at our expense. It's known your father and mother don't covet our possessions or our land. It sounds to me like Zach trusts no one but himself. Be careful, Ben. Remember who you are."

"I'll be careful, Cassie. I know who I am. I won't forget. I love the research. I love the intellectual pleasure of crafting a systematic argument based on fact. I love the sober judgment required to put together a case where justice prevails. Father taught me to pursue a conclusion based upon fact and not one held up by guesswork or theories. Zach's father says I have an outstanding legal mind. He wished his son was like me when it comes to intellectual pursuits."

Ben laughed and continued, "Zach will never be a great lawyer, maybe not even a good lawyer. It's humorous to see his eyes light up at the mention of barbecues and outings. You ought to hear him, Cassie. He sounds like a man reciting poetry when he talks of bourbon, leather and French perfume. I know Zach's life is not for me. You can trust me, Cassie. I'll be careful. So far Zach and I make a good team. I like him. He's easy to get along with. I'll let him get richer. I'll get smarter. I won't fall into that trap. I thought it humorous when Zach confessed that as a child he learned to manipulate authority, even his parents. I was the opposite. I've never wanted to manipulate anyone, least of all my parents. I still don't."

"Zach sounds selfish, like he would take advantage of anyone including his parents, including you, maybe especially you. Be careful, Ben. The way you described him it sounds as if Zach loves only himself. Remember your parents' advice."

"I'll remember, Cassie. Don't worry about me. I can take care of myself. I know who I am. I promise you, Zach won't rub off on me."

Chapter XXI
1826 – Zach's Warning
Chapter 21

November 1826 Milledgeville

Ben was looking forward to his meeting with Zach. It wasn't Ben's first visit to Zach's father's hotel. The food was excellent. This would be a welcome change from the plain table-fare in Ben's boring boarding house. He was weary of beans and boiled cabbage. More importantly Ben was looking forward to meeting Elizabeth formally. Zach had told him about her and painted her as exceptionally attractive.

"Glad you could join me," Zach said, greeting Ben on the three broad steps on the left side of the foyer, the steps leading to the private dining room.

"What would you like to drink before we eat?"

"Whatever you're having will be fine, my friend," Ben replied.

Zach made a motion to the tall African servant standing in the shadows.

"Ben, I want to tell you how pleased my father and I are with your work. Hiring you turned out a better decision than we could have imagined."

Ben didn't know what to say. He nodded in return.

"I knew you were the man for the job," Zach continued. "We're going to make money."

"I've never been afraid of hard work and I appreciate being paid for it," Ben answered. "Like I said, I'll give a fair day's work for a fair day's pay."

"That's the spirit, Ben. We appreciate the protestant work ethic around here. It makes us money."

The tall negro, in black with white gloves, moved about the room without making an audible sound. Ben's drinking glass, handed to him on a silver tray, sparkled in the light.

"Ben," Zach said, when they had their drinks in hand, "this is the best sipping whiskey there is. Since you don't know anything about alcohol, let me teach you how to enjoy it. First, take the smallest taste and don't swallow. Breathe slowly over your tongue. You'll get the full flavor of the whiskey that way. After you taste this, you'll never be happy with anything else, I promise you. Everything else will taste like snake oil."

Zach raised his glass and said, "A toast to you, Elizabeth and myself."

"To us," echoed Ben.

They clinked their glasses and Ben sipped. As Ben breathed in as instructed, his mouth seemed to explode with new sensations. Even though Zach assured him this whiskey was the best, the strong liquor was revolting, more like medicine or some kind of nasty horse liniment, not something anyone could enjoy. It left a trail of fire from his mouth to his empty stomach. Zach was right. He had never tasted anything like it. It was terrible. He thought he would choke.

As soon as he caught his breath, Ben returned the toast, "To our friendship, may it last forever."

Ben relaxed and began to take his father's advice and listen more than he talked.

"Elizabeth will be here shortly. Before you meet her, you should know a few things. First, she's the most attractive woman in Milledgeville, maybe in all of Georgia. She's one of a kind, for sure."

"How's she different?"

Zach took another sip of whiskey, "I know Elizabeth. She and I have been business associates since childhood. Neither Elizabeth nor I have siblings. We were both spoiled rotten, still are. We have been groomed to understand business and be wealthy. Elizabeth needed a male business partner. I needed a female business partner. She and I have been looking for someone like you. We have a strong interest in politics. We chose you as the addition to my father's firm with a view to perhaps becoming a future partner, a political ally. Therefore, since you're going to be involved in our business dealings, you need to know about Elizabeth, about us. I don't want you to get off on the wrong foot with her."

"I'm ready to listen, Zach. Tell me about Elizabeth."

"When we were little, Elizabeth and I learned we could get away with anything if we were careful. You might say we learned to play our parents, to play all adults really. Elizabeth and I make a good business team."

Zach laughed again with an easy laugh that made Ben feel comfortable. Ben reflected he had never played his parents and wasn't sure what Zach meant. It didn't sound like something to be proud of.

"When we were young Elizabeth and I learned to stay out of our parents' way. It became a formula we've carried into adulthood. We've made a science of avoiding authority. She and I are our own authority. This is my point."

Zach paused and leaned over towards Ben and shook his cigar towards Ben's face for emphasis.

"Now that we're adults, we take care of ourselves and our future. We enjoy money more than ever. We learned our continued happiness requires a liberal income, that's what Elizabeth and I work for. Acquiring wealth is a game, a serious game."

Zach looked at Ben and shook his cigar towards him once again.

"It's the only game, my friend. We became experts at getting our own way. The point is, Ben, the skills Elizabeth and I learned as children we use now as adults, we've made the acquisition of wealth our sole business."

"Do you play chess, Ben?"

"Yes, Father taught me to play when I was small. Do you play?"

"Yes, I'm intrigued with the game," Zach replied.

Zach waved at the negro servant, signaling he wanted another drink.

Zach leaned back in his big chair and examined Ben carefully.

"One day we'll have to see just how much strategy there is in that country boy mind of yours, Ben. I'll put you to the test before long. One evening we'll have us a good chess game. You can learn a lot about a person by playing chess with them. Have you heard of Francois Philador?"

"No, I don't think so," Ben said. "I'm not familiar with that name. Ruy Lopez is the only chess name I know. It's the name of the opening Father taught me."

Zach waved his cigar again towards Ben as if it were a wand.

"Philador was a French chess prodigy. He has an oft quoted saying about chess, 'Les pions sont l'ame du jeu'--'Pawns are the soul of chess'. Elizabeth and I play occasionally. She finds the game boring but she usually wins. She has a brilliant mind, devious at times, but brilliant. She wins because she is willing to sacrifice her assets, to sacrifice pawns initially but later she'll give up anything to gain the advantage. She plays by her own rules. She loves to open up the board and attack. She's vicious."

Zach took another long sip of whiskey and observed Ben again.

"She's a fearless competitor on the chessboard. She's likewise fearless in business. Remember that, Ben. To Elizabeth, life is one big chess game. People are pieces and wealth the ultimate prize. There are things Elizabeth and I want and we're willing to play the game, to manipulate the board, to sacrifice pawns or any other piece to win the prize. We look for nothing short of checkmate and we don't care how we get it. We're willing to play any kind of gambit to defeat our opponent. We're going to take care of our future and make it secure. If we don't, who will? I promise you, with Elizabeth on your side of the board, you'll win the game every time. That's my point. If you want to take care of your future, you'll be friends with Elizabeth, not an opponent."

Zach laughed and Ben laughed with him. Perhaps it was the alcohol that Ben wasn't used to or the sumptuous surroundings or Ben's willingness to please but under the laughter Ben felt an undercurrent of unease.

"Well, I hope Elizabeth doesn't think of me as a pawn to be sacrificed."

"My word no, Ben," Zach said with a broad smile. "Let me suggest you think of yourself as an intrepid knight carefully selected by his queen to lead a courageous charge, capture the enemy fastness and secure vast amounts of treasure for her royal coffers."

Zach continued with another chuckle.

"Don't misunderstand me, Ben. A couple of years ago Elizabeth and I decided we needed a man like you, a chivalrous knight if you will. My father needed a new man at the firm and you were our choice to fill both positions. You're going to work for my father and, if you want to, you can work for Elizabeth and me at the same time. I think it would be more accurate to say you'll partner with us, not work for us. The three of us will work together. We'll be a team. We'll play the game together. We've been watching you since you went to work for my father and we've decided to make you privy to our business. If you want to be rich, really rich, all you need to do is listen to us. We're experts. Don't worry about being sacrificed. I can assure you Elizabeth wouldn't treat you in such a cavalier fashion."

Ben didn't know what to say. He wasn't sure he was understanding everything Zach had been talking about, but he did understand Zach's desire for money and power. Zach and Elizabeth sounded as if they could, and would, accomplish their plans. This was interesting. What part could they possibly want him to play?

"Zach, I appreciate you taking the time to fill me in. I'm looking forward to meeting Elizabeth. With your introduction, she is even more intriguing than before. Is this job I've been selected for secondary to the one I have at the law firm? I'm confused. I thought I was hired to work for your father? I thought you and I both worked for your father?"

Zach laughed, his face beginning to turn bright pink from the whiskey.

"I understand your confusion, Ben. There's no conflict. Your first responsibility is to Father. You'll represent Father's clients and help him make a lot of money. However, with my father's full knowledge and blessing, Elizabeth and I have a secondary job for you. We're always looking for ways to make more money outside the firm. Elizabeth and I, and Father too, wanted a young, handsome, intelligent man like you. We wanted a trustworthy man, a man who could win the confidence of others, who could represent the firm, run for a state-wide office, and maybe an office in Washington City, the House or Senate. We want to begin with representation in the Georgia legislature."

Ben sipped his drink and listened to this exuberant lawyer continue to share his grand plans. He had certainly chosen to work for a progressive law firm. That was clear. Ben liked his work but he wasn't sure about the political angle Zach was talking about.

"On the surface," Zach continued, "Elizabeth and I may appear normal, but we have a hidden agenda. We want to travel the world and bask in the golden sun of unlimited wealth. You'll discover Elizabeth to be determined. She gets what she wants. She always gets what she wants."

Zach paused to sip his drink and relight his cigar.

Ben replied cautiously, "I want to say first of all that I couldn't agree to anything that would violate your father's trust in me. I couldn't participate in anything illegal. I wouldn't do that. I don't want to be prudish, but I want to be aboveboard from the beginning. I will never go behind your father's back."

Zach signaled for another drink, laughed, and waved at Ben with the hand holding his expensive Cuban cigar. Ben couldn't help thinking of Zach and his cigar as if he were a wizard, his magic dispensed by a wand of tobacco.

"I understand, Ben. Don't be silly. Elizabeth and I aren't going to do anything illegal or even dubious. Nothing we do is shady. Father wouldn't allow it. Father knows everything Elizabeth and I are involved in, well, almost everything, and he approves. We're honest, at least as far as the letter of the law is concerned, but it's a big, interesting world out there with plenty of opportunities for those willing to use the tools available. Father has ambitions, but Elizabeth and I have ambitions that go far beyond the walls of Father's stuffy old law firm and we're willing to use every tool available."

Ben was beginning to enjoy what he was hearing. He liked the privileges that came with his job. He could get used to this. His future looked brighter than ever.

Zach paused for a long while and puffed his cigar, blowing the silvery smoke casually towards the ornate ceiling.

"Ben," Zach said lazily, still looking at the ceiling, "you wouldn't mind living in the nicest house in town, visit the capitals of Europe, have a wardrobe full of French fashions for your wife, a houseful of servants and everyone tipping their hat when you passed? You wouldn't mind hiring the best tutors for your children, would you? What's wrong with that? That's what we have in mind for you, if you, my friend, are willing. We're thinking of your best interest, Ben. We want you to be successful."

Zach continued without giving Ben the chance to answer and Ben was content to listen. He had dreamed of touring Europe.

"Ben, I understand Elizabeth and you should, too. She isn't complicated. If you're agreeable, the three of us are going to work together, but here's the warning about Elizabeth and why I invited you here today. This is what I've been trying to tell you. I guess I talk too much but that's alright. I like to talk. I'm relaxed when I talk. Here's my point about Elizabeth. I'm going to give you a warning. She's dangerous."

Zach paused, took a sip of his whiskey and a lingering puff of his cigar. He leaned back again in the leather padded armchair and watched his silvery cigar smoke slowly rise.

"I'm warning you, Ben. Elizabeth is business, all business," Zach said quietly. "Elizabeth is beautiful but Elizabeth loves Elizabeth. Elizabeth will never be in love with anyone but Elizabeth. If she were to marry, it would be for money, never for love. Elizabeth uses men. Beware, Ben. She will use you. You've been warned. I've seen men sucked into her web, consumed and discarded. Elizabeth will never love a man. She's the master of the pawn sacrifice. To her, men are pawns. She loves money and she loves herself."

"You make her sound cold-hearted, Zach," Ben answered. "Why would I want to work with a person like her if what you say is true?"

Zach swirled the clear liquid in his expensive glass, watching it go around, and continued with his warning.

"That's a good question. That's exactly what I wanted to talk to you about. You'll want to work with Elizabeth because she's a brilliant business partner you can trust. Elizabeth will help us make a lot of money. You can depend on her implicitly in business, just not in matters of the heart. I'm not sure she has a heart, Ben."

Zach laughed, broke into a big smile, leaned over and slapped Ben's shoulder. Zach was enjoying the whiskey and the conversation, as was Ben.

"Don't get me wrong, Ben. I like Elizabeth. She and I are best friends. We trust one another. I would do anything for her. I trust her with my life but not my heart. She's not the kind of woman I want to be the mother of my children, if you know what I mean. She hates children and doesn't care for anyone but herself. The only man she would be happy with is a groveling drudge, a menial to do her bidding. She will always be queen on her personal chess board and there will be no rival, no king or knight, only one all-important queen. Ben, life's a game and we keep score with money. As long as you're aware of Elizabeth's greed and accompanying cold heart, you'll be fine, Ben. That's all I'm saying. I wanted to tell you this today to protect you."

"What makes you think I need protection?"

Zach paused and stared at Ben with a quizzical look.

"Ben, Ben. You are naïve. You're a child. You know nothing. I don't think you have any idea what I'm trying to tell you. Elizabeth is beautiful, charming and tempting. I'm afraid, my friend, you'll forget my warning the moment you meet her. You mustn't think her capable of love. Never allow yourself to believe you could make her happy. If you fall for her, she'll use you up. I learned that lesson when I was a boy and I've never fallen for her again."

Ben responded lamely, "Well, Zach, it sounds like you don't really want me to meet her. You make her sound dangerous, like someone I should fear. Why would I want to do business with a cold-hearted woman like her?"

Zach leaned forward towards Ben and looked him in the eye for a few moments to cement his words.

"I laid it on thick, didn't I?" Zach said, leaning back again. "It's simple. We'll work with her because she'll help us make a great deal of money. Like I told you, she has a brilliant business mind. As a business partner, Elizabeth is perceptive. I want you to meet her. That's why I hired you. That's why Elizabeth hired you. Elizabeth and I need a man like you, just don't get involved with her personally. She'll break your heart. Mark my words."

Zach paused for a moment and shook his glass towards Ben's face as if he were shaking his finger in a warning.

"We chose you, Ben. We chose you because of your country boy innocence and good looks. You're smart and people trust you at first meeting. You have a way with people. You were the missing piece in our master plan. You were the valiant knight missing from our chess board. Now that you're here, we intend to send you into the fray, right onto the floor of the Georgia House. It took us a couple of years to find the right person, but you're our man. We're sure of that. Remember, to Elizabeth everyone is a servant. Trust her in business, never in love. That's my warning, Ben. I know I've laid it on thick but that's what I wanted to tell you this afternoon."

"Well," Ben replied, "you paint her as the most egotistical, selfish woman I've ever heard of, but I hear what you're saying. You're telling me she's a good business woman and I should be careful. I have ambitions of my own. I don't think I want to accumulate as much as you two, but I would like to acquire some security for later years. You and Elizabeth come from a different background, Zach. We have different values. My parents taught me, 'do unto others as you would have them do unto you'. It sounds like you and Elizabeth believe you should take it away before they know it's missing."

"You're humorous, Ben, and not far from the truth. I'll be frank. Elizabeth and I will use anything and anyone to get what we want, as long as we don't go to jail. We use the law, but there is another side to Elizabeth. She can be fun. There's nothing wrong with you spending an afternoon with her. I hope you two have many, but I know better than to fall for her, and you better not fall for her either. That's all I'm telling you. She broke my heart a long time ago. I learned my lesson. If you allow her to steal your heart, she'll tromp it under her feet. You'll curse both me and the day you met her and remember every word of this conversation."

The tall negro servant refreshed their drinks once again. Ben marveled how he moved without making a sound. Both young men, now slightly red-faced, were beginning to feel the effects of the strong whiskey.

"Ben," Zach said, as he swirled his drink, "the most beautiful woman you've ever seen will walk up those stairs in a few minutes. Everything I've tried to hammer into you will disappear. When her fragrance fills your head, you'll behave irrationally. I've seen it time and again, but I don't think you've been listenin'," Zach said, slightly slurring his words.

Ben made the decision to be wary of this mercenary woman who cared for no man. He already had the love of his life in Cassie. He could be certain he wouldn't fall for the woman Zach had described. He was too smart for that.

Ben, unused to the liquor, noted Zach's warnings were actually having the opposite of their intended effect. Although he hadn't met her formally, he had begun thinking of Elizabeth as the ultimate challenge, the grand prize rather than a selfish woman to be avoided. What if he could win her heart?

What a trophy she would be, but he was thinking nonsense. He was yet to meet Elizabeth. He mustn't forget Cassie.

On schedule, Elizabeth walked up the three stairs from the foyer to the private dining room. The two finely dressed young men stood. She was dressed in white linen with ruffles, a pale green satin bow in the back with open shoulders and just the proper amount of exposed white bust. She might have stepped off a fashionable Paris street.

She curtseyed. Zach introduced her and the three sat close together.

"My word, Ben," Elizabeth said in a low husky voice looking straight into his eyes, "you are handsome. I think you're even more handsome than Zach, and you definitely have the most beautiful eyes I've ever seen. It's a pleasure to make your acquaintance, Ben Lowry."

As Zach had known, Ben was not prepared for this meeting. He was instantly undone by Elizabeth's opening remark. He found himself only able to mumble a near-incoherent reply.

"A pleasure to make your acquaintance, ma'am."

When Elizabeth appeared, everything Zach said disappeared from Ben's mind. Ben immediately thought her the most beautiful creature imaginable. Ben hoped the conversation wouldn't turn serious. He understood he was quite unable to think clearly.

Elizabeth, sitting between the two young men, spoke softly.

"As much as I would love to spend the afternoon with you two handsome men, my visit must be brief. I wanted to meet our new partner. Alas, I cannot stay. I do so want to stay with you but I must join my parents. I wanted to meet you, Ben. I'm not disappointed, not disappointed in the least."

Ben was hardly able to follow the conversation and remembered little of it later. He had never seen a woman wearing clothing with such power and this was his first encounter with French perfume.

After the introduction and a few moments of small talk, Elizabeth stood and extended her hand to Zach, "I wish I could stay all evening, but I promised my parents I would dine with them. I assured Father I wouldn't be a minute late. I'm enjoying your father's new chef, Zach. I've never eaten cuisine like this outside of France. I think the food here is better than Paris, to tell you the truth. All Milledgeville is in a fuss. You better be careful or my father will steal him away. You know how my father loves his food."

Elizabeth, facing Ben, gave him her hand and moved close.

"It's been a pleasure to meet you, Ben Lowry," she said in a low voice. "I'm not disappointed, not in the least. You are handsome," she said, never taking her eyes from his. "You'll have to bring me to dinner here one night, Ben Lowry, just the two of us so we can get to know one another properly. I want to know all about you, every little detail. Will you bring me here, Ben?" she begged.

Ben stuttered his reply in a voice much too loud.

"Of course, I would love to take you to dinner, Elizabeth. It would be a pleasure. I would be honored, I'm sure."

Elizabeth, continuing to hold her hand in Ben's, looked straight into Ben's eyes without blinking and asked immediately, "Would this Friday evening about seven o'clock be good for you? We'll have a nice wine and a wonderful meal. I want to know everything about you from the day you were born. After our meal you can drive me home."

Ben was captivated, stunned, unable to think or respond intelligently. If Ben had been observant, he would have noticed Zach's big grin.

At that moment Elizabeth's parents entered the foyer. Elizabeth gave the young men a polite curtsey.

"Ben, I can't tell you how much I'm looking forward to Friday. I find you an unusually attractive young man. I truly do."

She walked down the three stairs to the foyer. She didn't look back. Her fragrance lingered.

4 December 1826

From the *Georgia Journal*-28 November 1826-page 2

Legislature of Georgia, In Senate, Friday, Nov. 17

"....Mr. Coffee laid on the table a resolution instructing the Committee on the State of the Republic to inquire into the propriety and practicability of extending the jurisdiction of the State over the whole of her chartered limits...."

8 December 1826

Ben told me about Zach and Elizabeth and their plans for the legislature. He believes they will help him do something for the Cherokee. Ben said they are intelligent, understand business and come from well-to-do families. After my trip to Milledgeville, I find it much easier to imagine such things.

I love Ben's boyish innocence. I am not jealous but I warned him. Ben may be a good lawyer, but he has a lot to learn about the unseen world of avaricious American business men. I hope he remembers his parents' advice.

Milledgeville December 1826

"Ben, what did you think of your dinner with Elizabeth Friday?" Zach asked, "How did that go? I heard you two had a nice meal. She's an engaging woman, isn't she? Did you fall in love with her or did you take my advice and guard your heart?"

"She is beautiful, Zach, I'll grant you that. You were right to warn me. Yes, I enjoyed the evening, but I'm sure I was poor company. I felt awkward the entire time. My mother tried to teach me social etiquette, but I'm afraid I was an inattentive student. Elizabeth did most of the talking, which was fine with me. I'm sure she thinks me a boring farm boy with no conversation skills.

I've never been in the company of a sophisticated woman like her, Zach. She's nothing like my mother. Without your warning I'm sure I would have fallen for her right there at the table and turned into a blubbering puddle of jam."

"I warned you about her, didn't I?

"You were right, Zach. She's the most charming woman I could imagine. It's hard to believe her charm is assumed."

"Remember, Ben, she's interested in money, large amounts of money, and she'll use you to get it. Elizabeth and I are in search of talent. That's why you were chosen. You'll make a good politician because everyone will think you trustworthy. They love your schoolboy naiveté. That's what we want. Elizabeth is like a cat with a mouse. When she's finished playing with her captive, she'll devour her plaything and search for another. Enjoy her fashions, perfume and coquetry, but don't fall for her. She'll break your heart. However, if you want a shrewd calculating business partner, Elizabeth is your woman."

"Elizabeth, what do you think about our boy?" Zach asked. "Can we groom him to task? Will he make a successful politician we can control? That's what I want to know."

"He'll do fine," she answered. "He's nice-looking, malleable and incredibly naïve, just what we need. He'll make the perfect hand-crafted politician. He thinks everyone is honest. We have the right man, Zach. Eventually he'll figure out how the world works, but by then we'll have him so confused he won't know up from down. By the time he figures things out, we'll have put so much money in his pockets, he'll eat out of our hands. He'll be entirely dependent upon us and afraid we'll abandon him. He'll be easy to control. It'll be nice to finally have our own personal politician, and besides, I like him. He's amusing."

Elizabeth laughed unusually loud.

"With Ben, I can have my cake and eat it too. Did you see how he melted like a schoolboy when I flirted? You should have seen him at dinner. He drooled like a fawning dog the entire meal. It was humorous. We couldn't have picked a better man. If he balks, we'll find us another. There are plenty more where he came from.

Chapter XXII
1827 - An Afternoon with Zach
Chapter 22

2 January 1827 - The Cold Moon - Un ol v ta ni

It is cold, terribly cold. Animals walk across the frozen river. Five Feathers and I must break ice and carry water for the chickens and hogs. Edudu says it's the coldest he remembers.

4 January 1827

"(604) An Act to prevent the Testimony of Indians being received in courts of Justice.

Be it enacted by the Senate and the House of Representatives of the State of Georgia...after the passage of this act, no Indian, and no descendant of an Indian, not understanding the English language, shall be deemed a competent witness in any court of justice created by the Constitution and laws of this State. IRBY HUDSON-Speaker of the House of Representatives, THOMAS STOCKS- President of the Senate.

Assented to, December 26th, 1826 G.M. TROUP, Governor."

11 January 1827

Chief Pathkiller died 7 January in 'Di'ga-duhun'yi, Turkey Town, one of our largest towns by the Coosa River. Pathkiller became principle chief in 1811. He was a good man. William Hicks has been appointed chief.

29 January 1827

Bad news upon bad news. Two weeks after his appointment, William Hicks died. Who will be chief now? Sadness follows sadness.

2 February 1827

From the *Georgia Journal* - 16 January 1827

"The surveyors...employed on the lands lying between the new treaty line and the Georgia boundary have been arrested in their progress by the Indians. Here is another impediment to the occupation of the country this year. It is excessively provoking for there is no time to be lost...the lottery will be late going into operation...this impertinent interference with the affairs of the people of Georgia will meet with severe retribution."

17 March 1827

From *The Athenian* – 9 March 1827

"The claims of Georgia on the General Government for services rendered by the militia in the years '92, '93 and '94 have at last been allowed by the House of Representatives....The amount is $129,375.62. One great cause of dissatisfaction with the General Government will be removed. There then will remain no main subject of contention but the extinguishment of the Indian title to the Cherokee Territory within the limits of this state."

21 March 1827

Huff's Boarding House - 16 March 1827

My Dear Father,

I'm sure you have been reading the newspapers. Georgia has seized all Creek land in the pine barrens. They want to complete that seizure by occupying Cherokee land in the north. The thought of Indians having title to land drives them mad.

The General Government has revoked the tainted Treaty of Indian Springs but it's too late. All Creek homes and assets in Georgia have been confiscated. Creek removal is fait accompli. Now Georgia insists the government honor the Compact of 1802. I have no confidence in our government to act justly. What will you and Mother do if the Cherokee are also evicted? Whatever the outcome you can depend on me. Please share this letter with Cassie. I shall continue to be, Your loving son, Ben

2 April 1827

I watched river otters at play. I have never seen anything as singularly lovely, especially the mother with her kits. Across the river they have a slide and play as if they were human children. I cannot imagine a creature that enjoys its existence more. They swim by my rock and greet me as they pass, noticing everything. Their big eyes observe my every movement.

Milledgeville – May 1827

"Elizabeth was visiting Mother yesterday and was asking about you, Ben," Zach said with a grin.

Their waiter silently served their drinks, never making eye contact with the guests.

"She's interested in you, young man. That's for sure. She asked me all sorts of personal questions about you."

Zach changed the subject.

"Elizabeth's father is lookin' to add to his domestic staff. He heard my father bought a hundred niggers at the Charleston market last week. He wants the pick of the litter. Father will make a pretty profit, I imagine. He knows a bargain when he sees one, especially when it comes to niggers. Father's going to keep the best for the hotel."

Zach slouched back in his chair and puffed his cigar, relaxed and talkative. Zach talked. Ben listened.

"He never keeps field hands or women with children. He says there's a couple of excellent blacksmiths in the bunch. If he can find a good manager, he'll get a livery up and running in Macon and turn it over to me. I can make a tidy profit, I'm sure. Since we got rid of the Creeks, Macon is growing like crazy. Life is good, isn't it, Ben?"

Zach didn't wait for an answer.

"Have you and your parents ever owned slaves, Ben?" Zach asked.

"No, we've never owned slaves. My mother and Father are missionaries and have strong views about slavery."

Zach gave Ben a sidelong glance, laughed, tossed down the rest of his drink in one gulp and motioned to the waiter in the corner for another.

"Well, I guess some folks think of slaves as more than what they are, but if you ever hear them talkin', you'll know they're not exactly what we would call human. They sound like a bunch of monkeys jabbering about a banana."

The negro waiter delivered Zach's drink on a polished silver tray.

"Get yourself a slave, Ben, at least for show. It would let Father's clients know you're with us here in Georgia. Everyone needs a good servant. Talk to Father. He knows how to pick the ones who won't run."

Ben made a face. Zach noticed and laughed.

"What a face, Ben. Be careful with your body language. I don't care what you or your parents believe, you don't want anyone thinking you're an abolitionist, do you? If people thought you were opposed to slavery, they'd run you out of town on a rail. If Father thought you were a nigger-lover, you would be gone today. You'd be farming somewhere in the backwoods. Once you're branded an abolitionist, you're done for in the south. There are no abolitionists in business or politics in Georgia, Ben. Not one."

Ben answered in a low voice, "I know, Zach. I agree. I'll watch what I say. I like working for your father. I won't rock the boat."

"Good for you, Ben. Our economy would collapse without slaves. If we didn't have niggers who would pick the cotton?"

Ben noticed the tall waiter almost invisible in the shadows, watching and listening to their conversation. Ben wondered what he was thinking.

"I don't know what the abolitionists are so concerned about. Niggers ain't the same as us, Ben. We treat slaves right well here in Georgia, right well indeed. Father spends a lot of money on them, responsible folk do. Everybody takes care of their stock. Father puts new clothes on them, pays for their boarding and doctorin' and he's getting them new shoes. Why, I couldn't believe Father's bill for nigger shoes alone. My father is good to his niggers. They don't have any reason to complain, do they?"

Ben said in a low voice, "I saw a man horse-whipping a slave the other day in public. It was a terrible scene. I didn't like it."

Zach grinned and gave Ben a sidelong glance as he took another puff of his expensive cigar.

"Ben, you don't know nothin' about nothin', do you? Ever' now and then an uppity nigger needs to be put in his place. Once you've been in business for a while you'll understand. If you don't whip them in public what good is a whippin'? You see that, don't you? Niggers ain't got money, Ben. You can't fine 'em like white folks. You can't take nothin' from them cause they ain't got nothin'. The threat of fines and jail time works for white folks but it don't work for niggers. They had rather be in jail than work. Father says a good whippin' ever' now and then is a good thing so they know their place. We can't have them gettin' uppity, can we? First thing you know they'd be thinkin' they have the same rights as American folks. Can you imagine living in a town full of free niggers? Who would want that?"

Ben was watching the tall waiter in the corner, wondering how much of this conversation he had heard. Zach finished his drink and signaled for another. Ben was anxious for Zach to change the subject.

Ben wouldn't rock the boat. He wanted his job. He would do exactly as Zach had instructed. No one could succeed in Georgia, or anywhere in the South, who was publicly opposed to slavery. Landowners needed someone to pick the cotton and do the hard work involved with agriculture, it was true.

Zach, well lubricated and never at a loss for words, continued to taunt Ben to see if he could bait him into compromising his position.

"One more thing, Ben, don't ever refer to a nigger as a person. A nigger is a fellow or a boy. You have to keep them in their place. Niggers ain't men. If you start calling them men, it might give them the idea you think they're equal in some way. First thing you know we'll have a bunch of god-damned Yankees down here talkin' up some modern French claptrap about equality. That won't work in Georgia, and it especially won't work if you run for office. But don't you worry, Ben. I'm here to keep you straight. I'll keep your foot out of your mouth."

Ben was glad of the dulling effects of the alcohol and he certainly didn't want to enter into an intellectual conversation about slavery. Ben wanted to work. He wanted to work in Milledgeville. He wasn't interested in egalitarian philosophical debates about forced servitude. He would listen, enjoy the whiskey and avoid all discussion of slavery. He knew better than allow himself to be baited into a discussion, public or private, that could ruin his career.

"Ask Father's servants here in the hotel if they're not well taken care of?" Zach continued. "I had rather be one of Father's niggers than a farmer. Yes sir, Father takes care of his niggers. He can send his slaves to town to do business with money in their pocket and they come back."

Ben knew better than to comment on Zach's observations. Ben dare not bite the hand that was feeding him.

Zach, weary of teasing Ben, changed the subject.

"Elizabeth asked about you, Ben. I told her you were looking forward to seeing her again. Are you? I told her you were. She has her eye on you, my friend. The word is she thinks you're especially handsome."

Zach chuckled and changed the subject once again.

"How do you like these glasses, Ben?"

"I've never seen anything like these before," Ben admitted, as he examined the glass carefully, turning it slowly before his face in his long slender fingers, happy that Zach had changed the subject away from slavery.

"Without a doubt, this is the most beautiful glassware I've ever seen. I love the design, Zach, but why so heavy? Where did they come from?"

Ben wasn't interested in glassware. He wanted to hear more about Elizabeth and was wondering what she had said about him.

"This glassware is beautiful," said Zach.

"My father heard it called flint glass. It's striking, isn't it? Father was in Ireland last year. When he saw this Waterford Crystal he ordered a supply. He replaced all our glassware in the hotel with Waterford. One of the ingredients in this glass is lead. You didn't know they put lead in their glass, did you? That's why they're so heavy. Aren't they beautiful? Some folks call this lead crystal. We don't have anything like that here in Georgia, do we? All we have here is timber, cotton, slaves, cornbread and Indians."

"What do think about the Cherokee problem, Ben?"

"I liked living among the Cherokee," Ben replied. "I understand their simple lifestyle and their distrust of Americans. I like their contentment. They have a carefree existence in a strong community. Their view of corporate ownership of land gives identity and place to their people. They feel part of a greater society. To tell the truth I love wandering the woods, listening to the wind in the pines, drinking cold water coming out of the side of a mountain, lying on a soft bed of pine needles on a lazy spring day. I understand why the Cherokee wouldn't want to abandon their lifestyle."

Zach puffed his expensive cigar watching the smoke curl upwards.

"Well, Ben, I like the woods and huntin'. I like shootin' animals. That's a sport I can go for. I love sittin' on the side of a hill and seein' how many squirrels I can pick off. Father and I killed thirty-five one morning last year."

Ben recovered his thoughts and ignored Zach's remarks about hunting.

"My father could have all the paying students he wants down here. He hasn't earned anything teaching Indians, although everyone respects his noble intentions. I know why he wants to teach in Cherokee Country, but there's no money in it, never will be. Mother and Father need to look out for their future. I appreciate the advice you and Elizabeth have given me. I'm already beginning to save."

"Ben, I don't want to talk about abstract morality or the beauty of nature, I want to know, my friend, what you think of this whiskey? Smooth, isn't it?"

Zach had a big smile on his red face.

"Where did you get it?" asked Ben.

"Ben," said Zach, "I got this whiskey from a friend of mine who's just come from the Hermitage, that's in Nashville. This whiskey comes from Andy Jackson's private still. He sent this down himself. Jackson has a famous nigger who runs the best still in Tennessee."

Zach held up his glass and continued in his planned speech.

"This is the best Tennessee sour mash you have ever tasted, ain't it, Ben?" I ain't never tasted better myself. Jackson himself sent this whiskey to you personally through my father's firm, with his compliments."

Zach had Ben's full attention.

"That's right," Zach said, leaning over almost in Ben's face to emphasize his point, eyes slightly out of focus, holding his glass up as if making a toast. "I've been waitin' to tell you that. Jackson himself sent this whiskey to the newest and most promising young lawyer in the south. That's you, Ben Lowry, in case you don't know. You're already gettin' a reputation as far away as Tennessee. What do you think about that? Ole' Hickory himself has taken notice of you, young man, all the way from Nashville. He thinks there's good things in store for you. Jackson knows you're goin' to be gettin' into Georgia politics. He wants you on his side. He knows you're smart."

Zach's nose had a red tip exactly as if someone had just pinched it.

"Ben," said Zach, "we have to make hay while the sun shines, don't we? Well, your sun is shining, Ben. If you don't think about yourself now, you'll end up an old man with nothing, livin' on charity."

Ben continued to sip Andrew Jackson's whiskey and study Zach's face. He liked what he was hearing.

"You can have a prosperous future, Ben. You can retire by the time you're forty, if you're smart. My father recognized your potential and wrote Ole' Hickory," Zach continued without a pause. "Everyone needs help in this world. Ole' Hickory needs help, I need help, Father needs help and you'll need help, too. Political help is what I'm talkin' about. Quid pro quo, Ben, quid pro quo, the three most important words in politics."

Ben was enjoying Zach's vision.

"Elizabeth and I think you're the right man in the right place at the right time, Ben, but you need a little help from your friends. Who knows, you might even get a woman like Elizabeth in the bargain."

Zach shook his cigar toward Ben's face to make his point.

"I'll guarantee Elizabeth will be on your arm when you go to Washington City. She wouldn't miss that for the world. Elizabeth would make a pact with the devil for something like that. You can count on her, Ben."

Zach laughed out loud and Ben couldn't help joining. This was turning into a most relaxing afternoon. Zach painted a wonderful scene. Ben really could see himself with Elizabeth on his arm walking into a formal dining room, chandeliers sparkling and every eye on the handsome young couple as they were seated next to the host. Ben could smell her perfume. Ben didn't have Zach's confidence but he wouldn't rule anything out. He puffed his expensive cigar and considered Zach's imagined limelight.

"I confess, I do like your lead crystal and I'm learning to like Andrew Jackson's whiskey," Ben said. "I like women in silk and lace, French perfume and moonlight nights. I do like Elizabeth. Oh my, yes. I like to look at her, talk to her and smell her. I like to think about her. Have I gone too far, Zach? I could get used to all this."

Ben knew he was saying things that would have been better left unsaid.

Zach, grinning from ear to ear, gave a circular motion with his hand and cigar signaling for Ben to keep talking.

Ben obliged.

"What I like best is that the next president of the United States is taking an interest in us way down here in Georgia. It's flattering. I want to know if you were serious when you said Elizabeth would be on my arm in Washington. Did you mean that? Did she tell you that? Does she believe I can get elected to congress? Do you honestly believe that is something I can accomplish?"

"You mean when we get elected to congress, my handsome friend," Zach said, with a big smile and another wave of his cigar and a big laugh.

"Elizabeth and I are on your bandwagon. Include us in your plans, if you please. We want to help you. We're scratching your back now, Ben. When you're elected you can scratch ours, if you know what I mean."

Zach continued without waiting for Ben to speak.

"The three of us will be a team, Ben. And yes, I talked to Elizabeth about going to Washington City with you. In Washington City fortunes fall off the tree into your hand. A few years in congress and we'll never worry about money again. Why, Jackson himself will be askin' for favors.

Ben and Zach laughed uproariously at Zach's optimism.

Ben raised his glass.

"I propose a toast to the three brightest stars in Andrew Jackson's southern sky, Elizabeth, Zach and me."

They clinked glasses. Life was good for these two young lawyers. There were many perquisites in Ben's new life. His job required long hours but his off time with Zach was stimulating. He had never had a friend like Zach. Ben knew, in the back of his mind, he was approaching the fine line between enjoying the marrow of life and drowning in the pursuit of an epicurean lifestyle, but at the moment he didn't care. Life was good.

Zach took another big taste of the very good sipping whiskey.

"Ben, you'll qualify for the Georgia House on your next birthday. Then it'll be the United States House or the Georgia Senate when you're twenty-five. Which do you prefer? The House of Representatives in Washington or the Georgia Senate in Milledgeville?"

Zach didn't wait for Ben's response.

We'll skip the Georgia Senate, if you don't mind. Then, when you're thirty, we'll get you a United States Senate appointment, the biggest prize of all. After a few years, if you've scratched enough backs, the presidency of the United States could be yours, and why not? This is the land of opportunity. Americans take what they want, don't we?"

Ben couldn't believe what he just heard.

"It's lookin' like Jackson will support you all the way. In fact, I'm sure of it. I have that straight from his secretary. My father and I are going to support Jackson whole hog. Jackson will support you when the time comes. What do you think, Ben? The future I described can be a reality if you'll get on board. It's that easy," said Zach, staring into Ben's slightly glazed eyes.

Ben could not conceive of anyone wanting to use him for personal gain. Ben was incapable of thinking in such a devious manner.

"I would love that, Zach. I think you're right. Things are changing fast and only the forward-thinking will survive. I know that."

"I love your vision, Ben. When you've been appointed to the US Senate you'll have friends in every state, not just Georgia. You can push your private agenda. A United States Senator is king, you can help or hurt whomever. You'll have presidents comin' to you, ambassadors knockin' at your door. You're going places, Ben Lowry, and takin' us with you."

"That would be something, wouldn't it? Think of all the good I could do for folks if I was a Senator," Ben said softly.

Zach became more serious.

"Ben, someone will be a Senator from Georgia and twelve years from now someone will be elected president and it might as well be you."

Zach paused, cigar in one hand and drink in the other, and leaned over in Ben's face with a serious expression, "I been thinkin', Ben. I've chosen my goal in life. You're goin' to be the first person I've shared this with."

Zach put his cigar and drink on the table, leaned back staring upwards with his fingers locked behind his head, legs crossed at the ankles.

"Ben, when you've been elected United States Senator, but for sure when you're president, I want to be appointed ambassador to France. I never told anybody that. I want to live in Paris, Ben. Being ambassador to France will be the crowning achievement of my career. You'll do that for me, won't you Ben? I want to spend four years in Paris, eight if you get re-elected. I love Paris. Oh, my yes, I have fond memories of that town. Will you get me posted as ambassador to Paris? Will you do that for me, Ben?"

Ben, a little tipsy, laughed out loud and even the negro servant in the corner had to stifle a snicker when he heard Zach's request.

"Zach, you would be a perfect ambassador. You already dress like a dandy and you have about the same view of wine, food and morality. You'll be my first appointment, my first nomination will be Zach Mitchell, United States Ambassador to France."

The two young lawyers couldn't stop laughing.

"Ben, going to Washington City is the easiest thing you'll ever do, if you listen to me and Elizabeth. Don't worry. Speak in generalities and you'll be fine. Promise them the world in generalities. Never tell them what you really believe. Tell them what they want to hear. That's how to get elected."

"When you're in company, say the right thing, even if you don't believe it yourself. I don't care what you think about the Cherokee, niggers or a Chinaman for that matter. Keep your mouth shut about the Cherokee and niggers. We want to make money. Every landowner in Georgia wants to make money. If you make money for folks, you'll get elected again and again."

"Ben," said Zach, as he motioned to the tall negro waiting patiently in the corner, "give the boy your glass. I can't talk to anyone with an empty glass."

"Jackson will be president, Ben. We've already put an Ole Hickory Pole in front of our business. Jackson's party will win every seat in Georgia. People love a military man with backbone. We haven't had a president with Jackson's mettle since Washington. Folks love a fight and a fighter."

Zach laughed much too loud.

Ben was happy to listen to Zach's arcane opinions about politics. The effects of the alcohol made Zach's tiresome conversation enjoyable. Ben was wishing the evening wouldn't end. Zach repeated the same advice he had given earlier but Ben listened patiently, or at least tried to listen. He didn't care. He was enjoying the afternoon. He had never felt better.

"Jackson is unifying the country," Zach said. "Everyone knows we need an all-white English-speaking country. America must increase. We need room to grow. Indians must go, all of 'em. No French or Spanish either. Hell, we don't even want the British. We want their money but we've had enough of them. Be wise, Ben. We'll retire before we're forty and have everything we dreamed of."

Ben walked to his boarding house with his head spinning, not only from the whiskey, but from the most unusual conversation of his life. He had never expected this when he went to law school. Life was exciting but there was a disturbing darkness lurking at the edges of his mind. He sensed a discomfort in the shadows but he wasn't going to worry. It was pleasant to drink whiskey and abandon care, to think of Elizabeth and imagine what might be, both in Milledgeville and the nation's capital. He would love to walk up Pennsylvania Avenue with Elizabeth on his arm.

With Zach's help he could do things for those who couldn't help themselves. Everyone made compromises. He could do great things for the Cherokee after he was elected, great things indeed.

Ben thought of Cassie. Thinking of her dispelled the demons that gathered when listening to Zach. He would think of her more often.

Ben looked at the stars brilliantly shining above the darkened street. True, injustice does exist, but tonight all is well. He felt a euphoria after the evening's conversation with Zach. As he mounted the stairs he thought his future to be as bright as the stars above. It was a silly, worn metaphor but he could accomplish good things for the Cherokee if he were a Senator, and then there was the added thought of Elizabeth on his arm in Washington City. His thoughts seemed to stray often to Elizabeth, her eyes, the way she touched him, her fragrance. Everything about her lingered.

Ben slept fitfully, dreaming of a beckoning woman just out of reach, tempting, laughing, inviting, mocking. It wasn't like Ben to toss and turn so.

Chapter XXIII
1827 – The Approaching Storm
Chapter 23

6 June 1827 - Month of the Green Corn Moon – De ha lu yi

    Huff's Boarding House – Milledgeville 2 June 1827

My Dear Cassie,

    I can't wait to see you again. I think of you every evening as I walk to my room. I am comforted knowing you are not so very far from me, looking at the same evening sky.

    Zach thinks I'll be a good legislator and in time be elected to the United States House and possibly appointed to the U.S. Senate. The Senate may be a bit fanciful, but it's fun to think about. Zach is certain the Georgia House is within our reach. I enjoy conversation with Zach, but I had much rather be with you. It is usual that Zach is talking and I am listening, but I don't mind. I have a lot to learn. Our conversations would be so much more interesting with you there. You are missing from me.

    Always Yours, Ben xoxo

13 June 1827

    Ben was a good student and he's becoming a better lawyer, stronger friend and perfect lover. Once a month Ben makes the hundred-fifty-mile trip from Milledgeville. The stage is exhausting but fast.

19 June 1827

    I am overjoyed that Ben is visiting his parents, but I heard him and his father discussing political affairs, dreadful things that made me tremble. It was oppressively hot in the house. We sat on the porch on the long, wooden bench listening to Ben's warnings. Clouds were gathering in the distance. A storm was brewing.

    "Father, I'm sorry, but I bring bad news, the worst. The Compact of 1802 is to be activated. Governor Troup has removed the Creek Nation and now, in turn, Governor Forsyth wants to remove the Cherokee. Governor Forsyth is demanding the general government adhere to the terms of the compact."

    "Explain to me once again about the Compact, Ben," I asked.

"Of course, Cassie. Before 1802, Georgia had title to all the land to its west, all the way to the Mississippi River, what is now the states of Alabama and Mississippi. On 24 April 1802, Georgia made a deal with Washington City, Thomas Jefferson specifically, although James Madison signed the document as secretary of state. Georgia traded their western land to the general government for a million dollars plus the promise of future assistance in removing all Indians from their chartered boundaries. Jefferson assured Georgia the removal would be paid for by the general government and all land previously owned by the Indians would fall into the possession of the state at some unspecified date and not revert to the general government. Georgia insists it is high time the general government keep their part of the 1802 bargain."

As Ben talked, inky black clouds were building far to the southwest over our distant mountains. A storm was brewing. The freshening wind was delightfully cool, stirring small billows of dust in front of the house. Since reading Washington Irving's story, the sound of rolling thunder conjures up the image of an old bearded man watching little people bowling nine pins in some mysterious mountain hollow. The distant thunder warned us of the storm's approach.

"Did I hear you correctly, son? You're telling me Georgia insists the Cherokee be removed despite current treaties?"

"Yes, sir. That's exactly what I'm saying. Evidently, the previous treaties with the Cherokee were a ruse. In light of this agreement, the treaties were a stalling tactic intended to pacify the Cherokee until government assets could be gathered and the forced removal accomplished. Jefferson, and all presidents since, have intended to implement the compact no matter what Indian agents or any other government entity signed or promised. The government was hoping the Indians would leave of their own accord or be forced out by settlers. The compact supersedes everything, including treaties. I'm sorry to bring this news, Father."

Ben's news was difficult. I didn't want to interject anything into Ben's narrative or ask a question.

"I've always thought Jefferson honorable," Ben's father said, "a man who believed in equality. I've thought better of the American people, of our government."

"Father, Jefferson's government did believe in the equality, but that equality only existed for white men. The American Government, since it's conception, has believed in the advancement of European races only."

The top limbs of the trees were beginning to sway gently as the first strong gusts of cool wind swept down from the distant mountainsides. We were beginning to enjoy cooler temperatures after a hot, sultry day. There was another rumble of distant thunder, this time louder. The storm was closer.

"Father, Jefferson foresaw the four coastal states, Louisiana, Mississippi, Alabama and Georgia, as a military buffer to deter foreign invasion. He reasoned this four-state military shield would give the rest of the states time to deploy a defending army in case of invasion from that quarter. Secondly, the general government is afraid the Cherokee might side with a foreign power as happened in the Revolutionary War. The same is true of the Creek, Choctaw and Chickasaw. The Cherokee removal is set in stone, Father. Under no circumstances will the War Department allow the Cherokee Nation to exist. The government has instructed the War Department to remove every Indian nation east of the Mississippi outside the borders of the United States for national security."

Ben continued in subdued tones. Ben's father listened with bowed head.

"The ratification of the Cherokee constitution will trigger their removal. Cherokee leaders believe a national constitution will legitimize their continued existence as a nation within their present boundaries and avoid removal. From what I'm hearing, their constitution will have the reverse effect in Milledgeville. Georgia politicians view the ratification as a grave threat. The Cherokee constitution is being viewed as an infringement of the sovereignty of both Georgia and the Union."

The storm was fast approaching. The dark clouds had begun to obscure the bright sunlight bringing relief from the sweltering heat. As the gusts increased, the birds stopped singing. The rumbles of thunder were quickly becoming louder.

Ben continued, "Georgia ceded its western land to the general government for four things, first, a million dollars in gold, second, a promise to pay the entire cost of the extinguishment of the Cherokee nation, third, that the general government would never interfere in Georgia's internal affairs when dealings with Indians and lastly, the general government will supply the troops and other assets required for the extinguishment."

"When will the removal commence?" Ben's father asked in a whisper.

"My guess is it's in the works now. Georgia will survey all Cherokee land and complete the lotteries. The final removal will begin soon after. The writing is on the wall, Father."

Ben's father looked at the wooden floor of the porch as he spoke.

"Yes, son, the general government must keep their promise to their fellow Americans and break all promises to the Indian nations. I'm not surprised. Such is our history."

No one felt like speaking their thoughts. The wind increased. The storm was near. As we enjoyed the cool winds, Ben's father broke the silence.

"Who would have thought the Cherokee constitution would be the straw to break the camel's back. I can see what is happening, Son, but I know this is not the end. I won't live to see the day but the pendulum will swing. I hate to say it, but one day America will reap as it has sown. Such is the way."

The lightening was coming closer. The black clouds would be upon us soon. We continued on the porch reveling in the coolness of the blustery wind of the approaching summer storm. A few heavy raindrops fell on the dry ground in front of the porch, each exploding on the bone-dry soil in a little cloud of red dust. A noisy spattering of cold rain began falling in huge drops, then in another moment falling in blinding sheets. The gusting wind, brilliant lightning and pouring rain were upon us. We were engulfed in the cool ecstasy of the summer storm. We were surrounded by lightning, striking in rapid succession on all sides. The uninterrupted rolling thunder reverberated through the hills and echoed off the mountains. Water began to flow off the wooden shingles Ben and his father had cut and placed themselves. None of us wanted to return to the stuffy interior. We stood with our backs against the wall of the porch to escape the driving rain and experience the cool air as long as we could. I watched the rain and the wind in the trees as I listened to the thunder. The lightning was crashing in brilliant flashes.

Rivers of muddy red water began running through Mrs. Lowry's yard, the yard she swept clean every morning in her daily ritual. The bright orange streams rushed down the hill towards the woods and river beyond.

"Let's go inside," Mr. Lowry said softly. "I want to lie down."

The rain lashed against the small, curtained windows. The gusting wind whistled down the chimney with a supernatural howl. The storm was upon us.

Chapter XXIV
1827 - Cassie's Happy Thoughts
Chapter 24

9 July 1827 - Month of the Ripe Corn Moon -gu ye quo ni

We have achieved everything the Americans demand. We have a written language, newspaper, houses, farms, livestock, and barns. We are self-sustaining. We raise crops. We will have a national constitution, legislative body and established international borders. One thing we lack. We shall never be white. We will never be American.

24 July 1827

16 July 1827 - Huff's Boarding House

My Dearest Cassie,

You are missing from me, my dear, my best friend, my confidant. I love how we share secrets. As I write I pretend you are across the desk listening as I pen each word.

Zach, the owner's son, is teaching me about his father's business and life among influential landowners, but our time together is nothing compared with time spent with you.

Zach wants me to run for political office with the help of the firm. He plainly said he wants to ride my coat tails to power and wealth. Zach thinks my isolated upbringing makes me a perfect political candidate. I must close for now or miss the post. I'm missing you and hope to see you soon.

Your Loving Ben, xoxo

Milledgeville July 1827

"Ben, I love to walk into the hotel after a long day's work and have my drink and cigar put into my hand without a word. I can't tell you how much I enjoy that first puff and first drink. Life is good, isn't it, Ben?"

Ben nodded and sipped. He agreed with Zach. This quiet time in the hotel after a long day's work had become something Ben craved. He wanted to sit quietly until the alcohol began to work its magic. Ben noticed that lately he had actually begun to enjoy the taste of the alcohol. He wanted to relax. He would be silent and allow Zach to prattle on.

"Ben, I think you're amazing. I've never seen anyone like you. I avoid work and you search for more."

Zach waved his cigar to make a point.

"The very reason I want slaves and an overseer is so I don't have to work. I want leisure. That's my motivation. Money and power are my goals. After we've achieved quantities of wealth, we'll devote ourselves to pleasure."

Zach, already with his second drink in hand, was in a talkative mood.

"Ben, I like to think I understand how to use the greed of others to accumulate wealth. If you'll trust me, we can make a lot of money."

As was his custom, Ben sipped and listened. Zach's world view was diametrically opposite of that of Ben's parents. Zach's long-term plans to live a privileged life made it sound as if leisure was the be-all and end-all of human existence. Ben was amused how Zach repeated himself in a never-ending rehearsal as if he had no memory of previous conversations. Ben enjoyed the pleasure of not having to think after a long day. Ben curiously noticed that although Zach was only on his second drink, his cheeks were already turning pink.

"We hired you for two reasons," Zach said. "First, we wanted a smart young lawyer. You fit that bill perfectly. We've talked about this before, haven't we? Second, we want our own politician. Politics isn't complicated, Ben. It's arithmetic pure and simple. It's money and time. That's all. You'll qualify for the Georgia House when you're twenty, the United States House when you're twenty-five and the United States Senate when you're thirty."

"Zach, there's many a slip twixt the cup and the lip," Ben warned.

"Ben, Ben, Ben," Zach countered in mock criticism, "gettin' you elected will be like shootin' ducks on a pond. There are 213 seats in the House of Representatives in Washington City, but every bill must go to the Senate before it goes to the president's desk and becomes law. Did you know that?"

Ben laughed. "Of course, I knew that."

"There are only 24 states and thus only 48 senators. That's where the power is, in the Senate. If you want money, you have to have power. If you want power, you must have a Senate seat. You'll be elected to the house. That's not a problem but senators are different. They're appointed by their legislatures. A Senate appointment is the most difficult office of all. Give me enough time and I'll put you into the U.S. Senate. When you reach the age of qualification, we'll have the people in place. When you're ready, Father and I will call in all favors. That's when we'll find the pot of gold, Ben. 'Senator Ben Lowry'. That has a ring, doesn't it?"

"Perhaps we shouldn't count our chickens before they're hatched," said Ben with a smile. Zach continued as if he didn't hear.

"Senators pass all laws, approve treaties and confirm appointments," Zach droned on. "The House is a bunch of fuss and feathers schoolboys. A multi-term Senator is almost as powerful as the president. Father wants a

Senator in his pocket. We won't deceive you, Ben. That's our purpose in choosing you. We don't want to be rich, Ben, we want to be really rich."

Ben listened, giving Zach a thoughtful look as he considered what Zach had said. He sipped from the glass the servant in the corner never allowed to become empty. He wondered if Zach's political fantasies would be realized.

"Ben, you're learning. When you first came you were shy. It's nice to see you coming out of your shell. Folks are impressed by your expertise and wit and the women think you handsome. Elizabeth and I like the easy, country boy way you have with people. To be honest, I like the new sophisticated Ben who knows what he wants and is willing to take it. That's the American way, Ben. Take what you want."

Zach laughed and Ben noticed the tip of Zach's nose had become quite red, matching the pink of his cheeks.

19 July 1827

Ben is home. What a happy day. As we walked hand in hand to the river, I enjoyed Ben's conversation and the pleasantness of him being near me.

"Ben, I remember when I would kiss you first. Now you kiss me."

"Cassie, you're the sweetest. Of course I want to kiss you. You are beautiful."

I changed the subject.

"Ben, I'm excited about your decision to run for political office. I'm sure it's the right thing to do."

"I think you're right, Cassie. Father and Mother are excited, too. This is a good year for a young man to get into politics in Georgia. Things are changing with new faces everywhere. I'm looking forward to the challenge."

"The newspapers never say anything good about us, Ben. I never see an article defending our rights. Every week Edudu tells me of some new squatter moving in. All the militia cares about are slave patrols and drinking whiskey."

"I know, Cassie. Who knows what I can accomplish if I'm able to get into the legislature. Maybe I'll have influence, maybe not. I could never be elected if I openly support Indians. Just the fact that Father is a missionary is a liability. Andrew Jackson worries me the most. He's building a nation-wide power base. Zach told me all about that. The South is growing."

"The newspapers are impressed by his military reputation against the Creeks and Seminoles. The election next year will be interesting, Cassie. It's hard to vote an incumbent out. After the hard-fought election of '24, I'm certain there will be a lot of mudslinging between Jackson and Adams."

"What's mudslinging, Ben?"

"Politicians don't actually throw mud, Cassie," Ben said laughing. "It's a figure of speech. They throw dirty, untrue words meant to discredit their opponent. Jackson accuses Adams and Calhoun of a corrupt bargain that cheated Jackson out of the election of '24."

"What is the corrupt bargain Andrew Jackson is so angry about?" I asked.

"In the presidential election of '24, four men ran, Andrew Jackson, John Quincy Adams, Henry Clay and William Crawford. None of the four received a majority in the electoral college. According to the twelfth amendment, the president must be elected by a majority of the electoral college. One man must receive more than half of the total votes. A plurality is not enough."

"I remember, Ben. The newspapers were full of it for months."

"If no candidate receives a majority of the electoral college, the House of Representatives elects the president. That's what happened in '24. Jackson had the most votes in the electoral college but not a majority. He didn't get more than fifty-percent of the electoral votes as required. Therefore, the top three were voted on in the House in a subsequent election. John Quincy Adams won in the House with Henry Clay's help. Henry Clay was Speaker of the House. That cooperation between Adams and Clay caused Jackson to lose the election. Jackson has been angry about that since. He's still not over it. Clay persuaded his supporters to vote for Adams instead of Jackson. After Adams became president, he appointed Clay as Secretary of State. It's what we call quid pro quo. You scratch my back, I'll scratch yours."

"It seems to me everything in American politics is a backroom compromise, Ben. How can any American politician be honest?"

"I know what you mean, Cassie. A compromise is like building a tabletop out of boards and puttin' the middle board in last. If the middle board is too wide, which side do you plane? That's what I'll be required to do when I'm elected. I'll have to compromise if I want to accomplish anything good for the Cherokee. I'll never be able to oppose the government openly, but I'll be honest, Cassie. I promise. I won't lie to please folks or to get re-elected."

"I'm worried, Ben. Georgia has passed the law that a newborn can only be listed as white or black, not Indian. As far as the South is concerned, we Cherokee don't exist. It's white or nothing if you want to succeed. We can't vote or take a white man to court. We're aliens in our own country."

We paused for a long time before either spoke.

"Ben, let's talk of something brighter. We can't carry the weight of every injustice. We must make the best of what we have as we do every day. Can we talk about happy things? Can we talk about things that give hope? Can I share my happy thoughts with you, Ben?"

"Of course, Cassie. Tell me your happy thoughts. I want to hear good things. I'm as weary of politics and bad news as you are."

"Ben, my happy thought is I know you love me."

"That's my happy thought, too," Ben said smiling.

"I think about that all the time," I replied. "I want to share your dreams. I want a house full of your children. You, Ben Lowry, are my happy thought, whether you are by my side or in Milledgeville."

7 August 1827

Ben said his custom of including the letters xoxo at the bottom of his correspondence originated in Europe. His mother's relatives in Germany were using xoxo to end their correspondence long before they immigrated to the United States. The x represents a kiss and the o is a hug.

19 August 1827

The feelings Ben and I have for each other are natural, like breathing in and breathing out. Our passion fills my waking thoughts. Even when he isn't here, I feel his presence—enfolding me—protecting me.

Chapter XXV
1827 - Zach Plans
Chapter 25

Milledgeville – December 1827"

Ben and Zach were sharing their usual drink in their usual spot.

"Ben, this is December. We have eleven months before the election. If you want to make a lovely wine, you can't begin a month before you drink it. We need to establish your base and cut the legs from under your competition."

Although Ben was relaxing, he was listening carefully.

"Zach, you're right. I'm a novice. No one knows me and it'll take time to establish my name. I've thought about it. I say let's go to work. I'm all in."

"Good attitude, Ben," Zach raised his glass, "a toast to the brightest and one day most powerful politician in Georgia, with my help of course."

The young men clinked glasses, drank their toast and laughed as they began to seriously plan the campaign for the coming year.

Zach took a taste of his excellent sippin' whiskey.

"Money runs the world, Ben. Every politician in the world knows that. Altruism and politics have no common ground. People go to church to salve their conscience. Rich folks get into politics to get richer. You can have anything, including a Senate seat, if you have enough money. My father and his friends are planning on spending a lot of money on you."

Ben enjoyed thinking about the power and prestige of elected office and was perfectly willing to let Zach do the work.

"Go to church for morality. Go into politics for wealth. You can't deposit morality in the bank, can you, Ben? You told me yourself your father is as poor as a church mouse. A lawyer can be rich. A lawyer turned politician can be richer. Elizabeth and I intend for you to have everything you've dreamed of, Ben. You'll be a man of position, privilege and leisure. You'll be able to take care of your parents in style. Think about that."

Zach motioned to their servant to fill their glasses once again.

Milledgeville provided Ben with his first taste of class privilege. It was pleasant to have others perform life's menial tasks. His parents' days were filled with physical labor from daylight to dark. They did everything for themselves, therefore their life was simple. Ben's new friends never did their own chores. Under Zach's tutelage Ben's eyes were beginning to open to an agreeable lifestyle he had never experienced. He was beginning to understand Zach's motives. A life of privilege required money, lots of money.

Ben listened patiently as Zach continued.

Zach laughed out loud, "Ben, you need servants to have a good life. Servants cost money. Without money you'll end up with a complaining, overworked wife and a houseful of barefoot kids."

Zach was right. Ben didn't want to be a man of insufficient means.

Zach continued his alcohol-fueled speech.

"Time and tide wait for no man. Mark my words, Ben. You'll go to the top with our help. Another toast, Ben. To our success and friendship on the final leg of our journey into the vast political realms of the uncharted worlds of the rich and famous where we shall forever reside."

Zach and Ben once again toasted success. Ben had no political aspirations of his own. He considered his run for office as part of the job for which he was hired. Politics was Zach and Elizabeth's business. For him politics was a career path to help his father and the Cherokee. He had dreamed of helping Africans but recently found himself rethinking his views.

Ben's first year of employment had flown. He was comfortable in his role as the firm's number one lawyer. Times were moving fast. He could fulfill his dreams and accomplish at least a few of the more noble goals he and his father had discussed. Ben could see himself as an influential politician. It was a pleasant vision and, of course, he would enjoy the privileges along the way.

Ben enjoyed the frequent meetings to plan the details for his election in the autumn of '28, a presidential election year. Ben liked Zach. He liked Elizabeth. He had never been around people so full of life and energy. For years Cassie had been the center of his attention, but she was in New Echota.

Ben's regular meetings with Zach and Elizabeth were always business but perhaps, before too long, he could be alone with her. She was desirable. Most of the time he thought her unapproachable. Surely a beautiful, sophisticated, modern woman like Elizabeth would never be interested in a lowly country boy like him. She could have any man she wanted. Elizabeth would never be interested in him, yet she had given some veiled indications.

Ben knew what Zach said about Elizabeth was probably true, but what if she did learn to care for him? He could never be seen in public with Cassie, but he could daydream about walking down main street with Elizabeth. He could see her on his arm in Washington City. He loved that flight of fancy.

"Ben, we got a lot accomplished this afternoon. I'm ready for fun. I know a couple of Southern Belles who have indicated they want to explore the vagaries of international politics along with expensive imported wine and French cuisine I've specially ordered for the occasion. What do you say? Ready for adventure? Come with me. We'll have a great time."

Zach had teased Ben often with such escapades. Zach knew perfectly well Elizabeth would twist Ben into any shape she wished when the time came. He would leave Elizabeth to take care of Ben. Zach didn't want to move too fast and ruin their investment. Elizabeth would make the right decision.

For the time being Ben was determined not to violate his conscience. He had made promises to Cassie. He was prepared to resist Zach's straightforward temptations, but he would have done well to remember his father's warnings about the thin end of the wedge.

Ben responded with a grin, "Zach, I appreciate the honor. I'm sure your conversation with the young women will be grand, but I'm going to my room. I'm tired. I've a lot of reading to do. I don't feel like discussing international politics. You're the tireless one, Zach. You have fun. Maybe next time."

Zach gave Ben a playful push.

"You don't know what you're missing, my friend, but someone needs to work around here. I'll play. You work. I like that arrangement."

On slightly unsteady feet, Ben left the hotel for the short walk to his room. His thoughts strayed once again to Elizabeth. He imagined he could smell her perfume. He noticed an ache in his chest when he thought of her, an ache occurring with more frequency. As Ben got ready for bed he recognized from experience one of those nights when he would be thinking about all sorts of things well into the wee hours before sleep would come. His mind was too active for work. He would lie in bed and think.

Ben loved his job. His protestant work ethic, instilled by hardworking parents, was transferred to the world of law and thus into success and money. Zach's father was more than pleased with Ben. Everyone was surprised how quickly Ben's skills developed and how rapidly he had established a broad clientele. Ben's clients came back.

Georgia upheld the individual's right to own property and to leave it to heirs. It was curious, thought Ben, that in the Cherokee culture land was owned corporately. There was no fee simple in Cherokee Country, no deeds or personal ownership and there lay, as his father believed, the central problem. The Cherokee understanding of community, and by extension the ownership of land, was the leading cause of the clash with the invading American culture. Americans wanted private individual ownership, the ability to amass great wealth within a few leading families. Americans, like the Europeans from which they came, coveted the right of the few to prosper at the expense of everyone else. The Cherokee generally practiced corporate ownership and the sharing of wealth thus maintaining strong family ties across the wider community. Ben found the dichotomy most interesting.

Ben was no longer a child. He had learned nothing is black and white. He learned as a lawyer to turn a simple legal problem into shades of grey and watch his opponent founder. His job was to represent his client's best interest, to convince the judge that his client's shade of grey had a solid basis in legal precedent. If any dispute comes to litigation it means the issue isn't black or white, or it would have never been litigated in the first place. Ben represented his client, not a moral code. There are no morals in law. The law itself is moral. The law is always moral. The law is right. There are those who are law abiding and those who are lawless. Morality has nothing to do with the legal profession. Winning in a courtroom has to do with interpreting law in combination with precedent on behalf of one's client. The lazy lawyer loses.

Lawmakers represent society. Law is the consensus of the broader society and therefore moral. It wasn't theologians who understood right and wrong. Determining right and wrong is the sole prerogative of legislators. Ben's father would never agree, but Ben's father wasn't in the legislature. Ben's father had no legal standing.

The entire western legal system is built on Rule of Law, straight out of the courtrooms of Rome. Established law is the only way to govern society. Thus, the lawyer who wins in court is assured of the highest moral ground.

If Indians are removed by legal means, such removal becomes morally right. The law is always correct. From the moment Ben began to practice law, he began to see another star guiding his conscience. The Sunday morals his father espoused did not hold in the courtroom.

When legal authority pronounces judgment on right and wrong there are always mitigating circumstances. In law the legislature sets the position of the polar star. Societal probity cannot be fixed by ancient eastern religious texts. The legislature alone sets true north for society's moral compass. Society can only exist when it breaths the pure air provided by law, by the rule of law, overseen by courts, judges and lawyers.

His parents had one idea of morality, businessmen another. Ben discovered the lawyer's personal conscience, like his sidearm, must be checked at the courtroom door. Laws must be obeyed, otherwise society will collapse, there would be anarchy. Judges and courts are obliged to uphold the law on the books. Otherwise, society descends into chaos.

Laws came from Milledgeville and Washington. The simple life of a ten-year-old country boy raised by missionary parents had morphed into the complex adult society reflecting bewildering shades of grey, a confusing landscape of mists and fogs, a legal world that required a smart lawyer to lead his client through the dangerous morass covered by a shadowy gloom.

Ben felt liberated, empowered by progressive authors who applauded the freedom of an enlightened intellect. Although he respected and held to much of what his father had taught him, Ben chose to allow his two world views to co-exist as if there were no widening crevasse between, like saddlebags on his horse. On one side the world views of his parents and the other the law library and men like John Locke. Real life contained those who lie, cheat and steal at the expense of fellow citizens. Law existed to protect community. His father's imaginary Sunday dream world could protect no one. What could be more outdated than five-thousand-year-old morals carved into stone?

Civilization, as enshrined in the United States constitution, was infinitely superior to the casual existence of hunters and gatherers like the Cherokee.

He would carefully avoid discussing such with his parents. They would never be part of the progressive, democratic spirit fostered by the Jacksonian party. The United States was prospering as never before. Jackson, although sometimes pigheaded, wasn't afraid to lead from the front. Ben had to admit Jackson would make a good president.

26 December 1827

William Hicks has been appointed interim chief, John Ross secondary chief. Elijah Hicks has been appointed president of the National Committee.

I haven't had a letter from Ben in several days.

Chapter XXVI

1828 – Zach, Ben and Elizabeth

Chapter 26

10 January 1828 - The Cold Moon – Du no lv ta ni.

Ben's twenty-first birthday celebration is this afternoon. Ben is a lawyer and wants to be a lawmaker. Ben's friend says his election is certain.

11 January 1828

Ben left at dawn. His mother and I waved him goodbye until he was out of sight. I wish I could live in Milledgeville.

13 January 1828

Hurrah. We have a printing press in New Echota. I can't express my joy. We will be the first Indian nation to have a newspaper. Well-chosen words motivate deeds. I hope so. Our newspaper will make a difference in our ability to communicate. Perhaps Georgia will let us stay.

January – Milledgeville 1828

Ben shivered in the January cold as he and Zach walked to the hotel.

"I wish your father would keep the office warmer. I'm frozen, Zach."

"Don't be a wimp, Ben. If Father kept the office as warm as you like, everyone would sleep. Have a drink by the fire. That'll warm you up."

Zach gave Ben a slap on the back.

"Speed it up, Ben. Walk faster. Let's have a drink, get warm and plan your election campaign. I'm ready for a drink," Zach said.

"You're the schemer, Zach. I'm just a country boy lawyer, a cold lawyer."

"You're a country boy all right, but you're about the smartest country boy I've ever met. Ben, I don't understand how anyone can enjoy books the way you do. You read anything. You keep doing my legal work and I'll take care of this election. That's a good exchange, a proper division of labor, isn't it?"

Ben grinned, "Zach, I hate rubbing elbows with strangers. That's the onerous part of this thing for me. If you and Elizabeth will take care of as much of that as you can, I'll happily do your law work."

They entered the hotel and turned left up the three wide stairs straight to Zach's reserved table by the big fireplace in the corner. Ben had come to love Zach's father's hotel and their private space. On this dreary January afternoon, the fire was welcome. The servant took their coats and immediately served drinks. A young African, well dressed like all the staff, brought in a huge hickory backlog. As they watched, he scooped cold ashes, pulled the hottest coals forward and placed the seasoned backlog against the firebrick in the back. Ben could hear the seasoned hickory backlog begin crackling immediately. The boy returned with another armload of dry wood he put on top of the hot coals in front. In just a moment the wood was bursting into flame, in two moments it was roaring up the chimney.

Zach, as usual, leaned on the end of the mantelpiece, drink in hand, puffing on his big Cuban cigar. Ben was learning to enjoy privilege. He was glad he had been born an American. It was a pleasure to be waited on hand and foot. He couldn't imagine being African, having to work on behalf of the wealthy and worst of all, being denied literacy. He understood the reasoning behind American laws that prevented the education of those in bondage, but it made him shiver. He was glad he was who he was.

Zach placed his drink on the mantlepiece and cigar in an ashtray and turned his back to the freshening fire, lifted his coat tails and rubbed his back and posterior as he rotated left and right.

"It doesn't get better than this does it, Ben?" Zach said with pleasure.

"This is good, very good," Ben agreed. "I think this is the first time I've been warm all day. I'm glad I'm not the one who has to cut all this wood."

"For a country boy, you are a cry baby, Ben. I've seen little girls with more gumption. Get your mind off the temperature. Let's talk about your future."

"That's fine with me," Ben answered. "Talk about anything you want. I'm going to enjoy this fire."

Zach retrieved his drink and cigar, turned his back away from the fire and continued to lean against the mantel. With a wave of his arm he began.

"Your election is certain, Ben, but one never knows with elections. We've already done a lot of work and I don't want to waste the time we've invested.

Zach rotated before the fire once again to warm the other side.

"Ben, we've got to get your name out. I can get anyone elected, if I have time. We've got time, if we get busy. If we do this right, we'll have bigger fish to fry in the years to come. The Georgia House will be easy. The big prize is the United States Senate. That'll take time. That's why we're starting now with you at your age. That's why we hired you. Elizabeth and I are sowing the seeds for future success. You see that, don't you?"

Ben was listening carefully. He was enjoying his drink and the pleasant fire after a long day of intense study and research. Ben's father advised him to listen more and talk less. He didn't mind listening to Zach ramble.

"First, we'll solidify Father's friends. That'll be easy and they'll influence others. Elizabeth and I are working to secure the support of the wealthiest. We'll plan a series of breakfasts, dinners, socials and the like that will crescendo before the fall election. We'll see to it that every important person in Georgia shakes your hand. We'll tell folks you'll take care of them after you're elected. This plan will work. We'll find someone to scratch the rich folks' backs and they'll scratch yours on election day. Quid pro quo, Ben."

"Zach, you make this sound easy, but nothing is that easy."

"You're right, but I'm ahead of the game. This first election isn't difficult, but it does require a brain put together like mine, doesn't it? On your own, Ben, you couldn't get elected to a backwoods city council."

Zach, already slightly tipsy, laughed so hard at his comments he spilled his drink. Ben chuckled to himself as he watched the colorfully-dressed Zach standing beside the fire waving his arms as if on stage. Zach continued to make his points with hand gestures, drink in one hand and big cigar in the other. Zach reminded Ben of one of his mother's colorful banty roosters, strutting around the barnyard sporting brightly colored tail feathers for all to see, crowing to everyone and picking a fight with any and all who disagreed. That made Ben laugh out loud at Zach's expense. He couldn't help glancing down at Zach's new boots to see if they had spurs like a rooster.

Zach knew how to gain influence and he didn't mind work, as long as it was work he enjoyed, like backroom deals that put money in his pocket. Zach loved giving people what they wanted and getting things in return.

Ben continued sipping his Tennessee sour-mash. The whiskey gave his stomach a pleasant glow and warmed him all the way to his toes. This was the way to relax after a long day. Ben forced himself to drink the nasty stuff. He was getting used to the poisonous taste.

Ben didn't mind the idea of doing a portion of Zach's legal homework. He had never considered books, reading, research and study as work. He loved the library. Reading and study were pleasures, an avocation, not simply a vocation, something he would do without pay and had done since a child. Ben generally disliked socials, which meant less study time and a cloudy head the next day from the ever-present alcohol. He was amazed how it seemed everyone consumed alcohol and those who didn't were considered a stick-in-the-mud. Zach was actually doing him a favor by allowing him to help with legal responsibilities. Yes indeed, Ben thought, he and Zach did make a pair. He suddenly corrected himself and thought of Elizabeth and was reminded it was a trio, not a pair.

Zach turned to face the fire and warmed his other side. With his back to Ben, Zach continued, "We'll need money to get you elected. Raisin' money is easy. Gettin' a man to tell his friends he's supporting you, now that's the tricky part. When I'm trying to win a man's support, I ask myself what's the one thing this man wants above all else? When I know the answer to that question, I've got him, hook, line and sinker."

Zach lowered his voice and turned to face Ben, "What is it a man wants and is afraid to get for himself? When you know that about a man, he's in your pocket. It takes time to learn a man's secrets, but I have folks who work for me who can find out anything."

Ben was enjoying the fire. He had learned not to be surprised at anything Zach might say after he had a few drinks.

"Men motivated by money are the easiest," Zach continued, "but there are a lot of things men want besides money."

Zach, with both sides warmed, sat beside Ben in the high-backed leather chair, sipped his whiskey, blew clouds of silvery cigar smoke towards the fireplace and watched the smoke suddenly sucked up the flue.

"Ben, you're a quick study. I knew you would make a good politician."

As usual, Zach's cheeks and the tip of his nose were beginning to redden.

"Well, there's money, but there's also power."

Zach lectured on.

"Some folks don't care about money but would love to be on the city council or be mayor or judge or an important government contractor. Other folks thrive on orderin' others about. They want to be sheriff. People who want power are a bit more difficult to figure out. Jackson, for example, wants power. He wants to make executive decisions, be in the lead. Money is secondary to him."

Ben slumped down in his comfortable chair and watched the fire through the glass in his hand as it diffused the flames into various colors.

Zach droned on.

"Some want pleasure, some money and some power. Those who dream about a woman their wife doesn't know about are the stupidest, of course. Once you supply their need, you have both them and their pocketbook. Those folks will never feel comfortable about doing anything to make you angry once you know their dirty secret. They'll be afraid of you, and you can trust me, Ben, I know plenty of women who will help us."

Zach laughed again, "Understanding politics is easy, isn't it, Ben?"

Zach motioned to the tall, greying African waiter in the shadows to have their drinks freshened.

"Ben, about six weeks before the election, we'll have a rapid-fire series events culminating in Milledgeville. We'll invite the town. They ought to just go ahead and give you your seat. It's a done deal," Zach said, holding on to the mantelpiece to steady his legs and raising his glass high above his head for a tribute.

"Here's a toast to the smartest, handsomest, and soon-to-be richest legislator in the state of Georgia, Ben Lowry. You know I stretched the truth a bit about you being the handsomest, don't you, but then I'm getting used to tellin' folks things about you that aren't exactly true."

The two young men laughed with one another. Ben loved the moment. He enjoyed listening to Zach ramble on about different things even if he was sometimes monotonously pedantic. He and Zach were becoming friends.

At that moment Elizabeth and her parents walked into the foyer. Zach and Ben stepped quickly down the three wide steps to greet them.

"Good evening Mr. and Mrs. Cooper. What a pleasure to see you this cold January afternoon," Zach said. "Good evening to you, Miss Elizabeth. Would y'all care to join us before your meal and warm in front of our perfectly marvelous fire? We would love to have you join us and relax before dinner."

"No son," Elizabeth's father said. "Caroline and I expect guests shortly. Elizabeth may wish to join you. Would you like to join the boys, Elizabeth?"

Mr. Cooper's daughter lowered her eyes.

"If you and Mother would be content without my presence for a while. I would like that indeed."

"Go, my dear. Enjoy your evening. Your mother and I are going to our table. I need to sit down and have a drink. Join us when you're ready, dear."

Zach escorted Elizabeth to the warm leather chairs in front of the welcoming fire, "And what would Bethy have to drink, may I ask?"

Elizabeth's eyes sparkled.

"Hello, Elizabeth," Ben said as he kissed the back of her extended hand, never taking his eyes from her face. "You can have anything you desire this evening, my dear, up to and including my very soul."

The three laughed together at Ben's words. They seemed to get along perfectly, always on the same page.

Zach asked again, "And what does our Bethy want to drink this evening?"

"I'm like Father. I need a drink to warm my frozen toes. I'll have a double bourbon and water if you don't mind."

Ben's eyebrows raised. He had never seen a woman drinking straight whiskey. The usual feminine choice was a sickeningly sweet mint julep, a sherry or a dainty glass of white wine.

There was something overpoweringly attractive about a beautiful woman who threw caution to the wind, who drank bourbon in public. He liked her carefree attitude. He laughed to himself as he imagined her joining the men and smoking a big cigar with her whiskey. Elizabeth, in her element as the center of attention between two young men, made herself comfortable.

"You look most lovely this evening, Elizabeth," said Ben with a polite little bow as he sat beside her. "We are at your service."

Elizabeth was a striking woman who knew how to dress. With her unlimited clothing budget and her father's business connections, especially those in France, there wasn't a young woman in Georgia better turned out. With the addition of her expert coquetry, an art form she practiced daily, she was a most desirable woman, at least on the outside.

Elizabeth smiled at Ben. He sat as close to her as he dared.

"Why Ben Lowry, are you flirting with me? Mother says the best compliment a girl can have is a flirtatious beau. I agree. Mother told me a girl of modesty and breeding will flirt to gain the upper hand and thus defend her virtue. I love a battle of wits with a handsome young man and you, Mr. Ben Lowry, are exceptionally well-armed. I would never have to defend my virtue in the presence of such a gallant man as yourself. You would always defend my honor, wouldn't you, Ben? Could I depend on you to defend my dignity as a chivalrous southern gentleman should?"

Elizabeth, her eyes sparkling with amusement, gave Ben the most flirtatious smile she could manage and accomplished that which she intended.

Ben was undone.

Zach puffed his cigar and looked sidelong at the exchange, chuckled to himself and took a sip of his drink. He knew Elizabeth's ulterior motives when it came to men, pecuniary motives that coincided with his, motives that had brought Zach and Elizabeth together years earlier and made them two of the most influential young people in Georgia society.

Ben flushed. He thought Elizabeth more captivating with every meeting. The only time he had been alone with Elizabeth, that one time at dinner, he found her enchanting. Her perfume turned the room into springtime. Ben was having trouble even remembering why he was here. The unwanted thought came into his mind that Cassie never smelled like that. Now was not the time to think of Cassie. He wanted to think about Elizabeth. He needed to concentrate on the fascinating woman beside him that made him tingle from head to toe.

Elizabeth politely asked, "I understand you made your final decision?"

"Yes, ma'am. I did," Ben answered. "Zach will manage my campaign. He says my chances of election are excellent. I can do good things for the people of Georgia. I'm sure we'll be successful with your help."

"Spoken like a true politician, Ben," Elizabeth said as she leaned backward and looked at Ben with playful eyes and unsuccessfully restrained a laugh as she covered her mouth with her white gloved hand.

She continued mischievously, "So, you plan great things for the good people of Georgia, do you? Your legislative career will be filled with noble ideas and wonderful deeds of chivalry as you, prince valiant, perform an endless series of altruistic actions on behalf of your constituents? Am I right?"

Elizabeth was in a carefree mood. She couldn't restrain her teasing. Ben was quite unable to answer. Elizabeth lightheartedly continued.

"My dear Mr. Lowry, with that attitude you'll go far in politics, I assure you. For a moment, you almost had me convinced you were telling the truth."

Ben had to concentrate with all his strength to process what Elizabeth was saying and make an intelligent reply. He found it hard to breath because of a confusing swelling in his chest. She continued her breezy attitude with a wave of her hand.

"You're not just another handsome lawyer, Ben Lowry. You're ambitious, talented and determined. I like that, my handsome philanthropic friend. You'll be elected to high office and history will record you responsible for countless charitable deeds, no doubt. You'll be known throughout Georgia as the purveyor of compassion, emulated by schoolchildren everywhere."

Ben couldn't help being attracted to this beautiful, witty woman who enjoyed life to the fullest and wasn't afraid to poke fun at societies' most cherished institutions. He loved her openness. He loved the way she combined clever speech with body motions to communicate her interest in him. Surely she liked him. He always felt he had her full attention when she was near, as if she were truly interested in what he had to say, attentive to his every word. He knew she was flirting, perhaps even toying with him, but he didn't care. All he wanted was for her interest, genuine or feigned, to continue. He didn't want this moment to end.

Elizabeth continued with a grin.

"It occurred to me, since I am free, white and twenty-one, that an aspiring politician like you might consider helping little ole' me achieve my personal goals? Would you consider assisting me in exchange for my political support? I promise to show you every gratitude imaginable. I would be eternally grateful. I promise you'll never regret your decision to lend me a hand."

At the end of Elizabeth's little speech all three laughed louder. Ben couldn't wait to spend more time with this amusing woman whose bright green eyes shone like stars and made his blood flow hot. He had never met anyone like her. Not even Cassie had made him feel the way he felt at this moment, but then, when he was in New Echota he never drank whiskey. Ben, despite what he had been taught by his parents, did his best to believe he could manage his mind through an alcohol-induced fog. Ben knew there were important differences between Cassie and Elizabeth. When he was with Elizabeth he chose not to think of those differences. Ben had never met a woman with a quick mind like Elizabeth, none except Cassie. He must think about Cassie later. Now was not the time.

When the laughter subsided, Zach continued with obvious amusement.

"I don't wonder if your newfound goodness will result in the great accumulation of personal wealth, both for yourself and your associates. Quid pro quo, Ben. Everything we do is for our future."

"Ben," Elizabeth interrupted, "I was wondering if you and Zach might need the advice of an erudite woman who knows the ins and outs of Georgia society in places other than smelly taverns? The three of us might form an entertaining and profitable relationship. I have access to parlors you two can never enter. I've been bored. I'm interested in a challenge."

With this little speech, she allowed her head to tilt backward. She gave another teasing laugh that communicated her interest. She knew very well she was the center of attention. Ben, if he had been thinking clearly, would have noticed with each of Elizabeth's actions his interest was growing. Between Zach, the dulling effect of the alcohol and the seductive charms of Elizabeth, Ben was as helpless as a newborn.

Elizabeth accidentally touched Ben's trousers just above the knee. He hoped she didn't see the resulting shiver. She saw. Elizabeth had plans for Ben. This rustic specimen might be more exciting than others she had conquered. He was certainly healthy, tall and well groomed.

The inconspicuous African waiter, never making the least noise, refreshed their drinks, quietly observing the three young people from his corner in the shadows.

"I don't think we need to take this under further advisement, do you?" Zach said. "I pronounce our partnership in Ben's election a done deal. Let's drink to future corporate profits. I propose a toast to the most prosperous triumvirate in the history of Georgia and to the second-most handsomest lawyer and his election. May he be crowned king of Georgia."

They clinked their glasses and drank. All three believed the words of the toast would be fulfilled and Ben would be elected to the Georgia House, the beginning of an influential and profitable political career.

Ben was watching Elizabeth to see how she reacted when she sipped the strong liquor. Her facial expression didn't change. Her eyes and mind were as clear as when she entered the room. She might as well have been sipping lemonade. That told him something.

"Bethy and I have been putting our heads together, Ben. Would you like the three of us to begin meeting every Tuesday afternoon for a regular planning session here in this room? You'll benefit from the intellect of the most sought-after belle in town and gain access to clandestine feminine enclaves. How about we meet here every Tuesday and work on our plans?"

Ben and Elizabeth agreed. Zach stood on unsteady feet with a silly grin and raised his glass once again.

"Another toast then. To many a Tuesday in the delight of one another's company and to our acquisition of a cornucopia of pleasure and wealth, gifted by the singular political success of one Ben Lowry, future king of Georgia."

They laughed even more loudly, touched glasses and decided two in the afternoon would be the perfect time. They could have a few drinks, plot and scheme for an hour or two and dine afterward. Elizabeth swallowed the rest of her bourbon in one gulp, stood and extended her hand to Ben.

"Would you young men pardon me? I must be a good daughter and join my parents and their insufferable guests. I'm looking forward to seeing you more often, Ben. We will certainly become the best of friends. I'm sure of it."

Elizabeth excused herself. Ben's eyes followed as she stepped down the three wide steps. At the bottom she turned left to join her parents. She didn't look back. He had never met a woman with more self-confidence. She had the most beautiful facial features and figure he had ever seen. Before she was out of sight he was wishing to see her again. Would he ever have the courage to call her Bethy? Why did she never look back?

Chapter XXVII

1828 - Ben and Elizabeth
Chapter 27

17 January 1828 - Month of the Cold Moon- Du no lv ta ni

As I read Ben's letters I imagine myself sitting across from him as he is writing each word. He and Zach meet each Tuesday preparing for his November election. He will be successful and accomplish great things both as a lawyer and politician and for the Cherokee. I wait impatiently.

January 1828 - Milledgeville

It was Tuesday, finally. Ben made himself comfortable in Zach's private corner beside the big fireplace. If it weren't for his inherent frugality instilled by thrifty parents, and the fact that Huff's Boarding House was just around the corner from his office, Ben would have moved his lodgings to the hotel long ago. He would love to spend every evening here and have a quiet place for reading. He loved the hotel.

Recently Ben had been thinking more about his Tuesday sessions with Zach and Elizabeth, especially about Elizabeth. He had to admit he was more interested in politics because of Elizabeth's involvement. Tuesday afternoon was the highlight of his week.

Elizabeth, arriving late, walked into the hotel foyer alone. Ben chuckled to himself, thinking about the strict time-keeping among businessmen in Milledgeville. He preferred the Cherokee casual approach to appointments. In the American culture Ben had learned most folks are conscious of the passage of time to the minute. They divide their day into the smallest of segments. 'Time is money' he was often told.

Among the Cherokee there is no such awareness. The Cherokee are never rushed to accomplish anything. Ben liked that, he liked that a lot. In Milledgeville he felt pushed and shoved as if every hour of the day were a matter of increasing urgency, as if he were racing from the time he rose until the time he undressed for bed, driven by some heartless taskmaster with a big watch in his hand.

Among the Cherokee no one would be upset if a man was a day or two late for a meeting. Tardiness was expected. How different Americans are, Ben thought. How we put ourselves under pressure. That couldn't be healthy. He smiled as he felt for his expensive gold pocket watch on his new gold chain and laughed at himself as he rose to meet Elizabeth.

They met at the top of the three wide steps to the private dining room. She gave Ben a bright smile and extended her hand. Ben escorted her back to their cozy spot by the fire. He noticed her eyes never left his face and she walked as close to him as possible. He had never met a woman like this. He loved the way she looked up at him. It made him feel important. He couldn't describe the strong emotions Elizabeth evoked in him. Ben found it impossible to believe Elizabeth's interest was a charade as Zach had warned. Whatever the truth, he couldn't stop the tingling sensation that crawled over his entire body when he was close to her. He was never more alive than when she was near.

Their regular servant, the tall, slender, well-trained negro, politely asked their pleasure in perfect English. If Ben had closed his eyes, he would have never known by his speech the servant was African. There was no accent and no indication he was illiterate. On one occasion Ben thought he had detected a bit of a French accent and had overheard him speak fluent Spanish to a visitor earlier in the year. He wondered where Zach's father had found this 'boy' who moved soundlessly, spoke multiple languages and waited on them with impeccable manners. Ben noticed one of the African's incisors was missing and a neat pie shaped notch was cut from the top of his right ear. Ben had learned those disfigurements were put there by previous slave owners to easily identify a runaway. He mustn't think about such things. He must concentrate on the beautiful woman in front of him and give her his full attention. Ben's mind deferred to Elizabeth.

"What would you like to drink, my dear? Our usual?"

"Oh no," she responded. "Don't you think we should have something special? I think a nice glass of white wine would be in order, don't you, Ben? When we were in Bordeaux last year I enjoyed their lovely Chardonnay, but perhaps a German Riesling would be nice? What do you think? And when we've finished here with our business, we might take a little ride into the country if it's not too cool, and later we could have a romantic dinner at the hotel. Do you know how to be romantic, Ben? I think you do and we have so much to talk about. I can't wait to hear everything you have to say."

With that speech, Elizabeth squeezed Ben's arm. He couldn't help blushing like a schoolboy. She laughed easily at his shyness. Ben loved her soft, musical voice and the way she teased him. He understood she was flirting, and flirting was exactly what he wanted, what he needed. He craved the feminine attention she was giving.

Ben ordered two glasses of their best German Riesling.

"Zach left for Savannah early this morning," Elizabeth said. "He sends his apologizes for his absence today. He'll be gone the rest of the week and maybe next. He thought you and I should talk about our plans and continue to get to know one another. I think that's a good idea. We do have a lot to talk about. I'm one of those people who must know everything about a person I'm interested in. How can I ever help you if I don't know everything about you?"

Her eyes sparkled as she spoke. Ben gulped. He knew he appeared clumsy to the refined Elizabeth who seemed to be in full control of every situation. She and Zach were never ruffled. He envied that. He wanted confidence. All too often he felt his emotions uncontrolled, easily read by others. Elizabeth couldn't have more poise if she were a veteran actress on the stage of a crowded theatre. Zach and Elizabeth were never frustrated, never irritated. He liked people with self-assurance. He wanted to develop that same discipline. His rustic upbringing in Cherokee Country led to his shyness in the unfamiliar social circles of Milledgeville. He hated the idea of appearing socially awkward. He was embarrassed by every faux pas and the smiles they raised among Milledgeville's upper class who noticed his every lapse of etiquette.

The silent, white-gloved waiter brought the polished silver tray with their wine in the sparkling crystal glasses.

Elizabeth raised her glass, "To the success of my friend Ben and his certain election."

They drank the toast. Her eyes never left his. He knew she was studying him, looking inside his mind. He knew his body language made him an open book. His mother had told him he was a bad liar. She was right. He had always been a failure at deception and, like most folks with a good heart, was far too trusting for his own good. He could never attribute dark motives to others. Growing up in a selfless home where he had been encouraged to express himself, Ben had never learned to conceal his emotions. Ben's upbringing made him trusting and gullible. His mother had counseled him he should tell the truth in any situation. The truth, his mother said, was always the most valuable currency.

Ben had little worldly experience. He had never been betrayed by a friend or acquaintance. It would never occur to Ben that Zach and Elizabeth could be pseudo friends. Ben's naïve mind couldn't believe anyone would pretend friendship and later discard that friend.

When he looked at Elizabeth he felt as if he were in the sunshine of the first day of summer and she was the sun. He wanted that feeling to continue. He felt his emotions stirring with pleasure, a pleasure he had only experienced with Cassie. He thought again of Zach's warning. Surely this beautiful woman sitting beside him was not as callous as Zach had portrayed. Surely some of her flirtations were genuine.

Elizabeth had long been a shrewd business woman in a man's world. She knew exactly what she was doing around men. She operated with a single goal in mind, personal enrichment. Zach understood Elizabeth completely. They were two peas in a pod. He knew her for the clever business person she was and had no problem enjoying her friendship despite that knowledge.

As adolescents, Elizabeth and Zach learned relationships with the opposite sex were for sport, never to be taken seriously. Any love relationship, much less marriage, would be a mistake, detracting from and delaying their plans for acquiring financial security. Life was about using any means available to acquire wealth. Hedonistic pleasures were a perquisite, an occasional by-product. They considered permanent relationships and unconditional loyalty counterproductive, interfering with their long-term goals.

Ben was the opposite. His mother and father were unselfish, magnanimous. Their transparent generosity was the reason the Cherokee permitted Ben's parents to work in Cherokee Country. The council had complete confidence in Wilbur and Eleanor Lowry and trusted them with their children. Ben had seen his mother on more than one occasion give a hungry Indian, a complete stranger, the last morsel in their house.

Elizabeth was sitting as close to Ben as their upholstered chairs would allow. She smelled of Paris. Her bare arms and perfectly done hair were more than Ben could manage. His heart raced. He found himself forgetting to breathe normally and more than once caught himself staring.

The waiter refreshed their wine.

"Zach and I will help you get elected any way we can, Ben. How can I personally assist? Tell me what you and Zach have been planning."

Ben didn't know what to say and only managed to stutter.

"I don't really know, Elizabeth. I'm an absolute novice. Other than talking to my clients about my candidacy, I don't know what to do or what to say. What do you suggest? You and Zach have plenty of ideas. You've done this before. Surely Zach has told you what he's been doing."

Elizabeth leaned her shoulder against his as if to warm herself and continued in a low, controlled voice, "Ben, I know important people. I'll convince them you're the person to assist their business. That's what I'm going to do. I'll tell them you'll help them make money. That's it in a nutshell. Quid pro quo. They help us and we help them. People want to get ahead and we'll help them do that, you'll help them when you're elected. You're the perfect man to be in politics. I trusted you the moment I met you and I must confess my heart fluttered a bit. You're handsome. Oh my, yes, very handsome. First impressions are important in politics, perhaps the most important thing. You should appear handsome to the women, innocuous to their husbands and wise to everyone, a confident man who can get things done for his friends. Zach and I hired you because of your trustworthy appearance. You have a rare gift, Ben. Your innate intelligence and education are obvious at first glance. You have an honest face. The fact that you're an uncomplicated country boy is in your favor. When someone talks to you, they're immediately struck by your command of language which communicates wisdom. You have a friendly manner that puts folks at ease. They like you. No one would ever dream you could be a liar."

Elizabeth, with her easy, girlish manner, touched his arm allowing her hand to linger a moment longer than proper.

"Oh my yes, Ben, I trusted you the first time I saw you and I have a lot of ideas how I can help you. I love your ambition. You have the assets a man needs. I do like your assets, all of them. Zach and I will insure your career all the way to a Senate appointment. You know that, don't you? Right now, Ben, you're the number one interest in my life. If you succeed, I will succeed. What could be better than that? I would dearly love my new best friend to be a Senator from Georgia. You can trust me to always tell you the truth."

She laughed as her blond curls bounced on her bare shoulders. Ben was defenseless. Elizabeth knew exactly what she was doing. Young men are so easy, she thought. Elizabeth wanted Ben to be successful and she wanted to guide that success. She wanted control, complete control of her own personal politician. If her plans worked, she would be incredibly enriched. If her schemes failed, she would move on to Ben's replacement. She always had a backup plan. She never kept all her eggs in one basket. Ben wasn't the only young man in Georgia interested in politics. He happened to be the one at the moment most likely to make a success of his political career, with her help, of course. Plus, he was amusing. He wasn't much of a romantic challenge, but there was the distinct possibility he would go far with her amorous coaching.

Elizabeth continued, "You'll be elected to the Georgia house this autumn. After a few years we'll skip the Georgia Senate and go up to the U.S. House. If we play our cards right, the U.S. Senate could be ours the first year you qualify. What do you think? Zach and I believe you're the man."

She laughed. Ben's mind raced through the ten years Elizabeth had just described, visualizing himself appointed by the Georgia legislature to the Senate. He would have his own desk in Washington City and Milledgeville. The business world would be lined up outside his door. That was exactly the kind of thing he had wanted when he became a lawyer, to have influence with lawmakers in order to have political influence on behalf of the Cherokee. He had never dreamed such personal success possible, not in so short a time. Elizabeth's dream was almost believable. Perhaps, with the help of Zach and Elizabeth, it might happen. He could help his father and the Cherokee.

"I suppose that might be a possibility," Ben replied. 'We'll do good things for our fellow Georgians and we'll have fun doing it. I'm like Zach. I had much rather do this than be a farmer."

"May I make a suggestion?" Elizabeth asked.

"Of course," Ben replied.

Ben didn't know it, but he would be doing everything Elizabeth would ever ask from this moment forward.

Elizabeth's voice took on a serious business tone.

"Our initial plan is simple. We target men in the upper levels of society who control large groups. Slaves, Indians and laborers count for nothing. We ignore them. They're meaningless. White women are important only as a secondary influence, but in general we ignore them, too. In addition to the traditional methods of influence, Zach and I sometimes reach men through their wives and daughters. I assure you, Zach knows how to gain the confidence of a woman, even an older woman. It's amazing how silly older women can become when a handsome young man like Zach pays them attention. He finds women of all ages a challenge, especially the more experienced. He loves the game and plays it well."

Elizabeth, with a cute pout as if she were confused and seriously wanted an answer, paused for a moment and looked into Ben's eyes as she lightly placed her hand innocently on his thigh as if unaware of her actions, "Do you like women, Ben? Do you like me? Do you find me attractive, desirable?"

Flustered and unable to speak at such an odd question coming out of the blue, Ben could only mutter in reply. All he could think of was Elizabeth's hand. The room had disappeared into a swirling mist of Elizabeth's creation. He had to use every ounce of his inner determination to speak intelligently. He didn't want to babble to this clever, beautiful woman.

He took a deep breath, "Yes, Elizabeth, I like women. I do. You know I do. I like you. I always have. I've never met anyone like you."

Elizabeth kept her white gloved hand on Ben's thigh for a few moments longer before she returned it to her lap.

Surely everyone in the hotel heard Ben's heart beating. Elizabeth understood healthy young men and what went on in their minds. To her, young men were a means to an end, never an end in themselves. She loved the game, but it wasn't a game she wanted to play at home. She despised clingy men. She would make any exchange with a man if it meant she could gain control of both him and his assets. A man without assets, no matter how attractive, was worthless. Ben, although he presently had little monetary worth, was a clear means to a lucrative end, a tool, like a powerful carriage horse whose only value was in its ability to take one to one's desired destination. Ben would deliver her into male halls of power, her horse in the big race.

It amused her to think of men as if training animals. She knew few women willing to do what she did, but few women had her ambitions, few would reap the rewards. She wanted financial security. Perhaps this handsome, naïve young man would help her achieve both. If not, she would move on.

"Well, Ben, that's exactly what we'll do. We'll make two lists, one of men on our side. We'll keep them hooked, but that list is easy. We won't lose a one. The critical list is the influential men who don't support you. I will concentrate on those. Zach will concentrate on their wives and daughters."

She laughed out loud.

Ben didn't know what to say and answered, "I'm not sure I'm up to that, Elizabeth. I really don't want to be deceptive. Do you think I can actually plan to influence folks I have never met?"

Ben had one glass of wine too many. He was finding it impossible to think about election strategy. All he could think about was this beautiful creature beside him. He wanted to hear her talk. He wanted to listen to the musical sound of her voice. He wanted her to surround him, to never leave his presence. How could one think when she was near?

Elizabeth laughed out loud and once again gave Ben's thigh another lingering touch as if to accent her point. She leaned against his shoulder.

"Ben, do you know how to be polite to a woman and pay her attention? Can you listen without appearing bored? That's all you do to gain influence over a woman. You have excellent social skills. Everyone likes you. I like you a lot, probably too much. Be yourself. Zach and I will coach you on the political issues. You thought you were going to talk to men all the time, didn't you? You have a lot to learn about politics, Ben. The people in power don't care what you believe. They don't care if you're honest. They want to know if you can help them when they need help, help them make and keep money. That's how you get elected."

Ben didn't know what to say in answer and muttered a reply.

"I'll do the best I can. I'll promise to help."

"Ben, if you learn to pay a woman attention, she'll think you're as cute as a puppy dog. She'll tell her husband to vote for you. Don't look away when she's talking. Never interrupt. Listen to her every word. Occasionally tell her how intelligent she is. If she asks a question, preface your answer with, 'that's a good question'. Never look at a clock. Tell her how impressed you are with her thinking. If someone interrupts, continue to listen to her. Give her your full attention until she's finished talking. When it's time to go, ask her permission to leave. If you do that, you'll be the only man in her life who does. Without trying, you might have unexpected pleasure along the way. That would be alright, wouldn't it? You like women, don't you?"

Elizabeth continued in a voice that Ben found hypnotic, mesmerizing, a voice that transported him to a place of unending pleasure.

"I can do that," Ben replied softly.

Elizabeth was smiling. She knew exactly what she was doing.

"Ben, there are women who would happily spend an afternoon with you and never let their husbands know. Remember, I have access to parlors. I hear things I wasn't meant to hear and I can read between the lines. I would make a good spy, don't you think? In politics, information is of greater value than money. Zach and I have quite a circle of helpers who gather information."

Ben finally collected his wits enough to answer.

"Elizabeth, you would make an excellent spy. Sometimes I wonder if you know what I'm thinking."

She smiled and nodded in agreement.

"I do the same with the men as you do with women. Men are easy, easier than women. I listen and laugh. I ask about their work. I praise their intelligence and business acumen. I tell them they're handsome. In a few minutes they're unable to escape, unwilling to escape. Men are easy."

Ben's head wasn't clear. He wanted Elizabeth to continue talking to him, to continue looking at him. He didn't care what she said or did, as long as she was near. The waiter filled their crystal glasses once again.

"Don't think ill of me," Elizabeth said. "I know how men think. I know when they don't think, if you know what I mean. I'm a business woman. You wouldn't hold it against me if I asked someone a favor at the most opportune moment as a matter of business, would you? You would do the same. I understand business. I have something men want and why wouldn't I use my most valuable asset? A smart girl can have her cake and eat it too, if you know what I mean. My power over men will not last. I need to make hay while the sun shines. The time to act is while we're young and healthy."

Ben looked at this beautiful woman who could be so marvelously candid, who wasn't afraid to broach any subject. He had never met a woman so straightforward. She was intelligent, cultured, finely dressed and the most ambitious woman he had ever met. She was at this moment the sole object of his desire. He wanted her no matter what the risk. This beautiful woman knew exactly what she wanted and wasn't afraid to strive for it. She appeared innocent yet she could drink bourbon and water and never flinch. He liked that about her. He knew she would help him get elected and achieve his career goals. He was certain of that now. He knew he could trust her to accomplish what she said she could do. He was in good hands with Elizabeth and Zach.

Ben knew exactly how a young man felt around an attractive young woman. Elizabeth's frank talk excited him. He was vulnerable, but he didn't care. He loved Elizabeth at his side and her hand on his thigh. All he cared about was that this moment of intense pleasure in Elizabeth's company would never end. He would gladly throw caution to the wind.

Elizabeth observed carefully. Young men were predictable. She loved to have fun occasionally. It was time she had some fun with this handsome young lawyer with his powerful hands and athletic physique. It was time to spring the trap, set the hook. It was time to put her plan into action if she wanted to go to Washington City on the arm of a successful politician.

Perhaps this handsome young man would become an ongoing interest. She didn't care. One never knew what untold adventures would come one's way on the morrow. She needed to consolidate gains and secure her future. What she was about to encourage in Ben would, of course, give her pleasure but she had chosen this young lawyer to be her ticket to the United States Senate. If he became a Senator, she would be on his arm, no other woman. She would see to that. It was time to act. This was a young man she could control. If Ben didn't get an appointment to the Senate, she would find a man who could. It was a wonderful thing when business and pleasure coincided, a wonderful thing indeed.

"Ben, I have permanently reserved a suite on the top floor for out-of-town clients and such. In the business of politics it's important to be prudent, don't you think? The staff associated with our suite were selected with care. They never remember what they have seen or heard."

Ben was speechless. He felt as if he would burst with desire.

She continued, "I decorated the suite myself. It has the best of everything. We have a private balcony with an exquisite view. I have some interesting French prints I brought back from Paris. If I remember correctly, you just had a birthday, didn't you? I think today is the day for your belated birthday gift. You'll love it. I brought it from Paris just for you."

Elizabeth extended her hand to the flushed young man.

In the sweetest of voices she said, "If you'll accompany me to our room, you can admire my handiwork. We'll have a look at those French prints and you can receive your gift. Shall we? We keep our room cozy. I ordered a nice fire just in case. I promise you'll be comfortable there, I promise."

She was standing close by the end of her speech. Ben's chest was on fire as she pressed against his coat, her manicured hands resting on his forearms, her head thrown back. She looked up into the young man's blue eyes.

Ben stammered, "Of course I don't have any appointments and I would love to see the suite. I'm sure it's lovely. It would be a pleasure."

They had a lot of work to do to get Ben a Senate appointment. She and Zach had long planned on having their own personal politician. Nothing could be more lucrative. Ben fit the bill. Maybe Ben was the man, maybe not. Time would tell.

As the two left the room, the white-gloved, greying African servant with the missing front tooth collected the empty crystal glasses. The young couple reminded him of a time long ago when an attractive young woman had looked at him as this woman was looking at her man. Tray in hand, he leaned against the mahogany mantlepiece and enjoyed the warmth of the fire for a moment as he let his mind wander to the days of his youth. His eyes followed the handsome white couple. With only eyes for one another, they walked up the wide, carpeted, circular staircase arm-in-arm to their private suite. As they mounted the stairs, she pulled her body tight against his and allowed her head to rest against his shoulder.

The wintery sun hung low in the southern sky, dimly lighting the frigid Georgia capital. With no promise of warmth, its dull rays flickered across the modern skyline. For a moment the weak shafts of sunlight reflected brightly off a balcony window of a third-floor suite in a sumptuous hotel. The sun set. Milledgeville descended into an icy, winter darkness.

Chapter XXVIII
1828 - The Phoenix
Chapter 28

10 January 1828 - Month of the Cold Moon -du no lv ta ni
　　Ben's birthday today. I wish he were here. Rained all day.

11 January 1828
> From the *Georgia Journal* – 7 January 1828 – page 3
> "...We now have six mails per week from Milledgeville to
> Augusta...a stage goes once a week from this place to
> Tallahassee. There is also a stage going once a week, from this
> place to Athens. The facilities of communication between the
> seat of government, and various parts of the state are thus
> rendered very great..."

9 February 1828 - Month of the Bony Moon Ka ga li
> From the *Georgia Journal* – 4 February 1828 – Page 2-3
> "House of Representatives, Mr. Lumpkin, from the
> committee on Indian Affairs...Cherokee Indians have organized
> an independent system of government with a view to a
> permanent location in the States...The committee has seen their
> constitution...no doubt can be entertained of their determination
> to locate permanently in their current abode. They declare...their
> present boundaries shall forever remain unalterably the same
> and that the sovereignty and jurisdiction of their Government
> shall extend over this country which they occupy...The
> committee are of the opinion that good faith and justice require
> of this Government promptly to discountenance the formation of
> such Government, so far as it may,...assume a permanent
> jurisdiction over the soil, or in any way alter the tenure that they
> have heretofore held their land; because an idea of this kind must
> prove fallacious and injurious to the best interests of the Indians
> themselves...the sooner they are assured this cannot be
> permitted, the better it will be for them; and they will the more
> readily ...join their brethren in the west...To arrest the idea of a
> permanent location of the Cherokee Indians within the limits of

the State of Georgia, the motive is peculiarly strong, arising from the compact with that state, whereby the United States are bound to extinguish the Indian title to the lands within it,…With a view to the fulfillment of this contract…your committee would earnestly recommend that a generous and liberal provision be made to accomplish that object, as the best course, which can be pursued by the United States, to prevent conflicts, which may disturb the harmony of our citizens, and prevent the degradation and ruin of the Indians."

21 February 1828 - Thursday
Wonderful news. We have our own Cherokee newspaper printed on our own press. Our dream is real. The first edition was printed today.

24 February 1828
The *Cherokee Phoenix* 21 February 1828 - page 1--first edition
"CONSTITUTION OF THE CHEROKEE NATION: Formed by a convention of delegates from the several Districts, at New Echota, July 1827. We, the Representatives of the people of the Cherokee Nation in Convention assembled, in order to establish justice, ensure tranquility, promote our common welfare, and secure to ourselves and our posterity the blessings of liberty; acknowledging with humility and gratitude the goodness of the sovereign Ruler of the Universe in offering us an opportunity so favorable to the design, and imploring his aid and direction in its accomplishment, do ordain and establish this constitution for the government of the Cherokee Nation.

Article One: Sec. 1. The boundaries of this nation embracing the lands solemnly guarantied and reserved forever to the Cherokee Nation by the Treaties concluded with the United States; are as follows and shall forever hereafter remain unalterably the same--to wit--…"

We are the first Indian nation to have a written language and newspaper. In 1821, our Nation adopted Sequoya's syllabary. We have eighty-six characters which represent syllables. What a magnificent accomplishment.

Mr. Boudinott, our editor was educated in Connecticut at a Congregationalist foreign mission school, Harriet and Elias married. She and I have become friends. I love their children.

28 February 1828
Grand news. I am allowed to assist the newspaper as an unpaid apprentice. Now that we have a national voice, surely the political landscape

will change. It will be possible for people all over the United States to understand what is happening to the Cherokee.

I sat with Harriet watching her children play. She told me about the prejudice she and Elias faced when they married.

"Cassie, Elias and I are so happy with the newspaper and I'm glad you're helping. I love New Echota. I wouldn't want to live anywhere else. Elias and I have a wonderful life here, but it wasn't so when we married. The Congregationalists in Connecticut felt it their Christian duty to educate the heathen, but they didn't consider a converted Cherokee man their equal. Even after their conversion to Christianity, the Christian faithful continued to refer to Cherokee men as savages. When I announced my engagement to Elias, most everyone in town was angry. I still don't understand."

"How can anyone understand that sort of thing," I said.

Harriet sat silently for a long while staring into the trees across her tidy front yard. I allowed her time to think. I knew her memories were traumatic. I have similar memories, memories I keep hidden.

"Americans believe the teachings of Christ are for Indians as long as the new converts are not included in white society," Harriet said. "To the Congregationalists, a non-white person cannot be allowed in. 'Love thy neighbor' in Connecticut means love your American neighbor. Do unto others as you would have them do unto you in Connecticut means do unto white people as you would have them do unto you. I experienced this firsthand. When I was a girl I was taught we should imitate Christ and treat all people with his unselfish love, but in Connecticut those words were meant for white ears. They believe the Great Commission, but they don't want the converted heathen to mix with their children. That's what I experienced first-hand."

Harriet continued, "I know what would have happened if the story of the good Samaritan had taken place in Connecticut. If the injured man lying beside the road had been Cherokee or African, the good folks of my congregation would have walked by, just like the priest and Levite."

Harriet continued in a pensive voice.

"Cassie, I'm glad to be away from that bigotry. When I announced Elias and I were to be married, I saw what they believed written on their faces. I've chosen to forgive and let what dwells in their hearts be their problem. They'll have to stand that last day and answer for their actions before the righteous judge of all men. Their judgment has nothing to do with me. I can trust Him not to make a mistake. His judgment will be just. I choose not to keep a record of wrongs. I pray for them every day."

"Harriet," I said, "what happened in Connecticut I've seen here. Americans maintain strict racial purity. I believe that's the reason for our removal. They don't want their children playing with our children. They don't want our men to marry their daughters. I'm thankful Mr. and Mrs. Lowry are satisfied in their hearts to allow a Cherokee woman to marry their son. They love me as if they were my own mother and father. Somehow, they learned not to see people as white, Cherokee or African. They see everyone as equally in need of acceptance. If the Americans remove us, nothing will change. We will be forgotten and Cherokee Country will become white, totally American. Their exclusive society will continue, an all-white privileged society.

"Cassie, I'm so happy for you. You are fortunate to have Ben's parents in your life. I wish my family had been like them. I'm happy here with Elias. We have friends and the children are happy. I would never go back north. Elias and I were even shamed in the newspaper."

"What?" I exclaimed. "They wrote about you in the newspaper?"

"Oh yes, Cassie. When we announced our engagement my friends in the choir wore black armbands. They believed my decision to marry Elias to be a mortal sin. To them my marriage to a Cherokee was the same as renouncing Christ. That was a bad time in my life. I'm glad that's behind me."

Harriet stared into my face with her hand on my arm.

"My own brother, Stephen, burned me and Elias in effigy on the village green in front of a crowd. Even the missionary society responsible for Elias' conversion opposed us. They were embarrassed, I suppose, and needed to defend themselves before their peers."

As we talked Harriet's children played peacefully before us. I was glad they would not be reared in such an ugly environment.

"Because of my engagement to Elias, they closed the mission school. They decided to fulfill the great commission in distant lands only. I can still quote the newspaper article from memory.

> "The foreign mission school proclaims our unequivocal disapprobation of such connections...and the conduct of those who have been engaged in or accessory to this transaction, as criminal; as offering an insult to the known feelings of the Christian community."

"Christian leaders promised the Cherokee the privileges of a civilized life. The cultural success of America was given as the example of what happens when people become Christians. Elias accepted Christ, spoke perfect English and became a scholar. It wasn't enough. When he fell in love with an American girl he was threatened with death. Cassie, I'll be buried here in Cherokee Country where I'm accepted. This is home. Here no one judges my children's worth based on skin color and facial features."

"You're welcome here," I told her. "I'm glad you're here, Harriet."

"New Echota is my home, Cassie. I have chosen higher things. I'm afraid what's happening to the Cherokee is history repeating itself. A year before Elias and I married, Major Ridge and Sarah Northrop married. They, too, had a terrible time with friends and relatives. They were written about in the newspaper like we were by a man named Isaiah Bunce. He wrote, 'The girl ought to be publicly whipped, the Indian hung, and the mother drowned'. I find human behavior astonishing sometimes, don't you, Cassie? It seems to me if a Christian chooses to be unforgiving, that person has chosen to say Jesus' sacrifice for all humanity was ill-advised. I choose to forgive. I will not return evil for evil. That gives me peace."

Harriet and I agreed with one another that, after this day, we would never talk about these things ever again. We have chosen to forgive and to never harbor grudges against anyone.

3 March 1828

I love printing and newspapers. I'm overjoyed to be an apprentice exercising my talents. It is a joy to write in multiple languages and translate. Proofing galleys is a pleasure I can't explain.

12 March 1828

I celebrated our first issue of the *Cherokee Phoenix* with Mr. and Mrs. Lowry.

"Wilbur and I have been here going on ten years and we've seen marvelous improvements. We are so proud of you and your people and your newspaper, Cassie," Mrs. Lowry said with a smile.

"Thank you. The newspaper will strengthen our nation."

Mrs. Lowry frowned.

"From what I'm reading, Milledgeville views Cherokee political organization as a threat. It's my guess the American government will continue to be the enemy. Americans do not want a co-existing civilization for any Indian nation, especially the Cherokee. I'm pessimistic, but perhaps the Phoenix can change enough public opinion. I hope so."

20 March 1828

From the *Cherokee Phoenix* – Page 3

"...a motion was made in the House of Representatives, by Mr. Wilde, a member from Georgia, to take measures to ascertain, what white persons have assisted the Cherokees in forming the late constitution...It has been customary of late to charge the missionaries with the crime of assisting the Indians, and unbecomingly interfering in political affairs...Our object...was to correct the mistake, under which some may labor, and to declare once for all, that no white man has had anything to do in framing our constitution and all the public acts of the nation...We hope this practice of imputing the acts of Indians to white men will be done away."

Chapter XXIX
1828 – Ben and Zach Make Plans
Chapter 29

28 May 1828 – Month of the Planting Moon – A na a gv ti

From the *Georgia Journal* – Page 4

Mr. Woods - Indian Immigration

"...I will now Mr. Chairman, examine into the situation of the country which the Indians now possess within the limits of the several States; and into the advantages which they enjoy in their present homes. The Indian lands lying within our borders is that portion of their original possessions which they have never sold or transferred to us, or any other Government. We are told by one of our sovereign States..."It belongs to her and that she must and will have it: that we are bound, at all hazards, and without regard to terms to procure it."...Sir, the same argument may be urged, or rather the same language may be used by all the other States, within the limits of which there is any Indian territory. It was by virtue of the same sovereign right, that the Pope, in the name of St. Peter, gave to Spain all the countries which Columbus discovered. It is the right which power gives..."

June 1828 - Milledgeville

"Ben, I've arranged an event and your attendance is required. This is late notice, but you must be there. The host is one of Father's important clients, a personal friend of Jackson and our largest local landowner."

Zach slapped Ben's tired back.

"Besides, my friend, Elizabeth would be terribly disappointed if you didn't come. She's looking forward to seeing you this evening."

"Zach, where do you get your energy? I've worked late every night this week doing my work and half of yours. I don't know if the thought of seeing Elizabeth is enough to give me strength. I want to flop across my bed and sleep for two days. I'm exhausted. Let's have a drink and a bite to eat. Perhaps I'll rejuvenate. I know I need to go if I want to win this election. I'm willing to do whatever it takes. As you say, time and tide wait for no man."

Ben and Zach walked the short distance to the hotel and went straight to their corner by the big fireplace.

Since his first meeting with Elizabeth, the good whiskey, Elizabeth's scent and the hotel had become intertwined. Ben loved everything about the hotel including the beautiful intriguing woman who had become such an important part of his life. After sitting down with his first drink, Ben was already feeling better.

"Our plan is simple," Zach instructed. "Everyone you'll meet tonight is wealthy and a potential supporter. Pay attention. Listen when people talk. Look them in the eye. At the appropriate time during every conversation, promise them that after you're elected they can come to you with their problems. Promise them they'll get what they need. Tell them all you want in return is their public support and their vote. Simple, isn't it? Quid pro quo."

Zach continued without allowing Ben time to respond.

"After every conversation ask permission to leave their presence. There's nothing as ingratiating as requesting a person's permission to leave their company. Elizabeth and I will provide you with special targets. We'll direct you to the most important men and women. Don't worry about anything. We'll tell you what to do. You'll be elected, Ben. It's a certainty. There's not a chance of your opponent winning if you follow our plan."

Ben was tired but Zach appeared tireless. Even during their comfortable carriage ride Zach continued coaching his protégé.

"Elizabeth and I will assist you all evening, so don't worry."

Ben changed the subject, "What will Elizabeth be doing?"

"Glad you asked, Ben. She's goin' to keep an eye on you. She's an expert at events like this. To tell the truth, she'll probably get you more votes than I will. She'll find the important men who have an eye for a pretty woman. When she's finished flirting they would vote for the devil himself if she asked."

Ben was thinking how true Zach's statement was. He had never seen a woman more desirable. She was perfect. Ben found it remarkable that she was interested in him, a plain country boy with no social skills.

"Elizabeth and I are also experts in discretion. We know how to get people's attention and also how to avoid it."

Ben looked sidelong at Zach and marveled at his openness, nonexistent morals and careless attitude.

"How did you two come up with this clandestine circle of 'friends' you can trust in dubious circumstances to supply you with information? You two are amazing," Ben said with admiration.

"We learned years ago how to tactfully manage our parents, Ben. I guess we learned to apply those principles to our business associates. Over the years we've put together a team, a group of individuals who work for us, slaves mostly, but there are others. We have folks workin' for us you wouldn't suspect, some highly placed in society. They earn extra money now and then just for keepin' their ears open. We're motivated, Ben. That's our secret. We're motivated like no one you've ever seen. We want to be rich. We want to be so rich we'll never have to work and we won't have to worry about anyone taking our wealth, not even the government. To tell the truth, we want to be the government."

Zach leaned back in the open carriage with his hands behind his head, legs crossed, boots resting on the seat opposite. He stared into the clear June sky recalling some of those successful moments.

"Ben, over the years we've put together a covert group of trusted employees, social detectives you might say. We pay for information that's useless to most folks. We turn information into money. We're generous with our employees. Money can buy anything. We reward those who work for us, but they know there's a penalty for betrayal. We've had to punish offenders, employees who couldn't keep their mouth shut. Word gets around. We choose our associates because they value money above everything. We get what we pay for. You can't skimp when buying prudence. I don't think you want me to tell you much more than that. I may not have completely satisfied your curiosity, but let's leave it there. The less you know about that side of our business, the better. All you need to know is everything we do is legal and above board. Who knows what you might say one night to the wrong person when you've had a little too much to drink. I've told you enough."

Ben didn't want to know more. He would let Zach and Elizabeth handle the murkier side of politics. That was their business. They were good at it and, as long as it was legal, that was all he cared about. He was responsible for himself, no one else. Zach's father paid him each month and he earned every penny. He was honest. He wouldn't worry about the morality of others. That was none of his business.

Their carriage rolled up the long, perfectly smooth, gravel drive lined with mature oaks and arrived at the entrance to the magnificent, white columned, plantation house with its broad, white marble steps. This was a splendid house with extensive gardens manicured to perfection. They were met by perfectly dressed servants who assisted them down and opened doors. Ben was always impressed when he visited a well-to-do home. There was a good life to be had in Georgia. He was pleased to be a part of it.

Inside they met Elizabeth. Ben's weariness melted. They were served their first drink. Rejuvenated by the alcohol and the excitement, Ben felt like he could go till midnight. Maybe Zach's company was good for him.

It was a well-attended event during which Zach and Elizabeth planned to showcase Ben. Because the plantation owner was a client, Zach had been allowed to add important names to the invitation list. The election was still months away, but there was no time to lose, Zach said. Nothing should be left to chance. This event, and events like it, were stepping stones to Ben's election and the success of Zach's father's firm.

Elizabeth assumed her charming professional self. Ben thought her even more irresistible than the last time they met, if that was possible. As they conversed, sipped champagne and assessed the crowd, Elizabeth moved close to encourage Ben.

"Men are predictable. From across the room I can tell what they're thinking. It doesn't require a special skill to read their mind, if one has the right assets."

She laughed out loud and tossed her hair in a most disarming manner.

"If I want to influence a man, I get him to notice me and then I play hard to get for a while. I make it appear as if I'm gradually becoming more interested. It works every time. First thing you know, he's following me around the room like a puppy dog. Once he begins following, I capture him with an easy laugh, a warm smile, a toss of my head and then finally I let him look into my eyes. I touch his arm, move in closer and the trap snaps shut. It happens every time, without fail."

She moved in close to Ben, stood on her tip-toes and whispered into his ear, "It's easier than shootin' fish in a barrel."

Elizabeth laughed and smiled.

Ben loved her infectious laugh, easy smile and sparkling eyes, eyes that invited him in. He loved the way she made him feel. He had never felt that way around any woman except Cassie, but Cassie was a long way from Milledgeville and Cassie never wore clothing or perfume to match Elizabeth. Cassie would never fit into this kind of society.

Elizabeth was right about her assessment of men and their desires. That's exactly how she had captured him months ago. Ben had become aware of a permanent, uncomfortable ache in his chest, an ache only relieved by Elizabeth's physical presence. He was thinking about her more and more every day, thinking of ways to relieve the ache.

"I do the same as Elizabeth," Zach said, with a casual wave of his hand, "except in reverse. I get information from Elizabeth and her scouts who are privy to the private conversations and gossip of women. She tells me who will be vulnerable to my influence. I have to tell you, Ben, this job can be pleasurable at times. I love mixing business with pleasure. Elizabeth and I knew as soon as we met you we could take you far in politics. You have what it takes and your popularity is growing. It's our goal to take care of you, for our mutual benefit, of course. You're safe with us. You can trust us, Ben, but like the old proverb, 'don't look a gift horse in the mouth.' "

Zach and Elizabeth laughed and Ben joined them. He couldn't imagine two better friends. The trio separated and began to promote Ben's cause among Georgia's wealthy and influential. Ben knew he needed to mingle with the guests but it seemed he couldn't take his eyes off Elizabeth. He didn't want to talk to the important men and women. He wanted to talk to Elizabeth.

Zach gave Elizabeth the names of men to 'work on'. Elizabeth and Zach circulated, listened and promoted Ben. They wouldn't close every deal this evening, but they would lay the groundwork for more meetings later in the year. It was amazing how easy it was to gain influence with a little personal information and bold promises. Zach and Elizabeth had a file on every person of importance in Georgia and some beyond, especially in Washington City. They knew their favorite wine, if they liked to hunt or fish, if they were inclined to drink too much, if they gambled on horse races or cards and if they were happy at home. They gathered household gossip from slave staff. They knew if important men were neglecting their wives, which might be information of greater worth. Zach and Elizabeth's extensive network of scouts, men and women, both white and negro, gave them an insurmountable lead on Ben's competition.

Elizabeth's ultimate goal was to go to Washington City as a Senator's wife, to walk the halls of power. She and Zach had chosen Ben believing he might be the man. She knew she could bend him. He was putty in her hands as were other up-and-coming young men in the Georgia political arena. Elizabeth wasn't one to put all her eggs in one basket. Ben's career wasn't the only one Elizabeth was watching and promoting. The first man to win the Senate appointment was the man Elizabeth would assist. Time would tell which man would receive, at least temporarily, the grand prize.

As Elizabeth strolled the beautiful home and gardens, she marveled at the dullness of other's lives. She felt pity for those whose days were filled with the tedium of a home and childrearing. It would never occur to Elizabeth that loving a man and raising children could fill a home, and thus a woman's life, with happiness. To Elizabeth, taking care of a husband and keeping a home was a prison sentence. She was interested in that which gave broad financial advantage and thus ultimate freedom.

As Ben made ready for his bed after a tiring evening, he smiled at the memories. The social had been a great success and so would be the election. He knew he could trust Zach and Elizabeth. Ben fell asleep the moment his head touched the pillow.

Ben looked forward to the Tuesday planning sessions. Tuesday and its marvelous afternoon with Elizabeth and Zach had become the highlight of his week. Occasionally Zach would be away on business. Ben was never suspicious. It would never occur to Ben that anyone, especially Zach and Elizabeth, would actually make plans to take advantage of him.

When Zach was absent, Elizabeth and Ben would discuss upcoming events, the important men and women yet to be 'persuaded' and how they could 'gift' them into their camp.

"The most important single principle in politics is this," Elizabeth instructed, "a gift obligates. If you give someone a nice gift, it's their natural response to feel obligated. They want to give in return. This isn't a mystery,

177

is it? If you want to receive, you must give. That's in the Bible, isn't it, Ben, 'Give and you shall receive'? It's true in the Bible and it's the first principle of politics. After all, politicians are human, well, most of them anyway."

Elizabeth laughed, a loud carefree laugh. Elizabeth allowed her hand to innocently touch Ben's chest and move down his shirt.

"Give and you shall receive, Ben. Give and you shall receive. You do know the importance of giving when necessary, don't you?"

Ben quivered uncontrollably. He knew exactly what she was doing but was powerless to quell his response.

Elizabeth smiled.

"When one person gives the other cannot help but return the favor. You know that very well as a lawyer, don't you? It's called quid pro quo, isn't it?"

Her finger touched the outside of his trouser leg by his knee and lingered. The spot burned as if on fire.

"You see how giving works? I give to you, you automatically want to give back. You can't help it. One day, Ben Lowry, I will think of something quite special I want. It will be my turn to receive. I'll expect you to give. I give to you. You give to me. We'll have a good time, Ben, you and I. I give to you and you give to me in an ever-widening benevolent circle. I do love to give. We'll have fun, Ben. Oh my, yes. This could last a very long time."

Elizabeth threw her head back and laughed. He would give her gifts. He wanted to give her gifts. He wanted to give her everything at that moment. He couldn't wait to give to her. He didn't realize it yet, but he would give her anything, including his future. Ben trembled.

She was right. The things Zach and Elizabeth had done for him made him feel obligated. Although they had never asked for anything in return, he knew if they did ask, he would give without hesitation.

Tuesdays often found them sharing a bottle of wine and a romantic meal after their meeting. Ben's letters to Cassie were becoming less frequent. He never wrote Cassie or his parents on a Tuesday.

Elizabeth and Zach were on the same page. Zach knew Elizabeth didn't love Ben. She would love only herself. Ben was a tool. People were expendable chess pieces. Moving them about life's complicated board provided amusement. Elizabeth thrived on the complexities and risks of life the way some enjoyed puzzles. Her relationship with Zach, Ben and a dozen other men was one of treading near the edge. Ben was a passing challenge, a simple means to an end with an occasional bonus. Elizabeth's relationship with any man was a means to an end with the physical satisfaction of pleasure on demand, no strings attached. Those were her rules, an inviolate principle from which she had never varied.

Chapter XXX

1828 – Ben Elected to Georgia House
Chapter 30

13 October 1828 - The Trading Moon - Nu da de qua

Ben made a surprise visit and brought gifts.

"Father, a gift for you, a box of books. They're not new, but they're the ones you wanted and a few I thought you would enjoy."

Ben handed his father Robert Southey's *Life of Wesley*.

"Thank you, son. I've been wanting this. The Wesleys have a strong influence on both Creek and Cherokee. Thank you."

"Mother, here's your gift."

His mother could only stare at the new blue tailored dress and bonnet with matching handbag and scarf.

"Ben, I don't know what to say. I'm not used to gifts like these. This dress will cost you dearly, I'm afraid. Now you must take me to Savannah. Where could I wear this around here? I think a trip is in order."

She laughed and everyone joined. It was a wonderful moment.

"You, dear Mother, are worth it. I'll take you, Father and Cassie to Savannah, London and Paris, if you want to go."

Ben handed me my gift, two silver bracelets with a clever geometric design.

"But that's not all I have for you, Cassie. I have another gift."

Ben handed me a copy of Grimms' Fairy Tales translated by Edward Taylor. I was thrilled. I would much prefer a book over clothing or trinkets.

"Nothing is too good for you, Cassie," Ben said.

"Ben, you are the most thoughtful man in the world. You couldn't have given better gifts."

Later, Ben and I talked about everything, his job, Zach and Elizabeth, his political aspirations, the Cherokee and our desire to stay in our homeland. We had a perfectly lovely afternoon.

"Ben, what thoughtful gifts. Up here we have a different view of life than folks in Milledgeville. I love the bracelets and the book. At this moment I understand the American's desire to always have more."

"Cassie, I've thought a great deal about things since I went to Milledgeville. You're right. White folks do want more. The Cherokee are

179

satisfied. The growing American economy is putting pressure on the Cherokee. Georgia wants more land, specifically Cherokee land."

"I know, Ben. Squatters are everywhere."

"Business is booming on the whiteside, Cassie. Cotton is king. The price of everything is going up, land, commodities, slaves. You should see Milledgeville during harvest. The cotton gins run night and day. Cotton bales line the streets waiting shipment downriver to Savannah."

"I've seen what the squatters do, Ben," I answered. "They take our land, cut everything that grows and shoot everything that moves. Wherever the Americans go, they clear the land, burn everything and kill all the animals."

"I know, Cassie," Ben answered. "That's the problem. Everyone believes Indian land is for the taking. Every town in Georgia is growing. Milledgeville has been transformed from a frontier town into a cultural center, the envy of the South, a charming inland city with a busy social life. I'm enjoying my time there, but there's not a day goes by I don't wish you were there with me. I'm a country boy at heart, Cassie. I'm a fish out of water down there. Maybe one day folks' attitude towards the Indians will change and you'll be welcome. I miss you every day we're apart."

I was happy listening to Ben as we strolled along the worn paths around his parents' home. As we sat on a large lichen covered rock in the autumn sunshine we held one another silently for a long time. Ben's words didn't give me a lot of hope for the future of our country.

"Cassie, I remember the first day I saw you. You were a timid little girl who hardly spoke a word, but I could tell from your eyes you were smart. I knew that first day we would become friends. We've had many wonderful days together, haven't we?"

"Our future together is all I think about these days, Ben."

We were silent for a long while.

"Cassie, we're not children in Father's schoolroom. Our childhood is past. We need to think about our adult lives. One day I would love to live with you in a big house with lots of children and servants. Would you like that?"

Before I could answer he continued. He was excited thinking about our future and the delights of city life. I loved his thinking, even if I wasn't welcome in American society.

"Cassie, in a few years after I've saved enough for us to set up housekeeping, we can move somewhere, maybe up north, or even go to the western territories with the Cherokee and other tribes. It would be a tough life out there, but we would be together. That's what I want one day after I've saved enough."

I heard Ben's words and thought about him and his job in Milledgeville. He was over-dressed for New Echota and had an expensive horse with all new tack.

"Ben, there will be legal work out west. The Choctaw, Chickasaw and others are being removed. A good lawyer who understands Indians could find work. We wouldn't be rich but we would be happy. We would have a nice home, a little farm with horses, hogs, chickens and a couple of Jerseys. We could train our children and have a school. Maybe we could have a newspaper. We could read every evening and have a houseful of books."

I didn't say more. We have plenty of time to save for our life together in a place where our children will be respected. I must be patient.

Ben and I talked, walking the paths near his parents' home.

14 October 1828

Ben left at dawn. I couldn't contain my sadness. I cried.

30 October 1828

John Ross is the new chief. Everyone wishes him well. Today is Ben's election day. Zach thinks Ben and General Jackson will be elected.

1 November 1828

Ben is busy. His visits are less frequent. I understand. Who would want to travel that distance in a jarring, jerky, dirty old stagecoach.

4 November 1828

If Ben is elected, he wants to buy a house in Milledgeville for his parents. His father could have a successful school there.

Milledgeville - November 1828

Ben would probably one day marry Cassie but it wasn't the right time to marry. That was well into the future. For the time being he must consider his career. Zach had cautioned him to allow plenty of time for the sowing of wild oats before any serious commitments.

After he had acquired adequate wealth, he could find a place to work where a mixed couple could live in peace, maybe in the west. There wouldn't be much of a living in the territories and life would be hard, but at least his children would be treated normally. Ben had been reared by good parents who loved the Cherokee culture. He appreciated how, for the most part, the Cherokee accepted Africans as equals with no silly measurement of physiognomy or skin tone as a gauge of human worth.

Ben had work to do. He had his career to think about. Marriage and Cassie must wait, perhaps for a long time. Elizabeth could help him wait, he reasoned. His mood always brightened when he thought of her. He wished he could see her more often. He could easily imagine Elizabeth sitting in a rocker beside the fire holding their baby, a baby who would be accepted throughout

American society, have every advantage, a child with a grand future. It made a lot more sense to marry a woman like Elizabeth.

Zach and Elizabeth were teaching Ben about life, how to get ahead. A person without money is useless. Well, at least that's how Zach and Elizabeth had instructed Ben. Cassie could in no way further his career, therefore, according to Zach and Elizabeth, she was meaningless.

Ben was feeling a need for Elizabeth's companionship more frequently than their regular Tuesday afternoon. Maybe he could arrange a relaxing business trip to Savannah with her. That would be fun. There were clients they could see. If the stars aligned, one day he and Elizabeth might be a couple. He remembered Zach's warnings about Elizabeth, about her selfishness, but then people could change. People did change. Perhaps Zach was wrong. Ben's time with Elizabeth was always sheer pleasure. He would love to see her several times a week or even every evening, instead of just Tuesday. Perhaps one day she would feel that way about him? Surely, under the right conditions, he could win Elizabeth's heart.

Perhaps Zach was right and a future with Elizabeth was a pipe dream, but he couldn't get her out of his mind. He decided he should go to his room and write his parents and maybe send Cassie a nice letter, too. Yes, he would write Cassie and clear his mind.

6 November 1828

Huff's Boarding House – Milledgeville - 3 November 1828

My Dear Sweet Cassie,

Great news. The votes are counted. I am elected. I'll be the youngest member of the Georgia House. I wish you could come to the ceremony. I know you're as happy about my election as I am. I can't wait to work on behalf of you and your nation.

Zach and his father are hosting a victory celebration tomorrow evening. I wish you could share my success.

It appears General Jackson was elected to the presidency in a landslide. That's a disappointment but we can hope for the best.

With my election our plans are coming together. In four years, when I'm twenty-five, I'll stand for the U.S. House. In 1838, when I'm thirty, I'll seek a Senate appointment where real power resides. That's when I can achieve something substantial for your people. There is much we can do between now and then. If nothing else I can help the Cherokee know what sinister goings on are hatched in the backrooms of Milledgeville.

I'll visit soon. I miss you terribly. As the French say, 'you are missing from me'. I shall be holding you in my arms a few days after you receive this letter.

Always yours, Ben, xoxo

Milledgeville – November 1828

"We're proud of you, Ben," Zach's Father said.

"You've represented us well. Your election was quite an accomplishment for my firm. My bottom line will be blacker this year, significantly blacker. I promise this won't be the last time I go out of my way to take care of you, young man. Keep doing what you've been doing and I'll see you rewarded, handsomely rewarded, I say. I take care of my people."

"Thank you, sir. I appreciate everything you've done. I pledge to do my best for you and our supporters. I want you to know, sir, your hospitality is superb. This must be the most elegant hotel in the South."

With whiskey fueled enthusiasm, Zach's father slapped Ben on the back.

"From the moment I met you, Ben, I knew you were the man we needed. Folks like your country boy manner. I don't have to tell you my son Zach has blossomed since you came on board. He's enjoying his work once again. You two are good for one another. I have you to thank. Keep up the good work."

"I shall do the best I can, sir," Ben answered.

"Now that you're in the legislature," Mr. Mitchell said, beginning to slur his words, "remember who put you there. Quid pro quo, Ben. Every one of our clients will know I have my own man in the legislature."

Ben replied with a quiet thank you. Zach's tipsy father paid no attention.

"Ben, put these Cubans in your pocket. Don't tell our Virginia friends. If anyone asks, tell them they're pure Virginia leaf. If you like 'em I'll give you a box. I think Cubans are superior to anything that comes from Virginia. I been smokin' 'em since '17 when they lifted the ban."

Ben was listening. He had learned to pay attention no matter how uninteresting the conversation.

"I've got to mingle now, son," Zach's father said. "Remember how much we appreciate your work. When you take your seat, remember who put you there. We've great plans for you goin' forward, young man. Get busy. Do your work tonight. Two hundred of Milledgeville's finest are here. They all need a pat on the back from you. Every wife here wants you to speak to her. I know you're tired, but I want our firm to represent every one of them when they need us. This is your night, Ben. You're the celebrity. Circulate, young man, circulate. After tonight, take a few days off. In fact, I order you to take a few days and recuperate. You've earned it."

"Yes sir," replied Ben.

"Well, we did it, didn't we?"

Ben turned.

Behind him, arm in arm, stood Elizabeth and Zach sporting big smiles and sipping imported champagne.

"I was wondering when you two would get here," Ben said with relief. "I was beginning to feel lonely. I owe this night to you two, but I'm not sure I would have gone into politics if I had known how hard this is. Running for public office is harder than farming."

"Well," Zach said, laughing and giving Ben another slap on the back, "that's politics, isn't it? You'll get used to it. Get busy, Ben. Tell everyone to come to you when they need anything. Tonight it's all work for you. Your election is money in the bank. You have to make promises to any and all if you want the money to keep rolling in."

Elizabeth leaned up towards Ben's ear and slipped her arm through his. Standing tip-toe she whispered, "Without a doubt, Ben Lowry, you're the most handsome man here. We'll have a good time later. My poor heart skips a beat every time I see your handsome face."

She pressed her body tightly against Ben and gave him a lingering kiss on the cheek. Then, with her lips touching his ear, she whispered once again.

"I'll see you later upstairs. I'll be waiting. Hurry."

She leaned away, hooked her arm back around Zach's and said louder with a dreamy voice and a playful smile, "Ben, I'm smitten. When I'm around you I'm as giddy as a schoolgirl. You're irresistible. You've become the most eligible bachelor in Georgia, but don't forget me in the midst of your electoral success. I'm your greatest admirer. I can't think of anywhere I had rather be than on your arm. I'll be the most jealous woman in Georgia if I see you with another woman tonight."

"Bethy," Zach chuckled, "he's going to be popular with the ladies, maybe even more popular than I am, and that's sayin' somethin'."

Elizabeth, standing between the two young men, held on to both men's arms and all three laughed.

Elizabeth continued in her most seductive voice, "Ben, I've a special gift I picked up for you in Paris in anticipation of your victory."

She gave Ben's arm a squeeze and kissed his cheek. Once more on tip-toes she whispered into his ear, "Don't keep me waitin' or some other handsome man may sweep me away in my disappointment. When you're finished, come on up. I'll have your surprise waiting."

They parted.

Ben immediately engaged his nearest supporter in conversation. As he went about his business, he thought of Elizabeth, their special room and the surprise gift. He was envious of Zach's effortless ability to call her Bethy. He wished he had the courage to call her by Zach's pet name, to whisper 'Bethy' into her ear when they were alone. Maybe tonight, after enough champagne, he would call her Bethy instead of Elizabeth. He couldn't wait. He couldn't wait until the day he could always call the beautiful Elizabeth his Bethy. He couldn't wait to receive his gift. He wondered what it could be.

9 November 1828

    My Dear Cassie,

Everyone is pleased with my election. We had a marvelous victory celebration at Mr. Mitchell's hotel. I wish you could have been there.

Now I can begin to do good things for your people. Everyone of importance has a home in Milledgeville. I wish you could be here. I promise to visit soon and tell you everything. I think I may have been born for a career in politics and law.

Good news for Georgia is not good news for your nation, however. The Cherokee population isn't growing in comparison. I don't know when this burgeoning influx of immigrants will end, but I promise to do everything I can to assist. Perhaps Ross and the others can stem the tide. I hope so.

I'm always yours, Ben, xoxo

Chapter XXXI
1828 - Cassie in the Forest
Chapter 31

13 November 1828 - The Trading Moon - Nu da de qua
   Ben came to celebrate his victory with us. He leaves before dawn.

16 November 1828
   Mr. Lowry wants me to write about the Cherokee interaction with the Americans. I want to forget everything about the whiteside except Ben and his parents.
   Two days ago I walked home alone from my work at the Phoenix.
   I wanted to surprise Elisi with a bag of hickory nuts. I know a nearby hidden valley with plenty of nuts just waiting to be gathered. Straying farther than intended, I walked alone down a long hollow on the opposite side of my community. I heard horses. Three mounted men rode into the hollow behind me. I recognized the militia uniforms. They are often seen around here searching for runaway Africans, but these men seemed to be following me. I hesitated, thinking the men might be lost. When I realized I was in jeopardy, I fled in panic. If I could get over the hill I might get within earshot of a Cherokee hunter. As I ran under a persimmon, my foot snagged on a saw briar and I went down hard, cutting my hands on the stones under the dry leaves.
   Before I could recover the men were upon me. As I sat defenseless, my back against the persimmon, the militia men stared down with expressions of amusement. As I tried to stand, the one closest, the red-headed man, dismounted, grabbed my arm and slammed me to the ground violently. His powerful fingers dug deep into my upper arm. I screamed. The man slapped my face several times in rapid succession. Blood from my mouth ran freely onto the leaves under my head. I fell back stunned, unable to resist.
   As I began to recover, I felt the man's powerful fingers digging into my arms. I cried out in pain.
   "You Indian bitch, shut up," the man growled. Don't be makin' so much racket."
   He slapped me harder than before. I felt my lower lip split against my teeth. The blood ran down my neck, dripping onto the brown leaves under my head.
   "She's a hellcat, ain't she, Clement?" the man on top of me said.

"We'll tame this one, so we will. She'll be a pussycat when we're finished, by god."

I struggled.

"There ain't no need to fight. We won't hurt you. We're goin' to have some fun. You don't mind if we have a little fun this afternoon? We're not goin' to hurt you, we promise. I been lookin' for somethin' like you since I come here and you're a good-lookin' thing for an Indian. You're prettier than the last one we did, ain't she, Clement? She ain't nearly so fat. This one's got teeth."

I continued to struggle but my attempts to free myself were useless. The powerful man held me even tighter. The stones bruised my back as he held me to the ground.

"You don't like to give it up easy, do you bitch?"

My struggles were hopeless. My eyes were closed.

"Be still, and shut up. For god's sake, shut up."

His sour breath was in my face. I heard his teeth grinding as he strained to keep me pinned under his heavy body. He slapped me again and shoved me downwards. The stones hurt my shoulders. I opened my eyes. My fear turned into anger. I struggled, twisting, turning and kicking the man in his back with my knees as he straddled my torso. My attempt to free myself further infuriated the man on top of me.

"She's a feisty one, John. All the better, don't you think? I want lively action, don't you, John? I like a saucy woman who makes noise and carries on, don't you? Are you going to make noise for us, bitch?"

"Make noise, bitch. Nobody can hear you out here."

The tall man called John dismounted. He stood beside me staring down as the red-headed man held me. I felt my lips beginning to swell. I spit into the red-headed man's face. As my spittle dripped from his beard he smiled as if I had given him pleasure. The pain in my back and arms was intense. I felt a rising nausea from the pain and the acrid odor of the man above me. I began to retch into the leaves beside my head. The earth around me smelled of decaying persimmons.

The red-headed man put his lips almost against my ear. His dirty red whiskers brushed my face.

He whispered, "You're gonna pay for spittin' on an American, you arrogant bitch. I don't mind you spittin'. I don't mind nothin' you do. Fight and spit. The more, the better. When I'm finished, you'll think twice about spittin' on a white man."

The red-headed man slapped me again. He held my hands together above my head with his left hand, with his right he began ripping at my clothing. I kept my eyes closed. I knew what he intended.

"Damn you, John, grab her arms. I can't do this by myself, you son of a bitch. If you don't help, I'll kick your ass all over these woods. I mean it. Hold her, John. Hold her arms, dammit," the man shouted at his tall companion standing next to him.

The man named John hesitated.

"I don't know, Liam. Maybe we should let her go. This won't stop them printin' that newspaper. I didn't sign up for nothin' like this. Let's go back and have another drink. I'm thirsty."

I had a glimmer of hope.

The red-headed man snapped at his companion, "God damn you, John. It ain't like we was doin' nothin' wrong. We're doin' what we've been told and havin' fun doin' it, that's all. This ain't no white woman. She works at that damn Indian newspaper. Indians don't need no newspaper. Next thing you know they'll be wantin' to be like us. It ain't right, is it? Indians ain't no different than animals, are they? She'll probably like it anyways, like a brood mare or a nigger woman. God damn it, John, get down here and help or I'll kick your worthless ass all over these woods."

The man named John did as he was told. He knelt at my head and held my wrists so the red-headed man straddling me could have his way with his hands free. I felt the warm afternoon sun shining through the leafless limbs shining directly onto my face. I kept my eyes closed.

"You're right, Liam," the man named John said. "I never thought about that. I couldn't do this to an American woman, Liam, but she ain't white. Indians ain't like us. She ain't no different than a nigger woman. You're right."

The man named John held my wrists. The tall man, Clement, held my ankles. I might have successfully escaped from one man, but I couldn't escape three. I wished for some way to make myself unconscious so I would have no memory. The reek of the man's breath and the stench of his unwashed clothing burned my nose.

"John, if she hadn't vomited, it would've been perfect. She looks better than most women I been with and she's got all her teeth. I don't like to do a woman with no teeth. We'll come back tomorrow for more."

He leaned down, his face almost touching my nose.

"What do you think about that? We'll be back lookin' for you. We know where you come from. Don't run next time and we won't slap you around so much. I wouldn't a hit you this time if you hadn't run. Don't make me mad. It ain't good to make me mad, an' don't spit on me. Don't make me mad. I'll hurt you if you make me mad."

"She's ready for you, Clement."

Before he rose, he lowered his face once again. This time his face and beard pressed hard against my cheek as he whispered.

"I like you, bitch. We'll be lookin' for you. Don't run next time and don't make me mad. I don't like it when folks make me mad. Stay away from that damned newspaper. I don't like newspapers."

The man named Clement who had been holding my legs spoke, "Liam, I can't let go till you hold her ankles. She's a hell cat. If I let go, she'll kick my teeth out."

Liam stood pulling up his trousers. He and the man named Clement exchanged places. I closed my eyes and turned my head again. I wish I had kept my eyes shut from the beginning. Every visual image of that day is burned indelibly into my memory. I cried softly to myself with my eyes closed. The sun continued to shine through the leafless trees and warm my face. I felt an ant crawl over my forehead. I was physically and emotionally exhausted. I imagined I could magically prevent what was happening by averting my mind and my eyes and somehow transport myself to another place. Perhaps I was experiencing an evil dream, some ghastly nightmare from which I would suddenly awake and the horror above me would dissipate like a morning mist. It was not a dream. It did not dissolve. I will remember.

When the men finished, I spoke in English.

"Why are you doing this? Please let me go. I want to go home."

"The bitch speaks English. Imagine that. We got us here an educated heathen. Where in the hell did you learn English?"

The Irishman standing over me began to shake with rage. He fell to his knees upon me trembling with anger, pinning my arms to the ground once again. His face contorted into an unrecognizable mask of exploding passion as he screamed obscenities, venting his anger in a spray of tobacco-laden spittle. As he held me down the sharp stones ground deeply into my back.

"You want to know why? We want to and we can. You're an Indian and we're Americans. That's why. We do what we want in Cherokee Country. We know the law. There ain't no law again' what we're doin'. We make the law here."

With every sentence his face got closer, his eyes wilder, his voice louder and his words more indistinct.

"We do anything we want to in this damn country. We'll take you and anything else we want. This is America. We're the law. Nobody cares what we do with you. You're nothing."

The red-headed man spat directly on my face from only a hand breadth. He slapped me once again as hard as he could. His breath was coming hard and fast as if he had been running. He sagged over me as if the voicing of his outrage had used all his energy. His head was jerking side to side, his eyes flitted left and right. He looked into the woods with a blank stare.

"Liam, Liam, Liam, Liam," the man named Clement shouted as he grabbed the back of the red-headed man's shirt and tugged him backwards.

"That's enough. Leave her alone. Quit shoutin' at her, Liam. We need to get out of here before somebody comes. Somebody might hear you. Get on your horse. We need to get out of here. Let's go, Liam."

189

The red-headed man stood and took the reins of his horse. Before he mounted he leaned over and spat into my face again. I began to whimper. I felt the splash of his spittle. I could feel it run down the side of my face and drip onto the dry, autumn leaves where it mixed with my blood.

"Come on, Liam. We need to get out of here now. Let's go. I don't like this. What if somebody hears? You been shoutin' loud. Let's go before somebody comes. I don't want nobody to see us. Let's go get another drink. I need a drink. I don't want no trouble."

The man named Liam mounted his horse. His face contorted, twisted with emotion. I felt the warm rays of the afternoon sun shining on my face.

"We didn't do nothing wrong," Liam muttered as he mounted. "It ain't like she was an American woman."

I closed my eyes as they rode away.

My back hurt. I pulled my knees to my chin and lay quietly on my side.

I slept.

When I awoke the woods were silent. For a few moments I didn't know where I was. I was lying partially exposed. I shivered as I lay in the leaves in the evening chill. Suddenly the entire wretched scene came back. I burst into hysterical sobbing. I pulled my knees to my chin once again and covered myself with dried leaves. Thankfully, I lost consciousness once again.

The second time I awoke it was completely dark. My mind was numb, as if I were a different person. I remembered everything, but it was as if the horror had happened to someone else or I had read the story in a work of fiction. I moved in slow motion as if my body belonged to another. I watched my dirty hands sluggishly tidy my blood-spattered clothing. As if to erase the violence, I cleaned my body with leaves. I turned for home.

I mindlessly stumbled towards the river. Gratefully, no one was about. I could not bear to be seen. I did not want to explain. My only thought was to wash—wash away the uncleanness, the brutality. I wanted to cleanse my mind and body before I went home. I must bathe.

Alone and fully dressed, I slipped into the cold water of the flowing river. I wanted the spirit of our river to cleanse my flesh, to cleanse my soul, to restore. The icy water made me shiver. I didn't care. I needed to wash, to be restored. I wanted to turn inside out and let our river wash my soul and return me to the uncontaminated person I had been that morning.

I soon recognized my bathing as a cruel mockery. The Americans had written blasphemies on my soul with indelible ink using a stylus fashioned in hell. As I stood in the cold, flowing river in the darkness, I understood I would never be cleansed of the obscenity that was forever trapped within. No amount of washing could cleanse the hidden crevices of my innermost being. As I felt the icy water flow around me, I realized I would bear my shame of my violation forever. I would never be free. Every day for the rest of my life the abuse of those men would haunt me until my last breath. I was consigned to a prison I could never leave.

I vowed to never tell anyone. I did not want Five Feathers to learn what happened. My brother would quickly get himself killed avenging my humiliation at the hands of the Americans. He would die and my tragedy would be doubled. I will not tell Ben, Edudu or Elisi. No one must learn of this horror.

My attackers deserve retribution in kind but it will never be. I will suffer alone and allow the Great Spirit to return my world to balance.

Chapter XXXII

1828-29 - Edudu's Puppy
Chapter 32

21 November 1828 - Month of the Trading Moon -nu da de qua
Copied from the - *Georgia Journal* – Page 2 – 6 November 1828

"...the solemn promise of the United States made in 1802 to remove at their expense the Indians from the territory of the State, is yet to be performed....The rulers of that Tribe, who have since the year 1818 systematically devoted themselves to defeat any attempt to purchase out their permitted occupation of our lands, have as a last resort adopted a Constitutional form of government...a Government professing to be independent, is set up in defiance of the authority of the States of Georgia, Tennessee, Alabama and North Carolina, upon the territory and within the jurisdiction of those States....this attempt will not make any change in the relation in which they stand to the United States....This state of things cannot be endured....Our duty to the people and to posterity requires that we should act. Of the right of the General Assembly to legislate over all persons and all things within our territorial limits, on general principles, a doubt cannot be entertained....Believing that our right is undoubted, that the exercise of our sovereign power is required by the best interests of the State....What disposition is to be made of the Cherokee?...for incorporation, with equality of rights as a part of our political family, they are unfit....I recommend to you to extend all the laws of the State over the territory lying within our limits occupied by the Cherokees...we should unite in fervent supplication to the Ruler of Man and Empires, that he will direct us in all our deliberations, inspire us with a portion of his divine wisdom, and make us the humble instruments of his will, in promoting peace and harmony among the people and in establishing on the most solid basis the prosperity of the State."

John Forsyth - Governor

24 December 1828 - The Snow Moon – V s gi ga

The moment Ben's feet touched the ground his mother embraced him and Ben's father, still holding the reins of Ben's horse, gave his son a hug to welcome him home.

Mrs. Lowry prepared a nice tea. Ben didn't stop smiling from the moment he arrived. Christmas is a happy time.

"Father, I know this is a special time but I have news and it's not good news. The legislature, just this week, passed a comprehensive law pretty much revoking all Cherokee law within Georgia's chartered boundaries. I have the full text. I'm sorry, Father. They despise the Cherokee constitution. They view it as an attempt to compete with their government, thus the Cherokee nation will not be allowed to stand."

"I understand," Ben's father said. "We were suspecting something like this. I appreciate you coming up to tell me, even when you bring bad news."

"There's more, Father," Ben said. "Just this week Georgia passed new laws covering the counties of DeKalb, Hall, Habersham, Gwinnet, Carroll and others. On the first day of June, Georgia law will take effect in all these counties and all laws and customs in force by the Cherokee will become null and void, as if they never existed. The new Georgia law says no Indian or descendant of Indian shall be deemed a competent witness or party to any suit in any Georgia court. I'm so sorry. Practically this means all American debts to Cherokees are cancelled. A Cherokee man will no longer be allowed to take an American to court for non-payment of debts. In addition, the law says any Georgia court can call up the local militia to force obedience to the new laws."

10 January 1829

Ben brought two cute puppies he found abandoned on his way from Milledgeville. He gave one to his parents' friend. We gave the other to Edudu. Edudu has been wanting another dog since Spinner died. I have not seen Edudu with such a bright smile in a long time. If I had known how much he wanted another dog, Ben and I would have gotten him one sooner. Edudu's new puppy has longish hair, two white front paws and two dark back paws. I understand why the puppy follows Edudu. If someone gave me bits of bacon all day, I would lick his fingers and follow, too.

11 January 1829

"What will you name your puppy, Edudu?

"I never name my puppies, Walela. When puppy learns his name, he will tell me. Until then, I wait."

"Edudu, dogs cannot talk. How can the dog tell you his name?".

"My dear Walela, sometimes I wonder about you. Perhaps your mother found you under a corn stalk or sleeping in the melons one morning. Perhaps you fell out of Mrs. Possum's pouch. Of course dogs can talk. Everyone knows that. Anyone can hear animals talk if they take the time to listen, especially if they understand Cherokee. Animals don't understand the Americans. All animals understand Cherokee. You must hold your mind just right to let their thoughts through. Spinner and I talked every day. Do you not remember?"

"I remember, Edudu."

"I would sit on the porch and whittle and listen to Spinner tell me about his day and what happened in the woods at night while we slept. When Spinner finished talking, I would tell him about my day, what I was going to whittle or tell him when we would go hunting next. Spinner was my best friend. He was talkative. He always had something intelligent to say. Sometimes he would ask me to tell him stories. He loved stories."

"Yes, Edudu, Spinner was an amazing dog. How did you name Spinner?"

"Walela, you're not listening. I didn't name Spinner. He named himself. When Spinner was a puppy he would see his tail out of the corner of his eye and the chase was on. Sometimes he would chase his tail until he fell exhausted. One day while lying breathless from chasing his tail he told me to call him Spinner."

"When our new puppy is ready, he will tell me his name. It's important to allow dogs time to learn who they are. This puppy doesn't know his name, but he will learn. Our new puppy is already thinking about what he wants to be called. We must be patient."

12 February 1829

This article from *The Southern* was reprinted in the *Phoenix*

Copied from the *Phoenix* - 11 February 1829 - page 1

"They are not citizens…They are not the owners of the land they occupy. They cannot be subject to the tax law, to the militia law, or to all the civil laws…the federal government can never induce them to relinquish their present possessions, and that the immediate use of coercive measures alone can possibly prevent the total extinction of the Cherokee, who are constantly pressed on all sides by a constantly increasing white population. We have a large black population, who consider the Indians very little better in point of independence to the whites and as the Indians associate more freely with the blacks…more freely than with the whites…the discontent and envy of the former will be greatly increased. They must be driven from the soil from which they have an inherent attachment, and driven at the point of the sword and bayonet; for they have no right or title to their present homes…The plan is one that might easily be carried into execution by a few divisions of the Georgia militia."

14 February 1829

As I came home this unusually warm winter afternoon, I found Edudu whittling centers for our pine baskets. Oak shavings covered the porch and the ground in front of the porch. His new puppy was curled up beside him watching me as I approached.

"Edudu, how are you and dog this lovely winter's afternoon?"

"You mustn't offend puppy by calling him dog. Call him by his name."

"When did you give him his name, Edudu?"

"Dear Walela, you don't listen well to be such an intelligent woman. I didn't name him. Dogs find their own names. He found his today. It is the grandest name for a dog I have ever heard, maybe in the whole Cherokee Nation. It was well chosen. He told me today his name is Eagle Killer. Isn't that a splendid name?"

Puppy sat up proudly as if he understood us. He barked three times.

"A pleasure to meet you, Eagle Killer. Did you choose your name today?"

He again barked three times affirming he did exactly as Edudu explained. Edudu and I laughed. Eagle Killer jumped up on Edudu's lap.

"Tell me how he found his name, Edudu."

"This morning, Walela, after you went to the newspaper, Puppy and I went to round up the hogs. I wanted to bring the piglets and shoats closer to the house. I carried my walking stick. I should have taken my gun. We surprised a passel of wild hogs in a clearing. An old boar with long yellow tushes and mean little pig eyes came charging straight for me. Before I could run, Puppy jumped between me and Old Boar. Puppy growled and stood his ground. The hair on puppy's neck was standing. Old Boar stopped when he saw Puppy and heard him growling. Puppy, even though he was much smaller than Old Boar, wasn't afraid of the big yellow tushes that could rip him open. Before I had time to think, puppy attacked. Puppy sank his needle-sharp teeth into Old Boar's back leg above the hock. Puppy held fast. I was proud of him. Old Boar spun, jumped and kicked, trying to free himself from the iron grip of the little dog's jaws. After much twisting and turning, Old Boar shook Puppy loose at last. Puppy sailed across the clearing. Old Boar had enough of Puppy's sharp teeth. The old pig retreated as fast as he could into the underbrush. Growling and barking, Puppy chased Old Boar fearlessly. Puppy stopped at the edge of the clearing proclaiming victory. Puppy told everyone in the forest what a coward Old Boar was for running from a puppy. Puppy said he would give that ugly pig more of the same if he were foolish enough to return."

I laughed until tears ran down my cheeks. I could see every moment of the confrontation. The little dog was brave. As Edudu told his story, Puppy barked, confirming the truth of what I had heard.

"Walela, when little dog saw Old Boar was gone and wouldn't return, he turned to walk back to me from the far edge of the clearing. High overhead a pair of bald eagles were gliding in big circles looking for their dinner. Puppy looked up. When he saw the two beautiful eagles far above his head he sat on his hind legs and growled at the eagles, jumping, barking and threatening. He warned the eagles to stay away or he would do to them what he did to Old Boar. The eagles must leave his master alone. Little dog tried to jump and fly. He barked so loudly I think the eagles heard him because they flew away and never returned."

I observed the little dog watching and listening to Edudu. I looked at the little dog's intelligent eyes going back and forth between Edudu and me. I wondered if Edudu really did have the ability to awaken in an animal such intelligence as he described.

"After the eagles flew away, Puppy strode to my side, head held high. He sat down beside me. He told me he wasn't afraid of anything that walked, ran or flew. He told me I would always be safe with him at my side. He said I should never be afraid of wild hogs or anything that flies in the air. He told me his name was Eagle Killer. He said he wasn't afraid of anything, even eagles. I told him it was a good name. It is a good name, don't you think, Walela?"

"Eagle Killer is a remarkable name, I must say. It is the most impressive name for a dog I have ever heard. I don't think we need worry from this day forward. Eagle Killer will protect us from all harm. As I petted Eagle Killer, he licked my fingers. I listened. His voice was quiet and soft but I'm sure I heard him say, 'Thank you, Walela, I like your name, too'."

22 March 1829

Copied from the *Georgia Journal* – 16 March 1829 – page 2
From Andrew Jackson's Inaugural speech delivered in Washington City - 4 March 1829.
"…It will be my sincere and constant desire, to observe towards Indian tribes within our limits, a just and liberal policy; and to give the humane and considerate attention to their rights and their wants, which are consistent with the habits of our government, and the feelings of our people."

28 September 1829

Copied from the *Georgia Journal* – 1 August 1829 – page 3
"GOLD.—A gentleman of the first respectability in Habersham county, writes us thus, under date 22d July: 'Two gold mines have just been discovered in this county, and preparations are making to bring these hidden treasures of the earth into use.' "

12 October 1829

My Dearest Cassie,

Rumors are flying in Milledgeville. Georgia is infuriated by the Cherokee constitution, but the rumors of gold found in Cherokee Country is worse news, if possible. Men love gold more than their soul. The word from the Governor's office is that all Cherokee land where gold has been discovered will be immediately seized irrespective of treaties. All Cherokee who do not abandon land and assets will be imprisoned for four years at hard labor. In addition, Georgia is forming a special militia unit, the Georgia Guard, to assist their regular militia in enforcing Georgia law in the gold areas.

Every Cherokee family is to be evicted, no exceptions. Every Cherokee farm will be confiscated, no exception. All past treaties will be ignored as if they never existed. The Cherokee have no avenue for appeal. Please communicate this to your grandfather. Appeals to Washington City will be fruitless. The Militia and the new Georgia Guard will turn all Cherokee residents out of their homes as soon as possible. All who attempt to work their land will be imprisoned.

I am so sorry to communicate this terrible news. I cannot wait to see you once again. Pen and ink are much too impersonal for all that I have learned and desire to share with you.

Loving you always, Ben xoxo

15 December 1829

A law recently passed in Georgia.

From the *Georgia Journal*- 9 December 1829-page 2

"To prohibit the employment of slaves and free persons of color in the setting of types in printing offices in this state. To amend an act, passed on the 16th December, 1811, and also an act passed on the 19th of December, 1816, in relation to slaves and free persons of color."

20 December 1829

My Dear Father,

I can tell you by good authority that Andrew Jackson supports Georgia in the removal, but that isn't the worst. Mr. Jackson has given permission to Georgia to prevent white men from assisting the Cherokee. Unbelievably, that permission includes missionaries. God himself isn't safe from the American government. Missionary societies have little political power, but they write newspaper articles on behalf of the Cherokee and they are educated. Georgia wants to remove all American, white benevolent eyewitnesses from Cherokee Country. Take care,

Father. Do nothing foolish. Do not resist if questioned by the militia. They are a law unto themselves. Take no chances, Father.

John Eaton, the new Secretary of War, is a firebrand. He is one of Jackson's most ambitious cabinet members from Jackson's home state of Tennessee.

I feel helpless. I shall be home for Christmas. I will do my best to arrive on Christmas eve. Give my warmest felicitations to Cassie. Always, your adoring son, Ben, xoxo

25 December 1829

Excerpt from a bill that passed the Georgia Legislature on 19 December 1829 to go into effect 1 June 1830.

"...be it further enacted, That all the laws, both civil and criminal of this state, be...extended over said portions of territory respectively, and all persons shall, after the first day of June next, be subject and liable to the operation of said laws ...And be it further enacted, That after the first day of June next, all laws, ordinances, orders and regulations of any kind whatever, made, passed or enacted by the Cherokee Indians, either in general council or in any other way whatever,...are hereby declared to be null and void and of no effect, as if the same had never existed..."

When Elisi makes a mistake knitting, she will undo row upon row with one long tug on the yarn. The offending stitches are removed. They lie in an unruly pile on the floor at her feet.

One day, with one big pull upon the fabric of our nation, we shall unravel in one horrible episode to be forever undone.

Chapter XXXIII

1830 – Indian Removal Act - Edudu Goes Fishing
Chapter 33

10 January 1830 - Month of the Cold Moon - Du no lv ta ni
No sign of Ben. I hoped to see him on his birthday. I miss him terribly.

21 January 1830
From the *Phoenix* - 20 January 1830 – page 2
"THE INDIAN AND THE WHITE MAN, When Gen. Lincoln went to make peace with the Creek Indians, one of the chiefs asked him to sit down on a log. He did so. The chief then asked him to move, and in a few moments to move farther; the request was repeated till the General got to the end of the log; but the chief still said, "Move farther;" to which the General replied, "I can move no farther."

"Just so it is with us," said the chief; "You have moved us back to the water and then asked us to move farther."

30 March 1830
Jackson asked Ben to vote with his party. In return Jackson will support Ben. Ben is in a moral dilemma. He must sail between Scylla and Charybdis. He must maintain friendship with both the fox and the chickens.

8 June 1830
Huff's Boarding House - 4 June 1830
My Dearest Cassie,
Horrible news. On 28 May 1830 the Indian Removal Act has been signed into law authorizing the removal of all Indians from the United States.

I suspect the bill was written to please politicians in Georgia, North Carolina, Tennessee, Alabama, Florida, Mississippi and the western territories. With the passage of this bill, the deportation of Indians is legal and therefore no longer offends the American conscience.

I fear the immediate result of this law will be an instantaneous flood of squatters and ne'er-do-wells with an accompanying increase in the malicious activity of the militia.

I anticipate the worst. I shall visit as soon as I can. Beware.

Always yours, Ben, xoxo

10 June 1830

"What have you been doing today, Edudu?"

"I helped your Elisi in the smoke house. I brought water. Eagle Killer and I have been whittling. Eagle Killer hasn't stopped talking all afternoon. It's a good day. What have you been doing?"

"I went to school and worked at the Phoenix this afternoon. I brought newspapers and I have a letter from Ben. It's about the Indian Removal Act. It's not good news, Edudu. Do you want to hear what Ben has to say?"

Edudu turned and spoke to Eagle Killer lying at his feet.

"What shall we do, Killer? Shall we stay and listen to Walela's bad news or shall I get my gun and see if we can find a squirrel or maybe a fat turkey. Would you rather go fishing? What do you want to do, Killer, stay or go?"

Eagle Killer sat up and barked three times.

"Killer doesn't want to stay here and listen to bad news. He wants to go fishing and bring home supper. We have heard enough bad news lately. Would you like to come with us, Walela? I think you need to get away from bad news as much as I do. You read too much. Let's go to the river and cleanse our mind."

"That is a wonderful idea, Edudu. Let's go fishing and forget all this bad news. Fish never have bad news."

Edudu got his gun from above the fireplace and his special leather bag he carries fishing. I carried our basket for the fish and we began the lovely walk to the river. It was a warm day with no sign of rain. With the long afternoons of early-summer, we should have plenty of daylight to fish and be home before dark. Edudu told Elisi he was hungry for corn dumplings with ramps. They're my favorite, too. I was already hungry. I don't think anything is quite so tasty as a beautiful piece of fried fish on my plate, especially if that fish was swimming in the river that morning.

"Edudu, where is your fishing pole? I thought you said we were going fishing? Are you going to shoot the fish?"

"Of course I don't shoot the fish, Walela. I'm going to talk to the fish. I'll tell the fish to swim up to the bank and let Killer catch them. I know how to talk to the fish. You'll find Killer an excellent fisherman. I think nine fish today should be plenty."

"Where are we going to fish today?"

"I always allow Killer to decide where we fish, Walela. He's a better fisherman than I am. Eagle Killer will find the right spot. He knows about

200

hunting, but he did not want to go hunting today. I think maybe he likes to be in the water when it's warm. He knows where the fish are easy to catch. He likes a nice piece of fried fish and corn dumplings as well as we do."

When we got to the river Edudu walked slowly downstream. Eagle Killer kept walking. He finally stopped at a little cove where someone had built a weir of stones across the mouth of the little feeder creek not far upstream from where the creek joined the river.

"This is the place, Walela. Killer said this is the place where he will catch all the fish we want."

Eagle Killer was wagging his tail and running back and forth beside the creekbank near the water. Sometimes he would pause and stare down into the depths and then run back and sit in front of Edudu and bark.

"I'm going to close the door to the river and spread this magic powder, Walela. This magic powder will allow me to call to the fish in their language. I'll tell them to swim to Killer and jump into his mouth. We shall quickly fill our basket."

"Edudu, are you telling me you're going to let Killer catch the fish all by himself? We're not going to use a pole or a net?"

"Yes, Walela. Killer will catch the fish."

"How can a dog catch fish?" I asked incredulously.

"Walela, it's magical, didn't I tell you? I sprinkle the powder on the water and the fish fall under my spell. I talk and they listen. Watch."

Edudu took some sticks and waded to the middle of the stream where the water was trickling over the barricade of stones. He closed the weir using the sticks and smooth stones he pulled from the shallow water. It reminded me of times when Ben and I were younger and we would spend an afternoon playing in the water and building dams. Edudu repaired the weir and waded back to shore. From his bag he took several handfuls of a powdery substance and cast it over the still water. He sat down on a rock beside the creekbank and petted Killer, stroking him affectionately. Killer seemed anxious to begin fishing. He wagged his tail and barked.

We sat silently for a little while and finally Edudu spoke to Eagle Killer.

"Now, Killer," Edudu said, looking straight into Eagle Killer's eyes. "Now is the time. I want you to get us a fish. Go get us a fish."

Immediately Killer turned and walked to the creek until his front paws were submerged in the still water trapped behind the newly repaired weir. He moved slowly left and right with his nose almost touching the water. Suddenly, Eagle Killer dove head first into the creek. When he came up he had a big fish in his mouth. He dropped it at Edudu's feet.

"See what I told you, Walela. Killer is a fishing dog, probably the best in the world."

Edudu put the fish in our basket and sat on his rock. Killer sat quietly beside Edudu as if waiting for instructions.

I laughed to myself. I should have never doubted anything Edudu says about talking to his dog or about animals, birds or fish.

"What are you going to do now, Edudu?"

"I'll tell Killer to get us another fish. Watch."

"Now, Killer, bring me three fish. I need three fish. Bring three fish."

"How can Killer bring three fish?"

"Walela, you have a lot to learn. Killer will bring me three fish, one at a time. Killer can count, especially fish."

Edudu kissed Killer's wet nose.

"Killer, we need three more fish for our supper tonight. Catch three fish."

Immediately Killer barked his approval and ran to the large pool, looking into the depths. Once again his front paws were submerged. He moved to his left and right carefully. Suddenly he dove. Once again Eagle Killer surfaced with a big fish in his mouth. He dropped the fish at Edudu's feet. This time, without pause, Killer returned to the riverbank. In quick succession Eagle Killer caught two more fish. When Killer dropped the third, he sat up proudly waiting for a word from his master.

"Walela, are you ever going to believe Killer and I talk? I told him to bring three fish and he did? Do you think that a coincidence?"

"I believe you, Edudu," I said laughing. "I never doubted your words."

"Watch," Edudu said with a twinkle in his eye. "Killer, get three more fish. We need three more fish."

Killer immediately obeyed. He soon had three more fish, flipping and flopping in front of Edudu.

"I think, Walela, we'll get us three more fish. That will be plenty for tonight and tomorrow's breakfast and enough for us to share with Killer. I just have time to get them cleaned for your Elisi to cook them before dark."

I shall never again doubt my Edudu nor his marvelous companion.

16 June 1830

> *Georgia Journal* – 12 June 1830 – page 3
>
> "AN ACT To provide for an exchange of Lands with the Indians ... and for their removal West of the river Mississippi.
>
> Sec. 1. ... it shall and may be lawful for the President of the United States to cause so much of any territory belonging to the United States West of the river Mississippi, not included in any state or organized territory, and to which the Indian title has been extinguished...to be divided into a suitable number of districts for the reception of such tribes or nations of Indians as may choose to exchange the lands where they now reside, and remove there..."
>
> "Sec. 2 And be it further enacted, That it shall and may be lawful for the President to exchange any or all of such districts...with

any tribe or nation of Indians now residing within the limits of any of the States or Territories, and with which the United States have existing treaties, for the whole or any part or portion of the territory claimed and occupied by such tribe within the bounds of any one or more of the States or Territories where the land claimed and occupied by the Indians is owned by the United States, or the United States are bound to the State within which it lies, to extinguish the Indian claim thereto."

25 June 1830
Georgia Journal - 19 June 1830 - page 1
"...The European doctrine of the right conferred by the discovery of new countries inhabited by barbarous tribes, was, I thought well known. The discoverer claimed the sovereignty over the discovered country, and over everything under, upon, and above it, from the center to the zenith. The lands, the streams, the woods and minerals, all living things, including the human inhabitants, were all the property of, or subject to, the government of the fortunate navigator, who by accident or design, first saw the before unknown country. Such were the doctrines of Spain, England, France and Portugal claimed under a papal bull, which conferred upon the Crown empire and domain over every country newly discovered on the globe, not possessed by Christian people. This papal title was in perfect unison with the prevailing sentiments of an age, in which the decrees of the Roman Pontiff made and dethroned kings, established and overturned empires. All Christendom seem to have imagined, that, by offering that immortal life, promised by the Prince of Peace to fallen man, to the aborigines of this country, the right was fairly acquired of disposing of their persons and their property at pleasure..."

2 July 1830
Georgia Journal 26 June 1830 – page 1-2
Wilson Lumpkin's speech to the House.
"...But to those remnant tribes of Indians, whose good we seek, the subject before you is of vital importance. It is a measure of life and death. Pass the bill on your table and you save them; reject it, and you leave them to perish. Reject this bill, and you thereby encourage delusory hopes in the Indians, which their professed friends and allies well know will never be realized...The bill on your table involves but little that can be considered new principle. The only departure...is to be found in

that part which extends greater security and benefits to the Indians. The whole of my policy and views of legislation upon this subject have been founded in the ardent desire to better the condition of the remnant tribes…With the Choctaws and Creeks, treaties have also been made, assigning them countries west of the Arkansas and Mississippi. The Creeks have been flocking to theirs, and it is satisfactorily ascertained that they would all go, if the means contemplated in this bill were afforded to the Executive."

"The whole of the Choctaws are not only willing to go but preparing to go…The Chickasaws are anxious to emigrate…The Seminoles of Florida are also desirous to join their Creek brethren in the West…the Indians of Illinois, Ohio and Indiana have been emigrating for many years past, and the cost of their journey has been paid by the government…Our most enlightened Superintendents and Agents have all become converts to Indian emigration: our most pious and candid Missionaries have also added their testimony in our favor."

"Georgia, sir, is one of the good old thirteen states…She claims no superiority…Our social compact upon which we stand as a state gives you the metes and bounds of our sovereignty…our State authorities claim entire and complete jurisdiction over soul and population, regardless of complexion…Her boundaries are not only admitted by her sister States, but by this General Government, and every individual who administers any part of it, Executive or Legislative, must recollect that the faith of this Government has stood pledged for twenty-eight years past, to relieve Georgia from the embarrassment of Indian population…It is known to every member of congress that this was no gratuity to Georgia. No, sir, it was for and in consideration of the two entire States of Alabama and Mississippi."

6 August 1830

The Federal Union - 31 July 1830

"…the president has concluded it proper to suspend the present mode of enrolling and sending off (Indian) emigrants in small parties as heretofore….those who prefer to remove will be supported by the government in their removal, free of any expense to them, and have a full, and just value paid for such improvements as they may leave, that add real value to the soil, and maintained for one year after their arrival in the west, by which time they will have prepared, by opening farms, and otherwise for the support of themselves and families...liberal terms will be extended to them, their limits beyond the Mississippi will be enlarged and all things done for their protection....This suspension of present operations is designed to afford the Cherokee an opportunity to ponder their present situation...The president is their friend. He seeks not to deceive or oppress them. He feels for them as a father for his children. If they leave it will be of their own free will. If they stay it will also be of their own free will. There will be employed no force any way, but the force of reason and parental council, unless it shall be to protect them in their removing."

13 August 1830
> *The Federal Union* - 31 July 1830 page 3
> "Mr. Wirt, late attorney general of the United States, has been employed by the headmen of the Cherokee to carry their case before the supreme court of the United States. The Cherokee claim to be a sovereign and independent nation....A more wicked and unprincipled project could not have been suggested....it is impossible for two sovereignties to exist in the same district...the sovereignty of the Cherokee could only be asserted by dividing Alabama and Georgia and establishing a new nation....which would be a flagrant violation of the constitution...if sustained, the Cherokee Nation would be viewed as equal to whites....under the pretense of sustaining the pretensions of the Cherokee to sovereignty and independence the opposition are obviously striving to overthrow the State governments and dissolve the union...."

22 August 1830
The Americans want us to speak English, obey white laws, wear white clothing and abandon our customs. They insist we become Americans. White politicians in Georgia consider us an uncivilized embarrassment. How can a people from another continent cross a wide ocean and claim our land for their own and justify the claim?

26 September 1830
> *The Federal Union* - 11 September 1830 – page 3
> "THE CHEROKEE COUNTRY. There is no subject which more urgently imposes itself upon the serious consideration of the people of Georgia than the one with which I have headed this communication. Independent of the just right we have to its possession, there are other reasons of great weight which

demand a speedy change. The peculiar condition of the country at this time –presenting the disgusting scenes of licentiousness, riot, tumult and blood shed—endangering the peace of that portion of the state which lays contiguous to it –requires of our next legislature not only prompt but the most vigorous regulations. It is known that the Indians are utterly incapable of preserving the internal quietude even were the right conceded to them—and that it is totally impractical for the General Government to do so is equally certain...The General Government has acknowledged our right of jurisdiction...The General Government has held out to this unhappy and deluded people the most liberal inducements to prompt them to emigrate—and in return for those friendly overtures she has been met by taunt, insult and derision...The course which and interest both point us to pursue is plainly marked out. Let the next legislature take actual possession of the country—elect the necessary judicial officers...appoint surveyors—have it surveyed and disposed of in the usual manner...Their own good now requires our interference...situated in the midst of the whites their condition will be wretched and degraded—being so completely unfit for the enjoyments of civilized society...we can but deplore that perversity and obstinacy which they exhibit in refusing to embrace the liberal and philanthropic propositions of the Government. Newton."

29 September 1830

Georgia will require all white men to be licensed to work in Cherokee Country. This law is said to protect us. Ben believes it a crafty maneuver designed to remove the only whites who want to see the Cherokee prosper. Ben says all missionaries will be refused a license.

Excerpts from Andrew Jackson's speech in Congress celebrating the Indian Removal Act.

"It gives me pleasure to announce to Congress that the benevolent policy of the government, steadily pursued for nearly thirty years, in relation to the removal of the Indians beyond the white settlements is approaching to a happy consummation. Two important tribes have accepted the provision made for their removal... and it is believed that their example will induce the remaining tribes also to seek the same obvious advantage."

"The consequences of a speedy removal will be important to the United States, to individual States, and to the Indians themselves. It puts an end to all possible danger of collision between the authorities of the General and State governments on account of the Indians. It will place a dense and civilized population in large tracts of country now occupied by a few savage hunters. By opening the whole territory between Tennessee on the north and Louisiana on the south to the settlement of the whites, it will incalculably strengthen the southwestern frontier and render the adjacent States strong enough to repel future invasions without remote aid. It will relieve the whole State of Mississippi and the western part of Alabama of Indian occupancy, and enable those States to advance rapidly in population, wealth and power."

"It will separate the Indians from immediate contact with settlements of whites; free them from the power of the States; enable them to pursue happiness in their own way and under their own rude institutions; will retard the progress of decay, which is lessening their numbers, and perhaps cause them gradually... to cast off their savage habits and become an interesting, civilized, and Christian community...Toward the aborigines of the country no one can indulge a more friendly feeling than myself, or would go further to reclaim them from their wandering habits and make them a happy, prosperous people....What good man would prefer a country covered with forests and ranged by a few thousand savages to our extensive Republic, studded with cities, towns, and prosperous farms....and filled with all the blessings of liberty, civilization, and religion?..."

Chapter XXXIV

1830 - The Quilt – Enemies of Georgia
Chapter 34

2 October 1830 - Month of the Harvest Moon – Du ni nv di

The northern and southern states continue to feud. The quarrel is growing. Edudu thinks the dispute will end in war. Americans love war.

27 October 1830

I dream of my own newspaper and school, Ben as my husband and a house full of children. I would then have everything I love and be the happiest of women. I have wasted a day when I don't read.

29 October 1830

Yesterday when I arrived at Mrs. Lowry's house, she was worrying her apron, an action that betrays her state of mind.

"What is the problem, Mrs. Lowry?"

"Everything's good," Eleanor said, with tears beginning to come into her eyes. "I'm sorry for my uncontrolled emotion. I had every intention not to cry in front of you. I have something to tell you, but I want to let it wait until after school. Everything is good, Cassie. I promise."

Eleanor gave me another embrace with no words. I could tell she was concealing something of importance.

"Finish the children's lessons. Get your work done at the newspaper. Wilbur and I have a surprise for you. Everything is good. Mr. Lowry and I are quite content. Don't worry. Be patient until this afternoon, I'll tell you everything. Today is a good day."

"I promise not to worry," I told her.

When I returned that afternoon to the Lowry's home Eleanor had a nice tea ready. I sensed something was wrong but what the problem could be was impossible to guess. Mrs. Lowry set out fresh cream, hot bread and fresh baked sugar cookies. This was an unusually nice tea but with an undercurrent of sadness.

We shared small talk. Mr. and Mrs. Lowry gave no clue to what was coming.

Mrs. Lowry filled our cups for the last time.

"My dear Cassie," Mrs. Lowry said, "you are the daughter Wilbur and I longed for. You are a gift. It has been our pleasure to have you in our school and in our home. We want you always in our lives. Wilbur and I have watched you grow from a child into a brilliant young woman. Even if you and our son were not in love, we would cherish you as our daughter. If your mother and father were alive, they would be immensely proud. We count it an honor to have known you and a double honor for you and Ben to be together."

I felt tears coming.

"You helped Wilbur in his school for years, and you and Ben—well, it's obvious you and Ben were meant to be together, which is a bonus for us. We couldn't be more pleased. I can't wait till you two give us grandchildren. I couldn't wish for a better daughter-in-law. We love you dearly."

Mr. Lowry was silent. Up to this point he had said not a single word and that was unusual.

Mrs. Lowry continued.

"Cassie, I shall now share with you the source of my disturbed emotions you witnessed this morning."

Eleanor glanced at her husband. Her hands were working her apron.

"Cassie, Wilbur and I have heard ugly rumors. We're afraid for your nation, the school and our future. Ben warns of sinister things afoot now that Andrew Jackson is president. We're afraid, but we shall trust our Maker. We'll never abandon you, Cassie. Of that you can be certain. Missionary work is all Wilbur has ever wanted or will ever want. That's one of the things that made me fall in love with him all those years ago."

She glanced at her husband and gave him a pat on his arm that reflected a lifetime of devotion. Her hands continued to twist the apron in her lap.

Mrs. Lowry continued, "My parents sold all their belongings when they emigrated to the United States as newly-weds. They had money for passage and little else. They began a new life here with no regrets. Likewise, Wilbur and I have no regrets concerning our decision to give our lives in service to the Cherokee, none whatsoever. I miss Mother and Father terribly. I think about them every day."

Mrs. Lowry dried her eyes with the corner of her apron. I was speechless in the presence of such strong sentiment.

"I have three things my parents brought from Germany," Mrs. Lowry continued softly. "I have Mother's tea service, Grandmother's wedding quilt and my parents' wedding rings. That's all. Wilbur and I have laid up another kind of wealth in a place more secure, a place where thieves can't break through and steal. Wilbur made it clear to me when we married that we would never be affluent. Wilbur and I don't believe a person can take wealth with them when they pass, but we firmly believe we can send it on ahead."

With that speech Eleanor sobbed for a moment quietly. Mr. Lowry held her and said nothing. Mrs. Lowry quickly regained her composure, sat up straight and dried her eyes. With her hands clasped tightly in her lap, she continued speaking softly.

"Wilbur and I want to give you something, Cassie."

She looked at her husband.

"Now?"

He nodded.

Eleanor rose slowly and disappeared into the back room. She returned with a large parcel wrapped in brown paper.

"Wilbur and I want you to have this," she said, once again with tears filling her eyes as she handed me the parcel.

"Take it, Cassie. Open it now. It's our gift to you. Open it."

I untied the twine. Inside was a colorful quilt with the finest needlework I had ever seen.

"I don't know what to say. I don't know what to say," was all I could manage. I recognized the quilt. It was Eleanor's own wedding present she often displayed on her bed. I was overcome.

"It's yours. It's our gift to you," Ben's mother said.

"This is my mother's wedding present, given to her by her mother just before they emigrated. It's the quilt my mother gave me when I married. It was the quilt my grandmother was given before her. It is important to us that you have it, Cassie. It's an advanced gift for your wedding with Ben. Let this quilt be a reminder of our love that will forever keep you warm."

"We also want you to have this tea service, Cassie. From this day forward the tea set belongs to you, but if you don't mind, I'm going to keep it for just a while longer. We shall enjoy it together, but it's yours from our heart to yours. We'll give it to you at the appropriate time. It reminds me of my mother and grandmother. Perhaps one day you can give the tea service and quilt to your daughter on her wedding day. We love you dearly, Cassie. We hope in some small way these gifts communicate the depth of our affection."

Eleanor couldn't continue.

We paused, embraced, wept, and dried our tears. I have no words to express how good these people are and how much I care about them.

Mr. Lowry spoke quietly for the first time.

"Cassie, strange things will begin happening here soon, according to Ben. Ominous rumors are coming out of Milledgeville. While we have a measure of peace, Eleanor and I decided to communicate our love to you. Our hearts have been entwined with yours since you were a girl and will be forever."

I was completely overcome. Tears rolled down my cheeks. After we regained our composure, Mrs. Lowry spoke.

"Cassie, this quilt has reminded me of my family's love every day since I married Wilbur. It's yours. If one day we're separated, let this quilt remind you our hearts are beating in time with yours. If my mother and my grandmother were here, they would love you as we do."

"Stay with us a while longer, Cassie," Mr. Lowry said. "Let's go out on the porch. I have news. As much as you read the newspapers, you may already know what I'm going to say, but I want to share the latest from Ben that provoked the giving of these gifts."

When we were seated in the fresh air, Mr. Lowry began.

"Cassie, Ben has confirmed the rumor that all American men in Cherokee Country will be required to swear an oath of allegiance to Georgia. We will be required to apply for a license to continue to work here, a license missionaries will be denied. Georgia has claimed legal sovereignty over all Cherokee land within its chartered limits. Milledgeville doesn't want you or your people to receive encouragement from anyone, especially educated American missionaries with a developed sense of justice. The new law is an obvious pretext. The governor referred to us missionaries as the 'enemies of Georgia'. I will be forced to discontinue my work."

"How can that possibly happen, Mr. Lowry? How?"

"I don't know, Cassie. I suppose Georgia doesn't want anyone assisting the Cherokee, not even God. Georgia is afraid of missionaries. That tells me something about the conscience of politicians. The United States is not a Christian country, not even close. I thought it was, but it isn't. This government's integrity is a thin veneer covering the commercial self-interest of the well-to-do. Americans want your land and what may be under your land. Cassie, we asked you here because Eleanor and I may be forced to leave without warning in the near future."

"How could anyone consider you their enemy?" I said incredulously. "Even the Militia wouldn't do that to you, would they? I don't understand."

Mr. Lowry continued softly, "Ben says I shall be forbidden to work here in order to hasten your removal. Ben believes Georgia will act soon, therefore Eleanor and I decided to give you the quilt today. You and your people are at the center of our heart."

Mr. Lowry continued in a most serious tone.

"Some missionaries say they'll leave and I don't blame them. I don't know what the Guard or the Militia will do, but I labor for someone infinitely more powerful than the government of Georgia. I don't know how long Eleanor and I will remain here in our home. I do believe if God wouldn't spare His own son, we can't demand special treatment."

I felt myself beginning to cry again.

"Since the discovery of gold, greed has flourished. Human behavior today is as it always has been. They will take what they want. The American government possesses the same self-indulgent appetite as the Romans. Georgia covets the possessions of its weaker neighbors and vindicates their desires with a veneer of self-justifying law."

Mr. Lowry continued, "One day I shall stand in the dock before the judge of all men. I shall be required to give answer for my actions. I'm

211

understandably nervous about that meeting. I have complete faith in Him. I do not trust Georgia. I will not bend to their will, not one iota. As flawed as I am, I shall obey my Lord. As someone once said, it is neither safe nor right to go against one's conscience. I have made up my mind. I can do no other. I will not accede to cynical, pernicious demands from Milledgeville."

"Cassie, when we're gone, you'll be alone, isolated in a sea of angry white foam. Indians have been accused of atrocities when the real outrage is being perpetrated by invading Americans in a blind quest for fee simple land. A bitter winter is descending. The Cherokee, along with the Choctaw, Creeks, Chickasaw and Seminoles are, I fear, doomed. The writing is on the wall."

Mrs. Lowry kissed my cheek and whispered, "Cassie, wherever you go, remember us. If one day you find hope impossible, wrap yourself in this quilt and recall our love. Our love shall follow you all the days of your life."

Mrs. Lowry kissed my cheek once again.

"My dear Cassie, Wilbur and I have a third thing we want you to have. You have the quilt. It will keep you warm in our absence. We're going to give you the tea service, it will cheer and refresh your soul. The third gift we will give you when the time is right, but not quite yet. Wilbur and I want you to have our wedding rings. When you have our rings, you will possess everything our parents brought from Europe and everything Wilbur and I hold dear on this earth. Our life will then be completely merged with yours."

I was overcome. I objected.

"I can't take your wedding rings. That wouldn't be right."

"For the time being Wilbur and I will continue to wear the tokens of our eternal love. You have the quilt. One day soon we'll give you the tea service. As your wedding day draws near, we shall give you the rings. We want you and Ben to have them. We'll not be allowed to take them where we're going."

That was the end of the conversation. We sat quietly on the porch listening to the little song birds and watching the squirrels chase one another around the huge trunks of the red oaks. The clouds moved slowly across the blue sky. There were no more words.

12 November 1830

Ben came for a visit. It was much to brief but I loved ever moment. He had good news he wanted to share.

"Cassie, I did it again. I've been re-elected to the Georgia House."

"I'm proud of you, Ben. I was worried that your connection to your father and the Cherokee would have reflected poorly on your re-election."

"I was elected by a wide majority, Cassie. Zach and Elizabeth worked hard. They did it. They've built a strong political base. Now comes the hard part. I've got to repay these folks with good service."

"How do you repay all the people who voted for you?"

"Taking care of people is my job. Folks give me support. They tell their friends to vote for me. They may even contribute money. In return I do them favors. Quid pro quo. That's what government is for."

November - 1830 – Mitchell's Hotel – Milledgeville

"Ben, we did it again, didn't we? You, Zach and Elizabeth did a great job. I can't tell you how pleased we are. Keep up the good work, son. Take these cigars like I gave you last time. This could become quite a profitable habit if you keep gettin' re-elected."

Ben's re-election moved him one step closer to the grand prize, an appointment to the United States Senate. Once again Elizabeth presented him with an election night surprise. Life was good for Ben in Milledgeville. He had become a leader in the white community, an American politician of influence and privilege.

Chapter XXXV

1831 - Roses Transplanted – Missionaries Jailed
Chapter 35

11 March 1831 - The Windy Moon – A nu yi

Ben and his father discussed the new law.

"Father, the law has passed. How it'll be enforced, no one knows."

"I understand too well, son. My fellow missionaries are frightened. Most are leaving. Your mother and I shall stay. We'll not submit to patent wickedness, for that's what this is. Your mother and I made a pledge long ago. That oath was not to the State of Georgia. It was a much higher promise."

"I understand, Father, but the Governor will act. I'm sure of it. From what I'm hearing, at some point he'll strictly enforce this law. They despise the fact that you teach the Cherokee to read and write. They believe the Cherokee incapable of education and the Phoenix the work of American missionaries."

Mrs. Lowry spoke quietly, "What a strange world in which our own government believes only Americans should read and write."

"Yes, Mother. What's worse, Georgia believes missionaries have been secretly influencing Ross to defy Georgia's demand for emigration. The governor wants the public to accept his policies and he needs a whipping boy. Since the removal bill has become law, the talk about enforcing the Compact has increased. The writing is on the wall. Father, you have become the scapegoat, the declared enemy of Georgia, the Governor's very words."

"Greed for land and gold has fueled this law, I suspect," Ben's father said.

"I think so, Father. The discovery of gold has provoked Georgia to de facto claim all Cherokee land in defiance of treaties. They've set in motion the final lotteries. It won't be long before all Cherokee land from the Tennessee River through these mountains will be given away, every acre. All past treaties are defunct. There will be no further negotiations with Chief Ross and the Cherokee leadership. The state of Georgia will soon be sending soldiers to remove the entire Cherokee nation. It's a sad day, indeed."

We sat in the back under the big chestnut for a long time in the cool afternoon shadows behind the Lowrys' house. It was a magnificent day that betrayed nothing of the approaching darkness looming just beyond our national horizon. The birds were singing, the dogwoods beginning to flower and the forest was turning that special color of green only seen in early spring.

Ben continued, his voice hardly above a whisper.

"The new laws eliminate white eyewitnesses and provide a whipping boy. That's the bottom line, Father. Georgia doesn't want anyone of character to witness their impending actions. Out-of-sight, out-of-mind."

18 March 1831

Mrs. Lowry left word she had something important to share with me. I was devastated by her news.

"Cassie, the Guard came yesterday. Their young officer, no older than Ben, informed Wilbur we had been declared enemies of Georgia. We must swear allegiance to the state of Georgia and leave Cherokee Country or be arrested. If we stay they say our assets will be seized and Wilbur jailed. It was a terrible scene."

I put my arms around Mrs. Lowry. I had nothing to say.

"The Governor has given us one month, Cassie. With that terse warning the militia left for the next missionary home."

"I'll be here when you need me. I promise," I said, trying to comfort her.

"In some macabre twist of fate, Cassie, we have become the enemy of our own people. I would have never believed Christian missionaries would be considered the adversary. When the soldiers said they were doing this for our good, I laughed at the irony. I now feel a kinship with you and your people I have never felt before. What a price Wilbur and I paid for that privilege."

"I am so sorry, Mrs. Lowry."

"Cassie, what's happening to us is bad but nothing compared to what they will do to you. They want us out of the way in order to violently seize your country. I should have known this would happen when I read President Jackson's speeches about Indian removal. Wilbur is right. If God wouldn't spare his own son, why should he spare us? Wilbur didn't say a word to the young officer. Even after the soldiers were gone Wilbur stood on the front steps staring into the distance, his arm hanging at his side holding the single sheet of paper signed by the Governor. All I could think of was the sudden end of my husband's work represented by a single stroke of a pen."

Mrs. Lowry wept once again.

"I suppose this is our last spring here, Cassie. Our future is in His hands. Wilbur's not here. He rode to visit the other missionaries to talk about our future. I asked him to send for you to stay with me while he's gone. He told me he might not be back for a couple of days. Come inside and have a cup of tea. Please stay with me."

21 March 1831

Three days after being served by the Governor's office, a dozen missionaries met at New Echota to discuss the law requiring them to swear allegiance to Georgia and to be licensed to work in Cherokee Country.

"We discussed Georgia's law and our responsibility, Eleanor," Mr. Lowry said to his wife when he returned.

"Most are frightened of the government. They'll leave. At the end of the meeting we prayed and turned it over to God. That's all we can do. I'm staying. I'm not signing anything. I agree with Matthew, 'Seek ye first the kingdom of God and His righteousness and all these things shall be added unto you. Take therefore no thought for the morrow for the morrow shall take care of itself. Sufficient unto the day is the evil thereof'. Eleanor, my entire life I have served one master and that master has never been the governor of Georgia. I'll go to jail defending my right to share my faith with the Cherokee."

"I was hoping you would say that, Wilbur, but my heart is heavy. Whatever happens, I'm at your side."

"Eleanor, I could not have gotten this far in my life without you. I'm going to need you now more than ever. However, it's only fair to warn you, we can expect no help from the north nor from Washington City. We have been vilified in all the newspapers. We have been abandoned by our own."

25 March 1831

More bad news.

"I feel helpless, Cassie," Ben said as we sat on Elisi's porch. "Even though I'm in the legislature, there's nothing I can do. The Georgia House is behind Governor Gilmer one hundred percent. I must vote with my peers."

"I know, Ben."

"Come with me to Mother's house," Ben said. "We're going to dig up her roses and give them to your grandmother. If the Militia takes their house, Mother doesn't want them to have her flowers."

We spent the afternoon transplanting Eleanor's roses to the front of Elisi's porch. Elisi was thrilled with the first roses she has ever had. For years Edudu has protected the dogwoods and redbuds, making the adjacent woods look like a royal garden in the springtime. The roses will be a wonderful addition.

After we transplanted the roses, I spent the day with Ben, a wonderful day. My heart was heavy as I watched him disappear around the bend.

17 April 1831

My heart is broken. Edudu and I found the Lowrys' front door open, hanging crazily on one hinge. A note was pinned to the mantelpiece:

Dearest, Dearest Cassie,

Wilbur has been arrested, chained and transported. I leave immediately. I have no idea where they are taking him. I doubt if we shall return. I was able to gather only a few personal items and clothing before my hasty departure. The rest is for you and your grandparents. Take the chickens and everything you find in

the house, sheds and smokehouse before the Guard comes. Forgive me for not saying goodbye. I feel as if I am abandoning you. Forgive me. Until we meet again under better circumstances, you will be on my mind, night and day.
Mrs. Wilbur Lowry

18 April 1831

Edudu and I moved everything of value from the Lowrys' home. We caught the chickens. We found a cow lowing miserably in the meadow, her sack distended. We milked her to give relief.

27 April 1831

My Dearest Cassie,

By now you know Father has been arrested and transported. He refused to sign the document of allegiance. Father was beaten, chained, denied proper sustenance and forced to walk the to Milledgeville. The State has made an example of Father.

Georgia seized Father's house in New Echota as compensation. It shall become the headquarters for the Georgia Guard. How ironic a house built as a refuge for the Cherokee should be the headquarters of their oppressors.

I tried to persuade Father to sign the oath and remove to Brainerd but he will not. He stubbornly remains in prison. Father has never feared the consequences of doing what is right. I must say his behavior is consistent with his beliefs. I will come to you when duty allows. I will do what I can.
Loving you Always, Your Ben, xoxo

5 May 1831

My Dearest Cassie,

Father was sentenced to four years hard labor. I could do nothing. He would not sign the oath nor defend himself. How ironic my father was imprisoned for preaching Christianity without a license. Mother asks about you daily. Beware of white men ranging about in Cherokee Country. I fear their nefarious activity will increase with the removal of the missionaries.
Take care, my dear Cassie. Ben xoxo

Chapter XXXVI

1832 - Ben's Father Released – Ben Elected to US House
Chapter 36

8 January 1832 - Month of the Cold Moon - Du no lv ta ni

All the missionaries have gone. Georgia has mandated a third of the 160-acre lottery portions be designated as gold districts and divided into forty-acre lots distributed in a separate lottery. The drawing will be 22 October through 1 May 1833. Our leaders can do nothing to stop the give-away of our land.

9 January 1832

From the *Southern Recorder* - 5 January 1832 – page 2

"In relation to white settlers on Indian Territory, and State Jurisdiction.

Resolved by the Senate, and House of Representatives of the State of Alabama in general assembly convened, That this state recognizes a power in no one to dispossess white persons who have, or may settle on any lands known as Indian territory, not occupied by any Indian or Indians.

Resolved, that all territory within the boundaries assigned by the United States, and accepted by the Convention of Alabama as the boundary line of this state, is within the ordinary jurisdiction thereof, and subject to all its laws, civil and criminal. *Resolved,* That any exercise of jurisdiction on the part of the United States, by their courts or otherwise, over any portion of territory aforesaid, in the possession of any Indian tribe, which it could not constitutionally and legally exercise over that portion of territory, which is in the possession of the citizens of this State, is an usurpation of power on the part of the United States."

10 January 1832

"My word, Cassie, you're more beautiful than ever," Ben said. "I have missed you. I don't know why I don't take the time off more often."

"I missed you too."

"Cassie, I just want to look at you. Has anyone told you today that you have the most beautiful eyes in the world?"

218

"No one but you."

"Cassie, when you're close, everything is right with the world. When I'm near you, problems melt. Let's walk. I've a lot to tell you."

We walked to my special place by the river.

"I can't express how happy I am to be here, Cassie. I've thought of you and this place ten thousand times in the last few months. My fondest memories are here where I spent my boyhood, where I met you. I close my eyes and walk these hills in my mind. I smell the air and feel my toes sink into the pine needles. I feel the touch of your hand. Things change, don't they, Cassie? No matter how hard we try to keep things the way they are, things change. The world changes. Our lives change. Riding up here knowing Father is locked in prison is a horrible experience. I don't ever want things to change here or to change with you and me."

As I held Ben's arm I pressed myself tight against him.

"You're right, Ben. Some things change but my love for you will never change. How are your mother and father doing, Ben?"

"That's what I came here today to talk about, Cassie. I have good news, very good news. I just came from delivering my parents to Brainerd. Our new governor finally released my stubborn father from prison."

"That's wonderful news, Ben. Why did you wait to tell me?"

"I wanted to tell you down here by the river."

"That's good news, Ben, the best of news."

"Yes, it is good news. Father's out of jail now. I think having a Christian missionary in prison was an embarrassment to Georgia and especially the governor. The primary concession for Father's release was his immediate and permanent removal to Brainerd, leaving Georgia altogether. Father agreed, or at least they said he agreed. I'm not so sure that's actually the case. I know my father. He's stubborn. I think they released Father for political reasons to take pressure off the Governor."

"I wish I could have been there with you, Ben."

"I wish you could have been there too. I drove Mother and Father to Brainerd immediately upon his release before the Governor could change his mind. We left straight from the prison. I wanted to get him away as quickly as possible."

"Could we go up sometime to see your parents?" I asked.

"I would like that," Ben replied quickly. "The first time I can get away for any length of time I'll take you up. The folks at the mission gave Mother and Father a little one-room house. My parents are safe. That's the good news, Cassie."

"What's the bad news, Ben?"

"Father isn't doing well. He's not doing well at all. Mother and I are worried. Father has been released, but he's still in prison."

"What do you mean, Ben? What's wrong?"

"Father hardly eats. He's thin as a bean pole. His hair has turned pure white. He doesn't talk, not even to Mother, not a word. When I try to talk, he stares at me as if he doesn't know what's going on or who I am."

"I am so sorry, Ben."

"I suppose Father has taken refuge in some dark corner of his mind. Mother takes care of him as best she can. Father can't be left alone. She doesn't think he knows who he is."

Ben sat quietly and held me while I cried quietly against his shoulder. I thought of poor Mr. Lowry imprisoned in his madness.

"I don't know what the future holds, Cassie," Ben said quietly after a long silence. "I'm standing for the United States House of Representatives this autumn. Perhaps I'll be able to do something in Washington City for the Cherokee. I keep trying. It's several years yet before I qualify for a Senate appointment where the real power lies. Zach and his father want me in the Senate, but that's not what I want to talk to you about, Cassie."

Ben turned and faced me and held me tightly.

"Cassie, I have more bad news. Georgia will seize the remainder of Cherokee Country soon. I know your grandparents want to stay, but Georgia will make that impossible under any circumstances. I'm begging you, Cassie. You and your grandparents must leave for Brainerd immediately and prepare to remove west with the next group. You'll be safe there. You can't stay here. It's not safe. Ross will be ignored. Georgia won't let your grandfather keep one acre. The American government will get rid of the Cherokee. They're going to take every acre. I know your grandparents don't like the removal party, but they need to leave before trouble starts."

"They won't leave, Ben," I whispered.

"They need to leave now."

"I know, but Elisi won't leave."

"Cassie, terrible things will happen. You'll have to leave without them."

"I couldn't go without them, Ben. You know that."

"If you stay, you'll be at the mercy of the Guard."

"Elisi won't leave. I've told her what you said but she won't listen."

"Tell her again what I've told you. Maybe she'll change her mind."

"She won't go, Ben. She won't leave unless our Chief tells her to leave."

"He's wasting his time begging in Washington City," Ben said quietly. "You and your grandparents should leave, but I understand."

"I want to stay with Elisi and Edudu, Ben. I want to work on the Phoenix. Our newspaper is important. Chief Ross and the others are depending on us."

I could sense Ben's growing anxiety as we talked.

"I understand, Cassie. I probably wouldn't leave either if I were you. Your work on the Phoenix is important. I'll grant you that. Your newspaper is the best thing the Cherokee have done. To be honest I'm surprised the Guard has let it continue. Georgia understands the power of literature. That's why it's illegal to teach Africans to read."

"We're afraid of the Guard but there's nothing we can do," I said.

"I'm afraid too, Cassie, but I have more news. President Jackson is up for re-election. He's promised to support me if I support him, quid pro quo. I don't particularly like Jackson, but if I want to be elected I must support him. Don't think ill of me if you hear I've supported President Jackson."

"I'll be patient, Ben. Do what you can. I understand."

"I'll do everything I can for you, Cassie. You can count on me."

"When you're in Milledgeville, remember I'm yours, Ben. I'll wait as long as I need to, but could you come up more often. I miss you terribly."

22 January 1832

> From the *Cherokee Phoenix* – 21 January 1832 – Page 2
>
> "...a band of white men who are distinguished throughout the country by the appellation of 'The Poney Club' were located and permitted to reside upon Cherokee lands by...Georgia—and it is notorious that these men are visited by others of their own class from all quarters and many cases have occurred of their dismounting Cherokees off their horses in the face of day and escaping with them,--also of driving off whole gangs of Cherokee cattle and hogs from the woods where they range...it is an incontrovertible fact that the country is now more infested with this description of settlers than ever and the woods and public highways are almost alive with them..."

Soon, if my count is correct, we will have had eight separate lotteries giving away Indian land. How long can this continue? The surveyors come in direct violation of past treaties. My hope has fled. We are undone.

22 April 1832

> From the *Cherokee Phoenix* – 21 April 1832 – Page 3
>
> "Georgia has commenced her survey of Cherokee Country notwithstanding the decision of the Supreme Court of the United States. Our country is now overrun with surveyors, laying off the land into small sections about two hundred acres—The gold region is to be laid off into lots of forty acres. There are, we believe, about ninety-two districts nine miles square. One company of surveyors are sent to each district, consequently there are not less than five hundred and fifty men, employed in survey, under the authority of Georgia...marking trees or otherwise doing the thing which is expressly forbidden, by the act of congress of 1802—If the intercourse law, and the treaties

were carried into effect, which the president is constitutionally bound to do, these men, who are now employed in surveying the land would suffer the just penalty of the law...the fifth section of the law alluded to…that if any citizen shall make a settlement on any lands belonging to or secured, or granted by treaty with the U. States, to any Indian tribe, or shall survey or attempt to survey such lands, or designate any of the boundaries, or otherwise, said offender shall forfeit a sum not exceeding one thousand dollars and suffer imprisonment not exceeding twelve months. In the same section the president is armed with full power to take such measures and to employ such military force as he shall judge necessary to carry the law into execution."

1 July 1832
    From the *Southern Recorder* 21 June 1832 – page 1
        "Reading maketh a full man; conference a ready man; and writing an exact man; and therefore if a man write little he had need have a great memory; if he confer little; he had need have a present Wit; if he read little he had need have much cunning, to seem to know that he doth not….Lord Bacon."

30 August 1832
    There is division. Elias Boudinott has resigned from the Phoenix. He and Chief Ross disagree about the political future of our country. Chief Ross wants our nation to remain. Mr. Boudinott favors removal. Trouble is brewing.

30 September 1832
    The Black Hawk War is over. Hundreds of Sauk, Fox and Kickapoo were killed. Americans rejoice over our loss as if we were the incarnation of their devil.

12 November 1832
    Ben was elected to the United States House of Representatives by a wide margin, achieving his life's goals. I am proud. I can't wait until his next visit.

Milledgeville November 1832
    "Ben, here we are celebrating another political victory, your third. This has become a pleasant habit. I'm about to bust my buttons. I can't wait till you take your seat in the House. You can bet I'll be in Washington City in person to watch you take your oath. Everyone is pleased. I can't tell you how much this means to me and the firm."

Zach's father gave Ben a big slap on the back that took his breath away.

"Yes, sir. This is a grand day," Ben answered, thinking how good it felt to be elected once again to public office.

"This is the third time I've decorated this hotel's ballroom for you, Ben. We're proud as a peacock. We're the most successful law firm in Georgia. You, Zach and Elizabeth have turned a lot of government business our way."

Ben was smiling and waiting for a chance to say thank you.

Zach's father continued speaking without a pause.

"Ben, I have a little gift you'll appreciate. It's the kind of gift you can take to the bank. It will be on your desk when you get back to the office. I've been generous. Keep up the good work, son. This is just the beginning. We're in Washington City now. Next will be the Senate, but tonight enjoy yourself. You've earned it."

"Thank you, sir. I appreciate your consideration."

As he listened to Mr. Mitchell, Ben mused that things were working out well indeed. He was saving money. Things couldn't be better. Like the last election, Bethy had invited him up to the suite for her traditional victory gift. She assured him he would enjoy it far more than the last. He couldn't wait.

9 December 1832

More bad news. Georgia has created ten new counties from seized land: Cass, Cherokee, Cobb, Floyd, Forsyth, Gilmer, Lumpkin, Murray, Paulding and Union.

10 December 1832

From the *Federal Union* - 6 December 1832 - page 2

"Resolved: That the measures pursued by the President of the United States, for the purpose of inducing the Cherokee Indians to remove beyond the limits of the state of Georgia, are in a high degree acceptable to this legislature, and deserve the approbation of the people, as founded on the most liberal, just and generous policy: Which was unanimously agreed to."

13 December 1832

From the *Georgia Journal* – 10 December 1832 – page 2

"...Mississippi...revised their Constitution...ARTICLE 3, Legislative Department. Sec. 1, Every free white male person of the age of twenty-one years or upwards, who shall be a citizen of the United States and shall have resided in this State one year...preceding an election...may vote for any state or district officer, or member of Congress..."

18 December 1832

From the *Georgia Journal* – 13 December 1832 – page 2
President Jackson's acceptance speech to congress.

"...the hostile incursions of the Sac and Fox Indians necessarily led to the interposition of the government...the Indians were entirely defeated, and the disaffected band dispersed and destroyed...Severe as is the lesson to the Indians, it was rendered necessary by their unprovoked aggressions; and it is to be hoped that its impression will be permanent and salutary....I am happy to inform you that the wise and humane policy of transferring from the eastern to the western side of the Mississippi the remnants of our aboriginal tribes, with their own consent, and upon just terms, has been steadily pursued, and is approaching, I trust, its consummation...the conviction evidently gains ground among the Indians, that their removal to the country, assigned by the United States for their permanent residence, furnishes the only hope of their ultimate prosperity. With that portion of the Cherokees, however, living within the State of Georgia, it has been impracticable, as yet, to make a satisfactory adjustment...I directed the very liberal propositions to be made to them...they cannot but have seen in these offers the evidence of the strongest disposition, on the part of the government, to deal justly and liberally with them. An ample indemnity was offered for their present possessions, a liberal provision for their future support and improvement, and full security for their private and political rights....They were however rejected..."

19 December 1832

Fortunate drawers, assisted by the Guard, have evicted many families on the Coosa river. When mounted white men with rifles tell us they have a legal deed to our property, we have no choice.

21 December 1832 – Milledgeville
My Dearest Cassie,

I fear this year will not end well for the Cherokee. I heard the Governor's address to the legislature. I include an excerpt from his speech.

"The territory embraced in Cherokee County should be divided into counties of suitable size, and form, to promote the convenience of that portion of our population who may inhabit that section of the State; and the organization of such counties should be provided for without unnecessary delay."

I wish I had better news but truth does not come in season. I shall do my best to visit around Christmas time. I am not certain when my responsibilities will release me or how long I shall be at Brainerd helping Mother. I would wish to see you more often. I remind you once again in the strongest terms to encourage your grandparents to remove to Brainerd and go west with the next detachment. I promise to help them liberally if they remove. You cannot trust the misguided optimism of Chief Ross.

I am wishing you every happiness this joyous season. I think of you every day.

Yours Always and Forever, Ben xoxo

Chapter XXXVII
1833 - Final Lotteries - Georgia Sends Surveyors
Chapter 37

19 January 1833 – Month of the Cold Moon – Du no lv ta ni

Will the lotteries never end? With these last lotteries Georgia has seized every Cherokee house, farm and field. The end is near. What shall we do?

22 June 1833

We detest the symbol of American arrogance, their surveyors. They measure and squeeze until we can be measured and squeezed no more. We're like crawfish, always moving backwards to escape the encroachment of American law.

26 June 1833

Edudu told me what my brother and his two friends did. What they did was not good but who would not understand? Who would not defend their home and family against foreign invaders?

"Walela, Five Feathers told me something he did."

"What did he do, Edudu?"

"Walela, your brother will not be here for a while. He doesn't want the Guard and Militia to see his face because of something he has done. I don't know how long he will be gone, but do not worry. Your brother has a noble heart. He cares about the future happiness of others. He cares about you. He will never abandon us. He will certainly be chief."

"Yes, Edudu. My brother walks with grace and peace, but he can be quick like a mountain lion. I am never afraid when he is near. My heart is always with him."

Edudu smiled.

"When Five Feathers was a boy we made his bed from the skin of the mountain lion to help him grow powerful and quick. Your brother moves fast like the big cat, with keen sight and smell. He is the best at ballplay and like you he is strong of mind."

"Yes, Edudu. I believe he will be a white chief or perhaps even a red chief if we ever need one again. He will protect us. He is wise and strong."

My mind is filled with words. My brother's mind is filled with the forest, hunting and the joy of providing for others. He is in tune with the heart of our

226

people, in tune with earth itself. Even Mr. Lowry believes my brother will make a good chief and should learn to speak better English against that day. I agree, but my brother does not like the English-speaking Americans who have covered our land like a white killing frost on a frozen winter's morning.

"I understand your brother," Edudu continued. "He thinks like a true Cherokee man of long ago. Men follow him easily. He has the power of Dragging Canoe."

"Walela, your brother is hiding but he did no wrong. Five Feathers acted in the name of our nation. His deed was not retribution but duty, an honorable act of courage that will help return the balance to our troubled land."

"Tell me the story, Edudu. What happened? What did my brother do?"

"Walela, Americans divide our land among themselves. They are parasites. They add Cherokee Country to their white maps. They increase. We decrease. They suck our life's blood like ticks and leeches. They came for Mr. Lowry, one of their own. Only a corrupt people, a people obsessed with themselves, would imprison a man like him. Mr. Lowry is a good man."

"What can we do, Edudu? We cannot resist."

"There is little we can do, Walela. When Chief Ross returned from Washington City he found fortunate drawers occupying his farm on the Coosa. Americans had occupied his home in his absence. When he returned they threatened him and his family with violence if they tried to stay. Even though he is chief, there was nothing to be done, nowhere to appeal. He walked away from the thieves. Our chief lost all of his property. American justice is for Americans. Such unfairness makes your brother boil with anger. One day soon they will have this house. To them we are animals, like the buffalo and the white tail deer, animals to be taken and destroyed without compunction or hesitation, forgotten with no remorse, our bodies left to rot. In the end, Walela, the Cherokee shall be pushed until we tumble off the end of the earth and fall to our death among discarded mountains of white, meaningless paper."

Edudu paused and said nothing for a long while. I was quiet and thinking about his words. Finally, he kissed my forehead and began his story.

"Walela, this is what happened. Your brother and two friends were hunting in the mountains to the west towards Alabama. It was a misty day with the wind whipping the dead leaves as they followed the trail of white-tailed deer down the smooth path on the mountain's backbone above Rising Fawn's farm. Misty clouds had descended onto the narrow trail. Your brother and his companions had a deer and two turkeys in their slings."

"As they rounded a boulder as large as a house they found themselves in the path of three armed Georgia surveyors. The Americans had guns. Your brother was in the lead. He was not afraid. He made no move to flee. He stood his ground. Your brother saw the men's pack animals nearby, tethered in a dense grove of scrubby black pines. The white men were sheltering under the overhang of the huge boulder beside the path."

"You need to get out of here, head west," the American man in the lead said sharply to Five Feathers. "Go down into Alabama and you won't be harmed. We won't hurt you. Drop the game."

The leader motioned with his gun barrel in the westerly direction he wanted your brother and his two friends to go, down the mountain and into Alabama. Your brother did not move."

The man spoke louder.

"Do you understand English? Drop the game and get out of here."

The leader of the American men pulled the hammer of his gun to full cock, the sound communicating the unmistakable presence of mortal danger.

The other two men cocked their weapons.

Moisture from the mountain mist condensed on the men's beards. Their long hair curled from under their hats. Larger drops of water from the tree limbs above occasionally dripped onto the leaf bed with an audible thump as each water droplet hit the ground.

The leader spoke again with undisguised hostility.

"If you linger, you'll be shot dead. Drop the game and get the hell out. I know you understand English."

The red-headed leader transferred his quid to the other cheek and spoke.

"We don't want you here. We got surveying work to do. Get the hell out. It's a good thing you came by. Now we can have fresh meat. Consider it payment for our work on your behalf here in Indian country, like taxes."

The three men were amused to see the defenseless, wet Cherokee men standing in front of them caught unawares, who would be forced to surrender the hard-earned results of their successful hunt.

"We're goin' to survey every inch of this state," the talkative red-headed man continued. "We been told you don't like surveyors."

The red-headed man spit to the side without taking his eyes from the Indian standing in front of him.

"They told us to look out for Indians like you. We're loaded. We're ready. Our powder's dry. Do as we say."

The red-headed man held his gun stock tight against his mid-section with the barrel at point-blank range. There would be no need to aim at the Indian man standing calmly in the middle of the mountain path before him.

"One wrong move and we'll kill all three of you where you stand and leave you for the varmints, won't we, Clement?" the leader growled to his friend behind him.

"We'll kill 'em right where they stand, won't we?"

The man named Clement grunted in agreement.

The red-headed man squinted in the mist and shoved the barrel of his gun towards Five Feathers in a threatening manner.

"Do you understand English, you god-damned Indian? Answer me."

Five Feathers nodded slowly in reply, never taking his eyes from the red-headed man. Your brother spoke with just enough force for the Americans to hear.

"I understand. I understand you Americans perfectly."

The three white men, becoming more nervous with each passing moment, were ready for trouble. Afraid of an ambush, their eyes flitted left and right searching for unseen adversaries sneaking up the mountainside behind them.

"You reckon there's more of 'em? Why don't they leave like you said?" one of the men said to the leader in front of him.

Five Feathers and his two friends had one unloaded musket, their unstrung bows and hunting knives, impractical against the three loaded smoothbores at close range. Five Feathers carried Edudu's old war club in a sling on his back, useless against firearms.

Five Feathers held his ground. His two companions would take their cue from him. They would follow Five Feathers' lead no matter the consequences. If Five Feathers chose to drop the game on the path and go down the mountain into Alabama, they would follow. If Five Feathers chose to fight, they would fight. They knew any attack against the white men would be desperate and could result in instant death.

The Americans expected the Indian hunters to retreat, leaving their game for the surveyors. Five Feathers was ready for this day. He had been ready for this day for many years. He would not be dispossessed.

The deadlock continued. The leader motioned impatiently once again with the barrel of his gun for the Indians to move down the mountainside.

Five Feathers did not move or retreat. He did not obey the command nor take his eyes from the red-headed man. To an observer the Indian hunter might have been a glistening statue cast in bronze as he stood proudly on the misty mountain path staring at the bearded face of the red-headed man. Five Feathers seemed to grow larger with every passing moment.

Five Feathers spoke once again just loud enough for the men to hear.

"This is our mountain. We will not leave. You should go home. We will not harm you if you leave now. Take your guns and your animals. Leave our country. Go back to the whiteside. This is not a good day to die on a lonely mountain path far from your home. Go back to your comfortable fireside, to your wives and children. Be wise. Go home."

Five Feathers stood firm in the middle of the worn mountain path that snaked for endless miles along the narrow crest. Occasional water droplets fell from the branches of the surrounding trees making occasional distinct sounds as if someone were dropping small pebbles into the leaf bed from the tree tops.

The Americans were tense and afraid.

Why was this Cherokee man fearless? Surely he must have hidden compatriots preparing to surprise the American surveyors from behind in an overpowering ambush? Why did he stand unafraid? The longer Five Feathers stood his ground, the more uncomfortable the men became. They scanned the woods for danger for some kind of trap yet at the same time afraid to take their eyes off this bold Indian hunter.

It seemed to them the Indian's expressionless face was carved from stone, possessed no emotion and felt no fear. He seemed to be completely unaffected by wind and weather. Except for his brief speech, Five Feathers had not moved or made a sound since he surprised the surveyors. His eyes never strayed from those of the red-headed leader.

Was this Cherokee man not afraid of death? Was he crazy? The uneasy surveyors sensed his strength, a strength that seemed to swell. Even though the Americans possessed superior weapons, they found the confrontation unnerving. Perhaps the Indian didn't understand. They didn't want to kill an unarmed man, even an Indian. Five Feathers, his face and arms glistening in the mountain mist, was standing slightly more than an arm's length from the leader, the man with the red beard and intense blue eyes.

"Let 'em go, Liam. I don't like this," one of the men said.

"We don't need their game. Let 'em go. Let's do our business. I tell you, Liam, I don't like this. You don't have to be a god-damn hardheaded Irishman and have your way all the time. Tell them to keep their deer and git out. Let's get the work done we was hired to do. Indians ain't worth the trouble. I want to go home. Let 'em go."

Five Feathers, the wind gusting around his leggings and his face shimmering, spoke again in a perfectly controlled voice, just loud enough for the men to hear.

"This is our mountain. We will hunt in our country. This is our land. We belong. You do not. You will not take our deer. You will not survey this mountain today. You three should go back to the whiteside. Take your animals and equipment. Ride home in peace. We allow you to leave. Go to your children and sit by your fires. Be happy. Love your wives. Play with your children. We will not harm you. Go now and live."

With every word Five Feathers spoke, the red-headed man seemed to grow more agitated. As Five Feathers finished speaking, the red-headed man spit on Five Feathers' leggings.

"Who the hell do you think you are?" the red-headed man shouted. "You're nothin' but god-damned Indians. I'm an American. I'm going nowhere. This is our land. You think you own this land because you hunt here? You Indians are stupid. This is our land. You're the one goin' to leave. I'll see to that."

The red-headed made threatening motions with his gun barrel indicating the three Indian men should take the path down the mountainside.

"Git down the mountain now, if you know what's good for you. Git down that mountain and leave us to do our work or I'll shoot you where you stand. I ain't afraid of you."

Five Feathers continued to stand still and tall, his arms hanging relaxed at his side. The Americans nervously watched one another and their leader, with constant glances behind in case of ambush.

Five Feathers spoke again, "If you do not go, American, you shall die today on this wet mountain. Ants will consume your eyes. They will crawl into your dead ears. If you do not obey me and leave this mountain possoms will feast upon your cold flesh this very night. Your wives and children shall await your return forever."

Five Feathers never took his eyes from the leader with the red beard. When he finished speaking, he stood as if carved of stone. The three American men didn't like this strange man standing unmoved in front of them threatening them with such a horrible end, even though they knew his threats were empty. Surely the Indian said these bold things because there were others lurking hidden somewhere on the mountain? Is that why this man exhibited no fear?

The Americans, although uneasy, continued in their arrogance, pretending courage. Each with his gun at full cock and his finger on the trigger. It was obvious the Cherokee men in front of them were helpless. The Indians would surely back down. They must.

The leader, doing his best to match the physical presence of Five Feathers, spit another stream of tobacco-laden spittle onto Five Feathers' leggings without taking his eyes from the Cherokee man.

"We got guns," the leader said arrogantly. "You got nothin'. We got the Militia behind us. We're Americans. We're goin' to take your game, Indian, and we're goin' to survey this mountain. That's right, ain't it Clement?"

Clement didn't answer.

The red-headed man continued with a loud voice.

"We don't want trouble, but we'll sure give trouble, and I mean now. I'm tired of you lookin' at me like a dumb-ass. I don't like you. I don't like Indians," he spat his last words bitterly.

"If you don't drop that game and get the hell out of here, I'll kill you for fun. Do you understand? Are you stupid enough to let me shoot you? I promise I'll kill you if you don't leave now."

The red-headed man laughed.

The two American surveyors, standing close behind their leader, were beginning to believe with certainty more Cherokee men must be hidden in the underbrush and they were outnumbered. What else could explain the bravery of the Indian standing in front of them who disregarded every order he was given and was ready to give up his life for a dead turkey and a dead deer as a matter of principle.

Liam, with the red hair and beard, continued his superior tone. The nervousness and volume of his voice increased.

"We're going to survey this land. It's ours. You're trespassing. We got a job to do. The law is behind us. Don't you understand nothin'?"

Each of the surveyor's words became louder until by the end of his short speech he was shouting. Although Five Feathers was standing almost close enough to touch the barrel of the man's gun, he was unmoved by the force of the surveyor's words. Liam's voice had risen to a hysterical scream as if the power of his words alone would remove the Indian from the mountain top. Five Feathers could see the man's finger on the trigger. The stoic Cherokee man had no intention of backing down. Everyone present understood the standoff could not continue. Everyone, except Five Feathers, knew how this encounter would end.

The surveyors didn't want to kill the defenseless Cherokee men, but their American pride wouldn't let them retreat. Five Feathers had been in this situation before. He knew exactly what he was going to do. It might cost him his life but he wasn't going to back down. The Cherokee man's behavior wasn't a put-on bravado, but a tested courage that came from a soul tempered by hundreds of years of Cherokee experience. The three American men began to think they would be forced to kill this stubborn Indian if they wanted to survey the mountain.

The red-headed leader spoke again. His voice a mad scream. Flecks of spittle flew onto the barrel of his gun and Five Feathers' clothing.

Five Feathers' gaze never wavered.

"There's nothing you or your two Indian friends can do to stop us. I'm not standin' here all day. We got a job to do. This is your last chance. I think you're just stupid."

"I don't like this," one of the men said to their leader.

"Let them go and let's get out of here. We can survey here tomorrow. I don't like this. I want to leave. I don't want to be here."

The red-headed man paid no attention to his companion behind him and continued wildly shouting at Five Feathers.

"For the last time, get the hell out of here and drop that game."

His two companions laughed nervously. If there was no ambush they were in a position of unassailable strength yet they didn't want to shoot the three Indians in cold blood who had done nothing but appear in their path.

The red-headed man continued, "Drop your game and run or I'll put a bullet in you right now, right there where you stand, you god-damned statue. What are you lookin' at? Do you think I'm afraid? I wouldn't be afraid of ten of you. This is it. You're done."

Liam began to raise his weapon to his shoulder and squint down the barrel of his smoothbore at the middle of Five Feathers' chest. The two American men just behind, believing Liam had at last decided to kill the Indian, took an awkward step backward over the dead leaves and uneven rocky ground on the narrow mountain path.

At the exact moment the two men stepped backwards, a buzzard caught an updraft in the valley below and soared over the mountaintop directly above their heads. Like an evil apparition, the buzzard seemed to mysteriously appear, gliding silently across the mountaintop, almost brushing the treetops in perfect silence. The massive bird's sudden appearance with outstretched wings caused the three Americans to look upward and flinch and to take another step backwards.

Five Feathers was watching their eyes. When the men looked upwards and moved backwards towards the security of their pack animals, Five Feathers leapt with blinding speed against the red-headed leader who had threatened him.

The Americans, distracted by the buzzard, allowed Five Feathers to act. He was much too quick for a response from either of the three men. The instant the white men were distracted, Five Feathers grabbed the war club on his back in the fingers of his right hand and threw it with perfect accuracy at the center of the forehead of the man with the red beard. At the same moment with his left hand, Five Feathers brushed aside the barrel of the gun. The heavy end of the club crashed into the American's skull. As the red-headed man fell, his rifle discharged harmlessly against the lichen-covered boulder at their side. The sound of the bullet's ricochet echoed off the mountainside into the valley below. The red-headed man crumpled to the ground in a heap, unconscious, blood flowing through his red hair onto the damp soil of the mountain path. He lay still. The other two men were caught completely unawares by Five Feathers' lightening attack and were paralyzed with fear. Both hesitated. Their delay was fatal. Before they could think or squeeze their triggers, Five Feathers had disarmed them both in a single flurry of movement. Five Feathers threw them both to the ground. In quick, powerful motions the Indian broke their arms over protruding rocks in the leaf-bed, their arm bones shattering with loud splintering sounds on the quiet mountaintop like the breaking of dead tree branches. As quickly as it began, Five Feathers' solo attack was over. He stood looking down at the three American surveyors sent by the state of Georgia to divide and give away his land, all legal by laws they had passed to justify their own actions. Five Feathers, breathing normally and with no expression, stared down at the three helpless men at his feet. Escape was impossible.

The red-headed man lay unconscious, his blood running onto the damp leaves from the deep gash in his forehead. The other two terrified men lay with broken arms, immobile, moaning in intense pain, whimpering, begging for mercy from this strange Indian, bigger than the mountain itself, who had somehow magically overpowered them without modern weapons.

"Please, please don't hurt us," the two men pleaded, groveling in the leaves at Five Feathers' feet. With their arms broken, they were unable to rise to a sitting position or stand. Their only hope of survival was to elicit some measure of compassion from the stoic Cherokee man who had, so far, shown no pity or weakness, but who they knew understood their language.

"We weren't really goin' to hurt you," the tallest white man said. "Tell him, Clement. Tell him we ain't like Liam."

The man named Clement said, "John's right. We wouldn't let Liam hurt you. Please don't hurt us. We're good men. We'll go home. We got wives and children. We'll go home."

The man named Clement began to cry.

The tall man named John pleaded.

"It was Liam. He's crazy. Please let us go. We promise we'll go home and never bother you again. We won't never come back. We promise. We like Indians. We've always liked Indians. We never meant no harm. We were just havin' fun. Clement was right. We weren't really goin' to shoot you. I ain't never shot nobody. We wouldn't do that. Liam never did shoot nobody, neither. We like Indians. No one will ever come again. We promise. Please don't hurt us.

As the two men lay writhing on the damp rocky ground on the mountain-top path, they continued to beg for their lives as the expressionless Cherokee man stood above them saying not a word and giving no indication of what he was thinking or what he would do next. Five Feathers' companions were as stunned as the Americans. They, too, continued to stand quietly watching the bizarre scene unfold in front of them. Who was this hunting companion of theirs, this Cherokee warrior who had risen to stand taller than the mountain?

At last Five Feathers moved. He slowly and deliberately knelt beside the unconscious man with the red hair. Five Feathers took the red-headed man's worn leather pouch from his shoulder. He dumped its contents onto the path. Just a few feet from the two conscious white men and in their full view, Five Feathers knelt, scraped back the dead leaves and scooped the empty leather bag full of soft, damp, loamy soil, never once looking at the pitiful men continuing to beg only an arm's length away. They stared at their attacker wondering what was to be their fate. What was he planning? With their arms lying at crazy angles and their eyes wide with pain, they watched as the Cherokee man filled the leather bag to overflowing with damp soil, Cherokee soil taken from the path on the top of a Cherokee mountain.

Five Feathers put the leather strap of the worn leather pouch across his shoulder and hung the leather bag across his chest, rolled the red-headed man onto his back and knelt with his full weight on the red-headed man's torso. The two American men with broken arms watched in horror.

Blood still flowed from the red-headed man's wound. Without any facial expression Five Feathers spit on the unconscious man's face.

"You would spit on me? Kill me? You would come to my mountain and spit on me for no reason? You would take our land and make our children homeless? You would kill those who never did you harm? You would take that which has never belonged to you? There is no law on this earth or where you are going to justify you taking our land."

Five Feathers continued to speak to the unconscious man lying on his back under him, talking as if the wounded man could hear.

"You wish to take everything we possess? You would take the land from under the feet of our children? You want Cherokee soil? I shall give you what you want. You shall have your desire. I shall give you all the Cherokee soil you can eat and breathe. You shall freely have the Cherokee soil you thirsted for. You shall take our earth to that place I shall send you today. I will fill you with good Cherokee soil for your journey."

Five Feathers, kneeling on the unconscious man's chest, took a handful of soil from the bag and began stuffing the unconscious man's mouth with the moist earth. The man wakened suddenly, opened his eyes in panic making choking noises as he tried to breathe. Wildly staring upward at the Cherokee man he had intended to kill, he began to flail with his arms and legs to free himself from the crushing weight on his chest.

Five Feathers ignored the man's attempts to free himself and continued forcing soil into his mouth, prying his lower jaw open with his left hand as he packed the damp earth deep into his throat with his right. The red-headed man thrashed and writhed but in vain. Five Feathers continued to hold the wounded man to the ground. He stuffed his mouth with black soil until saliva and soil mixed came out the red-headed man's nose in great black bubbles as he made a final gasping, choking noise and breathed his last.

The white man with the red beard lay dead, motionless, his sightless blue eyes staring into the grey clouds moving slowly above the mountain path. Another buzzard glided low across the mountaintop. A gust of wind whipped dead brown leaves onto Liam's ashen face and his red beard. The other two white men began blubbering incoherently, begging for their lives.

Five Feathers' companions had not moved or spoken since Five Feathers had sprung into action. When the first man quit breathing, Five Feathers turned to the other two struggling on the ground nearby, their broken limbs useless. Unable to stand, they struggled on their backs. slithering between the rocks and trees, trying somehow to slide down the mountain away from this mad-man they believed would do to them as they had seen him do to their leader.

Five Feathers knelt beside the two men and spoke quietly.

"You came up this mountain to take our land. You want us to leave. You want to live in our homes, the homes we built for our children. You want to turn my Elisi and Edudu into the forest so you can sit at their fire, work their fields and eat from their smokehouse. You want Cherokee land. You pass laws to make your actions legal. I shall give you in abundance that which you so desire by an ancient law older, a law much older than you Americans."

The two men, in intense pain, were watching.

"You crossed the sea to take our country," Five Feathers continued quietly. "You should have listened to me and you would be on your way home to your children. You want to send us far away. Instead, I shall send you away, to a place from which you shall never return. The place where you belong."

The two pathetic men, trying to dissuade this Cherokee man from his intended task, began to cry and plead, hardly able to enunciate their words, tears mixed with spittle dripped from their beards as they continued to beg.

"We don't want your land. Please, please, please, please, we're sorry. We shouldn't have said those things. We won't say that again, will we Clement?"

"We won't come back," the other man said.

"We don't want your deer. That was Liam. We'll leave and never come back. Please don't kill us. We like Indians. We've always liked Indians. We don't want your land. We never did. It was Liam. We'll never come back."

"From your own mouth you speak truth. You shall leave this earth today and you shall never come back."

The two surveyors continued to whimper. Five Feathers paid no attention to their appeals. Without pity he knelt on the next man's chest. With one hand holding the man's head in place, he slowly forced small handfuls of the moist, sandy earth into his mouth until the man, his back arching and legs kicking madly, tried to free himself in an unsuccessful muscular spasm. He resisted until he, too, blew black, gritty bubbles out of his nose, choked, aspirated the mixture into his lungs and stopped breathing. He lay motionless, his mouth filled with the Cherokee soil he had coveted, his eyes glazed in death like Liam's, staring sightlessly at the scudding rain clouds flying low across the lonely Cherokee mountain they had intended to take from the Cherokee hunters.

Five Feathers' two friends shivered. Their shiver wasn't prompted by the cold mountain mist. They watched Five Feathers execute his judgment against the last white man, execute a law and its penalty, an ancient law older than Washington City or Milledgeville.

He squeezed the man's mouth open with one hand and slowly forced the earth in until the man choked on the black dirt and he, like the other two, foamed black bubbles of Cherokee earth out his white nostrils and thrashed in a final panic like an animal caught in a trap.

The three men lay dead, staring with sightless eyes at the iron-grey sky above the mountain path. Trailing from the mouth and nose of each was a black mixture of Cherokee soil and saliva. The raindrops, beginning to fall in a steady drizzle, began to wash their faces clean.

Five Feathers ordered his companions to throw the bodies and all their equipment into a nearby pit, not to keep one thing belonging to surveyors and to thickly cover the men with laurels. He ordered them to throw the deer and turkey carcass on top of the laurels. If someone happened by, they would smell the decomposing animals and investigate no further.

"That is what happened on the mountain top, Walela. If the Americans had not brought so much disease," Edudu said, "we would have many like your brother. We could defend our homes. Those like your brother are few. We cannot resist the Americans and their laws. Your brother will not abandon us. He will come back when it is safe. He would never leave you alone. He will be a leader in our nation."

"Edudu, I feel no sorrow for the three. I understand my brother. They are being repaid in kind.

Chapter XXXVIII

1834-35 – Council at Running Waters – Schermerhorn
Chapter 38

5 January 1834 - Month of the Cold Moon -du no lv ta ni
From the *Federal Union* – 1 January 1834 – page 2
"About five hundred artillerists, of the United States Army…passed through Milledgeville on the 24th of December…A part of them are destined for Fort Mitchell, a part for Mobile, and a part for Choctaw country."

26 January 1834
From the *Cherokee Phoenix* – 25 January 1834
"From the *Knoxville Republican* Sec. 1. Be it enacted by the General Assembly of the State of Tennessee, That the laws and jurisdiction of the state of Tennessee, be and hereby extended to the southern limits of the State, of that tract of country now in the occupancy of the Cherokee Indians…"

16 May 1834
Our newspaper has closed. We have no money for postage or wages or to purchase paper. President Jackson stopped government payments to force our emigration.

18 May 1834
The Guard frighten us. Since the missionaries were removed they have been commissioned to dispossess and steal. Georgia passed laws so we cannot bring suit against an American. No one sees or cares. Justice has departed. We are alone. Who can oppose the likes of Curry and Butler sent by the Governor himself to make our lives difficult?

Our crime is simple. We are not Americans. We are not white.

The president and the newspapers talk constantly of removal. Lewis Cass, Jackson's Secretary of War, thinks we are not fit to own land and must emigrate for our own protection. The American government assigns agents to help us. We are harassed and dispossessed at every turn. The future may become worse, but how can it be worse? They have taken all the good farmland in the river bottoms. Soon they will come for us in the mountains.

238

Ben is the light in my life. One day he and I shall be together. He will come. I know he will come.

31 July 1834

From the *Federal Union* – 23 July 1834 – page 2

Cherokee-Injunction Case, Judge Warner's Opinion, Delivered at the Convention of Judges, July Session, 1834

"This is a…contest between the rights of the state of Georgia and…the Cherokee Indians…The state claims the right to limit the Indians…In…1730 six of the principle chiefs of the Cherokee Indians…went to London, and acknowledged themselves subject to the king, in the same manner as were their white brethren of South Carolina. During the war of the Revolution, the Cherokee Indians took part with the British Crown…the American cause was victorious and the Indians conquered….Each state within its respective limits retained all the rights which belonged to the crown…From the Declaration of Independence up to the time of the adoption of the constitution…each state had the right to manage all affairs with the Indians within its own limits…The Cherokee Indians have never been recognized by the Government as a sovereign people…The states before the adoption of the Federal Constitution, having the exclusive right to manage the affairs of the Indians within their respective limits, and not having delegated this right, the conclusion is irresistible, that it yet remains in the states….That the Government of the United States "solemnly guarantied" to the Cherokee Indians the lands in their occupancy, within the limits of the state, is admitted; but the State of Georgia contends that she had prior and paramount right to all the land within her limits…It is plain to…everyone…the territorial rights of the states were to be considered sacred…It is therefore clear that the Cherokee Indians have not derived any vested rights to the soil within the limits of Georgia by virtue of the several treaties made with them and the Government of the United States…The supreme court of the State of New York…have exercised an entire supremacy over all the Indian tribes within the State, and have regulated by law their internal concerns, their contracts and their property."

12 November 1834

Great news. Ben has been elected to the U.S. House for the second time.

9 January 1835

The north wind has been whipping down the mountains bringing frozen rain and snow. Sleet makes music against the windows and the wind is whistling a tune in the chimney blowing a smoky downdraft. I love every moment of a winter storm. I feel sorry for Edudu carrying wood and tending to animals. Elisi and I put more straw in with the chickens. The poor things are so cold.

The storm was a surprise. Edudu said he never expected a storm from the northeast. The entire landscape is covered in its beautiful winter coat with drifts in many places as high as my knees and other places with hardly any snow at all. I feel sorry for the animals and the birds. I walked down to the river. It has much ice floating but it is not frozen across. I wonder where the river otters are? How do they stay warm?

24 January 1835

From the *Georgia Journal* – 20 January 1835 – page 2

"...within the present limits of the State, lies the Cherokee tribe...From whence does the State derive the right of jurisdiction? I answer—by charter from the Crown of Great Britain—the right which Great Britain had to these limits she acquired by discovery and conquest...Such rights are recognized among nations...and is not now open for discussion...as a question of international law the right is established."

4 July 1835

from the *Federal Union*-23 June 1835-page 2

"Our Cherokee Affairs: The terms of the treaty lately offered by General Jackson to the Cherokee are marked by unparalleled liberality to that misguided and unfortunate people and paternal solicitude for their welfare. It secures to the tribe a good and permanent home, and provides for distribution to each individual Indian...for their removal...Notwithstanding the magnitude of the price, the extraordinary liberality of the government has been approved by the American people....The assent of the chiefs to these treaties has generally been acquired by direct bribes...To the pure and inflexible patriot now at the head of the government, has been reserved the honor of reforming this corrupt and corrupting habit; of restraining the inordinate cupidity of the chiefs and of securing justice to the poor, weak and obscure Indian....Many of the most intelligent Cherokee are anxious for the confirmation of the treaty; but it is seriously apprehended that John Ross will resort to the most criminal measures to prevent its acceptance...that Indians of the Ross party, after the commission of the most flagrant crimes, may set at defiance, or may evade our constables, and sheriffs; that they may hold in contempt the array of our juries, and the authority of our judges."

"For a long course of years Andrew Jackson has evinced a steady friendship and a paternal benevolence for the Cherokee...The president has long been the faithful friend of Georgia and at the same time, with guardian care, he has attempted to provide for the real welfare of the Cherokee...These two men will not be censured for their measures in relation to the Cherokee, except by those who are determined to encourage these victims of delusion in their foolish rejection of the liberal offers of the President and their obstinate determination to violate the laws of the state and to oppress the friends of emigration...the honor of Georgia will sustain governor Lumpkin in his determination to maintain the authority of her laws for protection, from the ruffian violence of (Chief John) Ross and his savage myrmidons."

"Thank you, Walela, for reading to me. We have long known what the whiteside thinks. Americans hates us for no reason other than a wish to possess that which belongs to another. Our good chief has never advocated violence in any form, never at any time. He has been a hard-working representative to the Americans and promoted peace at every opportunity. Andrew Jackson says evil things about him because John Ross cannot be purchased."

One of Edudu's friends spoke, "I have not heard of a single crime committed by our chief or any of the men who work with him. Chief Ross tells us every time I hear him that we shall not use violence in any form. You read the American newspapers, Walela. What do you think?"

"I read their newspapers," I answered. "I know what they are saying and why. These accusations of violence are not true. The men who control the newspapers write lies intended to inflame the American populace over time, to bend public opinion to hate us. They receive and believe every bad thing said about us, even the stories that have been invented. Americans want to believe bad news because they want our land. Their politicians find it easy to deceive."

The men nodded and Edudu spoke, "Robbery, theft, intimidation, fraud, murder and rape have been committed against us for decades by Americans. It's useless for us to complain to their authorities. Every year it gets worse. They steal our livestock and anything else they want. Just a month ago I watched a group of Americans take most of my hogs. Even though I was standing there and told them the hogs were mine, there was nothing I could do. They laughed as they drove my hogs away. They know judges will not convict an American man for a crime committed against an Indian."

"One day, perhaps, our story will be told," I said. "I will write as long as I can hold a pen. Men can kill with lead, but there is no gun powerful enough to kill a noble idea once written."

Edudu spoke once again, "You keep writing, Walela. Maybe that will do some good. A grand council meeting has been called at Running Waters on John Ridge's farm. We will be asked to vote by Mr. Schermerhorn and Mr. Curry on the disbursements of annuities. We will be asked to decide whether the money goes to individuals as the Ridge and Curry people want or into the national treasury as our chief prefers. Schermerhorn and Murray, friends of Ridge, want the money to go to individuals, to their friends, of course. The removal party is doing their best to gain broad support among us at the expense of Chief Ross. I don't like this. It's appears Ridge and Curry are going behind our chief's back intentionally."

"What do you think will happen, Edudu?" I asked.

"I shall let you know, my dear, when I return from the meeting. I will listen and learn. I will listen and learn."

3 December 1834

"What happened at Running Waters, Edudu? Tell me.

"Our chief is a good man," Edudu said, with a smile. "Even when the Americans and the removal party sought to go behind his back, our people remained loyal and strong. Ridge, Schermerhorn and Major Curry were defeated in their attempt to undermine our chief's authority. They were defeated badly. I have a great suspicion, Walela, that Ridge and his friends are interested in acquiring wealth at our expense and they'll continue to work to defeat our chief. I find it hard to believe that Ridge and his friends hold the best interest of all Cherokee in their hearts—especially the poor Cherokee."

I was unusually impatient, "Please tell me what happened. I can't wait to hear the details."

"My dear Walela, you should have come with me. It was a magnificent meeting. Everyone behaved. There was almost no drunkenness and no violence whatsoever. We had dances, ballplays and wrestling and I talked with all my friends and told stories. I told a lot of stories late into the evening. We heard the speeches by Schermerhorn and his friends and we finally voted. The vote was big in favor of our chief. I am pleased. Perhaps we may be allowed to keep our farm, perhaps not, but at least the removal party was soundly defeated."

"That is wonderful news, Edudu."

Edudu looked at me and this time he didn't smile.

"I know a great deal about this world," Edudu said after a long pause. "We can admire a colorful stone lying on the ground, but pick that stone up and we discover slimy things crawling underneath. Life is like that. I know a great deal about the removal party. I hear things. When they talk it appears they have everyone's best interest at heart. Almost every day someone tells me what is going on down by the Coosa river, up at the Agency and other places. If someone damns the stream in one place it will overflow in another. I fear the defeat of the removal party at the meeting has only delayed the flood. The removal party is defeated for the moment, but they are secretly planning things. The Americans want rid of us and they don't care how. They will use the removal party as a tool. I hope for the best, but my heart tells me Ridge and the Americans will conspire."

28 July 1835

Good news. John Ross is going to move our printing press and all our printing equipment to Red Clay. We can begin publishing the Phoenix again. What wonderful news.

6 August 1835

It is hot, sticky and dusty. We need rain. The pleasant summer winds have been stilled. The house never cools.

24 August 1835

Terrible news. Without warning the Guard took our printing press, destroyed all our supplies, burned our building and scattered our precious type. It is rumored someone told the Guard about our plans to move the printing press north outside the borders of Georgia. Perhaps it was Stand Watie. I don't want to believe any Cherokee man would betray his own nation, but Edudu has heard things. I cried all afternoon. Our ability to send our newspaper throughout the United States has been destroyed. The right to speak truth is for Americans only. Mr. Lowry was right. Powerful men in Milledgeville understand. They know that words are more dangerous than lead, powder and iron.

I fear Edudu's words will prove prophetic. One cold morning the sun will reveal everything beautiful in our country frozen and lifeless, covered by a white killing frost.

21 November 1835

From the *Federal Union* - 13 November 1835 – page 3

"We have just had an interview with some gentleman on their return from the council from Red Clay, from whom we learn that the proposals, made to the Cherokee by the United States Government have met with final rejection. The two parties, whose views and actions have been so diametrically opposed to each other, met to confer on the possibility of so modifying the proposed treaty as to meet the conflicting views of the parties; and although the treaty and all its provisions were rejected, the parties so far united as to appoint a delegation, composed of both Ridge and Ross men, to meet and confer with the commissioners of the United States. Whether this conference will take place in the Cherokee Country, or at Washington, is not yet settled; but it is presumed they will meet at Washington: We leave to others to say whether this course of Ross is or is not finesse. But it appears to us that he wishes to gain time, and thereby see what regulations our present legislature will adopt towards the lands now occupied by the Cherokees, within the limits of the State.

If the present legislature should not provide for granting, indiscriminately, all the land in Cherokee Country, it is more than probable that he will still continue to reject the most liberal offers of the general government. But if the States of Tennessee and Georgia will adopt proper measures, there can be no doubt, but that they will, be forced to accept arrangements for their speedy removal West of the Mississippi river. Let Georgia grant all her lands, and Tennessee prevent their removal thither, and the result is obvious. –Cassville Pioneer, 30 ult."

Soldiers from Georgia crossed into Tennessee and arrested our chief and John Howard Payne.

From the *Federal Union* – 20 November 1835 – page 2

"There are four Cherokees in Milledgeville, who state, that in the absence of Col. Bishop, the second officer of the Cherokee Guard, with a detachment crossed the boundary of the State, proceeded to the residence of John Ross in Tennessee, seized him, and brought him a prisoner into Georgia. They state, that this outrage was perpetrated at the suggestion of Shermerhorn and Currie, agents of the United States, and that its motive was, to keep Ross from going to Washington, to represent the Cherokees with the Federal Government.... Mr. John Howard Payne also, a gentleman well known to the literary world, has been arrested under the suspicion of his having conspired with Ross, against the welfare of Georgia, and it is said his papers give evidence of the fact."

26 November 1835
My Dear Cassie,

I rushed to make the afternoon post. I want you to read the latest from today's paper. I fear there are, even as I write, backroom negotiations to destroy Cherokee unity. Zach thinks the same. He would know.

My guess is Shermerhorn has a hidden agenda straight from the White House. Treachery is afoot. I know Schermerhorn has written asking the President to refuse to negotiate with Ross and the national party. The President and Schermerhorn intend to cause divisions in the Cherokee leadership. They wish to sign a treaty, even if it's a treaty with a tiny portion of the delegates. When that clandestine treaty is signed, it will be immediately pushed through the United States Senate before Ross can mount objections. Georgia, of course, will cooperate with Schermerhorn and Curry in any backroom deal. Please share this with your grandfather and his friends. I will do my best to communicate this to John Ross himself if I can. This letter is for your eyes only. Do not let it out of your possession.

Loving you more every day, Ben xoxoxo

From the *Federal Union*, New Echota – 31 October 1835

Col. John H. Lumpkin

"…The Red Clay council has closed and the result of their deliberations have been of vast consequence to the Cherokee people—I considered that the Indian controversy now to be closed. The Ross party and the Treaty party have united, and have agreed to close the Cherokee difficulties by a general treaty. To effect this object the people in general council assembled, have elected twenty delegates, with full powers to treat at Washington City. Those delegates, to wit: John Ross, John Ridge, John Martin, Elias Boudinott, Charles Vann, Soft Shell Turtle, E. Hicks, John Baldridge, John Benge, James Daniel, Sleeping Rabbit, Joseph Vann, Richard Fields, Richard Taylor, Lewis Ross, Thomas Foreman, Jesse Bushyhead, Peter of Aquohee, James Brown and John Hass…the appointment of this delegation clothed with full power to treat, was ratified by the people….there were upwards of one thousand men signed the power of this delegation. This delegation then commenced a negotiation with Mr. Schermerhorn and as they could not procure from him positive terms, they have adjourned over to meet at Washington City, on the 20th of December next, to treat at headquarters….against Mr. Schermerhorn's official labor I have nothing to say; he has served his government with zeal and energy. But candor requires me to express my fears, that his zeal will carry him away from the true course which the government ought to adopt. I believe that he has written letters to the

245

President to reject the Delegation at Washington, and contrary to the will of all the parties of the Indians, has appointed the 3rd Monday in December to hold a treaty with the people at the New Echota....I feel a great desire to avert the great calamity of a people expelled out of their houses in winter, which leads me to make this appeal in behalf of my people....to the correctness of these views, I pledge to you my sacred honor.

Your Friend, John Ridge"

Why is Schermerhorn meeting in New Echota? Cherokee national meetings have been forbidden in our capital. I do not like this meeting when our chief is in Washington City. Georgia permits the removal party to hold meetings in Cherokee Country but John Ross and the national party must meet in Red Clay. A terrible storm brewing. I fear Ben is correct and the American government at the highest level is trying to destroy our nation.

Chapter XXXIX

1836 – Disputed Treaty Ratified – Gen. Wool Appointed

Chapter 39

3 January 1836 - Month of the Cold Moon -du no lv ta ni

On December 29, in the absence of our chief, a treaty was signed by Major Ridge, Elias Boudinott, John Gunter and seventeen others of the removal party with the representative of the general government, J. F. Schermerhorn. Why didn't they wait for Chief Ross? Under what devious authority did Schermerhorn, the Jackson representative, negotiate the treaty? The tiny removal party signed away our entire nation. Why did they go behind our chief's back? Why did Schermerhorn accept the signatures without our chief present and without a general council?

Did Schermerhorn purposely wait until our chief was absent or worse, arranged our chief's absence? Schermerhorn knew Chief Ross would not agree to any treaty that would cede our entire country. Many think Schermerhorn was acting deceitfully under direct orders from President Jackson.

4 January 1836

Harriet thinks her husband's friends pressured him. They believe it would be better to exchange our land rather than continue to struggle and perhaps lose everything. Perhaps our chief can work a miracle. Perhaps we should leave. How could they sign our country away for money when our chief wasn't here? The land belongs to all. The removal party represents a small portion of our people. There will be trouble over this.

According to the piece of paper they call a treaty, every Cherokee family must leave within two years. Edudu and Elisi will not talk about the treaty or the removal party. They trust our chief.

4 February 1836

The *Camden Journal* says South Carolina is sending mounted regiments to Florida to pursue Seminoles. They talk about how we violate the rights of Americans, of white people who are continually taking our land.

27 April 1836

The blackberry blossoms tell us spring has arrived. We'll soon plant our corn and vegetables. For one more year we'll enjoy squash, beans, cucumbers, pumpkins, watermelons and ramps. I love Dla-ya-de-i, polk-salad in English, gathered when young and tender. Edudu and I love them with an egg scrambled—so does Five Feathers. We gather the dark purple polk-salad berries for a rich dye when we're making pine baskets.

12 June 1836

The Schermerhorn treaty has been ratified by the United States Senate despite objections from Chief John Ross. Edudu and Eagle Killer walked slowly up the hill into the woods, Edudu's back bent like an old man.

From the *Georgia Journal* – 7 June 1836

"The treaty lately concluded the Headmen and Chiefs of the Cherokee Indians…for the purchase of all lands owned, claimed, or possessed by the Cherokees East of the Mississippi, as ratified by the President and the Senate of the United States has been officially published…The Indians are to be transported by the United States to the West of the Mississippi…"

14 June 1836

From the *Federal Union* - 9 June 1836 – page 3

"…it is the part of prudence to observe the Cherokees with a watchful and suspicious eye, even though they may appear to be quiet and peaceable…they have in fact given strong indications of hostility, which cannot be safely be overlooked. Since the failure of the Florida campaign, and the temporary success of the Creeks in Alabama…the Cherokees in Murray, and other counties in which they are numerous, have become sulky and insolent in their demeanor, and have declared that they will burn the houses of the whites, and do as much damage as possible. The Ross-men say, that Ross has told them that their land should never be sold; and that rather than leave it, as required by the treaty, and by the laws of Georgia, they will die fighting on it…should the Cherokees…commit any acts of hostility thousands of brave and generous Georgians…will rush to the assistance of their exposed fellow-citizens. An avenging storm, with desolating fury will beat upon the heads of the infatuated race. Woe to the Cherokees, if they should shed the blood of any of our people!"

18 June 1836

From the *Southern Recorder* – 14 June 1836 – page 3

"…Rumor states that Cedartown has been laid in ashes and from 12 to 16 families butchered by the Cherokees…that the Indian force now collected is computed from 3 to 500—that they insolently demand provisions from the whites, and are robbing them of their cattle…Therefore we anticipate that our volunteers…will receive orders…to protect their own homes, as the present seat of hostilities is only about a day's ride from here."

This newspaper article is a fabrication. There is no Indian force in Cedartown. There is no violence. No one is demanding anything from American settlers. No one has been murdered. No cattle have been stolen. There is no name attached to this article. What do the thousands of American newspaper readers think? I know what they think. Evil men want our land. Wicked men know the power of words and how to employ them.

7 July 1836
    From the *Southern Recorder* – 5 July 1836 – page 2
        "…we believe the Cherokees will remain quiet, at least for the present…the President has made a requisition for a brigade of troops on the governor of Tennessee, which will make its Head-Quarters at Athens, Tennessee, on the borders of Georgia, and adjacent to the Cherokees."

11 July 1836
    We are a tame and peaceful people. We build houses. We plant crops. We feed chickens, cows and pigs. We raise families. We have no army. We have no weapons. We have been preyed upon for a hundred years, yet the United States and Georgia speak of us as characterized by savage perfidy and violence. We have not disregarded treaty after treaty. We have not broken promise after promise. American perfidy, not ours, will be infamous.

From the *Federal Union* – 30 June 1836 – Page 2
        "The following letter from the secretary of War to the Georgia Delegation in Congress…shows that the Federal Executive has adopted, and is executing energetic precautionary measures to preserve the lives of our citizens and to guard the peace of our Cherokee counties against the dangers of savage perfidy and violence."

    War Department, June 18, 1836
        "Gentlemen—It may be agreeable to you to know, that with a view to prevent or suppress any hostilities among the Cherokee

Indians, a Brigade of Tennessee Volunteers, amounting to one thousand to twelve hundred men, one half mounted, one half infantry, will rendezvous at Athens on the 7th of July, and proceed immediately to Cherokee Country. Brigadier General Wool has been assigned to the command, and has been authorized, should circumstances require it, to call for additional force, and to take all measures necessary for the suppression of hostilities among those Indians, should any occur and for their immediate removal.

Very respectfully yours, your obedient servant,
Lewis Cass"

6 September 1836

The weather has been exceptionally hot. I'm anxious for the cool days of autumn. Bear Paws' mother came to see me today. The Americans have been selling more whiskey than ever and Bear Paws has begun drinking again. Our men asked the whiskey sellers to leave, but they laugh at us. American soldiers drink a lot of whiskey.

"Walela, I am heartbroken," Bear Paws' mother said, almost in tears. "I thought my son had stopped drinking whiskey, but once again he is causing terrible disturbances. I don't know what to do. Will you write a letter to my Bear Paws for me?"

"Of course I will, my dear Adsila. I have paper and pen. Tell me what you want me to write."

"I want him to know I have asked both the American God and our Great Spirit to help him stop drinking whiskey."

I wrote for Adsila:

My Dear Bear Paws,

I would give anything to save you from whiskey. You have been my joy since you were a happy baby.

Someone taught you to love whiskey more than you love your mother. Breaking my heart has become easy for you. This did not happen in one day. I do not blame you.

You are willing to wreck everyone's life for the pleasure of drinking whiskey and then you don't remember your awful pleasure. You and your bad wolf will soon perish if you continue.

My son, I have a new prayer. I no longer pray for your safety or that you come home to me.

I will pray that the Great God of all men brings you to himself no matter the cost.

My dear Bear Paws.

This is your mother's prayer:

God of heaven and earth I beseech you,

My son, Bear Paws, cannot stop drinking whiskey. In the past I asked you to keep him safe. I withdraw those prayers. I give you permission to do whatever it takes to get him to stop drinking whiskey. If he will not stop, you have my permission to rescue him from his madness and bring him home to yourself. You have my permission to use pain, suffering, or even death to rescue him—his death or mine or both.

I give you permission to break my heart if need be. I withhold nothing. I love my son. Please bring him to his senses. I wish nothing good for the Americans who sell whiskey. They vend sorrow and pain. I leave them to your judgment.

I give you permission to do anything you wish with my son or with myself—be it life or be it death.

This is my prayer, Adsila

My Dear Bear Paws,

I shall offer up that prayer every day to the Great God and our Great Spirit until you stop drinking whiskey or the Great Spirit takes you to himself. I pray for your rescue. If someone brings me news of your death, I will know you have gone home and are finally free from whiskey and your bad wolf.

If I hear of your death, I will know where to find you. One day I will join you there. We shall be forever free of those who sell death. I love you more than my own life,

Your mother, Adsila

I gave Adsila the finished letter in Cherokee. She said she would give it to Bear Paws and tell him to come by to have me read it to him. When she left, I cried.

15 October 1836

My dear Harriet is dead. She was on this earth for only thirty-one summers. She passed while young and vibrant. My friend leaves behind a husband and six beautiful children. Harriet suffered at the hands of her own family, rejected because of her love of a Cherokee man and now she has suffered the final human indignity, death. I want to experience endless days laughing again with Mrs. Lowry, teaching with her husband and sitting during long, carefree afternoons with my dear Harriet. I want to watch her children play. I want these things, but things change. Things change.

26 October 1836

Elias is sending the children to Harriet's relatives. Eleanor, Mary and Sarah are going to stay with their aunt, Mary Brinsmade, the sister who stood up for Harriet when she married. The boys, William Penn, Frank Brinsmade and Elias Cornelius will go to school in Manchester, Vermont.

14 November 1836

Ben is elected once again to the U.S. House, his third term. Martin Van Buren will be president, but I wonder if anything will be different. Ben's political future is bright and getting brighter. I wish I could see him more often. One day we will be together, it must be.

Milledgeville – The Grand Ballroom - Mitchell's Hotel

"Ben, here we are again. I don't know about you, but I'm getting used to our success. Third time's a charm. We're almost there. Your next office will be your appointment to the United States Senate. Everything is moving along as we planned. We've done well, very well. Your next election will see us win the grand prize. I'm grateful as usual. There will be a nice token of my gratitude on your desk when you return to work, much better than last time," Mr. Mitchell said with an alcohol fueled grin."

"Thank you, sir. I am grateful," Ben answered. "These eight years seem like a dream. Your business has grown. We've prospered beyond expectations. I have you, your son and Elizabeth to thank."

"Elizabeth and Zach have been busy, haven't they? I guess it's the energy of youth," Mr. Mitchell said with a wry smile.

"Ben," Zach's father continued, "there's something I've been wanting to talk to you about."

"Yes, sir. I'm all ears."

"You're becoming an important man in Georgia and Washington City, Ben. More people are taking notice. Folks are coming to you for advice and help with their business. You're popular and a leader in Georgia politics. I couldn't be more pleased. We need to let it be seen publicly you're a proud Georgian, that you believe in states' rights, the right for Southerners to own property free and clear. I don't want anyone to think you're not a patriotic American. The House of Representatives is one thing, but when you're in the Senate you'll have to toe the line. My friends believe you'll represent them very well, but if they're not sure you're a slavery man, you don't have a chance in Georgia. Folks have to be sure where your heart is on this matter."

"I'm fully committed to the rights of folks north and south to own property. That's not a problem with me, sir. Slavery is an institution that was here when the old thirteen became a nation. It can stay as far as I'm concerned."

"Good for you, Ben. That's the line you'll hold when you're in the senate. However, one of my wife's friends was wondering why she never sees you with servants, why you're always doin' for yourself. Ben, I know you don't own a single slave. That's going to be a problem if you want to be a senator. That's what I want to tell you. It's time to act. You have no choice in this matter. I could never support you in your senate bid if you're not fully on board. I'm sure you know what I mean."

"Yes, sir. I've thought of that," Ben answered. "Zach has often suggested I buy slaves, but I know nothing about the business. You know my background, sir."

"Ben, you've made us a lot of money and you're going to make us a lot more. Zach tells me you and Caesar get along well. He's heard you two talking. You're quite friendly with him, I understand. How about I give you Caesar, his wife, son and daughter as an election gift? They'll be a token of my gratitude. You've got money. Buy yourself a little house near the office and use Caesar as your personal servant, his daughter as your housekeeper and the boy as your driver. Everyone knows Caesar from my private dining room. When they see him with you they'll know you're a true Southerner. Givin' you Caesar is the best way to solve this problem, don't you think?"

"Yes, sir. Caesar is an excellent servant. I see your point, sir."

"If I give you Caesar, everyone in Georgia will know you own slaves, and besides, you need the help. Caesar's daughter is a seamstress and his son a farrier. You can make extra money hiring them out if you don't have enough for them to do. What do you say?"

"Sounds good to me, sir. I've always liked Caesar. I'll do whatever it takes to get that Senate seat. You know that, sir."

Chapter XL
1837 – Gen. Wool Removed – The Quilt
Chapter 40

8 March 1837 - Month of the Windy Moon -a nu yi

On 4 March, Martin Van Buren was inaugurated as the President of the United States. Will he continue Jackson's policies?

From the *Federal Union* - 4 April 1837 - Page 3

"**More of the Creeks**. The *Mobile Mercantile Advisor* says:- -Three Steamboats--the John Nelson, the Chippewa and the Bonnets O'Blue--have arrived from Montgomery with 1,900 Creek Indians, on their way to the far west. The John Nelson had 660--the Chippewa 800--and the Bonnets O'Blue 450. There are about 1000 yet to come, to complete the entire Creek Nation."

30 March 1837

Letter to the Cherokee from General Wool.

"Army Headquarters, New Echota, March 22, 1837 CHEROKEES:

It is nearly a year since I first arrived in this country. I then informed you of the objects of my coming among you. I told you that a treaty had been made with your people, and that your country was to be given up to the United States by the 25th May, 1838, a (little more than a year from this time,) when you would all be compelled to remove to the West. I also told you, if you would submit to the terms of the treaty I would protect you in your persons and property, at the same time I would furnish provisions and clothing to the poor and destitute of the Nation. You would not listen, but turned a deaf ear to my advice. You preferred the counsel of those who were opposed to the treaty. They told you, what was not true, that your people had made no treaty with the United States, and that you would be able to retain you lands, and would not be obliged to remove to the West, the place designated for your new homes. Be no longer deceived by such advice! It is not only untrue, but if listened to, may lead to your utter ruin. The President, as well as Congress, have decreed that you should remove from this country. The people of Georgia, of North Carolina, of Tennessee and of Alabama, have decreed it. Your fate is decided; and if you do not voluntarily get ready and go by the time fixed in the treaty, you will then be forced from this country by the soldiers of the United States.

Under such circumstances what will be your condition? Deplorable in the extreme! Instead of the benefits now presented to you by the treaty, of receiving pay for the improvements of your lands, your houses, your cornfields and your ferries, and for all the property unjustly taken from you by the white people, and at the same time, blankets, clothing and provisions for the poor, you will be driven from the country, and without a cent to support you on your arrival at your new homes. You will in vain flee to your mountains for protection. Like the Creeks, you will be hunted up and dragged from your lurking places and hurried to the West. I would ask, are you prepared for such scenes? I trust not. Yet such will be your fate if you persist in your present determination.

Cherokees: I have not come among you to oppress you, but to protect you and to see that justice is done you, as guaranteed by the treaty. Be advised, and turn a deaf ear to those who would induce you to believe that no treaty has been made with you, and that you will not be obliged to leave your country. They cannot be friends, but the worst of enemies. Their advice, if followed, will lead to your certain destruction. The President has said that a treaty has been made with you, and must be executed agreeably to its terms. The President never changes. Therefore, take my advice: It is the advice of a friend, who would tell you the truth, and who feels deeply interested in your welfare, and who will do everything in his power to relieve, protect and secure to you the benefits of the treaty. And why not abandon a country no longer yours? Do you not see the white people daily coming into it, driving you from your homes and possessing your houses, your cornfields and your ferries? Hitherto I have been able to some degree, to protect you from their intrusions; in a short time it will no longer be in my power. If, however, I could protect you, you could not live with them. Your habits, your manners and your customs are unlike, and unsuited to theirs. They have no feelings, no sympathies in common with yourselves. Leave then this country, which after the 25th May 1838, can afford you no protection and remove to the country designated for your new homes, which is secured to you and your children forever; and where you may live under your own laws, and the customs of your fathers, without intrusion or molestation from the white man. It is a country much better than the one you now occupy; where you can grow more corn, and where game is more abundant. Think seriously of what I say to you. Remember that you have but one summer more to plant corn in this country. Make the best use of this time, and dispose of your property to the best advantage. Go and settle with the Commissioners, and with the emigrating Agent, Gen. Smith, receive the money due for your improvements, your houses your cornfields and ferries, and for the property which has been unjustly taken from you by the whitemen, and at the appointed time be

255

prepared to remove. In the meantime, if you will apply to me or my Agents, I will cause rations, blankets and clothing to be furnished to the poor and destitute of your people. John E. Wool, Brg. Genl. Comdg."

3 May 1837

My Dear Cassie,

Important news, General Wool is to be replaced. The general government and the governors of Alabama, Tennessee and South Carolina want immediate action. They believe Wool is unsuited for the task. General Wool will face charges, probably a court martial, over past actions in Alabama. In any case Colonel Lindsay will be given temporary command of the army.

Come this May the army will act to remove the Cherokee.

I remain busy with my duties and my upcoming Senate bid. If you need anything, please let me know. I plan to visit soon. I beg you to persuade your grandparents to accept the benevolence of the American authorities. Removal will be for their own good.

Your Loving Ben, xoxox

22 June 1837

Chief Ross has called a big council meeting at Red Clay. Thousands will be there. Edudu is going.

11 August 1837

Edudu and Eagle Killer returned from Red Clay. Edudu is ill. It rained the last few days of the council. Edudu said it was impossible to keep a fire.

12 August 1837

When Edudu recovered from his illness, I asked about his trip.

"Tell me about the council. Is there good news?"

"Be glad you didn't go, Walela. Nothing was accomplished. It was wet. Everyone was miserable. I wish we weren't forbidden to have meetings here at New Echota. There were storms every day. There were maybe four thousand people and no shelter."

"Was there trouble, Edudu?"

"It was a peaceful meeting. Chief Ross spoke about his visit to Washington and Arkansas. He reminded us of the government's intention to force our removal. I learned nothing new. The last day Mr. Mason spoke. It was translated. The men listened and that was the end. Many had no more than a blanket stretched over a limb to shield them from the downpours. The men tried to keep their fires burning but with little success. I'm still cold."

11 October 1837

My Dearest Ben,

I cannot express how much I miss you. I know you're doing your best for us. It is said we will lose our nation. Our last hope is said to be that each family will be allowed to keep a little farm. Chief Ross believes we still have a chance for that. Edudu and his friends wait on word from Chief Ross.

I am not surprised to learn the final plans for our deportation are being made in Milledgeville. A few families have removed, but most will stay until Chief Ross tells us to leave. I read the newspapers. I understand, but my people are unable to comprehend the consequences of the approaching malevolence.

Edudu, Elisi and neighbors continue to plant and prepare for another year as if everything will be normal.

My love for you will never change, Cassie oxoxo

13 October 1837

From the *Georgia Journal* – page 1 – October 10, 1837

"...*The Cherokee Land Lottery* will contain all the names of all the fortunate drawers in the Land Lottery, and their residence, up to the first of January 1838, with an engraved map of each Land District in the Cherokee Country, immediately preceding the names in each district. *The Cherokee Land Lottery* will contain about five hundred pages, royal octavo size, will be printed on good paper, neatly bound and delivered to subscribers by the first of March 1838 at five dollars a copy..."

19 October 1837

Huff's Boarding House – Milledgeville - 14 October 1837

My Dearest Cassie,

I feel guilty for not writing more often. I miss you. Count on me to visit soon, probably before the end of the month. I need to get away and refresh my mind.

Life here is busy and confused. I fear your political assessment is correct. Everyone thinks Ross's attempts to persuade the general government to nullify the 1835 treaty are preventing the peaceful emigration of the Cherokee. I fear the government will accomplish the removal by means of military action. The American population surrounding Cherokee Country has grown sufficiently large to support the removal. I'm embarrassed to say everyone here is eager to accomplish your vanishment. Soon, Cherokee Country will be no more.

I beg you to persuade your grandparents to emigrate immediately. You must take advantage of the benevolent offers of the state of Georgia to aid their relocation. It's for their own good. Trust me. The American government is looking out for the Cherokees' best interest.

Yours Forever and Ever, Ben, xoxox

19 October 1837

With each infrequent visit Ben brings darker news. He warns we should not wait until soldiers force our removal. Edudu, Elisi and their friends will not leave until told by our chief. I will never leave their side.

28 October 1837

Ben and I had a wonderful day.

"Cassie, I can't tell you how nice it is to be here with you. I think this is the most peaceful spot on earth. No one's in a hurry here."

"We're never in a hurry. You should come more often."

"I shall. I need too. There is no one like you in my life and never will be. I should see you more often. I will come more often, I promise."

"All you have to do is get on the stage and come."

"I know."

"You could come anytime."

"I know, Cassie. You are good for me. This is the only place I can relax. You're the only woman I've ever met who understands. You're still my woman, aren't you?"

"I will always be your woman. You've known that since we were young."

"I've always known that too," Ben said.

"I'll never change, Ben. I have loved you and always will. You're my man, my only man. That will never change. I'll never change."

"I know, Cassie. You have a solid character. I can trust you."

"You're busy, Ben, but I want to see you more often. Perhaps we could see your parents again? I loved our trip to Brainerd."

"Mother wants me to bring you up again," Ben said. "She says your visit is the only thing that seems to brighten Father. He hasn't said a word in months. He may never speak again. Who would have thought my father, the smiling, laughing, confident man who taught others every day, who preached the gospel every Sunday, the man who made his living by talking, would end up a dumb mute."

Ben held me for a long time. Talking about his father was bothering him.

"I should take you to see him, Cassie. I promised Mother I would bring you to Brainerd."

"We need to do that," I said quietly.

"I'm going to see them again around Christmas or the New Year. I'll let you know," Ben said. "Would you like to ride up with me then?"

"I would love to ride up with you anytime," I answered quickly.

"We're agreed. Let's plan on that," he said.

"Every time I'm with you, Cassie, I realize how much I want you, how much I need you. One day I'll figure out a way we can be together."

"I know."

"We'll be married."

"I know."

"I'll come for you one day. I will."

"I know you will," I answered again.

"Americans will take our farm, won't they Ben?"

Ben didn't answer.

We watched the squirrels. I felt the wind blowing across the porch. Ben looked up at the sky. We held one another.

"We'll figure something out," he finally said.

"The easiest thing would be for you and me to emigrate together," I said. "We could make a good living in the western territories. We're young and strong. You could practice law and I could teach children and women."

"I would love to teach like Father," Ben mused quietly.

"We could live with my people. Wouldn't that be a good life?"

"It would."

"Your parents could go with us. We could leave now. Elisi and Edudu might go if you and your parents were to come with us."

"I don't know. I have a lot to do. I'm running for the Senate."

"We could have a good life. A very good life," I said quietly.

Ben held me.

"I want a houseful of your children, Ben. I could teach and maybe start a newspaper," I said. "You could teach, too."

"We could do that," Ben said as we watched the bluebird pair on the eave of the house. The male had a spider in his beak. He tried to give it to his mate but she refused.

"Cassie, we could go west but I don't want to live in poverty the rest of my life beyond the pale. I need to save more."

"If I'm with you, Ben, I would be rich. Let's go now."

"Let's wait till the right time, Cassie. Let's wait till I have saved enough so we can live comfortably. That's the right thing. You know what I mean. I have things I must do before we can live together."

"I know what you mean, Ben."

"I'm standing for the Senate."

"I know," I answered.

"I've saved some, but if you can wait, I can acquire enough so that we won't have to worry about anything. I'll save. We'll be well off."

"I never worry now, Ben, not with you."

"If we wait we can live anywhere, even Europe. Be patient, Cassie."

"I am patient."

259

"After my Senate appointment I can do anything I want, live anywhere I want."

"Let's go back to the river today, Ben. Let's have a romantic picnic. I want to spend every moment with you. I want your full attention every moment you're here."

"I love your place by the river, Cassie."

"Do you remember how we pledged our lives to one another?" I asked. "Do you remember that day? You don't have to answer that question," I said.

"I would love a picnic. I remember you said American folks are always trying to find happiness and the Cherokee are already happy. I've pondered that thought many times. In Milledgeville my soul is pushed, pulled, stretched and tugged in a hundred different directions at once. Everyone wants more."

"Let's don't talk about that, Ben. I'll get our picnic ready."

I returned with the quilt and our picnic. Today would be special. I could sense it. I could feel Ben's pleasure being where he grew up as a carefree boy. Since the moment he arrived Ben was looking younger, more alive. I could sense that he wasn't in a hurry to leave.

"It is nice to be in a place where folks are never in a hurry and everyone speaks to everyone," he said.

We walked hand in hand to our special place, the most peaceful spot in the universe. Ben chatted. He was at peace.

"You know, Cassie, I wish I could bring back the years I spent here as a boy. I wish I could turn back the calendar."

"I remember those days, Ben."

"I remember days with Father cutting firewood. There's not a thing about my life here that isn't wonderful. Cassie, your people don't care if one's parents are American, African or a mixture. Here everyone is respected. There are no half-children here, just fathers and mothers and families, everyone knows you by name."

"Ben, sometimes I think you're Cherokee at heart. You understand."

"Cassie. I feel as if I shed a great weight when I come here."

"Ben, from the moment you arrive I see you begin to relax as if you're casting off your Milledgeville skin. I want you to have everything good. My life is yours, Ben. I've waited ten years and I'll wait ten more if need be. Remember one thing, you'll never meet a woman who loves you more than I love you. I was created for you—for you alone, Ben Lowry."

Ben pulled me closer.

"I know, Cassie."

"You do?"

"In my better moments, I know you're the woman for me. I have to remember that. The minute I get off the stage in Milledgeville, my life becomes a madhouse. I must remember you're waiting for me here. I've things to sort out. I need to prioritize. I have some decisions to make."

"I know you don't think about me every moment you're not here. Anytime you see our moon, be it day or night, know there is someone looking at that same moon wishing you well, someone created for you alone."

"What a lovely thing to say, Cassie. I'll do that. When I look at the moon, I'll think about you up here looking at that same Cherokee moon."

We kissed tenderly.

Ben held me for a long time.

"I was hoping we would picnic today, Cassie. All the way from Brainerd I was excited about seeing you. I knew this day would be special."

"Every day with you is special," I answered softly.

"The last few months have been difficult with Father's illness. The removal is weighing upon me. Sometimes I feel guilty I can't do more."

"I know."

I pulled him to me.

"Come to me when you're unclean, Ben. I'll cleanse your guilt. I'll wrap you in myself and cleanse your soul."

We kissed.

"I shouldn't worry, but I do, Cassie. I worry about you and your grandparents. Being with you here in your place by the river helps make all those horrible things seem distant."

He pulled me to himself. We kissed passionately.

We sat pressed tightly against one another on the quilt by the river's edge enjoying the afternoon. It was unusually warm for late October.

"Cassie, I love these cloudless autumn days with a sky so blue it hurts your eyes. I can't tell where the air ends and my skin begins. I feel like I'm part of a piece of artwork, as if I'm a cloud floating on a blue canvas sky."

"What a lovely thing to say, Ben. You should write poetry."

We had our picnic by the quietly flowing river.

Ben pulled me to him. We kissed. I wanted more, much more. I wanted everything this beautiful man had to give, now and forever. I wanted to merge into his mind and life. I wanted to return the lifetime of love stored in my heart, love for him alone.

Our kisses could not be controlled.

After years of anticipation my world achieved its long-awaited balance on our big flat stone by the river's edge, on the quilt his mother had given us as our wedding gift. The kisses led into a never-ending embrace as we shared as only soulmates can. It was a perfect day. We were one in every way.

Ben whispered how much he loved me, how much he had always loved me. Years of patience were rewarded in one glorious afternoon. Our lives joined. Our love was consummated as we held one another, oblivious of the murmuring waters or birds singing, blind and deaf to everything save our beloved. As we lay wrapped in the quilt, I saw nothing but our glorious future. We fell asleep caring nothing for others who might disturb us by chance. I woke in Ben's arms, the boy I loved, the man who loved me. I felt everything evil that hovered above us had dissipated in one glorious afternoon.

Ben woke as I watched him sleep.

As we walked back up the hill the reality of Ben's departure loomed. The pain of that parting would be sharper than ever. As we got closer to the house I could feel his mood swing towards that of a successful lawyer and politician.

"Cassie, next year is a big year for my career. Things will happen."

"I'll wait for you, Ben."

"I'll do everything I can for you and your grandparents."

"I know you will."

"Cassie, you and your grandparents should leave soon. You must persuade them. When the army comes I won't be able to do much, maybe nothing. No one is sure what will happen during those last days. The removal will be a mess, of that I'm certain. I don't think the government understands how big Cherokee Country is and how many families there are to be moved."

"I know, Ben."

"Do your best, Cassie."

"I will explain everything again. I doubt they will leave. They're too old."

"Do your best to persuade them."

"They're set in their ways, Ben."

"This country has power over the mind. I'll grant that," Ben said.

"It's true, Ben. We belong to the land. Leaving is like forfeiting life."

Ben's voice lost the softness it had by the river.

"If I'm appointed to a Senate seat, I can write my own ticket."

"I know you can."

"The Senate is the big prize."

"I know."

"One six-year term in the Senate and I'm set for life. I'll have achieved everything I've worked for. I'll be in an excellent position to do something for the Indian nations. I'll take care of you, Cassie. I promise."

"I know you will."

Ben left in the afternoon amid his promises to return. Whatever may come, I had the best day of my life with the man I love.

21 November 1837

Elisi is certain. I'm carrying Ben's child. My beloved's seed is growing within me, the happiest thought I can imagine.

Chapter XLI

1837 - Ben's New Job – Bear Paws
Chapter 41

25 November 1837 - The Trading Moon – Nu da de qua

Ben came for a visit.

"Cassie, I've been troubled thinking how to tell you the news, but I must. That's why I came today. I've accepted an important job. You must understand I accepted this job because I didn't want someone unfriendly to the Cherokee in the position. I'll know what's happening in Cherokee Country and I can keep you informed. This job will be good for my future."

"What is the job?"

"I've been hired to help set up the government in the new counties. They want it done as soon as possible. It gives me no joy to tell you that. I have nothing to do with the removal, Cassie. My job is not military. I'll oversee surveying, registration of lottery winners and initial judicial appointments. I'll assist the governor with appointments and elections, everything to do with county government. They're going to take it all, Cassie. Every farm."

"I know."

"I told you this would happen, Cassie. I took this job for your sake. I wanted to tell you about it first-hand. I didn't want you to see my name in the newspaper."

"I know, Ben."

"Cassie, the date is the twenty-fifth of May. The governor's office has been liberal. I'll be supported by the military."

"I thought you would have nothing to do with the military?"

"I will have nothing to do with the removal. The military will help me facilitate setting up the local governments, that's all."

Ben was nervous but determined to finish.

"I promise I'll be good to the Cherokee, Cassie. You can count on me. That's why I came by today. I promise to do my best for you and your people."

I couldn't speak.

"The May date is set in stone, Cassie. This job is an honor, a big honor. Please don't think ill of me for accepting. I haven't changed."

"I still love you, Ben. I'll always love you."

"They needed a lawyer familiar with the Cherokee. This job will be a feather in my cap. It will help get the Senate appointment."

I could feel his discomfort.

"I'll wait for you, Ben. One day you'll come for me."

"I promise to come for you someday, Cassie. The government believes I can persuade some to emigrate. That would make everyone's job easier. They said working with Indians will serve me well in the Senate where all treaties are ratified. I would be chosen for important committees."

"I always thought you would do wonderful things, Ben."

"They needed a man like me to ensure a smooth transfer of land. They want to avoid retaliatory violence and newspaper coverage. No one wants trouble. That's why I wanted you and your grandparents to emigrate early."

Ben was wearing expensive clothes.

"In order to manage public opinion, it's critical that hostility be avoided," Ben said. "Georgia doesn't want undue national attention. Men in Milledgeville mean well."

"You're the only man in Milledgeville I trust."

"A peaceful exchange will serve everyone's best interest. After years of struggle your people deserve a happy outcome out west."

"They'll come for us there."

"No, they won't, Cassie."

"They always come."

"You'll be safe out west."

"They will come for us there. They always come. They'll take everything. We'll never be safe."

"Cassie, be reasonable. The American government is being kind to the Cherokee."

"Do you believe that?"

"Yes I do, Cassie. What we're doing is for their own good. It's not my fault the removal party signed that treaty. None of this is my fault. Don't blame me, Cassie. I'm an honest man doing an honest job."

"I know you believe that, Ben."

"Cassie, the removal can't be stopped."

I held Ben's hand and leaned my head against his shoulder as I watched our bluebird pair perched on the eave. I didn't care about anything he said. It was as if he was talking to a tree.

"Cassie, I'll do everything I can to help you. This job will allow me to help you more than I could otherwise. That's really what I came to tell you."

I heard the bluebirds twittering. They were flying looking for insects.

"Colonel Lindsey will oversee Georgia's part in the removal. It's rumored old fuss and feathers Scott will replace Lindsey. Scott's a good man, I hear. Removal is the best thing for your nation now."

Ben waited for me to say something to help him deal with his guilt. I found it impossible to speak. I wanted him to hold me and stop talking.

"Georgia is continuing to build removal forts and roads. I hate the fort they built here, right in the middle of town. It's a monstrosity, isn't it?"

"It's terrible."

"I'm sure it's the last thing you want to hear, Cassie, but the Militia and Guard will be in charge of the round-up. That's another reason I want you to emigrate early. I can't help you in any way when the removal begins."

I felt as if Ben were talking to himself.

"They're saying not one family will be left behind. This is the government's solution. I had to come by and tell you."

"I'm always glad when you come, Ben."

"I hope you don't hold this against me. I'm doing this for the Cherokee. I don't like this any more than you do. I couldn't refuse, could I? I couldn't stand by and do nothing. I couldn't allow someone in this job who hated you."

"Georgia hates us. I read the newspapers. All Americans want us to vanish."

"This job will be lucrative for me, for us. I'll be in a position to take care of you when this is over. That's why you should emigrate now."

"What did they promise?"

Ben looked away.

"I'll be paid in gold and receive a bonus of two thousand acres of bottomland. I'll have money when this is over, Cassie. I'll take care you."

"I don't care about the money, Ben."

"If I get the Senate appointment, I can take care of you. When this is over, I can build you and your grandparents a nice little house out west. I had to take the job, Cassie. You see that, don't you? It was the only thing to do."

Milledgeville November 1837

Ben had been honorable and spoken to Cassie face to face. He could now concentrate on his job without a nagging sense of guilt. There were things he didn't like, but life was like that. At least the bottomland could be held as an investment or sold. He could fund his retirement, his parents' retirement and even buy Cassie a little place out west. This job was the opportunity of a lifetime and then on to the Senate for greater things, but first things first.

Zach assured him the Senate seat was his. If he were a senator, Elizabeth would accompany him to Washington City. He was sure of it.

Ben was unaware of his transformation. He had allowed the crisp black and white principles of youth to blend with the colorless ethics of law and politics, coating his soul with layers of grey preventing him from identifying truth or detecting a lie. Unknown to himself Ben had become a puppet, a caricature, faintly resembling his previous self, controlled by political marionettes whose strings attached directly to his compromised integrity, all sustained by hollow promises of money, power and pleasure.

Ben reflected on his formidable task, but he was told he wasn't to worry about budget or staff. Governor Gilmer would personally take care of him as long as the job was done quickly and efficiently. Ben would do a good job and worry about Cassie when this was over. He couldn't concern himself about the stubborn Cherokee who refused to emigrate.

This job would get him noticed. It should put the icing on his political cake. He might even end up more popular in Georgia than Crawford. He was gaining a political reputation as a master of compromise and he could count on Zach and Elizabeth. They were as excited about going to Washington City as he was, perhaps more so. The closer he came to Milledgeville the more he thought about Elizabeth and less of Cassie.

He wanted to see Elizabeth. The thoughts of the hotel, her fragrance, walking with her up the long staircase gave him a sudden moment of intense pleasure renewing that familiar empty ache in his chest that was only relieved when she was near. He was impatient. He didn't realize how much he had missed her until this moment. How impressed she would be. She was exactly the kind of woman he desired, a woman who was comfortable in a man's world. This job would be his crowning achievement. What a pleasure it would be to have Elizabeth on his arm in Washington City.

In the end the Cherokee would thank him. Their problems were self-inflicted, a direct result of the shortsighted Cherokee leadership personified in John Ross. The removal party had seen the pragmatism of emigration. Why not take the money and leave? Why should the Cherokee believe they had a right to land in the State of Georgia? Cassie needed to be out west, not in the United States. The removal would be in her best interest. She would see that eventually. Two cultures had clashed and the weaker must yield. None of this was his fault. Sometimes for no reason bad things happen to good people. Removal was required for the good of the Cherokee.

Didn't they understand they couldn't stand against the legal rights of the United States of America? The Cherokee had been given a beautiful country out west where they could prosper. The Cherokee should be grateful. Many American politicians had gone out of their way, risked their careers to protect the Cherokee future by facilitating their national emigration. It was foolish to believe the Cherokee should have their own nation in the east. It was not practicable. Everything east of the Mississippi was American, as it should be. The United States was American, not Indian. Everyone knew that. Things change. In this case, things were changing for the better.

In any case, the Cherokee did not have the intellect to thrive. Indians were inferior, a sub-culture, a stone age society of illiterate hunters and gatherers. That didn't matter now. The Cherokee were finished. Georgia was part of the American dream.

Ben's thoughts drifted to his parents and their work in Cherokee Country. His parents had paid a high price for standing up for their beliefs. The years his parents had spent working for the Cherokee were a waste. Against good advice, his father had provoked the authorities and brought poverty upon himself. He had been warned of the consequences of opposing Georgia law. Civilization exists where the citizens remain civilized. If folks ignore law, anarchy results. His father knew that. The rule of law must govern a progressive society. Americans were law abiding, civilized. Indians were not, therefore inferior.

It wasn't his fault he worked for the state. It wasn't his fault he would oversee the giveaway of Cassie's land. He was doing what was right for the situation. Right and wrong should be judged on a case-by-case basis. There was no black and white in modern society. America was building a vibrant, modern, progressive nation, a leader among nations. This new world creation needed modern ethics to match. Five-thousand-year-old morals crudely etched in stone must be discarded.

Ben understood, as everyone should, the Cherokee were destined to disappear like Cooper's Chingachgook in *The Last of the Mohicans,* a prophetic novel highlighting the domination of the vibrant American culture and the disappearance of the Indian, as it should be. The Cherokee would be swallowed by the progressive American tide rolling across the North American continent from sea to shining sea. Like the Delaware, the Cherokee would and should disappear. Cherokee land would be developed by an enlightened culture—an American culture of education, science, music, agriculture and industry. Georgians wouldn't allow themselves to be hindered by weak-minded hunters and gatherers. Wide roads and great cities would replace undeveloped forests. The Cherokee must go, the sooner the better. It was his duty to serve the state. After all, he was free, white and twenty-one. It was his duty to be part of American political reform for the benefit of all.

Everything he did was for the good of the Cherokee. He should be commended, probably would be. Cassie would be better off west of the Mississippi and the sooner the better. He saw that clearly now. The American government knew what was best for the Indians' benighted culture.

26 November 1837
From the *Federal Union* - 14 November 1837 page 1
"Printed Maps of the LAND DISTRICTS IN CHEROKEE. Representing the Water Courses, Numbers, Names and Residences of the Drawer of each Lot.--For sale at the Surveyor General's office at $5.00 each. Persons requesting a Map of any District enclosing Five Dollars will be furnished without delay by mail. James F. Smith Milledgeville September 7, 1837."

29 November 1837

> From the *Federal Union* - 14 November 1837 - page 2
>> "Whereas, the time stipulated in the treaty with the Cherokee tribe of Indians for their removal...is approaching, and as it is the universal opinion of those best acquainted with...their removal, that difficulties will occur...which will endanger the lives and property of the citizens...without preventive measures being taken by the government...Be it therefore enacted, That his Excellency the Governor be, and he is hereby authorized to accept...four volunteer companies of mounted men, to be stationed, one in each of the counties of Lumpkin, Union, Walker and Murray, for the protection of the citizens of those counties..."

The Guard has mapped the location of all our homes in order to arrest us quickly when the time comes. There is no news from our Chief in Washington. I have heard nothing from Ben. We are being watched.

28 November 1837

> Huff's Boarding House - 22 November 1837
> My Dearest Cassie,
>> Events are approaching a climax. I beg you in the strongest terms to persuade your grandparents and Five Feathers to emigrate immediately. It is reported Cherokee families are planning a crop this spring. There will never be another Cherokee harvest in Georgia. There will never be another Green Corn Festival celebrated in Georgia. The 1835 treaty will stand.
>> At the end of May troops will remove every Cherokee man, woman and child. Persuade your family to leave immediately. If you delay I cannot guarantee your safety. I do not have a high opinion of the various militias, Guard or the civilian contractors who will be hired. Please heed this warning. I am privy to much information. If you emigrate now you will be in place for a crop this year out west. It's your only hope.
>> I miss you every day we are apart. Do not ignore this warning. Your Loving Ben, xoxoxoxo

"My dear Walela, perhaps our chief can persuade Washington City to allow us to keep our little farm."

"Edudu, I don't know what to think. I love these hills. This is the land given us by the Great Spirit. Some have left to find peace in the western lands, but my life is with you. I will never leave you or forsake you. Where you go, I go. Where you sleep, I shall sleep."

"Your Elisi and I have talked about removal, Walela. We will not leave until our Chief tells us to go. I am old. I want to be buried here with my ancestors in my best clothes."

"I promise you shall be buried properly, Edudu."

"I have my burial clothes ready. We shall be buried here in Cherokee Country, deep in the soil of our ancestors."

9 December 1837

We rose early. Killer was unsettled. He began barking in the front of the house. Edudu and I found Killer at the end of the porch barking at something. He was running back and forth to tell us to come and see what he had found.

"He's probably got Mrs. Possum cornered under the porch," Edudu said. "Mrs. Possum smelled those fish heads I buried under the rose bushes yesterday. She should have taken her babies and gone to her den before the sun came up. If she tries to get away now Killer will hurt her. I'll hold the dog. You get a stick and run Mrs. Possum from under the porch."

I kneeled down to look under the porch. I jumped backwards, leaned against the corner of the house and began to retch.

"Edudu, hold Killer tight. Don't let him go. Please don't let him go."

"Is the possum dead, Walela?"

"Don't let Killer loose, Edudu. Look under the porch."

I retched once again.

Edudu saw what I had seen.

Bear Paws was lying under the porch up against the house. He held a bottle in one hand. His blank eyes were staring. Ants were crawling over his face. He was dead. He had choked on his vomit. He had soiled himself. He smelled horrible. Americans sell whiskey to get our men drunk and then steal their possessions. Why would anyone want happy little boys to end like this? I hate whiskey. There isn't one good thing to say about alcohol, those who make it or those who sell it.

Five Feathers and I laid Bear Paws on the end of the porch. My brother pried the half empty bottle from Bear Paws' cold fingers, as if in death Bear Paws didn't want to be released from his curse. The bottle had the markings of the American traders. Five Feathers muttered a curse and smashed the bottle. Elisi covered Bear Paws.

"Tell Adsila, Walela. She should know before anyone else," Edudu said.

Chapter XLII

1838 – Blue Birds
Chapter 42

10 January 1838 – Ben's Birthday - Month of the Cold Moon -du no lv ta ni

I will have a baby, Ben's baby. Nothing could make me happier. My future is known. I am impatient for the child's arrival. I shall be a mother.

13 January 1838

Ben visited.

"Ben, do you have time to walk to our special place? I'll put a few things together for a picnic. Would you like that?"

"You know, Cassie, that's exactly what I would like to do. I need to relax and talk to you. The news from Brainerd isn't good. Father is declining."

"I'm sorry, Ben. I truly am."

"I know."

"How is your mother?"

"Mother was asking for you. I told her you were well. She's increasingly worried about Father."

"I miss her terribly."

"I know you do. She misses you, too."

"I hope your father gets better. I miss him."

We arrived at our spot by the river. It was cool. I brought my quilt. I put out the things from my pine basket. We sat hand in hand without talking and listened to the water. I was happy.

Ben held me.

Mr. and Mrs. River Otter swam past taking note of everything.

"Ben, I am a happy woman, the happiest of women."

Ben smiled. His smile helped me.

"I have loved you, Ben Lowry, since the day I first met you in your father's little schoolroom.

I saw in Ben's eyes a reflection of his youthful passion, the look I see when Ben and I are in our special place. I had to share the good news.

"Ben, I'm going to have a baby, your baby. Is that not wonderful news?"

I felt Ben become tense. I had hoped it would be joyful news to him. I knew I must allow him time to think.

"Cassie, are you sure?"

270

"There is no doubt. Elisi is certain. There is no mistake. I am with child. I'm going to have a baby, Ben, our baby."

Ben said nothing. I could feel his tension.

"I'm happy. I want you to be happy, too," I said quickly.

"I know we intended to wait," I said. "Some things don't come in season."

We were sitting on the quilt where Ben and I had conceived our child.

"I want you to be happy about our baby, your baby."

I began to cry.

"I am sorry, Ben, I don't mean to cry. I know you wanted to wait until after we married to have children. I wanted to tell you I was expecting our baby, the child you have given me, given us."

Ben pulled my head against his chest and began to rock me gently.

"I am happy for you, Cassie. Don't cry. Please forgive me. I should have responded differently."

"Are you really happy, Ben?"

"I'm happy. You're going to be fine, Cassie. Don't cry. You'll be a good mother. Everything will be good with your child. I'll see to that."

"Thank you, Ben. I know you'll be a good father. I want us to be happy."

"This is good news. You know I'm going to be busy with my new job, Cassie. I won't be able to come up as often as I would like, but don't worry. I'll take care of you."

"I know."

"I promise to see you as often as I can. Write me if you need anything."

"I'll let you know if I need anything for the baby."

"Don't worry, Cassie. I promise I'll help."

"There's more news, Cassie. It isn't good, I'm afraid.

"I know," I answered. "It's all bad news lately. I read the newspapers."

"The army says as many as 15,000 troops are coming. They're afraid your people might resist like the Creeks did in Alabama."

"I know. I've seen the soldiers and wagons. They're everywhere."

"There will be more than fifteen forts in Georgia alone, maybe as many as thirty all around. Ross is beating a dead horse in Washington City."

"Chief Ross is a good man."

"He's a good man but he's wasting his time," Ben said quietly.

"I've been reading the papers," I said. "I know you're right. It's hard to believe they're taking everything from us and nothing can be done."

"I know, Cassie. It isn't fair. It truly isn't fair. I've done everything I could. I promise I have."

"I know you have, Ben. I know."

"You have to leave, Cassie. If you and your grandparents don't emigrate, you'll be arrested and deported. It won't be pleasant. Once the orders are given, it will come like a storm. It's going to happen. Your grandparents and Chief Ross can't wish this away."

271

"I know, Ben. I know."

"I know what's going to happen, Cassie. Things will be bad."

"I'm afraid, Ben. We hide when we see the soldiers."

"Tell me what will happen to the children, Ben? Do you know? What will happen to Elisi and Edudu? What will happen to all the old folks?"

Ben held me tight.

"Edudu says the Guard has maps of all of our houses. They know where every family lives."

"I'm sure that's true," Ben said.

"Ben, I know you wouldn't be involved with anything like that."

"I'm a civilian, Cassie. I have nothing to do with the military."

12 February 1838

From the *Federal Union* – 6 February 1838 – page 2

"Speech of Mr. Lumpkin IN SENATE, Monday Jan. 22, 1838. CHEROKEE TREATY. Mr. Lumpkin said...While Mr. Ross continues to protest...the Government considers the treaty the supreme law...much has been done towards the execution of the treaty which cannot be undone...is not now far distant, when my course of policy of these people, from first to last, will receive the general approbation of all those who are well informed on the subject...Mr. John Ross and his associates...are laboring under great misapprehension, in regard to the true state and condition of these people...I have in my possession a document written by Mr. Elias Boudinot, late Editor of the Cherokee Phoenix, and one of the principal agents who negotiated the late treaty of 1835...a reply to the allegations contained in the writings of Mr. Ross...the Cherokee people are kept in a state of delusion and misapprehension in regard to their present condition...They unfortunately believe...Mr. Ross is here doing something to abrogate...the late treaty...this is a ruinous delusion...The time for their final departure is...May...and when the time arrives they must go: no power can...overturn this treaty...these people...ought to yield to the advice of better friends...who stand ready...to take them by the hand and lead them forth to their promised land of rest, where I trust these people will cease to be troubled by the white population...that it might be shown...that the Government was resolutely determined...to carry out with this people its benevolent policy...without which it is impossible the race can be preserved."

13 February 1838

From the *Federal Union* – 6 February 1838 – page 3

"OSCEOLA, THE INDIAN WARRIOR...departed this life at Fort Moultrie...the master spirit of this long and desperate war. He was the savage, treacherous, murderer of General Thompson...for which act, as well as...others, of like cruel character...he should have suffered the tortures of death more painful and ignominious than was reserved for his fate by an all-wise Providence. He was...consistent in hatred—dark in revenge—cool, subtle and sagacious in council. Osceola will long be remembered as the man, who with the feeblest means, produced the most terrible effects."

6 March 1838

From the *Federal Union* - 27 February 1838 – page 3

"...a letter was received last evening from an officer of the Army at Indian River...Gen. Jesop had captured three or four hundred Indians, men, women and children...Gen. Jesup is now near Jupiter...twenty-one Indians and one hundred and three negros have come in...It is also said that a considerable body of Indians are on an island southwardly, and are hemmed in by some of our troops...Gen. Nelson has killed fifteen Indians and taken nineteen prisoner."

Free Africans were captured with the Seminoles, their families broken apart and sold, the Seminoles deported. Every Seminole with African features is sold into slavery.

March 20th, 1838

I am weary of reading the American newspapers full of hate. They will never know us. They despise us living near. Perhaps we should leave, as Ben suggests. I shall ask Elisi again if we should flee the brewing storm, but I know her answer. She will never leave. She wants to be laid to rest in the country the Great Spirit gave us.

21 March 1838

From the *Federal Union* - 13 March 1838 - page 1

"What will this union be fifty years from now? The morning of 1887 will dawn upon this nation doubled in extent...fifty millions of freedmen will look upon the light of that morn and glory in the name...GREAT NATION. Splendid cities will then exist where now the Indian, the Lord of the dark forest around him, lies prone upon his copper face, dreaming of the happy hunting ground of his fathers, with whom must soon dwell the whole Indian race. On that day, a mere handful will be lingering on the borders of the great deep that must at length engulf them...the present dwellers of the earth will have then ceased their bustle...a new race of men--our children and our children's children will then manage the machinery of the world...and may the heavens permit us to continue our glorious career until all the nations of the earth become as we are."

5 April 1838

Why must we be deported by the Americans? Why must they possess everything? Edudu and I catch our chickens at dusk and take them to our special roost tree in our special enclosure. We stand under the tree in the twilight and toss the chickens into the lower branches where they stay for the night. After a few nights, our chickens come home to the same tree to roost without our help.

Elisi says the evil the Americans have released on our world will come home to roost over their heads. Evil, like our chickens, always returns to the owner. The deeds perpetrated against us will come back upon them in their twilight. Darkness will descend on their culture. On that day, they and their children shall understand injustice and be afraid.

From the newspaper,
"RUNAWAY...a bright mulatto boy named Alfred...so nearly white that he no doubt intends to pass as a white man and when he is discovered he will be with a white man...a liberal reward will be given to any person who will recover him and put him in my possession or in any safe jail."

Americans believe it a crime to pretend to be white when one is not. Can privilege only be transmitted by pure white blood?

From the *Federal Union* – 10 April 1838 – page 2
"In the Senate – Monday, March 26, 1838
CHEROKEE TREATY – Mr. SOUTHARD presented a memorial...signed by the deputation of Cherokee Indians, now in Washington...in regard to their situation under the late treaty, and praying Congress in some mode to interfere for their relief...with signatures of 15,665 persons of that nation.
Mr. Lumpkin said: I must express my deep regret at the introduction of this subject...the Senate should...put to rest all...hopes of the Cherokee people, that John Ross can effect the slightest change in the determination of a branch of the Federal Government, to execute the Cherokee Treaty of 1835.

"...this...treaty...was negotiated by a highly qualified and competent delegation of the Cherokee...the treaty was thoroughly discussed in this Senate and received its ratification...nine-tenths of the intelligent Cherokees have emigrated...or are preparing to go...There is no difficulty in regard to the executing of this treaty with the intelligent portion of the Cherokee people...the opposing Indians are ignorant and uninformed and these would...have cheerfully yielded...but for the wicked...operations of this man John Ross...Unfortunately he has been permitted to hold too much correspondence with the Executive officers of this Government...The twenty-third of May next...these people, so far as Georgia is concerned, must go, and go quickly. The citizens of Georgia hold grants for the lands on which these Indians now reside in that State, and the grantees are legally authorized by the laws of the State, as well as by Treaty, to take possession of their lands on and after the twenty-third of May next; and, sir, possession they will take; and the Indians will then be truly forced out of house and home...We have treated the Indians with all the kindness and forbearance which their interest required. But, sir, whatever conflict may arise, after the 23d of May, Georgia must, and will, be speedily relieved from this long-standing and vexatious perplexity...They must go or evil will come of it...all the combined powers of the Federal Government cannot abrogate or change this treaty, without the consent of the States interested, and that consent will never be obtained."

28 April 1838
From the *Federal Union*-Excerpt from page 2

"Major General Scott has made a requisition...for twenty companies of Militia of this state to be employed in removing the Cherokee...these companies are to march immediately to New Echota...This force, in addition to that made upon the states of Tennessee, Alabama and North Carolina and the regular troops will present a body of...seven or eight thousand men...sufficient to strike terror to...these deluded savages as are induced to resist the execution of the treaty."

"And earnest determination on the part of the government to have them removed is manifested, which...will be sufficient...to satisfy these Indians that Ross will not be able to have the time prolonged for their removal...Their remaining without evidencing any inclination to prepare for their removal indicates...it necessary that they shall be forcibly carried

275

off...we sincerely hope that every leniency may be exercised by our fellow-citizens and that their removal may be accomplished without loss of lives of any of our people, or the fatal consequences which would ensue to the Indians from their commencing hostilities."

From the *Jacksonville Republican*

"All accounts received from the Cherokee Nation heretofore, concur, in stating that the Indians were making no preparations for removal...they were planting corn and making other arrangements for a crop the ensuing season...Ross, we learn, has been solicited by those, whose feelings and opinions he should respect; but preserving in his obstinate and reckless determination to bring ruin upon his nation, he refuses to return, and replies, that his countrymen expect him to remain in Washington to attend to their business."

29 April 1838

At last, a letter from Ben. I hope he can visit before the end of May. My heart aches for him.

My Dearest Cassie,

I have been incredibly busy with my job and preparations for my Senate bid. I think of you and your condition often. I'm sorry I haven't been to see you. I will have business in your area soon and I look forward to visiting towards the end of May. Mother asks for you in all her correspondence. Let me know of anything you might possibly need to help in your condition. I will help you any way I can.

Your Loving Ben, xoxoxo

30 April 1838.

I read in the *Athenian* that mounted militia units from Alabama, Georgia, and North Carolina have formed and are on their way to New Echota to join the general government in the removal. American militia units are also on alert for runaway blacks hiding among us.

5 May 1838

No word from Ben. Troops are moving all around us. Mounted men are everywhere. We are afraid to leave our house. There are reports from every quarter of our people being robbed. Darkness has descended.

12 May 1838

Today we received a letter from General Winfield Scott by special messenger. Copies are being sent to every Cherokee community.

"Major General Scott, of the United States Army, sends to the Cherokee people, remaining in North Carolina, Georgia, Tennessee and Alabama, this ADDRESS:"

"Cherokee--The president of the United States has sent me, with a powerful army, to cause you, in obedience to the treaty of 1835, to join that part of your people who are already established in prosperity, on the other side of the Mississippi. Unhappily, the two years which were allowed for the purpose, you have suffered to pass away without following, and without making preparations to follow, and now, or by the time that this solemn address shall reach your distant settlements, the emigration must be commenced in haste, but I hope without disorder. I have no power, by granting further delay, to correct the error you have committed. The full moon of May is already on the wane, and before another shall have passed away, every Cherokee man, woman and child in those states, must be in motion to join their brethren in the far west."

"MY FRIENDS--This is no sudden determination on the part of the President, whom you and I must now obey. By the treaty, the emigration was to have been completed on or before the 23rd of this month, and the President has constantly kept you warned, during the two years allowed, through all his officers and agents in the country, that the Treaty would be enforced. I am come to carry out that determination. My troops already occupy many positions in the country that you are to abandon, and thousands, and thousands are approaching from every quarter to render resistance and escape alike hopeless. All those troops, regular and militia, are your friends. Receive them and confide in them as such. Obey them when they tell you can remain no longer in this country. Soldiers are as kindhearted as brave and the desire of every one of us is to execute our painful duty in mercy. We are commanded by the President to act towards you in that spirit, and such is also the wish of the whole people of America."

"Chiefs, headmen and warriors--Will you then, by resistance, compel us to resort to arms? God forbid! Or will you, by flight, seek to hide yourself in mountains and forests, and thus oblige us to hunt you down? Remember that in pursuit it may be impossible to avoid conflicts...Think of this, my Cherokee brethren. I am an old warrior, and have been present at many a

scene of slaughter, but spare me, I beseech you, the horror of witnessing the destruction of the Cherokee."

"…make such preparations for emigration as you can, and hasten to this place, to Ross' Landing or to Gunter's Landing, where you all will be received in kindness, by officers selected for the purpose. You will find food for all, and clothing for the destitute, at either of those places, and thence at your ease and in comfort, be transported to your new homes, according to the terms of the Treaty."

"This is the address of a warrior to warriors. May his entreaties be kindly received, and may the God of both prosper the Americans and the Cherokee, and preserve them long in peace and friendship with each other.

Winfield Scott, Cherokee Agency, May 10, 1838."

They have broken every promise except the one promising removal.

17 May 1838

I found Elisi crying to herself this morning.

"Walela, I am troubled. What will become of us?"

"Elisi, we are all worried. Five Feathers will be with us."

We sat on the porch holding one another.

"Walela, look at our bluebirds feeding their little ones," Elisi said happily.

We watched the bluebird pair coming and going under the eave of the wooden shingles at the top corner of the porch.

"They aren't worried," Elisi said. We shall take the days as they come just as the little bluebirds do. They need not worry nor shall we."

As we watched, a bluebird flew into his little hole with something in his beak. We walked quietly away from the house and sat with our backs against the white oak so we could leave the bluebird pair undisturbed and watch their coming and going as they fed their babies. Their color was bright in the sunshine as it filtered through the trees in the early morning.

"Walela, I wish we could come and go as these birds."

"I do too."

"I wish we could fly from trouble."

"Your Edudu said the bluebirds built their nest close to the porch so they can listen to his stories."

We laughed.

"I like to think about things like that. I like his stories, too. Everyone loves his stories."

"I think they nest here because I feed them all the skippers I find. I don't think they nest here because they like to hear stories," Elisi said, with a smile.

"I do not understand why the Americans must have our little farm," she continued. "Perhaps they want to sit here and watch the bluebirds come and go. Perhaps the soldiers will pass us by and allow mother and father bluebird to remain for another year."

"I hope so," I answered.

19 May 1838

From the *Georgia Journal*-15 May-1838-page 2

"Governor Gilmer - Gen. Charles Floyd to the command of the Georgia forces in Cherokee Country. The number of companies amount to thirty-one—Eleven hundred are mounted gunmen. The whole number of his command will be from 2,500 to 3,500 men. Gen. Floyd is required to repair with his staff, to New Echota and to report to Gen. Scott at Athens (Tennessee)."

24 May 1838

Renatus Floyd has arrived in New Echota with troops. He commands the Middle Military District with New Echota as his headquarters. Soldiers are everywhere. Where is Ben? I heard Elisi sobbing again last night in her bed. Crying is all we have. I held her all night.

I fear the end must come soon.

From the *Southern Recorder* – 8 May 1838 – page 3

"We learn, that the Georgia quota, are organized, and many of the companies on the route…to Cherokee. A fine spirit has characterized the country…and we feel great pleasure in saying, that probably a finer body of men, that that which will compose the Georgia Brigade, belongs to no service."

"…Gen. Charles Floyd, has been ordered to the command of the Georgia Brigade..."

"All that prudence, sound judgment and the most untiring devotion to the interests of the country…has been done. We can now only repeat our hope…that the removal of the Cherokees may be accomplished, and the rights of humanity, and the peace of the country at the same time maintained."

Chapter XLIII

1838 – One Day in May
Chapter 43

26 May 1838 - Month of the Planting Moon – A na a gv ti

At first light armed men burst into our house.

"You're under arrest," a soldier said. "Bring what you can carry."

Eagle Killer growled from under the table.

Six polished bayonets reflected the flames from the fire.

"Colonel Lindsey has ordered you to be brought to Fort Wool."

The soldiers put Edudu's wooden animals in their pockets.

"Here's some of them damned old Cherokee newspapers. Look at these books. What would Indians do with books?"

My terror changed to indignation.

"Those are my books," I answered proudly. "I read them all. I read the newspapers. Those things on the mantelpiece belong to us."

My brother watched each soldier's movements. He put his hand on my shoulder, the pressure of his fingers asking me to stay calm.

"Learning is wasted on Indians."

The soldier threw a handful of newspapers into the fire. As I sprang to rescue my newspapers, a soldier slammed my back with the butt of his rifle. My brother lunged to my defense. Another soldier crashed his gun butt into the back of my brother's head. Five Feathers fell unconscious.

Eagle Killer buried his teeth into the thigh of the nearest soldier.

A soldier ran his bayonet through Eagle Killer, pinning him to the oak floor boards, the bayonet buried deep into the wood.

The soldier put his boot on Eagle Killer, tugging his bayonet free.

A soldier kicked Eagle Killer. Edudu knelt to see to his dog. A soldier grabbed Edudu by the neck and slammed him backwards against the wall.

"Leave the damn dog alone. You can't bring dogs. No dogs."

I was glad Five Feathers had been disabled. My brother would certainly be dead if he had not fallen from the soldier's blow.

A rooster crowed. Ben had warned us this would happen.

We were ordered out of the house. The roaring fire was consuming my newspapers. An orange light reflected off the polished steel of the bayonets.

Edudu and I helped Five Feathers to his feet. Elisi bundled a few utensils along with my journal, pen and sketch book into my quilt. Eagle Killer was bleeding, moaning softly under the table.

The soldiers broke the windows, piled bedding, furniture, books, newspapers and Elisi's pine baskets over the table. I heard Eagle Killer moaning as they shoveled hot coals onto the combustibles. They left the doors open. Almost immediately orange flames were licking at the ceiling.

As we were forced away I saw tongues of red flame come through the wooden shingles. Mrs. Lowry's roses were in full bloom, brilliantly red.

Under the eave three baby bluebirds, their little pin-feathers beginning to grow, fled the choking smoke. Their perch burst into flame. The fledglings were instantly denuded, their skin blackened. The three baby birds fell beating the air with featherless wings. As each little bird hit the ground, a puff of dust was raised, their useless wings extended at crazy angles.

Using their bayonets as prods the young men ordered us to New Echota. Elisi carried our only possessions over her shoulder in my quilt.

Soldiers arrested our neighbors in their homes, in fields, on the way to the spring, wherever they were found and marched us all to New Echota.

My cousin Red Bird was born deaf. He fled the soldiers. They shot him in the back. Empty wagons driven by American men waited for the soldiers to remove families from their homes. We walked in eerie silence. Our column of misery grew constantly as soldiers added more families. My brother supported us every step. Blood stained his clothing but thankfully the bleeding had stopped. Elisi tended his wound.

I spoke to my brother. I was worried.

"I am afraid for you, Five Feathers. I know you are not afraid to die."

"I am not afraid, Walela. I will take care of you and our Elisi and Edudu."

"We need you," I said softly.

"I will take care of you. I don't mind dying, but not yet. You will be safe."

"Be patient, Five Feathers. These men will kill you. Become our chief and build our nation anew. You must help care for my son and teach him to hunt. Will you promise to do nothing foolish, no matter what you see or how these men provoke you? You can accomplish nothing violently against these men. If you retaliate, my baby and I shall perish. Our future is in your hands."

"I shall take care of your son. We shall live. I promise. We shall live."

I cried on his shoulder. As we walked along, he supported Elisi and me. My brother will be a magnificent chief.

Milledgeville 26 May 1838

When Ben heard the removal had begun, he left immediately for the Cherokee capital. As he neared New Echota he saw families under guard. He should have gotten here sooner. He hoped Cassie was well. The once peaceful town was overrun with soldiers, wagons and animals. It was a madhouse.

What Ben saw provoked the same reoccurring thought, the same self-justification. The problems the stubborn Cherokee encountered were of their own making. No one could blame the benevolent government. If Cassie had left last year, he could have arranged for her to travel comfortably, paid for everything and provided a servant. It made him angry to think about the inconsiderate selfishness, both of Cassie and the entire Cherokee Nation. The Cherokee were a stupid people. They brought all this upon themselves.

Ben would do what he could, but it was too late to do anything helpful for Cassie. He didn't have time to take care of everyone. He felt an angry wave of impatience. She knew better. She had caused him much inconvenience.

As he passed the old Cherokee burial grounds, he was appalled. Two dozen American men were madly unearthing graves searching for valuables. Cherokee gravesites had become fair game for scavengers. The graverobbers, completely ignored by the militia, had scattered the disinterred remains carelessly. Graverobbing, although not officially sanctioned, was allowed. This country would become American, everything above it, on it and below it. Indians were to be removed, even dead Indians.

For decades encroaching American interests had been patient. History would show the backward Cherokee had declined, overcome by the racial superiority of the forward-looking white, American culture.

The pigheaded Cherokee should have recognized they could not keep this beautiful land simply because their ancestors happened to have hunted here. The Indians were a decaying culture collapsing of its own ineptitude, a moldering anachronism in a modern, progressive world. They were a sub-standard culture with a sub-standard mentality, incapable of advanced civilization. It was good riddance.

Ben saw wagons loaded with household goods. One American farmer and his teenage boys were driving hogs, Cherokee hogs. Ben passed his father's old home, now the officer's quarters for the Georgia Guard, with newly constructed outbuildings. Ben wanted this moment in Georgia history to pass. There was nothing one man could do. He must continue to do the job the state of Georgia had hired him to do and let the military take care of the Cherokee problem. The removal wasn't his affair. It wasn't his fault. Cassie was out of his hands. Helping set up the new counties was his business. He was a civilian. The military and their actions, or inaction, was not his worry. None of this was his fault and, in reality, none of his concern.

New Echota was unrecognizable. The military had leveled most Cherokee structures and constructed the grotesque Fort Wool, the symbol of American racial ascendency. The State of Georgia owned New Echota, how ironic.

Fort Wool was out of place. Like all of the hastily constructed removal forts, it was built for storing military supplies, but mostly, he had been told, it was constructed to reassure the growing American population within Cherokee Country that their government in Milledgeville was committed to the security of American citizens. The removal forts were wooden shrines, built to reassure fortunate drawers of their government's commitment to American ethnic supremacy.

27 May 1838

We are held in the open, surrounded by soldiers. When the Guard destroyed our print shop they scattered our lead type. I found one small piece in our compound. Finding that little piece of lead type was painful, reawakening our loss of the Phoenix. Georgia will discard us with that same abandon. We are to be marched to Ross's Landing to be put on steamboats.

28 May 1838

All night there was a constant noise of the restless. The night air magnifies every sound. No one can sleep. The sky is our roof. The soil is our bed. We cannot wash. Our drinking water is dirty. Some say we will have tents, food and blankets when we get to Ross's Landing.

We have nothing to eat. As we were arrested Elisi bundled some utensils in my quilt along with my journal and sketch book. That is all we have. We need shoes. The soldiers took our guns and knives. Even though hungry, the children have been quiet. There are perhaps three or four hundred of us. We are not allowed out of our compound to relieve ourselves. It is sixty miles to Ross's Landing. Can Elisi and Edudu make the journey?

An old woman and a child were carried out this morning wrapped in their own clothing. Five Feathers said they have a few discarded slabs to fashion a coffin. They will be buried near the edge of the woods.

Ben rode through New Echota towards the river, to the one place he wanted to see, Cassie's secret place by the river, a place filled with memories.

He told his servant Caesar to wait on the rise. He rode down to Cassie's flat rock, still obscured by thick laurels and exactly as remembered. Nothing had changed. It looked exactly as it did the last time he was here with Cassie. He strangely expected to see her appear from behind the laurels.

He mustn't let sentiment cloud his thinking. He must be realistic. As he sat his horse there in the opening just a few feet from the water, memories flowed. Against his will he relived that afternoon with Cassie, a day he regretted fiercely. He wasn't ready to become a father. There was no question of marriage. Above all, he didn't need some self-righteous government official discovering and publishing his indiscretion.

He shouldn't have come. There were too many memories. He would think about Cassie and her baby another time. Unsatisfied, he rode towards New Echota wishing he had stayed in Milledgeville where everything was as it should be. As his horse walked up the hill, he passed an American man, a civilian, a new settler probably. He carried dead river otters, one in each hand. Their heads left furrows in the dust.

Ben was not prepared for what he had seen. New Echota was filled with memories. It had been a friendly place where he had played, worked and hunted with Cherokee friends. A place where he and Cassie had spent enchanting afternoons walking about the countryside sharing dreams. He had no ill will towards the Cherokee, none. If he would allow himself, he could see their side of the problem, but he didn't like thinking about that. He couldn't think about that and do his job. He would think about that when this was over and Cassie was out west somewhere. He couldn't believe the state of her community, completely stripped of inhabitants, American farming families already beginning to occupy vacant Cherokee homes.

Ben approached Cassie's homeplace. Nothing was left but smoldering ash under the scorched white oak limbs of the surrounding trees, his mother's charred rose bushes burned to nubs. It was a gloomy moment, even for the prosperous American lawyer turned politician from Milledgeville. For an instant Ben allowed himself to glimpse what had actually happened. He was witnessing the final moments of the collapse of a centuries old culture, a collapse orchestrated by powerful white Europeans greedy for fee simple land. He was a part of that orchestra, but he would think about that later.

Ben's expensive chestnut mare stood patiently in the warm Georgia afternoon sunshine of late spring quietly swatting annoying insects with her perfectly groomed black tail. She lightly stamped her feet to frighten away the maddening yellow horseflies from their never-ending attempt to bite her legs. She patiently waited for her master's next command.

Ben had never felt smaller in his life. What was he doing? Why was he here? What was happening? How could this have happened in this happy land of contented people? How could he have been a part of this day?

His thoughts came full circle. The treaty had been signed. They agreed to the removal. They had brought all this upon their own heads.

The silly Cherokee constitution, the useless Cherokee newspaper and the fruitless attempts to teach an illiterate culture to read was both tragic and humorous. He thought of the wasted trips to Washington City by Cherokee leadership pursuing a vain attempt to mimic American civilization and gain acceptance, an impossible task for backward people. They were never going to be civilized. Never would they achieve the high level of culture the surrounding American cities displayed. The Cherokee would never achieve equality, never. They were a patently inferior race. They would never be accepted on this continent in a thousand years. It made him laugh. They were like the donkey who wanted to become a racehorse.

29 May 1838

Over four hundred of us are imprisoned. We are held captive in our own capital. We are confined where our elders met and where we printed the Phoenix. Americans destroyed our old capital in Tennessee and have captured our new capital. We are evicted once again.

Our vanishment is complete. Three more died from ague and fever.

30 May 1838

At dawn we were ordered to Ross's Landing. We walked all day. We camped in an open field with a creek a few hundred yards away. At least we have fresh drinking water. We sleep on the ground. It will be a long night. We must not leave the perimeter or be shot. We relieve ourselves where we camp.

Chapter XLIV

1838 – Extinguished
Chapter 44

1 June 1838 – Month of the Green Corn Moon – De ha lu yi

The second day has ended. We're told we must walk fifteen miles a day. Elisi and Edudu are in the wagons.

My baby is growing. Walking is difficult. I am grateful for my brother. I am so terribly weary. I want to rest. I want to go back to my bed and sit on our front porch and listen to the birds.

The soldiers allowed some men to leave to persuade relatives in hiding to turn themselves in. Soldiers hold the family hostage until the man returns.

2 June 1838

We have no shelters, no tents. It's been bone dry. We will arrive at the river tomorrow. I am exhausted. I worry about Edudu and Elisi, tossed about on rough roads in the wagons. East of Ross's Landing at the Brainerd Mission is a woman who is praying to her God for our safety. I think of her.

More prisoners came. A woman delivered her baby beside the road. This evening, my brother helped dig the grave for the woman and her baby.

3 June 1838

We were herded into an enclosure by the river near Ross's Landing. We were not the first occupants. There is a stench. We are not allowed to leave our enclosure for any reason.

We have few tents, blankets, utensils, soap or clothing. The water is dirty.

I am too tired to think, unable to escape the odors and clouds of flies breeding in the mountains of manure lying everywhere around this military madhouse. Every morning there is a burial.

I had my first glimpse of a steamboat, the George Guess, the English name of Sequoyah who invented our syllabary. How ironic Americans would use a steamboat with a Cherokee name to deport us.

Contractors dole out meager rations of corn meal and salt pork. We often eat partially cooked food for lack of fuel and cooking utensils.

Elisi and I were in the line to receive our rations.

The man asked, "Flour or cornmeal?"

Elisi whispered, "Seluesi."

The man growled, "If you want to eat, speak English."

Elisi cowered before the man. I spoke politely in English.

"Sir, she is asking for cornmeal."

The man stared, his face contorted into an angry mask.

"I didn't ask you. Speak when spoken to."

"Why can't you learn English. Get the hell out, both of you. Nothing for you two. You don't appreciate what we do for you. Nothing for you two."

Two children were buried this evening.

4 June 1838

I woke with Elisi dead in my arms. My Elisi was always clean and bright with a smile and a good word for everyone. I did my best to prepare her for burial. Her clothing was torn and soiled, her hair dirty and disheveled. She would have been embarrassed. I cried as I held her for the last time.

In the afternoon soldiers from Fort Cummings at Lafayette brought more families. They had walked three days. They had received no food since the day before. In Lafayette an old woman had fallen, a heavy wagon drove over her unconscious body. She was buried beside the roadway.

Five Feathers and Edudu helped bury four others this morning along with Elisi. More are sick.

Ben, immersed in his work, learned the prisoners from New Echota had been moved to Ross's Landing. He had business in Gilmer and Murray Counties. Along the way he could visit his mother and find Cassie and then head down for more business in Walker County. This removal was a nuisance. He could try to get Cassie released into his parents' custody, but Georgia had no military authority at Ross's Landing. The removal was being overseen by Fuss n' Feathers Scott who would not likely allow any deviation from orders. Ben had to be careful. Perhaps it was best to ask for nothing. He had warned Cassie. He would do what he could, but she should have gone west earlier. This was her fault, nothing to do with him.

Ben quickly found Cassie's compound and left his escort and servant at the entrance. The soldiers granted the well-dressed Georgia politician immediate access.

When I saw Ben, the sun began to shine. I couldn't resist throwing my arms around him. I didn't care that I would soil his new coat. Ben didn't return my embrace. My brother and Edudu stared from some distance.

"Elisi died this morning, Ben. She was so sick."

My tears stained the sleeve of Ben's new coat.

"Elisi didn't understand, Ben. They burned our house."

Ben said nothing and made no attempt to hold me or kiss me.

"I'm sorry, Cassie."

"I asked for a doctor but the guards laughed. We buried her this morning."

"I am so sorry, Cassie. I'll do what I can. I promise. It's awkward for me to be here. I'm glad to see you're well."

"I know you are."

"I don't know what to say," Ben said. "I warned you, but that can't be helped now. I was afraid it would be like this. I understand how difficult this operation is. They're doing the best they can. There's nothing I can do right now, Cassie. I have to do my job. It will get better."

"I'm not angry," I said.

Ben looked around to see if he was being observed.

"Can you get us out, Ben? Is there some way for you to help us?

Ben didn't answer.

"We could stay with your parents in Brainerd."

"I'll do what I can, Cassie. I have no authority here. No one from Georgia has anything to do with Ross's Landing. This is Tennessee soil."

"It's terrible here, Ben. You can't imagine."

"I asked the captain if he would parole you into Mother's custody," Ben answered, "but he said he had orders not to let anyone out."

"Could you ask him again?"

"I will. I never imagined the removal would be this unpleasant, but I'm sure they'll soon get things right. Be patient. In no time at all you'll be in your new home out west and everything will be better than ever. I'm sure this is a temporary inconvenience. This is a complicated operation, Cassie. General Scott is a good man. He'll set things in order quickly."

"I don't think it will get better, Ben. The soldiers hate us."

"It will get better. They'll get supplies, tents, food and doctors. They're probably on the way now. I wouldn't worry if I were you."

"It's too late for Elisi."

"I'm sorry. There's nothing I can do, Cassie."

Ben glanced at my stomach. I wondered what he was thinking. I wondered if he was embarrassed by his own child? He probably was. Ben looked out of place in our pigsty. I understood his embarrassment. Ben is a good man at heart.

"Please help us get out, Ben. People are dying every day."

"I'll do what I can," he said quietly so no one could hear.

"We have no latrines. I'm hearing terrible reports about groups who have been removed ahead of us. I'm worried for our baby."

I cried. He took a step backward.

Ben loved Cassie but what was he to do? Events had taken a course of their own. He couldn't swim upstream. He had warned her. It wasn't his fault. He had a job to do with the state. He must fulfill his contractual obligations. He needed to get out of this stinking place before someone figured out why he was here. It was time to leave. He didn't want his security detail to suspect his relationship with Cassie. He didn't want to soil his expensive trousers. He had appointments later in the day.

I stood on tiptoes and whispered, "I'm sorry if I have embarrassed you. I know you don't want them to know this is your baby. I want to go home, Ben. Please help us. Your mother will take us."

A soldier approached.

"Sir, the contractors are preparing to distribute the daily ration. Sometimes it gets nasty, pushing and shoving and that kind of thing, sir. The Indians ain't violent but I wouldn't want you to get pushed around. Indians don't have no manners, sir. It's ugly in here, if you know what I mean, sir."

The private observed Ben's frown.

"Don't worry, sir. They'll be leavin' and everything will get back to normal like it should be. It ain't like they're white folks, sir. They're used to this. Dirt don't bother them. Before long they'll 'ave disappeared, gone completely. Everthing will be normal again. You'll see, sir."

Ben was annoyed. His trousers were soiled. Caesar would have to clean his clothes before his next meeting. This removal was nothing but trouble. He couldn't wait to get away from the filth and stench and the memory of uncontrolled passion and foolish promises.

"Cassie, I promise I'll do everything I can to get you out."

Ben gave Cassie's hand a parting squeeze. Perhaps he should do more to get her out. He mustn't draw attention to their relationship. Someone would put two and two together. He had risked enough just by coming for this short visit under the guise of an inspection. He had a Senate seat to think about. He would figure out some other way to help her. His primary responsibilities were to Zach and Elizabeth and to the firm.

A Cherokee woman married to an American man was exempt from removal, Ben knew, but marrying Cassie was not an option. How simple things would be if the Cherokee had agreed to emigrate. John Ross, the National Party and the other Cherokee leaders had brought this misery upon themselves. The pragmatic removal party had been right. Although a minority, they had seen the futility of a Cherokee homeland in Georgia. It wasn't his fault. It wasn't the fault of Jackson or the American government. Blame lay squarely upon the bullheaded Ross and the Cherokee leaders. They should have never tried to keep their land. They were an anachronism, backward and uncivilized, inherently unfit to exist in the modern world. They should and would disappear.

"I have to go, Cassie. I'll do everything I can."

"Please get us out, Ben."

"I'll do my best."

"You're an important man. You know people."

"I'll do everything I can. Don't worry."

"I'm not worried, Ben. I knew you would come."

"The army will get things right. You'll see," Ben said.

He gave Cassie's hand one last squeeze as she instinctively lifted her lips for a goodbye kiss. Ignoring Cassie's expectation of a parting kiss or embrace, Ben turned for the exit, head down. At least now he could tell his mother he had seen Cassie. If he had looked back he would have seen Cassie crying on her brother's shoulder.

5 June 1838

Edudu soiled himself during the night. He couldn't stand. I knew burying the woman he loved would be too much for his kind heart. I waited at the gate. The moment the white doctor appeared I begged him to examine Edudu. Perhaps, because I spoke English, it influenced him to grant my request.

I described Edudu's weakness and told the doctor his wife had died the day previous. As the doctor examined him, Edudu whispered in Cherokee.

"What did he say?" the doctor asked.

"He said you look like a kind man and you should help someone else."

The doctor closed his bag.

"Tell your grandfather he should rest. He needs hydration and nutrition. Broth would be good."

"Where will I get broth, doctor?" I whispered.

The doctor motioned for me to follow him out of Edudu's hearing.

"I understand, dear. I know very well what you're up against."

The doctor looked tired.

"I would give you what you need if I could. I've given away all my money. I have few medicines. I wish I could do more. I'll do everything I can for your grandfather. Let me introduce myself. I am Dr. Uriah D. Thweatt, at your service. Please ma'am, may I ask your name?"

"I'm Cassandra, sir, but everyone calls me Cassie."

A light entered his tired eyes.

"A pleasure indeed to meet you, young lady," he said crisply.

"Do you happen to know a Mr. Wilbur Lowry and his wife, Eleanor?"

"Yes sir. I know them quite well. Do you know them, sir?"

"Mr. and Mrs. Lowry have been friends of our family for many years. I talked to Mrs. Lowry this morning. She asked me specifically to search for you as I made my rounds. It was providential to find you in this madhouse, my dear. Mrs. Lowry has been intervening fervently on your behalf daily."

"I'm glad to meet you Dr. Thweatt."

"I'm so sorry I didn't recognize you sooner, young lady," Dr. Thweatt said. Mrs. Lowry told me how bright you are."

Dr. Thweatt's voice took on a more serious tone.

"I've encountered a great deal of resistance among the Cherokee. Some would prefer to die than submit to a white doctor, a sentiment I fully understand."

I nodded. I didn't know what to say.

Dr. Thweatt continued, "I could do a great deal more good for your people if I had someone like you to assist me. Mrs. Lowry suggested you interpret for me. She assured me I would benefit from your able assistance."

"Mrs. Lowry also suggested I use your brother to tote and carry. With the two of you as assistants I could increase my effectiveness. But, my dear, she didn't mention you were expecting. I'm not sure this activity would be best for your unborn child. You will be immersed in sickness and death all day."

"I would very much like to work for you, Dr. Thweatt. I would be better off with you, sir, than mired in this pig pen. Nothing could be worse than this. I would count it an honor to work with you and my child would be better off to have a physician watching over him."

"Well spoken, my dear. I was hoping to find you. I have already arranged with the army for your parole into my custody. I will vouchsafe for you and your brother. There will be no need to provide a hostage. You and your brother will be allowed to spend your evenings with Mr. and Mrs. Lowry."

Had I just heard the answer to my prayers?

"Would you and your brother be my aide, Cassie?"

"Oh, yes sir, yes sir. My answer is yes."

How ironic Ben's mother, isolated at the Brainerd Mission, had become our savior while her son, the powerful connected politician, could do nothing.

"It's done then. All is agreed," he said crisply. "I'll be back here this afternoon to check on your grandfather. I'll come at first light on the morrow to begin our work."

"We are ready, sir."

"If you'll permit me, I'll send word to Mrs. Lowry to expect you later, if that's agreeable?"

"We shall be ready, sir," I answered tearfully.

Dr. Thweatt left. Five Feathers and I did our best to make Edudu comfortable. Later that afternoon our Edudu called us to his side.

"My beloved waits. I must join her."

"You must rest now, Edudu," I said.

"Please lay me to rest close to my dear one," Edudu continued. "Care for your brother and your baby after I am gone, Walela. I must go. One day you and I and Five Feathers shall reunite with your Elisi. It will be a meeting of great joy. I must go. I have lived long and well. I have loved and been loved. Five Feathers, care for Walela. When you become chief, help Walela and her child remember who they are."

Edudu breathed his last.

Chapter XLV

1838 - Cassie and the Doctor – Reunion
Chapter 45

5 June 1838 – Month of the Green Corn Moon -de ha lu yi
Dr. Thweatt arrived as we finished burying Edudu beside dozens of mounds of fresh turned earth, mounds which will disappear with the next rain.

"I'm so very sorry, Cassie," the doctor said. "My heart is with you."

"We have nothing here, sir. Five Feathers and I are free to go with you. Elisi and Edudu are now part of the land to which they belonged."

"I'm so sorry for your loss. I'll come for you at dawn."

"Thank you, sir. I can't tell you how grateful we are."

"It's Mrs. Lowry you need to thank, my dear."

6 June 1838 – First day with Dr. Thweatt
The doctor met us at the entrance to our camp as the sky was beginning to turn pink over missionary ridge. It was wonderful to get out of the camp.

"I appreciate you and your brother's help more than I can say, Cassie. I apologize in advance, but I will not be able to compensate you two for your service. I will see you are fed, clothed and housed. That's the best I can do."

"Extracting us from that camp is enough, doctor."

"Mrs. Lowry will provide your meals and sleeping quarters."

"We're grateful, Doctor Thweatt."

"My dear, the fact that you and your brother speak Cherokee and Creek will allow me to help more people. You two are a godsend."

"We think you are the one sent by God, Dr. Thweatt."

"Whatever the case, I couldn't have ordered two better assistants."

Dr. Thweatt flicked the reins to speed his old mule.

"I want to visit both camps at Ross's Landing today and also visit the Creeks. They have been neglected more than the Cherokee, if that is possible. We'll not have enough time to visit them all, but we'll do the best we can."

"We're ready, doctor. My brother and I will do the best we can to help."

"I know you will," the doctor answered. "Forgive my old carryall, Cassie. It's as old as I am, but it will have to do. I wish I had a proper carriage."

"After what we've been through, sir, I feel like a princess."

The day passed in a confusing whirl. Five Feathers and I were exhausted. The emotion required to translate medical terms was grueling.

The doctor worked at the camps near Ross's Landing treating those who could be persuaded to allow an American man near. My brother helped with lifting, carrying and the deceased. For those beyond help, we did what we could. At the second camp a child was being carried out for burial as we arrived, having died of a bloody flux. The body was lashed to a slab with twine. One discolored, emaciated arm, no bigger than a stick of kindling, hung out of the ragged shirt that served as a shroud.

At the close of day the doctor's old mule, as tired as we were, plodded into the Brainerd mission grounds. Ben's mother ran to meet us. She almost leapt into our arms as we embraced. Even my stoic brother was emotional. I apologized for our unwashed condition but my apologies were dismissed.

"I'll see you two in the morning bright and early," the tired doctor said.

The doctor flicked the reins. The tired mule ambled away.

"We'll get you both a warm bath," Mrs. Lowry said. "I have clean clothes laid out. Follow me and I'll show your quarters. The mission is crowded as you can imagine. There are so many in need and we house as many as we can. Your sleeping arrangements are the best I could manage."

Mrs. Lowry led us to a corner stall in the old stable behind her cabin.

"We put up a few boards so the mules won't bother you. We put a floor on one side. The rest is dirt but you have fresh sawdust and straw. It will smell like a stable but that can't be helped. At least it's a clean stable."

"Better than us have slept in a stable," I answered.

"Your beds have clean bedclothes. You'll probably find the animals quieter company than your crowded camp. It's as nice as we could make it."

"It's a palace, Mrs. Lowry. It's wonderful."

Mrs. Lowry worried her apron, "Our outhouse is behind the stable. I would put you in our little cabin, but it's overcrowded with soldiers demanding accommodation. You'll have to let Missy sleep with you. The soldiers don't like cats. We feed her in the stable to keep little visitors away. She'll be good company. Sometimes I bring her a saucer of milk and sit with her a while and talk."

Mrs. Lowry took a deep breath.

"You'll be safe. You'll probably rest better here than in our little house. I've laid out your clean clothes in the washing shed behind the kitchen. Your bath water is warm. After you've bathed and changed, I'll have your supper ready. I'll wash your clothes tomorrow. I'm so glad to see you two. I'll prepare all your food while you're here. Don't worry about that."

Mrs. Lowry twisted her apron.

"I can't express how happy I am to see you two."

Missy purred and rubbed our ankles.

"We can't tell you how much Five Feathers and I appreciate this."

293

"My dear, at least for a while we shall enjoy one another's company like old times. I'm determined to make your every moment pleasant. I'm sorry to hear about your Elisi and Edudu. You have my deepest sympathy."

"Thank you," I answered.

"I feared greatly for them when I heard the arrests had begun. We're called on to bury elderly and children most every day. I don't want to talk about that now. I can't tell you how much I have missed you since Wilbur's imprisonment, but now you two are here, this is the happiest day I can remember in months and months."

"It's our happiest day, too," I answered.

"I wish I had something special to feed you. We have a good oven, but it's on the other side of the property and we don't bake every day. I fear all I have for you tonight is a plate of beans with fatback, old cornbread and a jug of buttermilk. When I heard you were coming, I saved a couple of fresh onions. They're not as good as the ramps you used to bring me, but they're fresh. There's plenty of cornmeal around these days, but not much in the way of fresh vegetables, milk, eggs or butter, but I'm sure it's better than what our stingy government has been giving you."

"The doctor will be calling at first light," she continued. "He works long hours, but he's a good man. Everyone loves him dearly. He's precious."

"He's a perfect gentleman," I responded.

"And thank you so much for everything, Mrs. Lowry. What you have prepared for us is a palace and a feast. Thank you, thank you."

Mrs. Lowry's hands began to twist her apron once again.

"We would have done more if we had more time."

I saw a look of consternation on her face. Something was bothering her.

"I guess you're wondering about Mr. Lowry," Ben's mother said.

"Ben told me about him. I'm afraid to ask," I answered.

"He doesn't talk. He stays in his bed most of the time."

"I'm so sorry, Mrs. Lowry."

"Sometimes he'll stay in bed all day. He never talks. I'm never sure if he knows where he is. Sometimes I come home to find him hiding under the bed. I wish you didn't have to see him like this. Since his imprisonment he hasn't been the same. I can't imagine the horror the Militia put him through. Maybe tomorrow evening you can visit with him for a little while."

7 June 1838 - Second day with Dr. Thweatt

Our night in the stable was our best night's sleep since our arrest. The animals had good manners. Missy kept us company. She slept curled beside Five Feathers' head most of the night.

Dr. Thweatt arrived before dawn and we were quickly off.

"There's a measles epidemic, Cassie," Dr. Thweatt said. "Measles spreads quickly under crowded conditions. It's a dreadful disease, dreadful."

"It was in our camp," I said.

"I wish I could do more," The doctor said. "The army has crowded families together without proper sanitation. They're asking for trouble."

"I know. We didn't have proper latrines," I said quietly.

"I know, Cassie. I've seen," the doctor said in a whisper. "If measles isn't fatal, the following pneumonia brings death. We can bleed them and administer an emetic, but that's about all. There's no rest for the weary."

I understood. I was too tired to talk.

Five Feathers helped bury six adults and two children. Many were beyond help and would pass soon. Five Feathers was busy all day.

8 June 1838 - Third day with Dr. Thweatt

Dr. Thweatt has been called to Fort Cass to report. We're to leave before dawn and be prepared to stay three days.

I don't feel like writing. My baby is stirring. Dr. Thweatt says my pregnancy is progressing perfectly, I'll deliver a healthy child.

Five Feathers helped dig graves, two children, five adults.

9 June 1838 – Fourth day with Dr. Thweatt

We left for the Agency before daylight. It is a forty-five-mile journey. Dr. Thweatt is to visit Rattlesnake Springs, Bedwell Springs, Mouse Creek number one and the East Mouse Creek camps and report to Fort Cass.

Several thousand are imprisoned near the Agency. We traveled all day. It was hot and muggy without a breath of wind, no sign of rain. Chickamauga Creek is the lowest in memory. Steamboats cannot pass the shoals. Only those of shallowest draft can make Knoxville.

It was a bumpy but a pleasant ride. I enjoyed the rest from our duties. We changed for a fresh horse early in the forenoon, then again at noon and one last time in the afternoon. We arrived at Rattlesnake Springs at twilight. Five Feathers and I slept under the carryall. Dr. Thweatt slept in the officers' quarters. Five Feathers did not dig a grave.

10 June 1838 – Fifth day with Dr. Thweatt

Dawn revealed what appeared to be a thousand prisoners in an open expanse. They were not nearly as crowded together as we were at Ross's Landing. I have no idea where they are from, I suppose North Carolina. We were immediately taken to an old man lying in a wagon. He had a quick, weak pulse, dry hacking cough, spitting blood.

Dr. Thweatt, already sweating profusely, turned away, leaned against the back of the wagon, wiped his brow and whispered, "The old man has consumption, much advanced. He's not long for this world. Make him comfortable."

Dr. Thweatt examined the young woman lying beside the old man. We were told she had recently delivered. He bowed his head. She and the infant were dead.

My brother helped bury four adults, three children.

Five Feathers and I slept under the carryall.

11 June 1838 - Sixth day with Dr. Thweatt

The dawn broke hot and sultry, no sign of much needed rain. Dr. Thweatt brought us a nice breakfast from the officers' tent. I felt guilty. Hundreds around me will wake and have nothing.

The sky is brass. The sickness, especially at Calhoun on the Hiwassee, is worse than ever. Our days pass in a haze, the faces blending into a single vision of disease, fever, vomiting, diarrhea, coughing, retching and death. I have bathed in impurity.

Dr. Thweatt was given some newspapers, the *Southern Recorder*. I was eager to read the first newspaper I had seen since our arrest.

From the *Southern Recorder* - 5 June 1838 – page 3

"...the rights of Georgia will never be compromised...We are likewise happy to be enabled to put before our readers the report of Col. Kenan, of the admirable conduct, and most successful operations of Gen. Scott, to whom was confided the critical duty of executing the treaty with the Cherokees. Our readers will perceive, that Gen. Scott has greatly added to his honorable renown, by the admirable efficiency with which he has performed the duty assigned him; and that he has found a most efficient right arm in our own Floyd—and what, above all, will be the most gratifying intelligence to the patriot and philanthropist, the simple announcement, that without the shedding of a single drop of blood, there remains not a single Indian in Georgia, except those who are in the keeping of the army and ready for instant removal to their home in the West."

From the *Southern Recorder* - 6 June 1838 – page 3

"To his Excellency, G. R. Gilmer:

Sir:--Having just arrived from the scene of operations in the Cherokee Country, I avail myself of the honor of communicating to your Excellency, the movements of my Chief, General Scott, within the limits of Georgia. Upon the 24th ult., he placed the Georgia Volunteers under the command of Gen. Floyd, in position; and on the 25th commenced operations. General Floyd, in person, commanded the first detachment that operated. The promptness and ability of his movement, gave the commanding

General the highest satisfaction, while it presented to the balance of the command, the most salutary example.

The number of prisoners on Tuesday last, was about 3000; and by this time, I do not think there is a wandering Indian in the Cherokee Country, within the limits of Georgia. The captures were made with the utmost kindness and humanity, and free from every stain of violence.

The deportment of our Georgia citizens, resident in the Cherokee counties, has been marked by a forbearance and kindness towards the Indians, that must win for them the admiration of every philanthropist. Permit me to conclude with the congratulation of our rights being so promptly and peacefully secured.

With the highest regard, A.H. Kenan
Volunteer Aide-de-camp to General Scott."

12 June 1838 – Seventh day with Dr. Thweatt
We have treated many children for Cholera infantum, known by vomiting, diarrhea, thirst, and muscle cramps.

We found a man lying under a bush beside a fence, lying on a scrap of cloth in his own filth, abandoned. Another scrap of cloth covered his middle. A piece of bark his only cover from the elements. The old man was unable to turn, relieve himself or communicate. He stared at us as we attempted to relieve his distress. His expressionless eyes followed us as we left him.

We met Dr. Grant, also working in the camps. He was a dentist, not a physician. I suppose a dentist is a better physician than none at all.

We see families eating partially cooked food. Civilian contractors often distribute spoiled rations. The water is generally contaminated.

Eight children and seven adults buried today. Measles is rampant.

13 June 1838 – Day eight with Dr. Thweatt
Dr. Thweatt was given a copy of *The Boston Recorder*. It quotes the southern newspapers. The north is being told we are emigrating of our own free will with the gracious assistance of the army. No one will ever read this journal. We will be forgotten. Five died today.

14 June 1838 – Day nine with Dr. Thweatt
Dr. Thweatt has been ordered back to Ross's Landing. We are exhausted, our supplies spent. Typhus is spreading, a nervous condition with trembling agitation, inflammation of the lungs, coughing, complete incontinence of bowels and urine, a ghastly death. The patients take on a wild look and mutter incoherently, at the point of confused rambling nothing can be done.

Today was dreadful, five dead of dysentery, six of nervous fever.

15 June 1838 - Day ten with Dr. Thweatt

We returned to the mission long after sunset, tired beyond words. We found Mrs. Lowry in bed shaking violently suffering ague and fever, alternating between shivering and high temperature. The doctor recommended she evacuate stomach and bowels. He administered quinine and warned she may experience a headache, nausea and roaring in her ears. I stayed by her side until she slept.

16 June 1838 – Day eleven with Dr. Thweatt

The doctor, Five Feathers and I returned to the mission in the late evening after a long day. Mrs. Lowry, weak but much recovered, met us at the stable and handed an official looking letter to Doctor Thweatt.

The doctor put the letter in his pocket and began to care for his mule and put his things away. All three of us stared at him without offering to help. He put his hands on his hips with an expression of some defiance. He patted his vest pocket containing the letter and looked at each of us in turn.

"You three want to know what's in this letter, don't you?"

"I was going to read it after I put our things away and fed the mule. I wanted to read this letter later with a nice cup of tea, but I guess if you three are so impatient, I'll read it now."

We crowded around.

"And I suppose you want me to tell you what this letter contains?"

He held the unopened letter in his hands and turned it over, looking at it from all sides as if to divine its contents. The delay was maddening.

"It's from the army," he said at last.

He sat on the stepover of the tack room. Missy hopped into his lap and began purring. We crowded around like children waiting for a treat. The doctor opened the letter with deliberate slowness. Mrs. Lowry and I pressed closer, not wanting to miss a word from this important letter from the military.

I had never seen an official letter from the army.

Doctor Thweatt slowly opened the single page letter and scanned its contents. His falling countenance revealed the news.

"The news isn't good, Cassie. A company of about twelve hundred Cherokee left four days ago for the western territory. Your detachment is being organized to leave tomorrow morning," the doctor said in a whisper.

I felt a pain in my heart.

"The parole I have arranged for you and Five Feathers has been revoked. I must deliver you and your brother to your detachment by first light.

Mrs. Lowry put her arm around me and wept softly.

"I am sorry but I must keep my pledge," the doctor said. "I obtained your parole on my honor."

Dr. Thweatt's entire body sagged. It was all he could do to sit upright, suddenly looking much older than his years. His wrinkled hand, still firmly grasping the letter in gnarled fingers, sagged onto his legs as if he had suddenly lost the strength in his arm.

"We're grateful for everything, doctor," I said. "It's not your fault."

"You and Five Feathers will accompany the detachment out west. I have been called to Charleston and then to Mission headquarters in the north.

The letter slipped from the doctor's fingers and lay on the sawdust.

Chapter XLVI

1838 – Cassie's Goodbye
Chapter 46

16 June 1838

United States Army Officers' Quarters - Ross's Landing

The Captain's charge to the escorting soldiers:

"Our mission, under orders from General Winfield Scott, is to escort the seven hundred and fifty Cherokee prisoners outside the borders of the United States as efficiently as possible.

The water level is too low for steamboats. We'll travel overland. The Indians are not allowed to pass through American settlements or towns. We cross improved farmland with permission. All damage to property will be paid for by the Indians through their conductor. Indians pay for all ferry crossings and have a daily ration provided by contractors.

Our primary task is to protect the American citizenry. The Cherokee are not to be trusted, especially the men. The mission will take approximately eighty days. I want to finish this assignment quickly.

The Indians are not allowed to leave the detachment for any reason. They are not allowed to buy, sell, trade or hunt. We especially want to keep them from whiskey. The government provides wagons for the sick and elderly. All others walk.

Hunting is forbidden. Since we're holding the women and children hostage, the men who sneak away will most likely return. I want to leave at first light. I expect to make ten miles a day. We travel rain or shine. We stop only to rest the animals and shoe the horses and mules."

17 June 1838 - Brainerd Mission

As we said our goodbyes, Dr. Thweatt waited patiently in the carryall.

"I'm so sorry," Mrs. Lowry said, beginning to cry, clutching my shoulders in her small, gnarled hands, her fingers disfigured by arthritis.

Mr. Lowry, silhouetted in the cabin's open doorway in his nightshirt, his shock of coarse white hair uncombed, stood staring into the distance with no indication he was aware of anything. He urinated off the side of the porch.

Mrs. Lowry wiped her cheeks with the back of her hand and stood as straight as she could.

"I'm so sorry, my dear. Please forgive me."

"There's nothing to forgive, Mrs. Lowry," I said.

"Forgive my failures, Cassie," Mrs. Lowry continued. "We tried to get you released into our custody but to no avail. They wouldn't listen."

"I know. You did your best," I answered.

"The authorities pay no heed to anyone at the mission. They care nothing for your achievements. Their only thought is to send every Indian west as soon as possible. I enjoyed the last few days more than I can say. You and Five Feathers are a gift from heaven. I want us to go west with you, Cassie. Wilbur never answers when I ask about that, but perhaps we'll come later. I'm sure he would prefer to spend his last days with the Cherokee."

"I'll be waiting, Mrs. Lowry. Please come."

"I wish I could be there when our grandchild is born," Mrs. Lowry said. "I'll talk to Dr. Thweatt. Perhaps I can take Wilbur west to be with you and our baby. Perhaps the journey west will bring Wilbur back."

"I hope you can come," I said.

"Cassie, I always wanted a little girl. If I ever had a little girl, I would want her to be just like you."

"Mrs. Lowry, I want to ask a favor. Years ago Ben made a sketch book which he gave to me. There are a couple of dozen sketches. They're precious."

Eleanor was looking at me with a strangely perceptive look.

"Would you please give these sketches to Ben for me? I want him to have this sketch book to remember me by."

"Of course I'll give it to him, dear. I won't let him forget you. He has been distracted. He's young, but he won't forget you. You can count on me."

Mrs. Lowry took me by the hand and pulled back the oilcloth. There was a small wooden flour box tied securely with twine.

"Last night Dr. Thweatt and I packed the tea service in old rags and sawdust for your trip. The box is sturdy. All I ask is every now and then when you have a cup of tea in your new home, remember our days in New Echota. Remember that the cup you hold in your hand I once held in mine."

"I'm so sorry, Doctor Thweatt. We're taking much too long to say goodbye but I may never see my Cassie again. I can't seem to let her go."

"You ladies take all the time you want," the doctor said.

"I've one last thing to say," Mrs. Lowry said. "The quilt and the tea service are the most precious things I have from my mother's family in Germany. The quilt you already have. The tea service is now yours, my dear. I shall pray for you every morning and evening. Perhaps one day you'll give the quilt and tea service to my grandchild on the occasion of her wedding and speak to the child of happier times in Cherokee Country, our glory days."

"I'll remember the stories. I'll write them down," I said.

301

"I didn't realize it then, but when we were together there in New Echota we weren't very far from heaven, were we my dear?" Mrs. Lowry said.

"Those were the best of days. I thought they would never end."

"There's one more thing. I suspect you have forgotten."

Mrs. Lowry withdrew a tiny silk purse from the pocket of her apron. In the purse were the two plain gold bands, shining in the predawn starlight. Mrs. Lowry handed them to me.

"They're yours, Cassie. I don't know how or where, but I trust the Almighty you will reach your destination and you and Ben will be united."

"I believe so, too. Ben and I will be together," I said.

"You and Ben will wed. That's why I'm giving you these rings. I want to be there that day. If we can't be there in person, Wilbur and I will be there in these rings. Take them, dear. If I could take my very heart from my body I would give it to you. Take these rings, remember us."

"I'll never forget you, Mrs. Lowry—never—never," I said.

"I look forward to our reunion, if not this side, then the other. I have loved you more dearly than can be said in words. Take care of my baby. Write the moment you arrive. I'll give Ben the sketch book. I promise. I'll see that Ben does right by you."

"I know he will," I said.

"Don't be surprised, young lady, if you see Wilbur and me coming round the bend to see you in your new home out west. I love you dearly."

Mrs. Lowry gave us a final embrace as we mounted the carryall and then we were on our way. In the morning stillness the ring of the iron tires on the hard-packed gravel reverberated off the surrounding buildings. I waved to Mrs. Lowry until we turned the corner by the graveyard.

Georgia Militia Camp

Ben felt a hand gently shaking his shoulder. For a moment he didn't know where he was. As he lay in the dim light of Caesar's lantern, he remembered he would have an exceptionally busy morning. During the last two months it seemed he had been in a different camp every night. As he swung his stocking feet to the canvas floor of the uncomfortable tent, he had the same thought he had every morning, he wished he were back in Milledgeville.

There was no end to the odd noises of men and beast that seemed to be amplified in the darkness in all the encampments. He was impatient to get back to quiet nights in his own bed in Huff's boarding house or, better yet, at the hotel with Elizabeth.

As his servant helped him into his trousers, he thought how he would prefer to be at the hotel. He cursed the removal. He mustn't torture himself and think of Elizabeth. He had responsibilities.

Ben sat on the edge of his cot and sipped hot coffee put in his hand by his resourceful servant. Ben hadn't brought the coffee. Supplies were scarce in this madhouse by the river. Caesar was capable, more than capable. He must remember to thank him. He probably bought this with his own money.

Ben sipped and reflected. He had been working all over the new counties to oversee the distribution of newly vacated Cherokee property. He had been dealing with fortunate drawers, surveyors, ignorant squatters and the inexperienced officials who tested his patience at every turn. Everyone wanted advice. His days were filled with nonsensical questions of semi-illiterate men in positions of authority who couldn't understand simple written instructions.

As his servant helped him complete his toilet in the dim light, he reflected on his awkward visit with his mother. He shouldn't have gone to see her. It was a mistake. His mother was a shell of her former self, barely able to care for his father. Ben was worried. He suggested once again he bring his parents to Milledgeville. He would put them in proper accommodations with servants and perhaps they could find doctors who could help his father, but his mother refused. It was their duty to support the work at the mission, she insisted.

Ben's mind returned to the reason for his early call. He had been informed Cassie's detachment would be leaving early this morning. He had promised his mother he would see her off. How utterly inconvenient but his mother would never forgive him if he didn't say goodbye to Cassie. Working for the government, he was used to doing things he didn't want to do. He would view this as just another unpleasant task. He might as well get it over with.

Ben washed in the small porcelain washbasin, dampened and combed his hair in the scrap of a mirror attached to the wooden upright and tidied his clothing. Caesar brushed his coat and helped him with his boots, boots Caesar kept shined to a mirror finish. He was expecting another hot, miserable day. The god-damned Indians continued to be a bother. He couldn't wait till they were gone and this was all over. For the thousandth time Ben thought how stupid the Cherokee were for trying to remain. They were nothing but trouble.

Ben swung his tall frame into the comfortable saddle in one effortless motion. At least his ride on his well-trained saddle horse was a welcome beginning to a dreadful day. His mare was a friend, a confidant who listened patiently, never criticized and instantly obeyed. He could count on her to never ask difficult questions or second guess his orders. She would wait all day and never complain. He had never owned such a well-trained horse. She obeyed the slightest touch of the reins on her neck, pressure from his legs or even a shift in his weight. Ben smiled. Riding his mare was the highlight of his job with the state of Georgia. What a strange thought first thing in the morning.

There was just the faintest hint of light in the eastern sky behind the big ridge to the east, the north to south ridge everyone called the missionary ridge. Stars were twinkling. It would be another beautiful, cloudless day, hotter than hell. He tugged at his collar remembering the heat of the day previous, once again wishing he didn't have to perform his first task of the day in obedience to his mother.

He leaned slightly to the left. His mare obediently turned onto the road towards Ross's Landing and Cassie's departure point. He noticed once again the low water level in the normally big Tennessee River. There was hardly a current. The river usually ran wide and deep and often flooded in late winter and spring. This summer it was the shallowest anyone had ever seen. The little creeks, tributaries and marshes feeding the river were nearly dry. This would be a terrible year for farmers in the Tennessee Valley.

Ben wasn't in a hurry. He allowed his chestnut mare to walk slowly towards Ross's Landing. He had plenty of time. He marveled how the sleepy Cherokee ferry crossing he remembered as a child had exploded into a bustling center of activity, a veritable city. Ross's Landing had changed in the last ten years.

When he was a boy this ferry crossing, just upstream from the big moccasin bend, was on the edge of nowhere. In the last two years Ben had seen Ross's Landing mushroom into a busy town and military center. He correctly reasoned it would soon blossom into an important American city with its strategic location on an important navigable river joining Tennessee, Alabama and Georgia.

This part of Cherokee Country had been coveted by American governments, both local and federal, for some time. Those who understood business recognized the importance of controlling the Tennessee River valley, necessary for the smooth flow of goods in the emergent markets of the South. The growth of a healthy business climate made removing the Cherokee a necessity.

Ben's father would draw a parallel with that of King Ahab and Naboth's vineyard, but that was his father's view, not his. The once tiny Cherokee trading post and ferry was this morning an all-white burgeoning American town, as it should be. The Cherokee right to occupy land had been legally extinguished. They were a backward bunch. Everything had been lawful and aboveboard. The Cherokee had no right to complain.

Ben halted on the crest of a small hill. The vista was magnificent. The rising sun was beginning to brighten the panoramic vision below him under a cloudless sky. The picturesque Tennessee River to his right was smooth as glass with a few small busy boats on early errands. Visible in the distance were the steamboat docks with several big paddle wheel steamers with barges lashed to their sides, useless until the water level in the river rose.

The two main prison camps, obscured in the morning mist, lay somewhere below him and to his right, close to the river. To his left up the hill and as far as he could see were an endless sea of tents and hastily constructed, low-slung wooden structures occupied by the United States Army, various military units, militias, hundreds of contractors and their wagons, their animals and mounds of supplies stored wherever they could find shelter. Mixed among all that and on the periphery were hundreds of recently arrived civilians, many ne'er-do-well scavengers taking advantage of the lawless nature of the vacuum left by the Cherokee departure.

Even the north side of the river, the old whiteside, had more activity than he remembered. Columns of smoke were beginning to rise from hundreds of fires. The columns of smoke in the still morning air gave the appearance of a giant forest of trees whose trunks reached to the stars. These fires would provide breakfast for some twenty thousand souls.

Ben continued to delay. He sat still, hooked his right knee around the saddle horn and lounged against the cantle, observing the remarkable vista. No one would ever see anything like this again, ever. In a week or two there wouldn't be a single Cherokee family anywhere. Georgia had its wish, an unobstructed border with Tennessee, Alabama and North Carolina. Travelers and business men would never have to pay another toll to a Cherokee gatekeeper. The way was cleared for the economic development of the entire southern region of the United States of America.

Tennessee and Georgia could now get on with the business of building a great nation of perfectly united states. Tennessee, Georgia, Alabama, North Carolina and South Carolina, now ethnically cleansed as the northern states had been previously, could prosper.

While Ben was delaying, the vista before him changed. The first rays of the morning sun rose above the eastern ridge, brilliantly illuminating the largest of the Cherokee prison camps. In a sudden explosion of light, the predawn mist cleared.

With the sun at his back Ben saw Cassie's detachment being prepared for removal. Against his will Ben viewed the scene through his father's eyes. He saw the Cherokee trapped under layer upon layer of white, American injustice.

It was as if a massive stage play was being acted out below him, a play controlled by insanity, written in hell, applauded by an approving audience.

"This isn't my fault," he said to himself. "I'm not responsible. If I had something to do with this mess, I would see they were treated better."

Ben tried to free his imaginative mind of unwanted images. He kicked his mare into a steady gait and rode down the hill to the staging area beside the river. He was determined to get this meeting with Cassie over and done with and get on with his business in Lafayette in the afternoon.

He was not looking forward to meeting Cassie. He found her love cloying, inconvenient. He needed to get back to Milledgeville. He wanted to be anywhere but here.

He must remind himself his Senate appointment would make all this worthwhile. He wondered about Zach and Elizabeth's progress on his behalf.

As he neared Cassie's enclosure, he reminded himself he was on the cusp of success. He couldn't help it if she was Cherokee. Her momentary discomforts had nothing to do with him. He would do what he could for her. Maybe he would buy her a little house when she arrived in the west and provide her with a modest income. He could do that secretly.

Ben left his servant with his horse. He was cautioned his visit must be brief. The Indians were already late for their departure.

Ben spotted a woman with a quilt draped over her shoulders, a quilt he recognized immediately. It was Cassie. Late in her pregnancy Cassie's face, normally healthy and brown, was drawn. She had lost weight and her hair was dull. She carried herself with a stoop as if bearing a heavy load, her face expressionless.

17 June 1838 – Ross's Landing

Ben came to see me this morning after Dr. Thweatt returned us to our camp. Ben will do good for us if he can. I know he will. We will be together.

Ben was embarrassed. That didn't matter. I don't care what Ben's job is. What is happening isn't his fault. The only thing that matters is that Ben is near. I will never tell anyone Ben is the father of my child. My wish is Ben and I shall be blessed with the happiness out west. I shall wait.

I waited for the embrace that never came.

"Cassie, I'm so glad to see you. I talked to Mother. She told me you might be leaving this morning. I wanted to see you before you left. I've spoken to the captain. He will personally make sure you're taken care of."

My last hope of rescue was denied. Ben could do nothing for me. My heart turned to Five Feathers. My brother and I must survive without Ben's help. There was nothing to say. Even in despair I was glad to have Ben beside me, even for a moment. He was uncomfortable. I understood his discomfort.

"I'll come to see you as soon as this is over, Cassie."

"I know."

"I'll see you are taken care of when I'm finished with my job. I promise."

"I know you will."

"In a few months I'll find you and your baby. If I'm appointed to the Senate, I'll send for you. We'll make a life in a place you'll be welcome."

I wanted to believe Ben's words.

"There's a lot of work for me now that the Cherokee are emigrating," he said.

"I know, Ben. I know you're busy."

"My staff and I are working night and day. This job will promote my career and my ability to help the Cherokee in the future. For the future good of the Cherokee, I need to do this, Cassie. I'm going to help you."

"I know you will, Ben."

"I took this job for the Cherokee. None of this is my fault. My career has been devoted to the Cherokee. You know that."

"I know you're not involved, Ben. I'll never be angry."

"If I go to Washington, I can mitigate some injustice and help the Cherokee in the west. Someone must do this job and I would rather it be me than someone who didn't care. There is much I can do in politics."

"You'll be a good Senator."

"I will be. I promise."

I looked into his beautiful eyes, eyes I had loved since I was a girl. I felt a sorrow to see the young man before me swept in a direction opposite that which he had intended. He believed his own words.

"I wish you were going with us, Ben."

"I wish I could go, too."

"I know you can't. I know you have an important job. You can't abandon that, but I wish you could come with us."

I understand. One's love for another can't be controlled or extinguished, manufactured or denied. Love is outside the control of the lover. Human love exists independently of human decision. As hard as I might try, I could never erase my love for this beautiful man.

"I will be thinking of you every day, Ben. Five Feathers and I will take care of our baby. Someday, Ben, we shall be together. I have always known that. Your mother thinks so, too. If it's a boy, I'll name him after you."

"You're sweet, Cassie. We'll be together one day. I promise."

"I will wish you well every morning and every night," I said.

"I'll do the same, Cassie. One day we'll be together. I promise."

"Ben, I am pleased you came."

"I'm glad I came, too," he said.

"Do you remember our promise about the moon? The moon that shines over Georgia is a Cherokee moon. Remember our promise to one another when you went to Milledgeville?"

"I remember," Ben said.

"When you look at our Cherokee moon, remember there is a woman who loves you looking at that same moon."

"I'll remember. I promise."

"Remember your baby when you see that moon."

Ben winced. What was done, was done. Cassie should find a Cherokee man. The child would be an Indian. It should be raised among Indians. Cassie was leaving going west. That solved many problems. Cassie and the child would be happy. With her gone he could safely continue his career. Perhaps he and Elizabeth would find a life together. He hoped so. Elizabeth would look grand on his arm, Cassie never would.

"I'll personally speak to the Captain about you and Five Feathers."

"Thank you, Ben."

"The captain is a good man. He'll listen. They've put a lot of work into this, Cassie. It doesn't look like it now, but the army is genuinely concerned about the welfare of the Cherokee. If there are problems on the journey, the army will put them right."

"I hope so."

"When you're settled, send me your address."

"I'll write the moment I arrive," I said.

A sergeant informed Ben it was time.

"Goodbye, Cassie. I have always loved you. Write when you arrive."

Ben turned away without a parting embrace.

Chapter XLVII

1838 – Ben's Denial - Cassie Deported
Chapter 47

Ben was relieved, glad the visit with Cassie was over. He wanted to be as far from Ross's Landing as he could. As he walked away he felt as if he had done something wrong, but he knew he was doing the best he could. If there was injustice, it had nothing to do with him or his government. The Cherokee brought this unpleasantness upon themselves.

Ben was walking with long strides. He wanted to get on his horse and down the road, into the fresh air of the quiet countryside, away from the river and the confusion. What he wouldn't give for a quiet drink with Elizabeth.

His next appointment was in the new county seat of Walker County, a nice ride south. It would be a lovely ride to Lafayette if he could get out of this damn madhouse and into the saddle.

As Ben started up the hill away from the forming detachment, a soldier gave Ben a long look. Ben was a curiosity, his fine clothes and polished boots out of place.

The young soldier spoke in a loud voice.

"I know you. I seen you in New Echota. You're that lawyer from Milledgeville, aren't you?"

Without breaking stride Ben answered, "You're mistaken."

Increasing his pace, Ben continued the short distance up the hill to the enclosure where his horse was held. He couldn't wait to feel the familiar comfort of the polished leather, the reassuring rhythm of hoofbeats and the power of a perfectly obedient animal under him, an experience that always brought a sense of normality. He wanted the pleasant smells of honeysuckle instead of urine, manure and unwashed bodies.

Ben found it impossible to raise his eyes from the path. He didn't want to see anything. He wanted to acquire no more haunting visual memories. Everything behind him was just where he wanted it, behind him forever.

A brace of mules in full harness approached. The mules, with the double tree hanging from the hames, trace chains jangling, would be hitched to a wagon in the departing detachment for the journey west. Ben stepped aside to let the mules pass.

"I know you," the man leading the mules said. "Your parents were missionaries down in Cherokee Country, at New Echota. I seen you down there. You're the one with that good-lookin' Indian girlfriend."

Ben wanted to get away. He couldn't get away fast enough.

"She had that baby yet?"

For a second time, and with a loud voice, Ben denied the accusations.

"No, that wasn't me. You're confused. I'm not the man."

Ben descended into a darker mood. He felt like an animal pursued. All he wanted was to get away, to be alone.

He had assumed his relationship with Cassie would be unknown at Ross's Landing. He wanted his past to be forgotten. If he could just get away from this place quickly, the soldiers would forget him. The Cherokee would be gone. He would once again become an unidentifiable man in the shadows.

Immediately to Ben's right was a small white tent with a couple of Georgia militia standing a lazy guard and a well-dressed civilian official. The sign on the tent read, 'Fortunate Drawers Here, State of Georgia'.

General Scott had been ordered to cooperate with the governors of the surrounding states. Thus, Ben was allowed the table for men who wanted to take possession of their lottery winnings in the Georgia counties that bordered the state of Tennessee. On Ben's orders, scores of these Lottery Tents were manned throughout newly vacated Cherokee Country.

The man was singing the old song,

'All I ask in this creation,
is a pretty little wife and a big plantation,
way up yonder in the Cherokee Nation.'

The song was fast becoming a reality. As Ben walked past the lottery tent, he fumed with impatience. He felt as if he would burst if he couldn't get away immediately. Delay was maddening. He needed to get on the road.

The Georgia militia stable was hard by the fortunate drawers' tent. Ben gave a sigh of relief as he took his reins from the hostler and mounted. Ben felt a sense of growing security as the hostler led Ben's horse through the crowd by the stable towards the unobstructed path up the hill.

Another teamster was noisily leading a fresh pair of draft horses in full harness down the hill. He called up to Ben in an extra loud voice.

"I know you," the teamster said as he passed. "You're that Cherokee lawyer. We sent your Indian lovin' father to prison."

Ben ignored the young man.

"You've got that pregnant Cherokee woman," the teamster continued.

Ben was sitting in the saddle above the crowd. Those standing near who heard the driver's words turned to watch and listen.

The teamster's remarks touched Ben's last nerve. He lost control. Why should he be singled out? He was doing his job, a good job. He always did a good job. This was unfair. He had been trying to do the right thing. He should have ignored his mother and not said goodbye to Cassie. It was a mistake to come to the river this morning of all mornings, a big mistake.

This unexpected third accusation, hot on the heels of the first two, struck Ben's exposed nerves, worn raw by weeks of worry. Ben exploded in a sudden release of hostility. For the third time Ben denied knowing anything about Cassie or any association with the Cherokee. He stood in the stirrups, leaned towards the young teamster below him and shouted at the top of his voice.

"Just shut up," Ben screamed. "Why don't you just shut up and leave me alone. Shut up."

Ben's voice got louder.

"I'm not the man. Do you hear me? I-am-not-that-man."

Why couldn't they leave him alone. His outburst was a surprise, even to himself. He felt trapped but the inconsiderate soldier deserved harsh words.

Ben's bellowing oath reverberated off the temporary wooden structures on the hills above and echoed over Cassie's detachment below. Everyone heard. In curiosity, onlookers, guards, soldiers and Cherokee alike turned to see this well-dressed man's uncontrolled shouting.

Ben was embarrassed. For the first time since he had walked away from Cassie, Ben turned her way. Their eyes met. She had heard. Everyone heard. Her upturned face wore no expression. She held Ben's gaze for a moment, then turned away to lean against her brother's shoulder.

He must not think about Cassie. He shouldn't have shouted. It was unfortunate if she had heard him, but none of this was his fault. Even his shouts weren't his fault.

Ben's horse walked south, up the hill and away from Ross's Landing and the river, past the old Cherokee post office and settlement near Chief Ross' old home. He followed the road deep into Walker County and the new county seat at Lafayette. He had a lot of work to do before his return to Milledgeville, and then his election campaign and, hopefully, it would be on to Washington City and his new Senate appointment. Zach taught him to have a thick skin when it came to critics. He should not have come this morning, but none of this was his fault. Cassie was gone. That was one worry out of his mind, permanently.

17 June 1838 – First day on the trail west
  Our first day is done. We walked all day. Where will this end?
  Buried Corn Tassel's child. Buried Flax Bird. Buried White Bird.

18 June 1838 – Second day on the trail
  Elisi and Edudu are gone. I have seen my Ben for the last time. My baby, my brother and I shall survive.
  Already the wagons are filled with sick and elderly.
  It was a long, miserable day. My feet hurt, my back aches.

1838 – Ben's Denial – Cassie Deported

Buried Big Field's child. Buried old Chesnut. Buried Four Killer's child.

19 June 1838 – Third day on the trail
Five Feathers and I help the American doctor. We have almost no medicines. We translate. The doctor's expertise is animal husbandry, an appropriate choice by a government that thinks of us as animals.
Buried Grass Hopper's child. Buried Johnson.

20 June 1838 – Fourth day on the trail
We try to help the sick but most choose to bear illness quietly rather than suffer the indignity of treatment by an American doctor who brought an ample supply of whiskey for himself alone.
The army stops to rest the draft animals. The soldiers' horses all have shoes.
No burials today.

21 June 1838 – Fifth day on the trail
Yesterday the solstice. Our days will shorten until we have eternal night.
I forgive Ben. When this madness has passed, he will choose his baby.
Buried Nancy's oldest child. Buried old Otiah. Buried Smith's child.

22 June 1838 – Sixth day
Our path west is easy to follow. To find us, follow our trail of tears.
I stopped to assist an old woman in the dry grass beside the road. A soldier ordered me to keep going. I checked the trailing wagons at the end of the day. The old woman was nowhere to be found.
Buried another of Nancy's children. Buried Tallassah. Buried Mary.

23 June 1838 – Seventh day
Another hot day. The birds sang this morning. I am tired.
The soldiers caught my brother hunting. They horsewhipped him. He was told not to leave the column or he would get worse.
Buried Anderson's child. Buried The Goose's wife and her stillborn child. Buried old Standing Turkey.

24 June 1838 – Eighth day
Twenty Cherokee joined us who had escaped a previous detachment. Their group was famished when they left it.
Buried Tobacco John's wife. Buried Nancy's youngest daughter. Buried Young Duck.

25 June 1838 – Evening – Ninth day on our trail west
We will endure. My brother will be chief.

Moses and Sally, brother and sister, died. Buried Hopkins' youngest.

26 June 1838 – Tenth day on the trail.

I am too tired to write. Ben's child lies heavy within me. No one mentions our past Green Corn Festivals. Five Feathers continues by my side. He will be chief in the west. Every morning I have nausea.

Five Feathers buried Falling Blossom's new baby that came early.

27 June 1838 – Eleventh Day on the journey west.

The soldiers stopped early to shoe. I think of Ben.

I'm tired. There is a stream close by. I want to bathe.

Buried another of Nancy's children. Buried July. Buried Tusla.

28 June 1838 – Twelfth day on the journey

I dreamed of honeysuckle and the Whippoorwill. He welcomed me home. I dreamed this poem. I awoke and found my pen.

Whippoorwill
I hear your call in the lonely night,
From seasons past,
You fetch me home on your glorious cry,
Whip-poor-will
You bid me in the night,
Wake me from my sleep,
Renewing our friendship,
I come to you,
To your call clear and bright,
Whip-poor-will
From shadows you invite,
Out of summer's mist,
From the warm silence of deep night,
Beside the river we love,
Deep and wide, our ancient home,
Whip-poor-will
All is still but you and me,
Sing your song of home,
Sing on invisible wings,
As I listen under the stars,
Your dark forest surrounds cozy and safe,
Whip-poor-will
What say you this night?
All is well with you and me?
You invite me to your tour,

To join your pleasant walk.
Whip-poor-will
You call me home,
To all good and right.
You call me to childhood,
My protection once again,
In darkness with no light,
I am secure in your night,
Whip-poor-will
Nothing shall harm in your place,
Your voice not forlorn,
Time is ours this friendly night,
Naught is lost,
Your call restores that which vanished,
Whip-poor-will
You guard the night,
You guard my soul,
You are my light,
My gentle bed,
Whip-poor-will
You and owl stand sentinel,
We cavort till dawn,
You are my nightly joy,
Spellbound I listen to your call,
Whip-poor-will
Shall you come another lonely night,
To grace my dream?
To bring my childhood,
Once again on tiny wings?
Whip-poor-will
Shall I hear your voice once more?
Will you bring that which is lost?
Will I see you again,
And hear your lonesome call?
Whip-poor-will

Buried Amachanah. Buried Denis Woff's child. Buried the child born untimely to Ahyoka. She did not bring happiness.

29 June 1838 – Day thirteen

I feel a weariness deep in my bones. I have no strength. It is difficult to walk. I have nothing good to write. There is no joy. The world will not miss us. No one will remember.

Buried Dirt Thrower. Buried Feather's wife.

30 June 1838 – Day fourteen

We stopped early beside a rock-filled flowing stream. The happy water is welcome. Even the soldiers are tired. Will there be a river in our new land?

My time is approaching. I wonder if Ben knows his baby will be born under a wagon or beside the road or under a tree. I hope Ben finds us. One day I will look to the horizon and see him coming to me. I know he will come.

My ankles are swollen. My back aches. I am heavy.

Buried Sarah Raincrow. Buried McDonald's youngest child, Sinda.

1 July 1838 – Day fifteen

We make one more day. We bury our dead. My brother and I walk together. Sometimes he almost carries me. Without his support I would go bouncing in a wagon and die with the rest. I watch the children with their mothers. I watch Five Feathers carry a tired child. I watch him play with the children, diverting their minds, teaching them about the birds, trees and animals. Five Feathers will be a good chief. He will not forget.

Our baby will come soon. At last I will be a mother.

No burials today.

2 July 1838 – Day sixteen of our journey west

Today was hot. We camped early by a welcoming stream, an oasis. The little creek, shaded by trees on both sides, is filled with smooth stones, the languid water running from one puddle to another. The children began jumping from stone to stone playing games, shouting and laughing. Watching the children play games in the water in the cool of the afternoon is the most pleasant sight I have seen since our arrest.

I stretched my legs, resting my swollen feet in the cool water listening to the river run over smooth rocks. Everyone's mood is lighter. Tonight I shall sleep next to this bubbling creek. I shall listen as it sings lullabies throughout the night. I wish we could stay.

My brother saw many rabbit signs this morning. No American farms are near.

My brother can escape any time and easily make his way westward and be free. He chooses to stay with me and my child.

Five Feathers told me he would sneak away and bring a rabbit for my dinner. I felt our spirits unite as I watched him disappear silently.

The baby feels heavy.

Five Feathers was reveling in his temporary freedom. An expert with a sling, he soon had two fat rabbits tied to his belt. He was enjoying the silence of the cool shade under the dense summertime canopy, relishing the simple ability to go where he pleased instead of where he was told.

Five Feathers discovered a dry creek bed running parallel to the road. During the rainy season the little creek would be a mad, tumbling stream impossible to cross, but today, after weeks of bone-dry weather, there was no water flowing, none at all. The only water in the creek bed was the occasional stagnant puddle filled with happy tadpoles and water spiders.

Wide, flat stones filled the creek bottom as if conveniently placed inviting Five Feathers to avoid the puddles and effortlessly walk dry shod. He would enjoy his freedom, casually walk a mile or two more and then slip back into the column unobserved to prepare the rabbits for his sister's evening meal. For a few moments at least, life was good.

Walking on the flat stones of the creek bed meant he could travel unobserved, obscured by the dense, green laurels on both banks. It was as if Five Feathers were walking down his own private hallway with high, emerald walls.

A sudden noise caused Five Feathers to stop instantly and turn. A short bow shot behind him were two armed hunters, both Americans. They stepped into the creek bed with their long guns raised, shouting for Five Feathers to halt. Five Feathers was not going to be detained by two clumsy hunters. He saw an opening in the laurels to his left and instantly leapt for safety.

Five Feathers remembered the last time Americans wanted to steal his game. These men would not have the rabbits intended for his sister. With a powerful athletic move, Five Feathers leapt upward and sideways for a small opening at the bottom of the solid wall of laurels lining the creekbank. If he could reach the opening and avoid the first salvo, he could slither through the laurels, easily escaping these inept pursuers.

At the same instant Five Feathers jumped, both men fired their rifles, guns that made a lead bullet spin and hold its intended line for great distances with uncanny accuracy.

In the middle of his leap, a single rifle bullet passed through the upper part of Five Feathers' chest under his right shoulder. The force slammed his body against the bare soil of the creekbank just short of the opening and his intended escape under the laurels. Bleeding profusely, Five Feathers lay still, his head and neck lying at an awkward angle, his left cheek pressed against the cool earth, his left arm extended upward as if reaching for a handhold.

Through their gunsmoke, the two men saw the Cherokee man fall. Terrified of a counter attack, the hunters frantically reloaded their weapons where they stood.

When the smoke cleared, the nervous men saw the wounded Cherokee man lying face down, perfectly still, a small rivulet of blood trickling down the near-vertical creekbank, turning a stagnant puddle below bright pink.

The nervous men approached cautiously, one step at a time, rifles ready. Five Feathers had not moved since he fell. As the two men reached the wounded Indian, they saw the location of the entrance wound, a round, black hole in the back of the Cherokee's leather shirt.

The first man approached slowly, leaned forward over the prone form of Five Feathers, carefully examining the entrance wound.

"John, that was a good shot. This 'un ain't goin' nowhere."

His companion who was still several feet away answered, "Watch him, Hank, don't take your eye off him. Keep your finger on the trigger. He may be playin' possum."

Both men, chewing tobacco, spat on the unconscious man. The brown spittle ran down Five Feathers' leather shirt and dripped into the puddle, mixing with pink water below.

"Well, John, this 'un's done for," Hank said. "He's shot clean through. The bullet come out the other side, I think. Watch him while I make sure he's dead."

Hank, rifle at the ready, held the muzzle of his weapon just inches from the Indian's body. With the toe of his boot the man named Hank kicked against Five Feathers' leg and jumped backward as if he expected the wounded Indian to suddenly leap upon them.

Even after the violent kick from the American, there was no movement from the prone Cherokee warrior. He was unconscious, or dead.

Emboldened, the man named Hank gave Five Feathers' leg a second vicious kick and jumped backwards, but still no response from the Indian.

"John, keep your rifle on 'im. He may not be dead now, but he soon will be. If he so much as twitches, pull the trigger. I'm goin' to put my rifle down."

The man named John, following instructions, put the wooden stock of his rifle to his cheek and nervously aimed the long barrel of his loaded gun at the prone Indian lying on his stomach on the slope of the creek bank. The man named Hank laid his rifle carefully on a large stone, well out of the reach in case the Indian suddenly revived. Kneeling beside the wounded Cherokee warrior, the man named Hank unsheathed his skinning knife, roughly grabbing a handful of Five Feathers' hair at the crown of his head. He jerked the hair upward and backward.

As he pulled Five Feathers' head backwards, the warrior's unconscious body began to slowly slide down the near vertical creekbank. As Five Feathers' body slid, the man continued to hold Five Feathers' hair in his left hand. Five Feathers' feet gently slid into the puddle of pink water below him, stopping his downward movement, disturbing tadpoles. The American repositioned himself for his intended task. Once again, the man yanked Five Feathers' head backwards away from the red soil of the creekbank.

With his skinning knife in his right hand, the man named Hank made a deep horizontal gash in the flesh of Five Feathers' head just above his right ear. In one motion and using all his strength, the sharp knife circled all the way around the Indian's head cutting deep, the blade making an audible crunching sound as the sharp blade ground against bone. With rapid strokes of a skilled hunter, the man named Hank separated the hair and flesh from the skull. When the last bit of flesh was severed from the bone at the back of Five Feathers' neck, the Indian's head fell, his face making a thud as his cheek slapped against the damp soil of the creekbank. The man named Hank held his prize high to be admired by his companion.

"By god, John, I've always wanted to do that. I've heard about it, but I never thought I would have the chance to get one. We're lucky to get this 'un. I thought all the injuns were gone," Hank said, holding up his prize.

The man named John relaxed and uncocked his rifle.

"I thought he would git away. Did you see how he jumped like a scared rabbit? He didn't get away from us, did he, Hank?"

The man named Hank washed his trophy in the pink puddle between Five Feathers' feet.

"We got him, by god, John. We got the last one, I reckon. We'll be famous. There won't be no more after these are gone. Yep, we'll be famous."

Hank tucked his prize in his belt.

"I can't wait till I get back and show ever' body what we got."

"We'll be famous, Hank," the man named John replied.

"It's a shame you can't turn that pelt in for a bounty like they used to. My daddy's old uncle made a lot of money from Indian bounties in the old days."

After the man named Hank cleaned his knife blade on the unconscious Indian's leather shirt, he cut the rabbits off the waist band.

The two hunters headed back the way they had come without a backward glance at the wounded man they left lying against the cool earth in the deep shade of the creekbank.

The resilient Five Feathers continued to breathe, short, shallow breaths, hanging desperately onto life as he lay on the slope of the creekbank in the cool shade of the evergreen laurels, his feet half submerged in the shallow puddle of pink water.

Five Feathers regained consciousness.

Weakened by loss of blood, he was unable to lift his head or open his eyes. His right arm was paralyzed from the passage of the bullet. Five Feathers slowly explored with his left, searching for a handhold to pull himself out of sight under the laurels. He needed to rest. He made several unsuccessful attempts to pull himself upward. Five Feathers was too weak to move. He lay still. He felt the welcome coolness of the damp soil on his cheek. He decided to rest quietly where he was and sleep. He never moved again.

2 July 1838 evening
I heard gun shots in the forest. Five Feathers did not return.

Buried Bigbear's grandchild. Buried Dreadful Waters. Buried Oolanheta.

3 July 1838 – Day seventeen of our journey west

My brother did not return. I am alone. My baby and I will begin a new life in the west. We must. I will protect my child. I will tell my child the stories of our village, our nation, Edudu, Elisi and Five Feathers.

Buried Rainfrog's daughter. Buried Timberlake's daughter, Alsey.

4 July 1838 – Morning – Day eighteen of our journey west

I am up before the sun. My discomfort increases. I feel my baby heavy within. Today my child shall be born. Tears shall end. I hear Mockingbird singing from the top of the tree welcoming me to motherhood and my child into this world. I await my joy.

Chapter XLVIII

1838 - First Johnson Reunion Planned
Chapter 48

The Johnson Family Farm – Tennessee

Abner cupped his mug of steaming black coffee in both hands and looked over the rich bottomland stretched below him. Most of what he saw was his. He inhaled the delicious aroma slowly as if it were a perfume.

"Martha," he said after a while, "there isn't anything in this world I can think of that rivals my love for you."

She beamed hearing those words. She loved it when Abner was romantic. He wasn't romantic nearly enough, but that was alright with her. She felt fortunate to have him. He was a good man. They had a good life in Tennessee.

He gave her a big grin. Their eyes met for a moment of shared intimacy. He adored her, always had. He couldn't imagine a day of his life without her.

"I'm lazy this morning, Martha. Since tomorrow's the Fourth, I'll take the morning off and help you get ready for your relatives' visit."

"That'll be nice, Abner. You don't take much time off."

"I want your first family reunion to be a success but I want to spend the morning with you. I'll do the chores this afternoon," Abner said quietly.

"You know how important family is to me," his wife said.

"I know, Martha. We'll have a get-together to remember. You're a special woman. I want you to know that."

She snuggled against her husband. While he sipped his coffee, they enjoyed the breaking July dawn, a welcome respite from their busy summertime routine.

She refilled his coffee. She felt a wave of sentimental emotion sweep over her which almost brought her to tears.

"I want to thank you again for the dinner bell, Abner. I love it."

They both looked up at the new bell proudly displayed just behind them.

"Now I won't have to shout for you to come in for your dinner. It's the best gift I've ever had. Thank you."

"You're welcome, my dear," her husband replied. I enjoyed gettin' the bell and puttin' it up for you."

Martha leaned on her husband's shoulder.

"I love comin' out here and ringin' it when I got your dinner on the table. I think it's the most beautiful bell I've ever seen. It has a beautiful ring. I love you, Abner."

Abner studied the black polished bell he had mounted attractively on a tall, shaped cedar post. His wife had mentioned she wanted a dinner bell last year to call everyone in from the fields. She deserved it. She worked as hard as any man. Her long hours cooking, preserving food, washing, managing the house slaves, taking care of the chickens, fattening hogs, and keeping their vegetable garden was a hard life. Abner was glad he wasn't a woman. She deserved the bell and more besides.

His thinking came full circle. This bottomland was good to him. In a few years he would purchase more land and more slaves. He could see the big house he would eventually build for Martha. She deserved a proper house instead of their tiny log cabin. He would build a respectable kitchen separate from the house with a big brick oven and a proper cookin' hearth with high ceiling. He would make sure she had enough help so she wouldn't have to sweat over an open fire all day. Help would be important with the new baby coming. He would put the female slave quarters out back so she could call on them anytime day or night.

Since all four of his female slaves were of childbearing age, or soon would be, he would have yet more slaves to work the farm, job out or sell. Healthy male slaves, even young ones, brought good money, even more if they were skilled. Young female slaves, if properly trained, would also bring good money when he got ready to sell them. In a few years Martha's slave girls would produce quite a few offspring he could market. He could buy more land and furnish her new house in proper style. Life was good here in Tennessee, very good.

Abner thought, once more, how he loved this farm and the rural life here. He wouldn't want to live anywhere else. His place here was like a Garden of Eden. Yes, he thought to himself again, the Garden of Eden couldn't have been any nicer than this.

Abner pulled his wife closer.

"You know, Martha, we're blessed. We have this farm and all the bottomland a man could want. We own our place. No one can take it away."

"I love it, Abner."

"It's paid for and we have the deed. I'm proud of this place."

"I know, Abner. I have you and we're going to have a baby."

"I couldn't be happier," Abner said.

Abner looked out over the crops that would soon be ready for harvest.

"Life is good, isn't it, Martha? What more could a man want? I wish my father and mother could be at your reunion tomorrow. I'm lookin' forward to the holiday. I got the tables built. We're ready for everything. I'll put the pig in the ground later this mornin'. Your brothers and their wives will bring even more food and we'll have the biggest family celebration since we been in Tennessee."

"Yes, we'll be eatin' high on the hog," Martha said and laughed at her reference to Abner's pig in the ground.

His wife smiled, gave him a sidelong look, and marveled once again how much she loved him. She was proud of her husband, proud of his hard work.

She didn't mind she was married to a quiet man. She had learned to read his moods and body language, but she loved it when he shared his mind with her. She treasured those moments when he talked to her. She laid her head on his shoulder and gave his arm a squeeze as they watched the sun rise.

Her gaze, as always when she sat on this bench, slowly traveled from horizon to horizon, left to right involuntarily. The view was breathtaking. That's why Abner's grandfather had built on this particular spot up on the hill. The panorama from her front door never failed to amaze her. She loved the view of the two peaks on the ridgeline on the other side of the valley and, like always, thought how their shape had the uncanny resemblance to some giant woman's breasts as she lay resting on the far side of the valley.

Martha's thoughts were interrupted by the distant sound of horse's hooves coming from the southeast, unusual any time but especially this early in the morning. The sound was getting louder each moment. Without a word, Abner got his rifle and bag.

Abner wasn't worried. Rural Tennessee had been safe for a long time. Andrew Jackson and his Volunteers had made sure of that. He walked down the hill and stood on the narrow wagon track that was the main east-west road through the valley. Six mounted men, United States Army cavalry, appeared walking their horses up the road toward Abner's farm.

They respectfully informed Abner they were the scouting patrol for a detachment of Indians being escorted across the Mississippi. The detachment would pass his farm on the morrow.

"It's about time we got rid of them damn Indians," Abner responded.

Abner was worried about Indian violence. He was more worried about the terrible stories he had heard of disease among the Indians. They were cursed. He could protect his wife from most everything, but he couldn't protect her from disease. He didn't have any use for Indians in any case. The lazy, sneaky bastards knew not to come around his place. His threats weren't empty. He wouldn't hesitate to shoot. Killing a sneaky Indian wasn't a crime in Tennessee.

The July morning was muggy. Abner's shirt, along with the uniforms of the soldiers, was already stained with sweat. Abner invited the patrol to the shade of the big red oak beside the cabin. The invitation was more than politeness. Abner wanted news. These men would have recent information, both of the army and things back east. The big news concerned this final removal of the Cherokee. He wanted to hear every detail. As soon as the soldiers dismounted and were properly introduced to his wife, she offered refreshment. The young men accepted.

As he watched the young soldiers rest in the shade, he wondered why any young man would want to join the army and put themselves through misery for thirteen dollars a month. A strong young man who wasn't afraid of hard work could make thirteen dollars a week.

Abner's wife ordered one of her girls to bring the men some sassafras tea sweetened with some of their precious sugar. The sweet, cool tea was everyone's summertime favorite. Abner had expanded their root cellar just behind the house. It was in the right place, always cool and dry as a bone, even in the winter. They used it to store vegetables and such and to keep milk, butter and eggs cool in the summer.

Abner's wife marveled how young these soldiers were, hardly old enough to grow whiskers. She felt a mother's compassion. Her first thought was that somewhere there were six mothers hoping their sons were being fed properly and had a clean shirt. It broke her heart. She touched her stomach again and felt the baby kick. One day she would feel the same for her adult children, but that day would be a long time coming. She wouldn't think about that now.

The young soldiers accepted the sweet sassafras tea eagerly.

After Abner heard the news, the Corporal addressed Abner formally.

"Sir, tomorrow a contingent of United States Calvary escorting about eight hundred Indians on foot will pass this farm headed west. We're takin' them outside the United States."

"Sir, there will be no danger. You'll have no trouble. They're Cherokee, sir. We haven't had a problem since we left Ross's Landing on the seventeenth, not the slightest difficulty."

"Thank you, men," Abner said. "I appreciate you comin' by. It's high time we got rid of the Indians and I don't care if they're Cherokee, Creek or Choctaw. I want them out of here. The sooner the better."

"That's what we're doin', sir."

"America will thank you when you get rid of 'em."

"Thank you, sir," the young corporal said. "May I ask, sir, which is the easiest route to take through this valley. What's your advice?"

Abner responded firmly, "I don't want those damned Indians anywhere near this farm or my wife, do you understand?"

"Yes, sir. We understand."

"They can go around our farm. Do you see that tree line on the other side of that big cornfield?" Abner pointed out the direction to the soldiers.

"Yes, sir. I see the tree line."

"On the other side of that cornfield and that tree line is a creek running the length of this valley east and west. On the other side of that creek is an old wagon track. You can take that. I don't want them on my farm."

"Yes, sir."

"When you come down this road, turn left here at my fence line. You'll come to a creek. Ford the creek and turn right down the wagon track on the far side, that'll take you west and out of this valley."

"Yes, sir. We can do that, sir," the corporal answered respectfully.

"There's no white folks over there and no cultivation. You can't get lost. You'll have easy goin'. Don't bring Indians through my farm."

"No sir. We won't bring them through your farm."

Abner continued, "Don't take down any fences and don't go through any of my fields. Do you understand?"

"Yes, sir. We understand perfectly, sir. We're happy to oblige. You can count on us, sir. We are here to protect citizens. The Indians will go through peacefully, sir. They go where we tell them. They know we're doing what's best for 'em. They're like a bunch of sheep since they were arrested."

"Sir, you can expect us tomorrow as early as we can get 'em here, maybe two or three hours after sunup," the corporal said. "If we can get those lazy Indians movin' and don't have to dig too many graves, we'll have 'em here early, well before noon."

"I would appreciate that, corporal. The sooner the better."

The soldiers rode back up the road the way they came.

"I wish the Indians weren't coming tomorrow, Abner. I don't like Indians. Tomorrow's the Fourth of July. I was looking forward to a happy day. I hope these Indians don't ruin our get-together," Martha said.

"Don't you worry, Martha. I'll make sure you have a good reunion."

"I hope so, Abner. All five of us haven't been together at one time since our parents died. My brothers are sayin' they want to start gettin' together every year on the Fourth. I would like that."

"I would like that, too," Abner agreed.

"Next year let's invite your people, Abner. Wouldn't that be fun?"

"I would like that. Yes, let's do that," Abner agreed.

"In a couple of years, think of all the children. It will be fun to have both sides of the family here next year."

Martha suddenly frowned.

"I do hope the Indians don't ruin our plans tomorrow, Abner."

"The Indians won't come near our place. You start getting things ready. Don't put anything out till after them damned savages pass. I don't trust them. Maybe this will be the last we'll ever see of Indians. I hope so.

Chapter XLIX
1838 – Nightmare
Chapter 49

4 July 1838 - Johnson Family Farm – Tennessee

Abner rose long before sunrise. He wanted to double check his preparations for the hundreds of Indians passing his farm later that morning. He went to the lean-to shed on the back of the barn and shook his boys awake. He would make sure they were vigilant. They would mind Abner, especially the two older ones. They knew exactly what he would do if disobeyed.

Well after sunrise and precisely as forecast the lead soldiers escorting the Indians rode slowly up the road. The detachment traveled at a snail's pace. Even before the leading horsemen came into sight, Abner had ordered his wife inside with her slave girls. He would take no chances. He had one of the boys watch the house, the pigs and chickens, the others were at the barn watching the stock. He had rounded up every animal he owned. His farm and belongings were as secure as he could make them.

Abner rode to meet the detachment. There were too few soldiers to control too many Indians, but there didn't appear to be anything out of order. The column was moving peacefully. He hoped the savages would mind their manners. If they didn't, he would give them what for.

The lead group of soldiers halted. The courteous Indian representative, a Cherokee himself, politely requested passage through Abner's farm. He explained the detour that Abner requested was five miles out of their way and unreasonably difficult, since the Indians were on foot, many without shoes.

"We'll take down and return all fences exactly as found. Any damage to your fences, crops or property will be paid for on the spot in gold. You, sir, can judge the monetary damage. It would be a Christian blessing if you would suffer us to pass straight through," the Cherokee representative asked politely with perfect English.

Indians would get no Christian blessing from him, today or any day. Indians weren't Christian. They deserved no good will, not from his god or any god. They didn't deserve anything as far as he was concerned. He was glad they were leaving. The army had orders not to bother landowners. That's the way the government always handled Indian removals. Jackson and the Tennesseans stuck together and took care of business. He was proud of the

Volunteers. They took care of their own. Abner didn't want the thieving Indians anywhere near his place.

"No. Absolutely not," Abner answered in a hard voice. "You'll not pass through my farm. You'll have to cross at the ford and take the road down on the other side of the valley like I told you yesterday. Keep your money."

"Yes, sir," the disappointed representative said in a low voice.

"There's good water on the other side," Abner continued. "I told you yesterday. I don't want Indians anywhere near my place."

"We understand, sir."

The representative was used to denial. White Americans owned everything. The inconvenience of the Cherokee was not their concern.

While the detachment was resting, Cassie doubled over with the agony of her first big contraction. Her water broke. She fell to her knees in pain. She would walk no farther this day. On the heels of the first contraction came another. Cassie's companions helped her to the welcome shade of an old white oak tree. They laid her on her quilt, the bed on which the child had been conceived and on which it would struggle to enter the world, the quilt given her by Eleanor.

There was one doctor, but he had few medicines and no way to minister to a woman in labor. She and her friends were on their own. Ready or not the child was coming.

After the discussion with Abner, the soldiers ordered the column to resume their journey, turning to the left across the creek and away from the Johnson farm as instructed. The July morning, already insufferable under a cloudless sky with no wind, promised the exhausted Cherokee another day of dust, sweat and tears.

Abner saw the knot of Indian women gathered in the shade of the big white oak down by the road. The tree was on his property. He shouted and waved indicating they should get back in the column and get on the move. None of the Indian women understood Abner's shouts.

Waving his arms, Abner shouted again at the Cherokee women.

"Get the hell out of here, you god-damned Indians. Get back onto the road and don't leave that thing here. Take it with you."

Abner wanted the detachment to pass as quickly as possible. He wanted the soldiers to take care of these stragglers. He was angry that Indians would stop on his property for any reason. He mounted and galloped the short distance to the white oak. He found four Indian women comforting a fifth woman lying on a quilt in the shade. As he approached he shouted again but to no avail. Cassie, in intense pain and beginning her delivery, couldn't be moved. Her friends intended to help. Abner intended otherwise. He fired a shot into the air.

Two young soldiers turned their tired horses away from their escort of the slow-moving column and walked slowly back towards the irate, gesturing farmer who was demanding immediate attention. Escorting Indians was a thankless task for these young, underpaid soldiers.

"I want these god-damned Indians out of here now."

"Yes, sir."

"Get them out now. Do you hear me?" Abner demanded. Get them away from here now. I don't want any Indians anywhere near my farm."

"Yes, sir," the young soldier patiently replied.

In obedience to the farmer's demands, the young soldiers turned their horses slowly towards the four Cherokee women under the old white oak tree. With gestures, the soldiers ordered the frightened women back into the moving column. When the women hesitated the soldiers used the bulk of their horses and their boots to push the women toward the main column.

Cassie, obscured from the view by the trunk of the large tree, lay on her quilt in the shade of the white oak in great pain. She thought of Ben and his mother. She wished Ben could be there. She hoped to catch a glimpse of Ben coming to help.

Ben didn't come.

Under the big white oak tree and all alone on a hot Fourth of July morning, Cassie delivered her baby.

Abner followed the soldiers and pointed back at the white oak tree, shouting.

"You can't leave that on my property."

The soldiers said nothing.

"What am I supposed to do?" Abner shouted.

"Sir, the trailing wagons are comin' by. They'll pick it up. The trailing wagons pick up all the stragglers, sir."

"I want her out of here now, this instant."

"Sir, I have orders to keep these Indians moving and get them out of this valley as you requested. We've a long way to go before nightfall unless you want the whole bunch to camp right here and wait for this one."

"No, I want them gone. I don't want them to camp anywhere near here," Abner said flatly.

"In that case I have to get them movin', sir. Don't worry. We don't leave anyone behind. I seen women like her have babies before, sir. After the baby's born, she'll be up like a cricket. If she don't recover, you'll have one less Indian to worry about, beggin' your pardon, sir."

"I don't like this one bit."

"We're only doing ten miles a day, sir. She'll catch up after the baby's born. No problem. Good luck, sir."

The young soldiers turned away.

Abner was enraged that he had been left to deal with the straggler lying beside the road under his white oak tree so close to his home. It wasn't fair he should have to deal with this on the day of his wife's reunion, of all days.

He went back up the hill and ordered his wife to stay inside a little while longer. It wouldn't be long and all the Indians, the contractor's wagons and the soldiers would be out of sight down the valley and the trailing wagons would pick up the woman under the tree.

"Martha, I'm going to stay up here with you till every last one is gone. I don't trust the sneaky bastards."

"I'm glad you're here, Abner."

"Don't worry, Martha."

"I'm not worried with you here. Can I open the door? It's hot in here."

"You can leave the door open and go outside as long as you stay close. I'm goin' to sit right here till they're out of sight."

"I'll get you something to drink," his wife said sweetly.

Abner watched until the last Indians and the trailing wagons turned left and crossed the creek on the other side of Abner's property.

"Abner, my brothers and their families will be here before long and you still have to dig up the pig."

"I know."

"I hope these Indians haven't caused my brothers a problem."

"The Indians won't be a problem."

"Do you think it's alright if I start getting things ready? I need to put the tables out. The girls and I have a lot to do if we're going to have our celebration. I want everything to be perfect."

"I got everything under control. I got one more thing I need to do, dear. You work around the house and let your girls tend to the cookin'. Don't you worry."

"I'm not worried, Abner. I'm not worried with you here."

The sound of the draft horses' clanking harness and trace chains had faded. His farm was secure. His Garden of Eden once again belonged to himself, except for one thing.

"I'm goin' to go check around, Martha. I won't be gone long. As soon as I get back, I'll help get everything together. We'll have a good time today, I promise. Don't you worry. I'm not going to let Indians spoil your reunion."

"I won't worry, dear," she answered.

Abner looked at his wife and thought that he loved her more at this moment than ever before. He hoped the unwanted problem under the tree had been taken care of by the American Army's trailing wagons. His wife deserved to have a carefree, happy day with her family.

Abner immediately went down the hill to check under the white oak. The Indian woman was still there. The trailing wagons hadn't noticed her behind the trunk of the big white oak. He didn't like this. He felt his anger rising. This was unfair.

He examined the Indian woman carefully. She was lying half on her side and half on her stomach, her face turned away from him. There was no movement. With the toe of his boot he shoved her shoulder, disturbing a yellow butterfly resting on the woman's black hair. The butterfly fluttered upward through the limbs of the oak towards the hot July sun.

He pushed her again with his boot, harder this time, but still no response. Unwilling to use his hands, Abner rolled her over with the butt of his rifle. Her eyes were open, unblinking, glazed in death, staring upward as if following the butterfly. Ants had already found her eyes and mouth.

The only sound in the deep shade of the white oak was the buzz of green flies. Abner stumbled backwards, tripped and fell to the ground. In a panic, and continuing to stare at the woman, he scooted backwards on the seat of his trousers away from the horror before him.

He didn't need to see this. His wife didn't need to know anything about it. He recovered from his initial shock. Half running, half stumbling, he hurried up the hill to get his pick and shovel. He had to bury it immediately. He didn't want his wife or slaves to see. No one must see. He didn't want anyone telling his wife what lay under the tree down by the road. A woman dying in childbirth on his property would be a bad omen. He must take care of this immediately. He would do this alone.

"What are you doing, honey?" his wife asked innocently as she observed her husband carrying tools.

"I'm burying a dead animal. Stay in the cabin. I won't be long."

Abner ran down the hill.

"God-damned Indians never cease to be trouble. They're trouble even when they're dead. We should have gotten rid of them long ago."

The prosperous American farmer was angry because of the inconvenience and the horror of what he was required to do. There was no way he was going dig a proper grave. She should have died somewhere else if she wanted to be buried properly. Indians didn't deserve a Christian burial in any case. They were savages, animals. She would get an animal's burial. If it was an American woman, he would dig a proper grave. They would say words over her and show respect, but she wasn't. There would be no words. This thing wasn't any different than a dead possum the dogs drug up in the night. He would scoop out the nearby wash, roll her in and throw some dirt over her. That would be good enough for an Indian.

Digging furiously, Abner quickly scooped out a depression next to the body deep enough to cover the dead Indian. Not wanting to touch the corpse, Abner pulled the quilt on which she lay until she rolled into the depression. He would throw the quilt over the body, cover it with a layer of earth, place flat stones on top and that would do. His wife would never know.

The limp body rolled into the shallow grave with a thud, face upwards, her glazed eyes were staring into his. As Abner leaned to fold the blanket over the body and hide the accusing face, he was shocked again. Beside the woman and obscured in a fold of the quilt and not quite in the grave, was a newborn, still connected to its cord. The baby's eyes were closed. It had a perfectly formed face and shock of black hair.

Abner turned and fell on his knees, his back to the Indian and baby. His stomach revolted. He retched, and retched again.

He wanted someone to finish this job. This was unfair. This was a holiday, a United States holiday commemorating the union of states. This was the United States of America. He was an American. He and his pregnant wife should be celebrating the fact that they lived in the greatest country in the world. He shouldn't be here doing this. The army should have done this for him. Indians were nothing but trouble. They should have been removed long ago. He hated Indians.

Abner gathered himself and breathed deeply. He stood, hardening himself to finish the job he must finish. With the toe of his boot, Abner pushed the newborn until it fell into the depression beside the corpse of its mother, its tiny arms stretched, reaching its mother, reaching to be held. It was a boy.

Abner wanted this to be over. This wasn't the same as burying a dead possum. He had shot a horse once. That was awful. This was worse. It wasn't right he should have to do this. This wasn't his fault. He hated Indians. The army should have taken care of this. He didn't want any part of this thing.

He quickly pulled the quilt over the two lifeless bodies, disturbing busy ants and green flies. He didn't want to be looking at the thing he was about to cover with dirt. As he pulled the quilt to cover the bodies, the baby moved, it pressed forward, reaching for its mother. Abner lost control. He covered the two with the dirty quilt.

Throwing the shovel aside, Abner fell to his knees shouting obscenities. Using his hands he worked madly to cover the quilt as quickly as possible with a thin layer of soil, sticks, leaves and grass. The American farmer kicked and pushed everything within reach to cover the dead thing which seemed to threaten his very existence. He must protect himself and his family. This Indian must be immediately removed from his sight. When covered, they would disappear, vanish as if they had never existed.

When Abner finished covering the bodies, he was exhausted. He sat on a nearby stump, his hands on his knees, head sagging, sweat dripping off his face and nose onto the freshly disturbed earth at his feet, each drop of sweat making an audible sound as it struck the ground.

His breathing gradually returned to normal. He dragged large flat stones to completely cover the soft earth of the shallow grave to prevent animals from digging. No one must see, ever. It must be covered, forgotten, erased. He would forget. He must forget. He would make himself forget. Everyone should forget. He would never remember this day ever again. He would see to it no one remembered.

Abner leaned on the long handle of his shovel. The Indians were gone, buried, their memory buried with them.

The Indians were gone. His community, the state of Tennessee and his nation were now pure. America was free of its contaminating nuisance. He must pull himself together. He had a lot to do this afternoon. Life could return to normal. He washed his face and hands, then washed again.

Years afterward Martha Johnson would wake in the night to the sobbing moans of her husband in his nightshirt, huddled on the floor behind the bed, arms above his head, trying to escape some invisible night-time horror as he cried, "Take it away. Take it away. Take it away. Not here. Take it away. Not here."

Chapter L
1838 – Ben's Reward
Chapter 50

26 September 1838 – Milledgeville – Ben Lowry's Law Office

With the removal of the Cherokee, Americans poured into northwest Georgia. Cherokee Country had been fully surveyed and mapped. Cherokee Country was no more. Every acre within Georgia's chartered boundaries was free of Indians with a fully functioning American government in each of the new counties. Ben's work with Georgia was finished.

Ben had a final meeting with government officials in his well-appointed office. The successful conclusion of the removal was a feather in his political cap, a huge step towards his appointment to the Senate.

Everyone was pleased. The fear of a war with the Cherokee, like the recent Creek war, had been averted. The Cherokee's claims were legally extinguished, the nation finally removed and the American conscience was clear. Ben would receive his share of the credit. The Cherokee were gone lock, stock and barrel. The few Indians who had escaped General Scott's roundup had nowhere to hide and nowhere to go. Those who had escaped north into the Smokey Mountains would soon be captured, or starved out of existence, which served them right for refusing to emigrate peacefully when told to. Everything was as it should be. At long last the American agreement of 1802 had been fulfilled. Life was good in the state of Georgia. America could grow and proper as never before.

A few thousand Cherokee yet remained in prison camps in Tennessee near the Agency awaiting cooler weather to complete the removal. The hardheaded Ross had at last grudgingly agreed to the self-removal of the entire Cherokee Nation. The Tennessee removal was winding down, but Georgia had already been cleared. Georgia newspapers boasted that the entire state was free of its Indian population for the first time in its history, both Creek and Cherokee. The stupid Seminoles on Georgia's southern border would soon be deported en masse by the efficient United States Army. Osceola was dead, foolishly allowing himself to be captured under a white flag. Life in Georgia couldn't be better thanks to the foresight of Andrew Jackson, the Indian Removal Act and the superior American government. It could and would be, America the Beautiful.

Georgia could get on with the economic development of the entire area within their chartered boundaries and not just the Piedmont. With the removal of the Cherokee, Georgia could take its rightful place as leader among progressive southern states, the largest state east of the Mississippi and one of the 'ole Thirteen'. America was growing exponentially. Thousands of acres of prime farmland had been opened in a matter of weeks, not to mention the vast tracts of virgin timber immediately available for harvest. Wide roads were being built to connect to its sister states of Alabama, Tennessee and North Carolina without the nuisance of Cherokee tolls. The removal of the Cherokee had been good for business. With the Indians gone, Georgia could grow.

Andrew Jackson's 1830 Indian removal bill had played out precisely as envisioned. Plantations, roads, railroads, canals and bridges could be built. Entrepreneurs and forward-thinking governments were raising money to develop the new idea of railroads to connect widely separated population centers. Railroads could ignore the river system and the great inland cities politicians had envisioned could be developed. All this was possible because of the removal of the benighted Indians, a wise move by the American government.

Everything Cherokee had been removed, even their bones. New Echota, the once proud Cherokee capital, was sub-divided and given to fortunate drawers, the remnants of the irresponsible Creeks apprehended, African runaways and their children properly returned to slavery.

Ben was looking forward to the meeting with the representatives of former president Andrew Jackson. He was excited thinking about the next step in his political career, a United States Senate appointment. Jackson, although retired, was still a powerful force behind his democratic party. Ben's appointment depended upon Jackson's favor. The meeting today with his representatives was all-important.

For the last couple of months Ben had been puzzled by the absence of Elizabeth and Zach. Ben had been out of town but it seemed no matter how hard he tried, he had not had time to visit with Zach and Elizabeth. He had no idea what was going on behind the scenes in Milledgeville. He would begin that process of catching up today.

The day of his return, he sent Elizabeth a note asking to meet that afternoon, or perhaps on their regular Tuesday. She scribbled two words on the returned note, 'Not Today'. Ben was puzzled.

He sent a second note a few days later asking Elizabeth to dinner, but once again the note was returned with only the two words, 'Not Today', scribbled on the back. There was no signature, no explanation.

Ben was confused. For the last year he had been under the impression Zach and Elizabeth were in the final stages of arranging his Senate appointment, that everything was progressing nicely. True, he had been busy but that was part of their plan. Elizabeth should have contacted him by now and Zach had been away from the office on business since Ben's return. Something was amiss. Ben was anxious to get his relationship with Elizabeth back on track. He missed her desperately.

Ben had fallen for Elizabeth. He was in love with her, head over heels. Every thought he had of her was accompanied by a terrible ache in his chest, an ache that could only be removed by her physical presence, her touch. Now that the removal was over, she had become the center of his thinking.

Why were Elizabeth and Zach not in contact? Surely she cared for him, at least a little? She had been such a carefree lover and indicated on many occasions the two of them were destined for big things. He must see her. He would figure out a way to be with her, to have her in his life. Maybe she would answer another note. He didn't want to live without her. He needed her. He must see her.

He would have to think about Elizabeth later. At the moment he had business to attend to with the two presidential envoys who had been assigned by the War Department during the removal as liaison between Georgia's governor, the President, the War Department and Ben.

The men entered Ben's office with an unusually cool manner. Ben perceived something was awry. Something had changed.

"Mr. Lowry, we're pressed for time. We shall get to the point. Both the President and General Jackson thank you for your invaluable service to your nation and the state of Georgia. You are an American patriot."

"Thank you, sir," Ben answered politely.

The government's messenger continued, "You did a splendid job assisting in the removal. You were the right man for the task."

"Thank you, sir," Ben answered politely once again.

"President Van Buren commends you for the successful completion of your mission and will recommend you be given the highest honor for service to your country. America is in your debt. However, it is not convenient for President Van Buren to receive you in Washington City. He will let you know when your visit will be appropriate."

Ben sensed that everything was not as good as he thought previously.

"In addition, President Jackson asked us to inform you he will send your invitation to the Hermitage when he deems it appropriate. Now is not convenient."

In that instant, Ben realized he had been played for a fool.

In so many words, the officials were dismissing him like a schoolboy.

He had been used. The postponement of his visit with President Van Buren was the same as being told he would never be invited.

He had become persona non-grata. The promised high level Senate endorsement was obviously canceled. He understood. Zach and Elizabeth had dropped him. Without the support of Van Buren and Jackson, he couldn't get elected to the city council. Only Jackson's men had a chance in Georgia.

How could he have been so naïve? It had been rumored Jackson and Van Buren would give their support to one of Ben's young, up-and-coming opponents, but he had refused to believe it. Now he knew it to be true.

Zach and Elizabeth had abandoned him, thrown their lot in with someone who better suited their ambitions. Zach and Elizabeth had moved on.

He suddenly saw himself as Elizabeth's intrepid knight. In return for all his time and trouble he had received the coup de grace on her big chess board, brazenly sacrificed in her egocentric gambit for social advancement and security. He was yesterday's news. How could he have not seen this coming?

Ben was now no more than a local lawyer, nothing else. His magnificent political aspirations were crushed. Nullification, that was the word bandied about in the newspapers. Now the word applied to him. He had been nullified. If he were to turn the three steps to the left as he entered the foyer at Mr. Mitchell's hotel, he would find his handsome opponent sitting with Zach and Elizabeth drinking expensive whiskey distilled at the Hermitage, smoking expensive Cuban cigars, spellbound by French perfume and tempted with visions of state dinners. His young replacement would be dreaming of a beautiful, carefree woman who would give him the most wonderful gifts in her private suite. Ben knew the routine. He had never resembled a valiant knight. At best he had been a miserable pawn, a jackass in the eyes of his peers who knew of his relationship with Zach and Elizabeth, perhaps they had known all along.

After the brief meeting and curt goodbyes, Ben stared out the window seeing nothing. His messenger returned with the third note he had sent Elizabeth just this morning. Ben was asking for their Tuesday meeting, a dinner together or any meeting. As she had twice before, she scribbled two words, 'NOT TODAY', across the bottom of the note.

He realized he would not see her today or any day. He should have listened to Zach in the beginning. He should have listened to his mother and father. He had thrown away his life in pursuit of a fantasy.

Ben leaned back in his expensive chair and stared at the note in his hand. A burning pain filled his chest as he realized his love for Elizabeth would be forever unfulfilled. Even after this third rejection he loved her more than ever. He loved her with all his heart. He always would. He wanted desperately for 'Bethy' to be in love with him.

Ben's mind sought frantically for some undiscovered method by which he could win her heart, change her mind. His thoughts began to spin looking for the solution to the impossible puzzle that would return her to him. She couldn't be that cold and insensitive, could she? Ben's mind and body filled with the pain of his unrequited desire for his lover, the woman he had mistakenly fallen for.

Ben leaned back in his chair. After the visit of the envoys it was obvious his lowly law career was all that remained of his grand dreams, all he would ever have. His political career was over. He would never again be elected to public office. He would lose many clients. Andrew Jackson, the governor of Georgia, Elizabeth and Zach, everyone in power had used him just as they had used hundreds of other eager politicians. Their glorious promises turned out to be arrogant vanities, disintegrating into nothingness, like the clouds of backroom cigar smoke in which they were born. His years of tireless labor were wasted. The expected taste of victory had turned to ashes in his mouth.

The glory of Tuesday was gone forever. He would never again walk up the hotel's magnificent staircase to spend heavenly afternoons. He would never again smell her rich perfume, feel the softness of her hair or the tingle of her touch. All that remained was a suffocating pain in his chest that grew with every evil thought of rejection. He had been a self-absorbed simpleton. He couldn't stop thinking of his love for Elizabeth. His mind was trapped in a vicious downward spiral of destructive malevolence.

As Ben stared through his white linen curtains into the busy street, he contemplated reality. He let fall the engraved notepaper returned from Elizabeth. Nothing mattered now. His life was over.

He looked at the hand carved chess set on the corner of his desk, the set Zach had given him not long after he went to work for the firm. He remembered their conversations about how Zach and Elizabeth played their game with human chess pieces. He recalled how Zach cautioned him not to lose his heart to Elizabeth, the cold-hearted temptress. He had ignored the advice of his mother, father and Zach. Of his own free will he had literally become that chess piece on Elizabeth's board, a knight sacrificed in her well-planned gambit.

What a mockery his life had become. With one bitter sweep of his arm Ben sent the mahogany chess pieces crashing against the far wall. His attraction to Elizabeth must have seemed comical to his peers. Behind his back he must have been viewed as a droll burlesque character, ridiculous, farcical, his romance with Elizabeth laughable, the actions of a naïve schoolboy. He had become an object of pity, an embarrassment to his clientele. As he stared out the window, the mist cleared. He had given up things more beautiful than any man could hope for in exchange for a meaningless pursuit of wealth and power, a delusion, a mirage, never an object of substance.

Cassie had gone west and taken her baby with her. He would probably never see her again. His father's health was ruined. The Cherokee were gone. His political career derelict. His reputation ruined.

Like the smoking ashes that had been Cassie's home, so was his life. He had given up everything he loved for something he could never possess. He had spurned the love of the most beautiful of women for an egocentric vanity, a chimera, an illusion impossible to achieve and never worth possessing in the first place. What could he do? How could he find joy or purpose now? His life's ambitions were shattered. He would never experience joy again.

In the blinding light of merciless self-examination, Ben realized he had become a sleazy reflection of Zach and Elizabeth, himself a user, no better than the bribe-taking politicians in the back streets of Milledgeville he had become familiar with while strolling the halls of power.

For the first time in years he thought of his mother's advice the day he left for law school, her warning about trying to look over the edge of the big stone mountain. He had gaily chosen the forbidden. Without ambiguity, he could see his father telling him about the dangers of the thin end of the wedge.

He had nothing to live for, absolutely nothing. Perhaps he should fall to a well-deserved death at the foot of the stone mountain, adding his bones to those of other foolish young men who believed lies, young men who insisted on finding out for themselves. Perhaps to cease to exist would be best.

He remembered the quote from Macbeth.

"Life's but a walking shadow, a poor player that struts and frets his hour upon the stage and then is heard no more, it is a tale told by an idiot, full of sound and fury, signifying nothing."

He opened his desk drawer. He examined the new twenty-two caliber Derringer Elizabeth had given him last year. It was a beautiful pistol. The precision weapon, with its modern percussion cap firing mechanism, had been ordered straight from the factory in Pennsylvania. As he held the weapon Elizabeth had given him he thought how she had manipulated him from the day they met and when he had served her purpose, she had, without a qualm, sacrificed him for personal advancement.

He didn't want the life she offered. He would never want that life. He didn't want anything she or Zach had to give. He saw that now.

He didn't want wealth, power or Elizabeth. He wanted things of substance. He wanted the things he had discarded. He wanted the things his mother and father had taught him to love.

He had thrown away gold and kept ashes. Like Esau, who sold his birthright for a mess of pottage, he had despised everything worth having for momentary gratification. Oh, that he could live his life over again.

The Cherokee were gone, his parent's life wrecked, his life wasted. He had been an accessory to the death of a nation. He was ashamed. He must bear the guilt of his actions and suffer the consequences. Oh, that there was some way to undo the evil he had been party to. There was not.

He looked at the pistol. Engraved in a flowing conjoined script on the handle were the names Elizabeth and Ben. The handgun was an appropriate gift. He wondered if she had foreseen this very moment. This pistol was the only thing he had left from his relationship with her, all he would ever have. How fitting.

How appropriate the only thing Elizabeth had ever given him of any worth was an instrument of death. He stared at the pistol in his hand. He faced the bitter truth that he was no different than Elizabeth and Zach. His life was as pointless as theirs. He was worthless. His life was empty, signifying nothing. He had deliberately disposed of his past and now he had no future.

Ben, seeing nothing, thinking nothing, stared blindly out the curtained window as he placed a percussion cap in the loaded pistol and cocked the hammer.

Chapter LI
Closure
Chapter 51

The edited manuscript is at the publisher. There remained one last task to allow Cassie to rest in peace, to complete the circle. To accomplish that task, I left about ten the next morning and followed the route Cassie would have walked when she was deported from Chattanooga in 1838.

I drove slowly, stopping often. Occasionally I would stare out the window and imagine the slow progress of Cassie's detachment down the very road I was driving. I searched for places the hundreds of prisoners might stop to rest or camp. I visualized Cassie's column stretching for the best part of a mile guarded by well-armed American soldiers.

When I stopped at a likely spot, I could see Cassie resting in the shadows, nodding towards me as she acknowledged my work.

I laid my head on my steering wheel and cried. Today's journey was different from the first time I came down this road, before I knew the answers to my questions. This time I know who lies under that old white oak tree.

The drive to the Johnson farm, less than two hours with modern roads, would have taken two weeks for Cassie's detachment. I recalled my original excitement searching for the two mountains. The old woman was right. There are things about this story I do not like, things I wish I had never learned. I suppose I was depressed by the visions made realistic by months of in-depth research. I could close my eyes and see the mounted soldiers prodding the men, women, children, grandmothers and grandfathers as if they were cattle.

I am embarrassed to be an American, part of a nation who has officially chosen to justify and forget. Since the day I was born, I have enjoyed the fruits of the land taken from Cassie. My family and I continue to profit from her loss. In that regard I continue to share the guilt of my 1838 relatives. My great-grandparents, grandparents, parents and I have enjoyed the bounty of a land stolen, the same as if it were a handful of cash and ten cartons of cigarettes taken from a convenience store. Are my parents the rightful owners of their property in Walker County? Well, they have a deed. In America that's all that counts, as long as it's legal, it's perfectly ok. Many centuries ago the Pope declared American ownership of Cherokee land legal.

I arrived at the Johnson farm just after noon and rang the doorbell. Mrs. Johnson, her daughter Ann and her granddaughter Cassie remembered me and invited me in with warm greetings.

"What's the matter, Katie?" little Cassie asked. "Is something wrong?"

"No," I answered. "I've been thinking about my research and the Trail of Tears. I guess the emotion of seeing you when you opened the door was a bit much. Please forgive me. I didn't mean to cry."

Cassie's mother walked me into the living room.

"Don't worry, Katie. Cry all you want to. Cassie and I are spending the weekend with Momma and Daddy," Cassie's mother continued, "and we're more than pleased to see you. We've talked about you often since the day of the reunion. Come on into the living room and sit down."

Mr. Johnson joined us.

When everyone was seated, I began.

"I have some news, good news. As you remember I'm a journalist interested in the Trail of Tears and the detachment of Cherokee that passed this farm in 1838 and I'm interested in the grave here on your property."

"If you recall," I continued, "I shared information I had about a Cherokee woman's journal, a journal she kept from 1820 until 1838. I'm finished with the transcription. I was wondering if you would like to hear some details, especially as they pertain to your family?"

"Oh, yes, please," little Cassie said quickly. I had their full attention.

I took a deep breath and began again.

"Here are some things I've learned."

"A Cherokee woman, her English name Cassie, lived in Cherokee Country near New Echota, near what is Calhoun, Georgia today. She was the journal writer. She was arrested in late May of 1838, probably on May twenty-sixth, and marched to Ross's Landing in what is now Chattanooga. She was in the very last of the summer detachments forced west before Chief John Ross agreed to a national self-removal."

No one said a word.

I took another deep breath and continued, "Immediately after her group of about eight hundred left Chattanooga, Chief John Ross, at last resigned to the loss of the Cherokee homeland, gave up all hope of compromise with the American government. He asked General Scott to allow the Cherokee people to remove peacefully as soon as the weather cooled in the autumn and traveling was not so dangerous. General Scott agreed. After Cassie was deported in late June from what is now Chattanooga, it is estimated about fifteen more detachments left for Oklahoma in the autumn, most from the Agency in Charleston, near Cleveland, Tennessee."

As I continued talking everyone was listening intently. I had their undivided attention.

"I have strong evidence that Cassie, expecting a baby any day, never made it past this farm. I will present the evidence in a moment. I came today because I thought you would want to know what I have learned."

"Please continue," Ann and little Cassie said in unison. They were quite impatient as they waited for me to tell them what I had discovered.

I looked directly at little Cassie's grandfather.

"First, Mr. Johnson, I learned something about the bow you have over your mantle. This may be a bit melodramatic, but may I hold it again please?"

"Yes, of course you can, young lady. I remember your interest in the bow on the day of the reunion. I remember you asked me all sorts of questions I couldn't answer."

Mr. Johnson retrieved the bow from its expensive velvet-lined shadow box over the mantelpiece.

I held the bow in my hands. I felt a queer, tingling sensation as if the bow had inner life. I remembered Five Feathers' Edudu said the bow was made of living wood and would be faithful to the hand that held it.

"I have transcribed the journal the Cherokee woman kept for eighteen years. I also acquired supplementary material from a friend of hers who was also in her detachment. I'm still not sure of her name but I'll probably figure that out before too long. I brought a copy of the manuscript. I would like you to read a passage from Cassie's book about a bow her brother made himself. It's about a bow similar to the one I'm holding in my hand."

"Of course, I would love to read for you, Katie," little Cassie said.

I handed Cassie the open book.

"Please begin reading at the blue pencil mark."

She began:

"Five Feathers and Edudu prepared for the hunt in proper Cherokee fashion. That evening, Edudu handed Five Feathers the bow. "Look at your bow, Five Feathers. What do you see?"

Five Feathers examined it carefully. Just above the grip the young man saw the delicate carving of five eagle feathers in a curious and clever design. Just below the handle was an equally artistic carving of the bust of a big male deer and proud antlers.

"Edudu, the feathers are beautiful and I love the deer and his antlers. It is our clan. I love what you have done with my bow and my name. Thank you, thank you, thank you. Five Feathers, you and Walela are of the deer clan. I thought this would be a special gift to carry with you the rest of your life. This is your bow."

Cassie finished. I took the manuscript from her. Without a word, Mr. Johnson walked over slowly, and with a sense of reverence, gently took the bow from my hands, examining the carving as if seeing it for the first time.

Finally, Mr. Johnson spoke to no one in particular, "I wonder if this is the bow that belonged to that young Cherokee man?

I have more information, sir," I said quietly. "Five Feathers, the young man little Cassie read about just now, was the brother of the woman who died on the Trail of Tears, the woman named Cassie. I think we can safely say the bow described in Cassie's journal is the very same bow you're now holding, Mr. Johnson. There's more to the story, but I'll come back to that in a minute."

Secondly," I said, bringing everyone back from their thoughts about the bow, "I went to Nashville and obtained a copy of the final forensic report on the examination of the remains in the grave by the road.

The report says the remains of the mother and child were wrapped in a quilt. The quilt, according to the pathologists, was handmade with unmistakable German cultural characteristics, from fabrics only available in Germany. The quilt was likely brought over by immigrants. The report deduced the woman and baby to be of European decent. They were sure until I presented them with Cassie's journal."

I asked Ann if she would like to read. She took the book from my hands.

"Ann, please read this excerpt from the journal of a woman who was on the Trail of Tears with Cassie and passed this very spot in July of 1838. This will shed light on what we already know. This woman and her journal made it the entire way to Park Hill in what is now Oklahoma."

Ann began:

"4 July 1838 - Walela was in labor all morning. Something was wrong. Walela was in great discomfort. Our detachment stopped by a big farm across from the twin mountains that resembled the breasts of a woman, the right taller than the left. Walela's waters broke. We laid her on her quilt in the shade under a big white oak tree.

Soldiers forced us away. My daughter and I hid across the road. An angry American man came shouting for the soldiers to take Walela away. We watched the man go back up to his cabin. We crossed the road to help. Walela was dead. I cut off a corner of the quilt to remember her. She and Ben had conceived her baby on this very quilt. We rejoined the detachment. I hope my children make it safely to wherever we are going and the man in the house will bury Walela and her baby."

"That's the same grave under our white oak tree, isn't it? Cassie is Walela, isn't she? Cassie is the woman, isn't she?" Ann asked.

Ann's eyes were filling with tears.

"The Cherokee woman and her baby boy are buried here, right here on our farm, aren't they?" Ann continued, "The woman buried under the tree wasn't an American, like they thought? Cassie and her baby were Cherokee."

I nodded in agreement and held out a remnant of old cloth for Ann to see.

"I found this in the pages of the second journal in Oklahoma. The forensic folks said it is an exact match. There is no doubt. The woman in the grave is the Cherokee woman, Walela. Her English name is Cassie."

"We pretty much know everything now," I answered. "Because we have her journal, we know everything that happened leading up to her arrival here. We even know she was going to name the baby Ben, if he had lived."

It was an emotional moment. No one spoke.

"And that's not all," I said to break the silence. "In the grave, according to the forensic folks, they found two gold rings, probably wedding rings. I understand you have the rings, Mr. Johnson?"

"Yes, Katie," Mr. Johnson answered. "I'll get them. They've been in the top drawer of Mamma's chifforobe since she passed."

He returned and handed me the little case.

"According to the journal Mrs. Lowry gave Cassie two wedding rings that originally belonged to Mr. and Mrs. Lowry. According to the forensic folks, the woman was holding the rings when she died. These are the rings that would have been used in her wedding if she had married her fiancé, Ben."

Mr. Johnson, muttering to himself, walked to the window overlooking the old white oak tree by the road.

"We're going to have to put up a new gravestone," he said to no one in particular as he stared out the window. "I'll order that tomorrow."

"She'll have to have a new gravestone," he mumbled again.

"I'll do that this week. I have to put up a new headstone. I'll do that."

Ann, her mother, Cassie and myself were crying.

"Now I know whose voice that was, don't I? Ann said. "Thank you so much, Katie, for all your work to bring us the truth. It wasn't right that woman should lie there all this time in an unmarked grave after what she went through. It isn't right."

I nodded.

"We owe you a big debt," Ann said quietly. "Cassie owes you a big debt. The Cherokee Nation owes you a debt."

It occurred to me that this little gathering in the Johnson living room was the only memorial service Walela and her baby ever had. I was pleased her story had been told. Ann, her daughter and grandmother and I ended up on the couch wiping our eyes and blowing our noses.

Mr. Johnson, standing transfixed at the window, whispered to himself, "Cassie and her baby are buried by the road. Her brother's bow has come home to be with his sister. I didn't choose this bow, it chose me. We're going to have to put up a new headstone, aren't we? I'll do that this week."

I knew in my heart I had accomplished the wishes of the voice and now the story had been told as requested.

I wonder if one day I will hear that voice again, perhaps in another time, in another place, under more joyful circumstances. I hope so. I would love to hear that voice again. In that moment I hoped Cassie's Great Spirit would bring the long-delayed justice to her and her people. I want very much to meet the woman who wrote the journal and whose bones, along with the bones of her baby, were unceremoniously buried on the Fourth of July, 1838, under the lonely white oak tree—buried and forgotten.

I wanted to hug her neck and tell her everything was going to be ok.

In that moment I knew I must name my first baby girl Cassandra Eleanor. We would call her Cassie. That would be my final token of respect.

The Johnson family now knows Cassie and her baby are buried in the grave under the old white oak tree and that her brother's hunting bow hangs over the mantelpiece as a sentinel. As I left the Johnson's and walked to my car, the long shadows of evening fell across the quiet rural Tennessee landscape. Everything was at peace, in balance. Cassie's story was delivered to the publishers. I had brought closure to the Johnson family, to myself, to Cassie, her brother and her nation, at least in some small measure.

I turned my car at the end of the driveway to head home. The last rays of the afternoon sun reflected off the simple granite gravestone there to my left as I drove away. The engraving just legible from the road, 'Mother and Child'.

I could trust Mr. Johnson to have another headstone in place soon. The low afternoon sun shone across the fertile fields of the picturesque Johnson farm, the landscape little different than it was a hundred and seventy-five years ago when Cassie last viewed this valley. I reflected on the baby boy born beside the road that day. Unbidden, my mind rehearsed the old woman's words in Tahlequah, "I think, my dear, the story may be pursuing you."

She was right. The story had been pursuing me. I knew that now. It was my privilege to have obeyed the voice and told her story. I felt a sense of gratitude as I began the drive back to Chattanooga.

The last resting place of a brave Cherokee woman from New Echota lay behind me in the long shadows as I gently accelerated my Camry past the old white oak towards Chattanooga and my small apartment off Vine Street.

A myriad of emotions poured over me as I pondered the life and death of the woman who had allowed me, nay, chosen me, to transcribe her journal. The visit with the Johnsons had been supercharged. I needed to decompress. My mind had been thinking too much about the things I had learned. I needed immediate relief. I pulled over just up the road from the Johnson farm, laid my head on my arms and sobbed uncontrollably one more time. When I finally got control of myself, I looked up as a small yellow butterfly landed on the hood of my car.

That little yellow butterfly had been sent. I realized that last of all it was I who had been granted closure. The little butterfly confirmed that my task was completed. All was resolved.

Since completing my research, I have a different view of life in our United States of America. I understand who it was who lived here before the Johnson family was given their federal land grant. I know who the people were who lived in Walker County before 1838. I know the meaning of the German word Mrs. Lowry shared with Cassie, lebensraum. I know too well. My father's farm and everyone around me are living on land seized from the Cherokee.

As my mind traveled back in time, I could see dozens and dozens of Cherokee towns up and down the network of rivers in Cherokee Country. I can see Cherokee mothers caring for children, fields of ripening corn, squash, pumpkins and beans, martin gourds all around the perimeter of their villages. I can see Cherokee families and their old folks sitting on their little front porch in the evening twilight whittling and telling stories and listening to the whippoorwills in the gathering dusk and the trills of the mockingbirds in the tops of the trees. I had a vision of the joy accompanying the Cherokee Green Corn festivals, the food, the families and the renewal of relationships, the connection with their past that maintained the balance.

Things change, I mused to myself. Things certainly change.

I found a tissue in my purse, wiped my eyes and blew my nose. I needed to get control of myself and drive home. I had thought about this enough for one day, for a lifetime really. I needed to finish my degree and get on with my career.

I regained my composure and glanced at Cassie's journal lying in my passenger seat, the very book that had come down this road all those years ago. As I drove east on the trail on which they wept, I knew I could never think of the Fourth of July in the same terms. As I was thinking, I heard a voice from somewhere say clearly, "Thank You, Katie, Thank You."

The End

Postscript I
Katie's Postscript

It's been a labor of love reading and transcribing the things Mr. Lowry encouraged Cassie to write in that old accounting ledger all those years ago. I loved every moment of my work. I couldn't really call it work. I feel more like an artist or a sculptor, but, of course, Cassie is the artist.

I was curious and tested my DNA to determine my heritage. Like many of my friends and neighbors, I had been told part of me was Cherokee.

As it turned out, eighty-five percent of me came from somewhere in the United Kingdom, probably England, ten percent from western Europe, probably Germany from my great grandmother's side and I'm six percent Scandinavian. I'm solid white.

From the moment my relatives stepped ashore on the North American continent, they began a process of ethnic cleansing that spread from sea to shining sea, Mexico and Canada included. Searching for lebensraum, my relatives removed hundreds of ethnic groups, cultures and languages to make room for their own.

Our modern collective American memory is short and selective. We don't talk about what happened to the peoples who lived here before we came any more than we talk about a family member in a mental institution.

We justify our behavior. 'It's not my fault' is a phrase we all learn early in childhood. I'm not nearly as proud of America as I was before I began my research. What we swept under the rug lies there still, forgotten.

Cassie's book is finished, the transcription complete, her wish fulfilled. I am not the same person I was on that day in Tahlequah when I first met the old Cherokee woman and held that mysterious old book in my lap wondering what it contained.

Yours Sincerely,
Katie

Postscript II
Author's Epilogue

The following is an excerpt from a letter from John Ross to Job R. Tyson of Philadelphia, written one year before the Cherokee deportation.

Washington City – 6 May 1837

"…we asked that if we were to be driven from our homes and our native country, we should not also be denounced as treaty breakers, but have at least the consolation of being recognized as the unoffending, unresisting Indian, despoiled of his property, driven from his domestic fireside, exiled from his home by the mere dint of superior power. We ask that deeds be called by their right names.

We distinctly disavow all thoughts, all desire, to gratify any feelings of resentment. That possessions acquired, and objects attained by unjust means, will, sooner or later, prove a curse to those who have sought them, is a truth we have been taught by that holy religion which was brought to us by our white brethren. Years, nay, centuries may elapse before the punishment may follow the offense, but the volume of history and the sacred Bible assure us, that period will certainly arrive. We would with Christian sympathy labour to avert the wrath of Heaven from the United States, by imploring your government to be just. John Ross"

Chief John Ross, well acquainted with the Christian scriptures, would have been familiar with the old Hebrew story that goes like this:

King Ahab wanted the beautiful vineyard next to his palace for an herb garden. The problem was the property was owned by someone else, Mr. Naboth.

Mr. Naboth wouldn't sell to Mr. Ahab.

The king said, "Mr. Naboth, please sell it to me."

Mr. Naboth, quoting longstanding national law, respectfully told king Ahab it wouldn't be right to sell ancestral land. No deal. He wouldn't sell.

Jezebel, the king's wife, was incensed. Jezebel thought no one should refuse her husband, the king, the highest authority in the land.

Since no one in government could get Mr. Naboth to sell his property, Jezebel came up with a plan to acquire his property legally. The Naboth's Vineyard Removal Act passed and became the law of the land. Mr. Naboth was removed

347

legally for his highly prized piece of real estate. Mr. Naboth was no more. The proud King Ahab and his lovely wife Jezebel took possession of Mr. Naboth's beautiful next-door vineyard.

And so, America was finally rid—oops, sorry, a slip of the pen. I meant to say, King Ahab was finally rid of the Cherokee—darn it, there I go again with that slippery pen. I meant to say, Ahab was finally rid of his inconsiderate, selfish neighbor, Mr. Naboth. The king had legal possession of the beautiful land of his desire. Ahab was happy. Even back then civilized people understood if you want something that doesn't belong to you, it must be acquired legally. When civilized folks want something that doesn't belong to them they know they have to go through their congress or a court of law to make their acquisition legal.

So, Ahab proudly took possession of the beautiful next-door vineyard and everyone lived happily ever after, right?

Nope. Not exactly.

Ahab took possession of the land he wanted but didn't live happily ever after, neither did Jezebel. Ahab had a lingering problem that came with his crafty use of his country's legal system. Ahab had forgotten there was a higher authority than the president—Sorry, I meant to say, there was a higher authority than the king. I just can't seem to control my dodgy pen, can I?

John Ross believed there to be a higher authority than the American president and the United States congress, a higher authority who keeps a record of injustice. That same higher authority sent a man named Elijah to have a talk with King Ahab at the very moment he was taking possession of his new vineyard.

Elijah said to the happy new landowner, "Where the dogs licked the blood of the innocent Naboth, so shall the dogs lick your blood and dogs shall also consume the flesh of your wife Jezebel." Oh dear, Oh dear.

Americans shared their King James Authorized Version with Chief John Ross. Is that old book nothing more than a collection of well-meaning Jewish stories, myths intended to placate old women and children? What do you think? Is there, perhaps, a higher authority who takes injustice seriously?

Ahab was hoping Elijah was blowin' smoke. How could anyone oppose the president and congress—oops, darn it, there I go again. I meant to say, how could anyone oppose the king and not expect to get stepped on?

If you happen to be in Washington D.C., go to the supreme court and read the story of Ahab and Naboth's vineyard in I Kings chapter twenty-one. I know that story is there in the supreme court building because it's in the book they used to swear in President George Washington himself.

The United States Federal Government holds title to 63% of all land west of the Mississippi. John Ross said if the United States seized Cherokee land by force there wasn't anything the Cherokee could do. He was right. Americans have taken the land away from everyone who lived here before we arrived.

If I were the President of the United States of America, I would keep an eye out for a man named Elijah walking up Pennsylvania Avenue.

In books and films produced for American amusement, Native Americans are portrayed as backward, brutal savages deserving extinction. Films like John Ford's *The Searchers,* validate the destruction of the Indians and American ownership of the entire American continent. In *The Searchers,* Indians are portrayed as vicious animals. Shoot on sight was John Wayne's mantra. Hundreds of stories like these in American literature and on American television justified the American seizure of the North American continent.

In 1826, James Fenimore Cooper's *Last of the Mohicans* portrayed his American protagonist, Natty Bumppo, better known as Hawkeye or Deerslayer, as the champion of a superior culture in the malevolent frontier world of heathen redskins. Hawkeye, representing the superior American race, defeats the wicked Mauga, wicked because he is an Indian and sub-human.

Native Americans in James Fenimore Cooper's *Leatherstocking Tales* are violent savages wholly without human kindness, animals to be taken and destroyed. The single exception is old Chief Chingachgook and his son. They alone demonstrated a civilized Indian character by their submission to higher American culture and their wise decision to allow their race to expire, as Henry Clay suggested.

Mauga disappears. The Mohicans conveniently abandon the frontier for the benefit of the superior Americans. Chingachgook understood Indians were inferior and the American superior, right?

In Washington D.C. you can find on file over 600 treaties ratified by our elected officials with the nations we encountered when we arrived. Not one treaty has been honored.

We worship the image of Andrew Jackson, Indian fighter, on our twenty-dollar bill as the consummate American hero. Andrew Jackson, along with George Washington, Abraham Lincoln, Ulysses S. Grant and Benjamin Franklin reside in our political Cooperstown.

From the beginning Americans began to rid the land of the Indians by offering a bounty for a dead savage. Since it was inconvenient to bring the body to the authorities to collect their reward, the bounty was paid if just the hair and skin of the head were presented, a hundred pounds sterling in colonial Massachusetts.

As late as 1990, Native American pelts were on display in American museums beside the remains of the extinct hairy mammoth and the dried bones of the Tyrannosaurus Rex. It wouldn't be until 1990 that the American Government passed the Native American Graves Protection and Repatriation Act.

A bill will soon be introduced in Congress to return the old Cherokee Capital of New Echota, located near Calhoun, Georgia, to Cherokee ownership, also the nearby Chattahoochee National Forest along with the Smoky Mountain National Park. All seized in 1838.

Contact your congressman and give your support to the restoration of Cherokee lands in Georgia and the Smoky Mountains. Perhaps America can avoid the consequences of John Ross's warning. Perhaps Elijah won't be sent to 1600 Pennsylvania Avenue after all.

In the words of the old woman in Tahlequah:

"When does the thief legally own that which he stole?"

Postscript III
The Inheritance

A man inherited a thousand-acre farm complete with equipment, outbuildings and a magnificent 4,000 square foot home. The farm could be traced back five generations. What a wonderful legacy. The proud son took possession of his ancestral property, a property filled with decades of family memories.

One day he discovered a secret drawer in his great-great-grandfather's old desk. The secret drawer contained hidden documents describing how his great-great-grandfather obtained the farm by intimidation, lies, deceit, bribery, violence and at last the brutal eviction of the rightful owners.

The man examined the newfound papers. With careful research his great-great grandfather's actions were documented. The facts were there. His great-great-grandfather was a crook and had acquired the farm from its rightful owners by grossly illegal means. His great-great-grandfather wasn't great at all.

As he read the secret documents, the man realized he knew the descendants of the dispossessed family. The deprived family had lost their station in the community with succeeding generations living in poverty and ruin while the family of the man who had stolen the property thrived.

His great-great-grandfather was a crook. That was a fact. He had inherited a farm that had been stolen. That was a fact. In light of his great-great-grandfather's crime, he had to decide if he would consider righting an old wrong. What about the people who had been dispossessed?

He had to answer the question: When does the thief legally own that which he stole? As he considered his answer, he could see his wife and children on the back veranda enjoying a lovely spring afternoon. He made his decision. He decided to tuck the incriminating papers back into the secret drawer and forget about them. He wanted his family to enjoy their inheritance no matter how it had been acquired. He would take care of his own.

Righting old wrongs would cost him too much and besides, it had nothing to do with him. It was none of his business.

21 March 2021

www.ingramcontent.com/pod-product-compliance
Lightning Source LLC
Chambersburg PA
CBHW051322250626
47155CB00007B/2415